David

Many thanks for all the encouragement during the 'hard' times.

Roberta Tait
(R. Frost Watts).
1987.

THE LUSHAI GIRL

Roberta Forrest

THE LUSHAI GIRL

Michael Joseph London

First published in Great Britain by Michael Joseph Ltd
44 Bedford Square, London WC1
1986

© 1986 by Roberta Forrest

All Rights Reserved. No part of this publication may be
reproduced, stored in a retrieval system, or transmitted in any
form or by any means, electronic, mechanical, photocopying,
recording or otherwise, without the prior permission of the
Copyright owner

British Library Cataloguing in Publication Data

Forrest, Roberta
  The Lushai girl.
  Rn: Forrest Webb   I. Title
  823'.914[F]   PR6073.E147
  ISBN 0–7181–2678–5

Set in 10/12 point Sabon Roman by
Wilmaset, Birkenhead, Wirral
Printed and bound in Great Britain by
Billings & Sons, Worcester

PART I

CHAPTER ONE

ASSAM. MARCH 1944

The Punjabi Lance Naik, guarding the coal bunkers, watched her from the shade of a gnarled baobob on the far side of the compound, and she could read his thoughts. He had been studying her for half an hour; regardless of caste, all Assamese girls were assumed to be prostitutes by these foreign soldiers.

She realised with dismay that she was staring back at the man, but before she turned her head away their eyes met and he smiled, then spat a thin stream of red betelnut juice on to the dry earth by his feet, making the gesture sexual and obscene. The soldier grinned, then hefted the sling of his rifle into a more comfortable position on his shoulder. She knew that in a few moments he would stroll over to her and there would be more embarrassment as she tried to reject his unwelcome attentions.

Acrid smoke from a neglected cooking fire beside one of the market stalls was drifting slowly across the wharf, beyond which lay the ancient paddle-steamer carcass serving as quay and office for the Brahmaputra River Transport Company. It was mid-afternoon, the laziest time of the day, and the only sound was the dull hum of insects. The coolies were lounging in the shelter of stacks of tea chests awaiting shipment downriver, while the market traders squatted motionless like shrivelled Buddhas beside their wares.

Apart from the Punjabi soldier and herself, it seemed to the Lushai girl that only the river was awake, its brown water swirling lazily around the mooring cables of the floating ghat, and lapping against the wooden piles which prevented it from eating its way towards the cantonment during the monsoons. Half a mile distant, and close to the far bank, a small country boat, overloaded with rice straw, drifted sideways in the current. Somewhere under its towering and unsafe cargo slept its crew; a small boy hung over its steering oar, and dozed.

From the corner of her eye, the girl saw the soldier begin to move towards her, but to her relief, after only a couple of paces, he hesitated then stopped, listening. She heard the sound of engines in the distance; a convoy from the military supply depot on the eastern side of the township, where lines of tents had been erected on the cricket ground and the area surrounded by coils of barbed-wire fencing.

The engine noise grew until the first of the lorries swung past the market stalls and into the wharf compound, its body lurching, swaying, as its wheels bounced over the deep ruts formed during the mud of last year's rains. Dust billowed. The arrival of five more vehicles moved the coolies from their resting place beside the tea chests. Had there been any breeze the men might have been able to escape the choking filth which now swirled about them, but in the still air of the afternoon it was impossible. They wrapped their headcloths protectively around their faces.

A British sergeant major, his bush-hat tilted forward to shade his eyes, jumped down from the first vehicle, beat red dust from his shorts, and then walked stiffly on to the ghat; he slapped the side of his leg with his leather-covered swagger cane in time to his steps. Sweat discoloured the back and armpits of his khaki shirt and streaked the dirt which had accumulated on his face in the short distance he had been driven. He stood on the edge of the grounded hull and stared downstream, impatiently.

A Military Police jeep bucketed its short wheelbase across the pot-holes and stopped near the edge of the quay. Its two Sikh occupants lolled back in their seats; one, a burly corporal, began swinging a horsetail switch in front of his netted beard to discourage the flies, which the arrival of the vehicles had tempted from the cool of the nearby trees.

The sergeant major glanced at his wristwatch, then clasped both his hands on his swagger cane behind his back.

The slatted door of what had once been the first-class passenger accommodation of the old hull opened and a European, stripped to the waist but in the process of pulling on a white shirt, stepped out on to the deck. He pushed his arms through the sleeves, stretched himself, then noticed the sergeant major. With a hurried movement he jammed the shirt into his waistband and buttoned it; on his shoulders were black epaulettes with gold braid. He ducked back into the cabin and returned a moment later wearing his uniform cap.

From somewhere near the bow of the hulk appeared a gang of Moslem seamen, their flowing lunghis distinguishing them from the coolies in loincloths.

The transport company officer walked to the side of the sergeant major, spoke, then pointed downriver. The girl moved forward so her view was no longer obscured by the lorries. In the distance, beyond the bend of the river and distinct above the trees, she could see the outline of the side-wheeler's stack, the dark smoke of its coal-burning engines mingling with the emerald canopy of the jungle. White steam burst through the smoke, and a few seconds later came the raucous howl of the steamer's klaxon; once, twice, and then its echoes thrown back by distant hills.

Birds scattered upwards from the trees, wheeling, soaring, screeching above the river.

The compound, wharf, ghat and market, came to life. The coolies moved into their work gangs, one group beginning to fill baskets with coal from the fuel bunker near the wharf edge. The drivers of the lorries, who had been smoking and chatting together, stubbed out their cigarettes and returned to their vehicles. The market traders began rearranging their wares, wiping dust from fruit and vegetables, stirring lethargic chickens to life inside their inadequate crates. Children carrying baskets of bread and sweetmeats on their heads appeared from nowhere, as did beggars.

A senior Indian clerk of the transport company, wearing a white topi and carrying a thick ledger under his arm, shepherded his office staff into a neat line beside the European officer. The Sikh military policemen climbed languidly from their jeep, armed themselves with bamboo lathis and stationed themselves near the unloading point.

The side-wheeler cruised slowly into view, the foam of its paddles creaming the brown water as the river pilot aimed the long narrow vessel up the deep-water channel near the far bank. The awakened crew of the country boat frantically sculled from the steamer's path, knowing the pilot would ignore them, and that if they were too close the bow wave and wash might sink them. Beyond the steamer, a high section of mud bank, undercut by the swell, collapsed and slid majestically into the river.

On the quayside, one of the Indian clerks struck a short length of hanging railway line several times with a hammer. The off-key bell notes were an unnecessary warning to the coolies that they would soon be required to work. It also served to inform the cantonment that one of the company steamers was about to berth.

The side-wheeler edged slowly across the river. A mistake in this delicate manoeuvre and she would be caught by the current, swing about and be swept downstream on to a sand bar; an action which would cost the company time and money and the pilot his job. Even at full-ahead the *Mahanadi* could make little more than five knots against the river. Her journey from the go-downs of Juggernautgunge had been slow and tedious, and the round trip from Calcutta to her most north-easterly port of call would take her two full months – time in which a good cargo ship from the port of London could reach the ends of the earth ... U-boats permitting.

The steamer was already old, her triple expansion engines made in the Birmingham factories in 1893, and the spars and shafts of her paddle-wheels cast even earlier in the foundries of South Wales. Normally, she carried only an Indian crew, the chief officer being a serang. But as the country was now at war, and the *Mahanadi* was carrying military as well as plantation stores, a British second lieutenant of the Royal Indian Army Service Corps stood on her bridge alongside the serang and pilot, and there were British NCOs and soldiers overseeing the crew and protecting her cargo. On her bow, beyond the corrugated-iron roof covering both her accommodation and a section of the deck cargo, was a machine-gun; the Japanese advance through Burma towards India was bringing the enemy aircraft dangerously close to some sections of the Brahmaputra.

The noise increased until it was almost deafening. The *Mahanadi*'s paddles churned the water. Men yelled to each other above the sound; the pilot to the serang, the serang to the seamen on the ghat as they heaved on the mooring ropes, the Indian tally clerk at the coolies standing beside their baskets of coal. The lorry drivers started their engines, revved them, and began to move closer to the quayside. The military policemen shouted and swore at the swelling crowd of tradesmen, sightseers and beggars, and cleared a path for the vehicles with their threatening sticks.

The girl, hating the crush of unwashed bodies, the stench, the noise, held up her notice-board, and felt self-conscious as she pushed her way through the crowd until she was almost at the side of one of the military policemen. He turned quickly, anticipating her bamboo pole with its painted board as a weapon; he opened his mouth to order her away, but then read her sign and impatiently motioned her past him towards the edge of the ghat. The thrashing of the steamer's paddles and the deep thudding of its engines stopped, but the shouting intensified. Gangplanks crashed on to the worm-eaten hulk. A platoon of Gurkha soldiers jogged heavily down on to the ghat, bowed under the weight of their kit and weapons. They formed a line beside one of the lorries and waited for orders.

The British sergeant major and the transport company officer jumped the gap between the quay and the steamer's paddle-box to avoid the congestion on the gangplanks. The *Mahanadi*'s purser ran to meet them as they began checking the off-going cargo against the manifest and military requisitions. The voice of the Indian clerk on the ghat sounded hysterical. Feet and vehicles fanned the dust again so it rose as a fine, choking mist, tasting of petrol, wood ash, sweat and excreta.

More soldiers, British and Indian, hurried ashore and arranged themselves in the compound, pestered by its occupants. The gangs of coolies began chanting rhythmically as they passed baskets of coal up to the steamer, and boxes of cargo down to the quay; every item recorded by the clerks. As the stacks of cargo on the ghat grew, the military policemen became as attentive as hens protecting their broods from scavenging kites; one unguarded moment and a crate would disappear, regardless of the nature of its contents. The illiterate thieves would be pleased or disappointed later, when it was broken open in some jungle clearing.

Perhaps the Englishman was not on board the steamer, the girl thought. He might have changed his plans – perhaps he was not visiting his friends after all. His leave might have been cancelled; it happened to local soldiers, she had heard, so it might also happen to a British officer. The description of him that Warren Sahib had given her had been brief; Petrie was very tall, had yellow hair, and would be wearing the badges of the 1st Assam Regiment. She assumed he would have blue eyes, most pale Englishmen had them.

Then she saw him; she was certain.

He stood at the head of the nearest gangplank, waiting for the coolies to pause in their unloading of a number of khaki ammunition boxes. When there was a momentary break in the line of men, he stepped between them. A bearer followed him with a pair of leather suitcases.

Once he had passed the coolies, the Englishman paused and stared at the mass of people in the compound. He was even taller than the girl had expected. His eyes seemed to catch the sign she held and his move towards her confirmed her identification. His bearer used the ends of the suitcases as battering rams to clear a way through the crowd and, as the officer drew nearer, the girl was forced to tilt her head back to look up at him. He was very young, she decided, perhaps no more than twenty. And his hair was not yellow but almost white where she could see it beneath his hat. She had been correct, though, about the colour of his eyes; they matched the warm blue of the afternoon sky.

He was the first Englishman whom she had ever thought of as handsome; she felt herself blushing.

Lieutenant Gerald Petrie had already decided that his trip to Gauhati was a mistake. The long journey from Calcutta had been uncomfortable and boring. Both the visit and the method of travel had been his father's idea. 'If you've got time,' he had written from London, 'I want you to go upriver to Gauhati. See what Jack Warren is up to on Number Three Plantation ... Let me have a brief report for the Board. Hope you'll understand it's important for the Company to known what's going on out there. Damn the war, it's costing us a lot of money. Use a BRTC steamer if you can. Give you the chance to see the country. Speak to Howard Everson at the Calcutta office, he'll arrange everything for you.'

The letter had briefly annoyed Gerald. It was enough, he felt, to be out here in India doing his bit in the services, without having to involve himself in the family business. He was physically and mentally exhausted by the months of jungle training and needed to relax with his friends; that was what leave was all about. His father had cursed the war for what it cost his company in pounds, shillings and pence, but conveniently overlooked the years it was stealing from his son.

Guilt forced Gerald to shrug his shoulders with acceptance and obey his father's request. So far, he had only taken from the

Company and given nothing in return. He owed it practically everything; his education, private income and former high standard of living in England. He had always known one day he must become involved in the activities of Petrie India Limited, so it might as well start now.

As his father had suggested, he contacted the Calcutta manager and Everson did, obsequiously, arrange everything, and in less than twenty-four hours – which was a lightning flash in wartime Bengal.

Instead of joining his friends on a drunken spree to celebrate their return to civilisation, Gerald had been entertained to a formal lunch at Firpos, and later, a more tedious dinner at the Eversons' home in Theatre Road. By the time he had managed to excuse himself and located his friends in the bar of the Queen's Hotel, they were inebriated and he still sober; so that even their purchase of a hashish-drugged parakeet, which almost wrecked the bar of the hotel, had seemed childish rather than amusing. He spent the last night with them feeling like an outsider.

Gauhati! The noise, dust and press of its grubby crowd irritated him. At this time of the afternoon, his friends would be lounging beside the pool of the Calcutta Swimming Club, iced drinks at their tables; yet he was facing three weeks of boredom in the company of someone he barely knew. Jack Warren must be at least fifty by now. Gerald couldn't remember his wife at all. 'A brief report,' his father had said. What did you report about that could take a full three weeks? What could you say when you didn't really know how a plantation should be run anyway? And you could hardly criticise the man's book-keeping if you didn't even know how accounts were compiled! Three weeks, three weeks. Once he had been shown around the plantation, what then? Dinners with Warren's cronies? Facetious conversations with people who were notoriously out of touch with reality? The guest's inevitable shikar for duck?

Gerald had seen the waiting girl from the paddle-steamer's deck. It would have been hard not to see her; the notice-board she carried on its pole was eighteen inches square, with his name printed in large childish letters in red paint. The girl was attractive enough, though; in fact one of the prettiest he had seen since his arrival in India, but the notice-board further annoyed Gerald; the crude form of identification was an intrusion. Why the hell hadn't Warren just told her to ask one of the steamer's crew? Any of the NCOs on the vessel would have known him; they'd shared the same squalid mess for the past week!

Gerald stared down at the girl. 'I'm Lieutenant Petrie.'

The girl smiled, then as it wasn't returned, lowered her eyes from his face. 'Sah'b.' He made her feel like a servant; reminded her of her place.

'Well, let's get out of here.' Gerald's temporary bearer began swinging the suitcases again. The crush thinned. 'Which way?' Gerald asked the girl sharply.

Dispirited by his coldness she led him past the market traders and a narrow street of mud and thatched 'shops' that were no more than bashas. The road widened to a small maidan with an incongruous military sign naming it Leicester Square.

A Morris Cowley saloon was parked in the shade of one of the buildings and as they approached, its chauffeur appeared from a doorway and snapped to attention beside the car. His salute was less an acknowledgement of Gerald's rank than an intention to inform him the driver too had once been a soldier. To ensure the information he was giving was not overlooked, the chauffeur saluted a second time before opening the rear door and bowing Gerald inside. The bearer had the suitcases snatched from his hands by the chauffeur who strapped them on the carrier at the rear; the bearer looked pleadingly at Gerald through the window. Gerald wound down the glass, and tipped him. The girl climbed into the front seat beside the driver, who leant unnecessarily on the horn for several seconds before finally putting the car into gear and easing out on to the empty roadway.

Although Gerald Petrie was unaware of it, the girl, Mary Sachema, had been looking forward to his visit. There was no entertainment on the tea plantation where the daily routine seldom varied, and while she was educated, few of the young tea workers could even read or write. She had little in common with them. The thought that a young Englishman would be staying as her employer's guest for a few weeks had thrilled her. Somehow, in a naive way, she had expected the pleasure of the anticipation she had experienced to be reciprocated. His coldness had brought her back to reality; he was British, and she an Indian.

She spoke little, answering only Gerald's few questions. She was wearing a strong perfume which he could smell in the back of the car, rich and heady. Her English was good, less accented than that of the Bengalese he had met further south. She was exceptionally pretty, he decided. And she had walked in the graceful upright manner which, his mother had once told him, was the result of carrying things on your head. He had been unable to judge her figure under the sari she wore. She was paler than he remembered the complexions of the plantation women of his childhood. But perhaps he was mistaken; after all, it had been twelve years since he had left Assam for school in England, and he had been only eight at the time. Childhood memories were often confused.

The drive to Petrie Number Three Plantation, one of seventeen owned by the Company in Assam, India and Ceylon, took half an hour. At first, across the low flat plain of the Brahmaputra valley and then into the foothills reminiscent of the central regions of southern France; only its vegetation betrayed it as tropical, dense jungle on the slopes of the far Naga and Khasi hills, thickets of bamboo, hibiscus and rhododendron, bright splashes of colour on the rolling landscape. An area of contrast, even in its climate: dry and parched except during the monsoons in its western valley, and yet including in its territory the wettest place on earth, Charapunge, where as much as eight hundred inches of rain could fall in a single year.

Although he was resenting his present visit, it was here that Gerald had been born and here that he had spent his childhood. It was the reason for him joining the Assam Regiment. He had been expecting to report to them at their depot in Digboi in north-east Assam after his jungle training, but the regiment had recently moved to Jessami in the Naga territory, where it was patrolling the region of the Chin river.

Once the car had left the river plain, with its paddy fields and scattered villages, the road became little more than a gravelled track winding into the growing hills. There were few signs of habitation, the odd bullock cart, crocodiles of field-workers and spiralling blue smoke above the scrub the only indications of small agricultural settlements hidden by screens of palms. The orderliness of the green shrubs on the side of a hill was Gerald's first indication that they were nearing the plantation.

The tea factory was a collection of sheet-metal and asbestos barns, starkly rectangular in their lush setting, functional and unattractive, with corrugated iron, stacked chests, concrete yards and wire fencing; a chokidar waved them past the gates. The driver swung the Morris on to an even narrower track, between hedges of overgrown rhododendron with flowers withered to dry brown clusters, and leaves ochred by the dust of passing vehicles.

Gerald could see Warren's bungalow ahead. It stood to the left of the track, high on a plateau cut into the side of one of the hills, its gardens shaded by a grove of old trees. It was a single-storeyed building with a low roof and a verandah on three sides. Its gardens were mature and well maintained, sprinklers like mobile fountains reviving the parched grass of its lawns and bringing miniature rainbows to its glades.

He realised that the Morris's approach must have been visible for perhaps a mile or so along the plantation track, for even as the vehicle approached the gardens he saw a bearer appear on the verandah and hurry to wait beside the steps. The bearer was joined, before the car stopped, by Jack Warren; Gerald would never have recognised him from memory. Warren's moustache was grey, yellowed below his nostrils by tobacco smoke; he was almost completely bald, the top of his head tanned, but his cheeks were florid. He was little more than five feet eight in height, but heavily built, with a stomach that bulged over the waistband of his cream slacks. He jerked the passenger door open as the wheels of the car skidded to a halt on the gravel of the drive.

'Gerald Petrie!' A thick-fingered hand was thrust at him even before he had begun levering himself from the cramped rear seat. For a moment he had difficulty standing, as his circulation brought pins and needles to his calf muscles. The hand waited. 'My God!' Jack Warren found himself head and shoulders shorter than the young man before him. Gerald shook the determined hand. 'My God!' said Warren, again. He stepped backwards and surveyed Gerald. 'Last time I saw you, you were that big.' He indicated the level of his stomach. 'Well, perhaps a bit taller, but not much. England has obviously done you a lot of good.'

A woman had appeared at the steps above them, diminutive, obediently waiting for her husband's introduction. Jack Warren waved an agitated hand at her. 'Gerald, you must remember my wife Evelyn.' He turned to the bearer. 'Bring in his luggage.' Then to his wife: 'Just look at him. I'd never have believed it. The spitting image of his father.' To Gerald: 'Did you know that? I suppose you've been told often enough. Well, come along in. Filthy trip up from Gauhati. Glad you've come, though. Get you a peg to wash some of that dust out of your mouth. Disgusting road in the dry season.'

It was late evening; the moon had risen over the bungalow's gardens and the rolling hills of the plantation. The lights of the bungalow pulsed to the rhythm of a distant and unheard generator. Gerald had bathed, changed and joined the Warrens for dinner. Now they sat in wickerwork armchairs on the verandah. Above them, moths and mosquitoes bustled around the white bowl of a lamp.

Gerald was having difficulty keeping awake; it seemed he had not yet finished travelling. There was no physical reason for his weariness. He had done no real exercise on the steamer, spending most of the time resting on a lounger, watching the passing river banks and chatting with fellow passengers. Perhaps it was the silence of the bungalow, he thought. There had always been noise on the paddle-steamer; noise and vibration. Here, even the servants moved soundlessly, adding to the strange monasterial atmosphere, which Gerald found disturbing. The plantation bungalow in which Gerald had spent his childhood had felt alive and vital; to leave it, then, had been traumatic.

There was a whisky bottle and water carafe on a low table between the two men. A few feet away, Evelyn Warren sat before a table of her own and dealt patience cards with the skill of ten thousand evenings.

Warren had searched his mind for subjects likely to be of common interest to Petrie and himself; it was difficult for him. The difference between their ages denied them friendships that might have been discussed, planters who had retired or who now worked for the company in its London offices. And Warren was uncertain of Petrie's involvement with the company and felt it unwise to question him. He knew the reason for his visit; Howard Everson had been considerate enough to warn him. The war had placed a comfortable distance between the plantation managers and their London directors, giving them a sense of autonomy they had seldom before experienced. Petrie's presence was a reminder that one day the war would be over.

War! A common subject! Warren said: 'I'm told your chaps are in the Chin hills. That where you're going?'

'Yes, I believe so. Report to Dimapur.'
'Looking forward to it?'
'Yes, I suppose so.'
'Damned unhealthy place, the Chin hills. Malaria, scrub typhus, cholera, yaws ... name it, and you can catch it there. You'll have to take care of yourself. Especially with those little yellow bastards.'

'Jack!' Evelyn sounded affronted.

'Good God, woman. Why do you think we all sleep with rifles in our bedrooms?' He puffed out his cheeks.

'He's being dramatic,' Evelyn said, peevishly. 'He knows very well that the reason we have the rifle is because we've been advised to have one handy. It's got nothing to do with the Japanese. It's the Indian National Army.'

'Well, it's the Japs who train them, and encourage them. Say they're going to liberate them; from us! Bloody traitors, the INA, I'd hang the lot of them.'

Evelyn spoke in a low voice, as though someone might be eavesdropping from behind a thick clematis which tangled itself around the verandah railings. 'They actually caught one a few miles from here. A Bengali, of course. He was trying to burn down one of the factories.'

'Typically useless act of vandalism,' added Warren. 'Made so much noise about it that the chokidar raised the alarm. Bloody fool of a manager handed him over to the State Police. If it had been me, I'd have strung the little blighter up on a tree; as an example.'

'He's not normally so bloodthirsty,' apologised his wife. She moved a jack on to an appropriate queen and smiled with satisfaction. 'He's feeling frustrated lately, about the war.'

'I just wish I was young enough to fight, that's all. I've missed both wars. Missed the first one because I was stuck out here. Your grandfather's fault. I wanted to join Skinner's Horse; played a lot of polo in those days; but your grandfather insisted on me staying in the Calcutta office. I should have been doing something useful.'

'You *did* do something useful, dear,' said Evelyn. 'You got tea to the troops. And you know what it would have been like in the trenches without tea; Willie Kempster used to tell you how grateful the Tommies were for their char. Besides, you're doing your bit now, through Frederick.' She looked at Gerald and smiled. 'You remember

Frederick, our son, of course? Oh, perhaps not. He was a few years older than yourself. I think he'd left here by the time you were born. Let me see, he's twenty-nine now.'

'I don't think we ever met,' said Gerald, knowing full well they hadn't.

'He's in the Engineers,' said Warren, proudly. 'A major. Got an engineering degree at Cambridge, came out here and worked for the PWD. When the war started, the blighter joined up. Indian Army, of course.'

'So you still see him?' asked Gerald.

'Only there.' Evelyn pointed through the French doors towards a tall, glass-fronted cabinet in the lounge. In it were photographs; in a heavily embossed silver frame a studio portrait of a young officer. 'Doesn't he look smart? Jack's very proud of him. We both are.'

'He's in Italy.' Warren perked up noticeably. 'At least, we think so. You get so little information these days. According to his letters, he seems to enjoy himself.'

'And, it's not as though his work is dangerous, really,' said his wife. 'I mean, not like an infantry officer who has to do the fighting. Infantry officers have a very high casualty rate, I believe.'

'Evelyn.' Warren cautioned her.

She looked quickly at Gerald. 'Oh. I'd forgotten. I didn't mean it was *particularly* dangerous, really. It's just that you have to do the fighting and engineers only build things.'

Waves of fatigue were making it difficult for Gerald to concentrate. He could feel his eyelids drooping, his head sagging. He forced himself more upright in the armchair and took a deep swig of whisky. Warren's voice droned on hypnotically.

For the past few days he had always awakened to movement, the shudder of the steamer's hull, the dull thumping of the engines. He had slept in a military bed-roll, on hard mattresses. It took him a few moments to remember where he was. He lay with his eyes closed, enjoying the sensation of a soft bed. A shadow moved across his eyelids. He opened them quickly.

Warren's bearer, white-coated like a surgeon and wearing a red cummerbund and turban, stood at the side of his bed with a tray in his hands. He placed it on the bedside table, then walked to the window and raised the bamboo chicks. Bright sunlight reflected from cream walls, forcing Gerald to shield his eyes.

'Good morning, sah'b.'

'Morning.' Gerald wished the man would leave and allow him to drift back into sleep. He had decided in his first week in India he would willingly sacrifice chota hazri for an extra few minutes in bed.

'Warren Sah'b says you will be riding, sah'b. He is sending his breeches for you.' The man stared at Gerald's feet resting against the footboard of the bed, and smiled. 'But I am thinking you will be wearing your own trousers.'

'I think so, too.'

The bearer bowed himself from the room as Gerald wedged himself up on an elbow and examined the tray. Its contents seldom varied throughout the continent; a cup of tea, a bowl of sugar, an orange, and two digestive biscuits! He had often wondered about the person who had devised it; digestive biscuits and an orange, every morning, at six a.m. He shuddered and stirred a spoon of sugar into the tea.

How had he got himself to bed? Had he been drunk? It seemed hardly likely after only three whiskies. But neither could he remember anything of the previous evening's conversation. The war? Warren had chatted about that; and, of course, his son. Damn! Falling asleep on your host wasn't the best thing to do on your first night as a guest.

Riding! He hadn't ridden for several years. Might be a useful bit of exercise, though. Warren obviously wanted to show him around the plantation before the full heat of the day.

He swung his feet lazily to the floor, stood and stretched. He could see himself reflected in the wardrobe mirror. 'Don't just shoot at any yellow skin,' someone had joked in the barracks. 'Make sure you can see slanting eyes as well!' Gerald grimaced at himself. Mepacrine had yellowed the tan on his body, tinting it golden; the MOs claimed the drug prevented malaria, but it was as bitter as pure quinine and even stained bed sheets with dyed sweat. And the men still caught the disease.

There were towels laid on a stool near the dressing table. He swung one around his waist, walked to the window and leant on the ledge. The sun was warm on his body. Beyond the verandah, two ancient gardeners dug at a patch of rock-hard ground with their powrahs, the blades chipping rhythmically, the men's backs bowed above thin hips and legs. They had been employed by Europeans long enough to know exactly how hard they should work; sufficient to keep the sah'bs uncomplaining, but not enough to make themselves perspire.

Someone, long in the past, had planned the gardens with care. The palms, standing sixty feet above the lawns, had matured many years ago and were sturdy and elegant; a group of neems trailed delicate aerial roots behind a small artificial pool, their long branches trimmed to form a shaded grotto around a stone garden seat. Bright flowers coloured the beds and scented the light air.

But the gardens ceased to exist once Gerald's eye was caught by the magnetic attraction of the hills, flowing like gigantic waves into the eastern distance, fading to purple mist where they joined the sky. They had seemed too far away and mysterious when he was a child; now they welcomed him. For the first time since he had arrived in India, he felt he was home.

The morning ride with Jack Warren revived many of Gerald's memories. He was surprised he had forgotten so much of his early life spent in so similar an environment. There was a disconcerting familiarity in the factory buildings, an impossible sense of *déjà vu*, the result of his great-grandfather's legendary frugality. The original founder of Petrie India Limited had used a single architectural plan for the development of every plantation he acquired. Known as Picey Petrie by his business associates, he had never drawn more money from the Company than the salary paid to his senior clerk. And even after receiving his baronetcy from Queen Victoria, his family had never been allowed to live in the style they associated with the title until after its first recipient had died.

It was close to noon when the men rode back towards the bungalow. The sun was high, its heat fierce, and the women labourers who had been working amongst the tea bushes were leaving the fields to seek the shade of their quarters close to the factory compound. They watched Gerald with curiosity as he rode by them, but if he glanced in their direction they turned their heads away or pulled a loose fold of sari across their faces. The sun had scorched their skin near-black, dried and mummified them, and it seemed to him that the jewellery they wore, heavy silver anklets, bangles, nose-rings and pendants, and the colourful cloth of their saris, were a pitiful attempt to compensate their bodies for the years of destruction.

He commented on their cheerfulness; they chattered like small flocks of starlings, only silent while the men passed. To his astonishment, Jack Warren responded with a vehemence he had not shown in previous conversations. 'They were better when they were ignorant. Better in the old days.' He paused as though expecting Gerald to question him, and then added, 'Damned American Baptists. We've got them to thank for a lot of our problems. Mission schools. Before we had them, everyone was content with what they'd got. Everyone knew where they fitted in. Education is the curse of Assam.'

'I'm afraid I can't believe that,' said Gerald. He had encountered similar attitudes with old India hands before, forced to listen to their windy arguments at his parents' dinner and lunch parties. He had never agreed with their views which he felt were old-fashioned and imperialistic.

'You will agree one day, my boy. Freddie's no different from you. Thinks his generation will find the remedies for all ills. Well, education isn't the cure-all out here. Education only breeds discontent; fills the ranks of the INA. And as sure as God made little apples, one day it will be education that pushes us all out of here.' They passed another file of women. 'They look happy enough, but by God we have to treat them carefully. Ask any sepoy which he would rather face, a mob of men, or a mob of women tea workers? Bet your life he'll chose the men.'

He sounds like my father, thought Gerald. The same condescending manner and derogatory way of acknowledging progress, of denigrating the views of the succeeding generation. Every serious discussion he had ever attempted to have with his father had ended in the same manner. 'You're not old enough ... not experienced yet ... can't understand ... influenced by misplaced socialism ... it's all bosh.' It was only as he had grown older himself that he had realised the vehemence was sometimes used to conceal ignorance. His father's formal education had ended at sixteen when he had been taken from college and employed as a junior clerk in the family business. At eighteen he was assistant manager on a plantation in Assam. His real education, as he often boasted to his son and daughter, was obtained 'out in the gardens, where it all happens'. It was narrow.

They were now within a hundred yards of the bungalow and in the shaded aisle of rhododendron that lined the narrow road leading to its compound. There was a solitary woman walking towards them, wearing a pale orange sari. Unlike the barefooted field workers, she wore chapplis and as they drew nearer Gerald recognised her as the girl who had met him the previous afternoon on the wharf. She made no attempt to cover her face, but when he said hello, smiled pleasantly.

'Who is she?' Gerald asked.

'Mary. Evelyn's servant. Attractive girl, eh?'

'Very pretty,' agreed Gerald.

'She's Lushai. A hill girl. Part Naga, perhaps.'

'I've met some of the Lushai men. We've got quite a few in the regiment.'

'A good looking lot.' Warren turned his head to watch the girl. 'Not really Indian; supposed to have come from Tibet or China; hundreds of years ago, of course. Fought their way down here, and drove out the local tribes. Related to the Nagas, and the Khasi.'

'I'm told the Nagas still hunt heads.'

'When they get the chance. But not the Lushai; we tamed them seventy years ago.' He paused, clicked encouragement to his horse, and then said: 'Never easy to get good servants upcountry; most of them prefer to work in the cities. Mary was quite a find. Evelyn thinks the world of her; heard about her through a friend who runs some kind of charity – women's stuff, you know: collecting children's clothes, whist drives and raffles at the club. Mary was at school in Shillong, but one of the nuns asked if a place could be found for her in service. A lot of the better looking girls end up as prostitutes; the nun didn't want that to happen.'

'So she's educated. I thought you were against native education.' Warren's convenient hypocrisy amused Gerald.

Warren failed to notice the jibe. 'Not in its place. We've got to have *some* education in the country, otherwise we'd have to import every clerk we need. Mary's exceptionally well educated by local standards. Apparently, her head teacher took a liking to her; so she was allowed to stay on an extra year at school until she was found a respectable position. She's been with us eighteen months. But her education helps us, rather than her.'

'How's that?'

'Well, in a way it demonstrates what I meant. If she hadn't been educated she would probably have married a labourer and had a couple of children by now. But she feels above that and, as it is, I don't think she's likely to meet the kind of husband she would like.

She talks to Evelyn about it sometimes. The girl has ambitions, but no opportunities. Perhaps she might find the kind of man she's looking for in places like Delhi or Calcutta, but she's here, up in Assam. And there's another problem, she needs a dowry and hasn't got one. Her father died when she was small. Tuberculosis, I believe.'

'That's hard on her.'

'Yes, perhaps,' agreed Warren. 'Out here, lack of dowry condemns a woman to spinsterhood. But she's lucky. She has a good job, and Evelyn likes her. She'll probably stay with us until I retire, and that's not for a few years yet. If she behaves herself, then Evelyn will try to find her another job before we go home. In the meantime, she eats well and has a roof over her head.'

'That's not much in the way of prospects,' commented Gerald.

'Prospects!' Warren laughed. 'Out here, Gerald, prospects are all part of the caste system. If you're the wrong caste, then the only real prospects are TB, malaria, beriberi, dengue fever and starvation. They're the prospects for over fifty per cent of the population. You can't start being sorry for every one of them. Not even the pretty ones.'

The aiya was so old it was no longer possible for her to walk upright. Her thin hair was white, contrasting sharply with the wrinkled chestnut skin of her narrow face. Most of her time was spent resting on the rickety bamboo charpoy in the darkness of her tiny room in the servants' quarters, but each day, a little after noon, she would rise, wash herself slowly at the trough in the compound at the rear of the Warrens' bungalow, then sit in the warmth of the sun until one of the kitchen staff brought her a scrap of food. She had been a servant of the Warrens for almost thirty years – employed a week after Evelyn Warren had discovered she was pregnant. Now, the aiya prayed daily to Christian and Hindu gods that they would permit her to sleep without waking; she knew she had become little more than a once-loved family pet, decrepit and useless, but kept alive by a lost affection existing only in its master's memories.

But the gods refused to allow her to die. They had not even given her the anaesthetic of simple-mindedness. Her body was shrinking away, dehydrating and seizing up, but her mind seemed determined to outlast the dried shell that contained it.

'Shall I brush your hair, grandmother?'

It was the Lushai girl, Mary. The old woman smiled with her

eyes. 'If you are wishing so.' She decided her reply had been ungracious and said: 'I will be grateful, child. My arms are stiff these days, so it is difficult for me.' She liked the young Lushai girl, and knew she was often lonely. The girl knelt and began brushing, long, even, soporific strokes. 'You are doing it well. Is Memsah'b Warren being pleased with your work?'

The old woman always spoke to Mary Sachema in English. To the other household servants she would have chosen Hindi, and with the outdoor workers, Assamese. Her use of English with Mary was an indication she considered the Lushai girl of equal household rank to that held previously by herself. Twenty-nine years before, however, when the Warrens had entrusted her with the care of their child, she might have felt differently.

'I think Memsah'b is satisfied. Though she never says it.'

'They are never saying it,' said the old aiya. 'Or very seldom. They thank you often, but never say your work is good; only if you leave them and are asking for a reference. It's their way of protecting themselves from us.'

'They will tell you if your work is bad, grandmother.'

The old woman gave a dry laugh. 'They are certainly doing that, my child.'

'But the European nuns would tell you if you worked well; at school.'

'Perhaps, but the nuns are not paying you for your work. Therefore it is a different matter. When you are being paid, then employment and wages are sufficient, the British are thinking.'

Mary was silent for a while, as she continued brushing, then she stopped and said, 'There. It looks very good.' She moved into a squatting position beside the aiya and pulled strands of white hair from the brush. After a few moments she asked: 'Grandmother, can there be any truth in dreams?'

'Dreams? My goodness me.' The old woman turned her head and peered at the girl. 'Yes, it is possible there can be truth in dreams. But often they are a deceit. There is more truth in the palm of a hand. Give yours to me.'

Mary held her hand towards the aiya, and the woman took it in her bony fingers holding it for a while before turning it, palm upwards, close to her eyes. 'My skin was like this, once, Mary. Perhaps not so pale, but just as soft. You are in love,' she added, positively.

'You can see that?' Mary leant forward and stared at her hand in surprise.

The aiya chuckled with delight. 'No, I cannot see that. But I am knowing it. Why else does a young woman question her dreams?' She peered again at the hand. 'I see marriage, children, happiness and sadness. Does that satisfy you?'

'Do you see a man?'

'Naturally I am seeing a man. Without a man, there cannot be a marriage.'

'But which man, grandmother?'

'The man who is in your dreams, of course.'

'Then you are teasing me.' The girl gently pulled her hand away from the aiya. 'Because I am sure that would be impossible.'

As Gerald had anticipated, he had become bored by his stay on the plantation. He knew it was not the fault of the Warrens, who were doing their best to entertain him. But five days had passed since his arrival, and the routine for each of them had been identical: chota hazri at six a.m., then main breakfast at nine, followed by Jack Warren's daily tour of the plantation and buildings. After tiffin at one p.m. the Warrens retired to their room until four p.m., when Jack would emerge to check the work in the factory or office, or to attend to any emergencies which might have arisen during his siesta. Some of his time would be spent examining books or statements prepared by the clerks, arranging wages or the payment of bills, and settling disputes between workers.

At six-thirty, he returned to the bungalow, downed two burra-pegs of Scotch, took a bath and changed for dinner. After that, there was the choice for Gerald of three-handed bridge, billiards, or conversation on subjects which had already become repetitive.

There was not even the opportunity for a visit to the Gauhati Club. According to Evelyn, it was no longer pukka; forced by the circumstances of the war to accept visiting allied officers as members. True, she admitted, the military kept the club supplied with whisky, even American beer, but the atmosphere had changed sufficiently to discourage the custom of its more discerning members. The Americans certainly did not know how to treat servants, and some of the British officers were little better. It had all become rather common, and extremely drunken. So the Warrens used it only rarely. They would be pleased to take him if he insisted; from politeness he declined.

However, despite his determination to keep his boredom to himself, he knew he had failed when after dinner Evelyn said, 'I'm afraid Jack and I are rather tedious, aren't we?'

'Good heavens, no,' insisted Gerald.

'Oh, come along now. Young people don't want us as company. Frederick absolutely hates it here. Well, I suppose he doesn't exactly hate it, but I think he feels it his duty to come along and stay for a couple of weeks every year. I know he's always glad when it's time to be going back. He much prefers us spending Christmas with him in Calcutta.'

'He ought to get himself a wife, and settle down,' said Jack Warren. 'But it's not too easy for him out here. There isn't exactly a surplus of European women in India.'

'You see,' added Evelyn, 'he was employed out here, not back at home, so he doesn't get UK leave. Still, perhaps he'll meet someone while he's in the army. Are you engaged?' she asked Gerald unexpectedly.

Gerald hesitated. 'Well, yes. I suppose so.'

'You don't sound too certain.'

Gerald laughed. 'I'm pretty certain, I can assure you. It's just I haven't heard from her for a while; it's normal, though. Our mail never seems to quite catch up for months, then we get a batch of it all at once.'

'Tell me about her,' suggested Evelyn, in a motherly way.

'I don't think I've ever been asked to do that before.'

'Dear me, weren't your parents interested?'

'Of course, but she's the daughter of a family friend. I never had to take her home and introduce her.' He paused. 'Name's Monica Purcell. She's nineteen, about up to my shoulder, and she has brown hair and she dances well.'

'Apart from her name, you've described every girl I ever took out when I was your age,' said Jack.

'Her father's a barrister. She plays tennis and I think she did rather well with her Higher School Certificate. And she drives a tractor.'

'Drives a tractor?' Evelyn looked appalled.

'She's in the Land Army,' explained Gerald. 'On a farm near Uttoxeter.'

*

The telegram informing the Warrens of their son's death was delivered personally, by the Gauhati Post Master, the following day. 'We regret to inform you that Major Frederick George Warren has been reported killed in action.'

It was delivered during lunch and Evelyn sat, with a look of horrified disbelief on her face, her hands tightly gripping the edge of the table, as Jack read it aloud in a flat, hollow voice. He put the yellow paper form down on the tablecloth and then said, 'Somehow I didn't think it would happen to Freddie. Assam makes you feel too damned secure.'

Gerald was walking alone. His boredom had been eclipsed by a feeling of sadness. He had never known Frederick Warren, but the grief the Warrens were experiencing was easily transmitted and it had been simple for Gerald to substitute his own parents for the two people who were comforting each other in the privacy of their room.

The atmosphere of the bungalow had suddenly become unbearable for him. It was as though a heavy blanket had been draped around the building to cut off the sounds of life outside. Even the air it contained seemed to have become cloying and liquid. He had determined he should leave as soon as it could be arranged. He felt certain his hosts would prefer to be on their own. Just where he would go, he wasn't certain. It was possible he might get a train down to Calcutta; in the circumstances the RTO might be able to arrange something. If not, then perhaps he should make his way to the military base at Dimapur; he would be a couple of weeks early, but it was unlikely anyone would object.

He had strolled away from the bungalow, following an unaccustomed track leading through a grove of trees. Behind him, the penetrating wailing of one of the servants in their compound grew fainter.

The afternoon sun was hot enough to have silenced even the birds. As he walked, the trees thinned to bamboo on either side of the track, the slender trunks a dense hedge restricting his view to the narrow path ahead of him.

He experienced a sense of uneasiness as though the impenetrable thicket concealed some hidden danger. It was so strong that had it been evening, he would have returned to the bungalow gardens, but now, in the security of full daylight, he continued. Momentarily he was in battledress, his Webley in his hand and a patrol behind him, anticipating an ambush. At any time, he felt, there might be a fusillade of shots, shouted orders, the crash of bodies hurtling into protective undergrowth. Was this premonition, he wondered? Was he going to die in some hidden patch of jungle, like this? And would his parents then receive their telegram: 'We regret to inform you...'?

The track widened to a clearing, a small reservoir supplying the needs of the factory; a square lake, an acre and a half in area, its banks greened by lichen, camouflaged by the garlands of creeper and vines, the surface of the water crowded with hyacinth. Tall banks of palms gave it shade, dissecting it with razor-edged shadows.

There should be a temple, he thought, overgrown, concealed, inhabited by cobras, decorated by a thousand carved statues. It had existed in his mind since childhood; since the tales of Mowgli, Bahgeera, Sher Khan. Perhaps that was what had given him the eerie prickling of his scalp when he had walked the jungle path? Only Sher Khan, the tiger, had been missing. And here, at the lake, at any moment the triangular head of Ka would slice through the water towards him.

'Petrie Sah'b.'

The voice, though soft, was unexpected enough to startle him. He turned quickly. The girl was sitting beneath the trees, the dark green sari she was wearing making her part of the jungle background.

Mary apologised: 'I'm sorry. I should have coughed.' The silence of grief which had pervaded the Warrens' bungalow gave her the courage to speak to him.

'And then I would have thought you were a leopard, for sure,' said Gerald. 'Don't they cough, too?'

'Yes, but like this.' She imitated the sound of the big cat, a deep growling noise, forcing the brief sound out with the muscles of her diaphragm. 'And I cough like this.' She put her hand to her mouth and coughed softly, then smiled at him.

'I think I would have known the difference.'

The girl smiled at him again. He walked slowly across to where she was sitting, deliberately taking his time so he could look at her more carefully. He had been wrong in describing her as simply pretty; she was actually very beautiful. Her skin, unlike that of so many of the country's inhabitants, was totally unblemished, was ... paler than coffee, darker than cream. He had seen a fawn, once, in a field of wheat at harvest time; the doe had stood her ground, guarding her new-born offspring, even when the chestnut cob which pulled the harvester had been forced to step aside to avoid them. The girl's skin was the colour of the fawn, and her eyes were like those of the doe.

The girl was seated on a concrete inspection cover, its surface cushioned by a thick layer of moss which gave an illusion of antiquity.

'Playing truant?' he asked.

'Truant?'

'Absent from school, without permission?'

'School? Oh, I understand what you mean.' She took his remark seriously. 'Oh, no. No one works at this time. And today, especially, I am not needed.'

He was surprised to see the eyes watching him moisten. 'I was only joking,' he assured her. 'Not criticising.' The girl's cheekbones were higher and more pronounced than those of most Indians, a hint of oriental ancestry. The delicate structure of her body made him feel ungainly as he sat next to her.

'I come here almost every day,' explained Mary. 'It is quiet and cool.'

'Like the jungle.'

'No, not like the jungle. The jungle is always wet. And there are many things in jungles which I do not like.'

'There are many things in them which I don't like, too,' admitted Gerald, thinking of the training of the past few months.

'Did you know the Memsah'b's son?'

'I never met him. I'd forgotten they had one until they spoke about him. It's a damn shame. A lot of good men are being killed; they'll be missed when it's all over.'

'They are being missed, now.' Mary frowned. 'The Memsah'b is missing her son. And the aiya is sad, too. She is wailing in the compound.'

'I heard her. I didn't realise it was his aiya.'

'She is very old. But Memsah'b's son was also her son. So she is mourning as well.'

Gerald had forgotten his own aiya, a fat, jolly woman, who had been more part of his early childhood than his mother. He had been told, much later, that she had even wet-nursed him. He wondered if she was still alive; he hoped so.

'They say you are of this place.'

'Once. A long time ago. My father ran a plantation further north. But we've all been in England for many years.'

'Home!'

'Yes, it's home.'

Mary, her forearms crossed, leant forward on her knees. Gerald could see the back of her head. He had thought, when they had been travelling in the car, that she had oiled her hair; it was a common habit, and made the hair shine. Now he saw its sheen was natural. She spoke again: 'When I was very small, before I went to school, I thought there was a country called Home, where all the Europeans came from. I heard it called that, very often. Even the Anglo-Indians who were born here called it Home. I was surprised to learn there was no such country.'

'Don't the Lushai call their hills home?'

She nodded. 'But only when we live there. Wherever we live is our home. Here is mine.' She spoke like a teacher to a pupil. 'But not in the case of the British. The British can live wherever they like, but their home is always in England.'

'And you think that's a bad thing?' asked Gerald.

Mary sat more upright and turned her head to face him. This time she did not look away as their eyes met. 'It may not be a bad thing for the British.'

There was a positiveness to her words which he had not expected. 'Why?'

'Because home is where you keep your most valued possessions. Home is where you can become your true self.' She hesitated and then said: 'Perhaps it is better for the British to become their true selves only when they are home.'

'That's nonesense. Is that what the nuns taught you?'

'No. But the nuns come here when they are young. They *never* go back. They are buried here; therefore, they are different. But, I can read, and I do read. I read your books, I read your newspapers and I read your magazines. All the British are not burra sahibs. They do not have servants in their own country. Some may have them, but most are chotta sahibs. And they work like us, digging coal in the ground, on the railways, making roads.'

'So you don't really like us?'

'I didn't say that.' She blushed, deeply. 'I meant to...' She was interrupted by urgent shouts from the direction of the path.

An elderly man, breathless, his eyes wild, burst into the clearing. 'Sah'b.' He ran to Gerald and grabbed him so violently by the arm he was dragged to his feet. 'Sah'b, *juldee*...' The man burst into a gabbled flow of Hindi which Gerald failed to understand.

He noticed the girl's face was now so bloodless her skin had become translucent. She silenced the man with a single word, and then said, urgently: 'Sah'b. You must come at once. There has been an accident.'

He followed her as she ran. A chappli slipped from one of her feet; she kicked off the other and left them where they lay.

There was a crowd of servants blocking the doorway of one of their living quarters when Gerald and the girl arrived. She shouted at them in Assamese, and they moved quickly aside. The room was in darkness, its one small window shuttered. It smelt musty, like the interior of a long unopened tomb. For a few seconds Gerald lost the girl in its gloom, then saw her, kneeling beside a low charpoy. He joined her.

Sunlight was filtering through the cracks in the shutters and doorway, and glistened strangely on the still figure. With horror, Gerald realised its significance. He wrenched the girl away from the bed. Mary struggled, resisting him, but he lifted her easily and carried her out into the compound. There were crimson bloodstains on her sari and on her feet. She saw them and screamed, but he held her even more tightly until she buried her head, sobbing, on his shoulder. He had seen the cut-throat razor lying in the blood on the old woman's body.

As the light of the fires became stronger than the fading day, Rasid, the bungalow khansama, brought her soup, a thin broth which Mary could not eat. She sat on the line-house steps, hunched miserably, her sari pulled over her head, so motionless she might have been dead herself. Vijaya was dead; the one friend with whom she could discuss her life, her dreams, her longings, sometimes her problems. Vijaya had known so much, had travelled to the cities, and been so wise. Yet she had killed herself rather than live in a world without the child, the man, she had fostered. She had killed herself because of her grief. No, because of her love.

The nuns had said it was a sin to take one's own life, because life was a gift of God, and to reject it was to reject him. But that was Christian thinking, and Vijaya had been Hindu; the choice had been hers to make. Was there a different God, different gods? Were gods created in the minds of people, or people in the minds of greater beings? Vijaya had once said to her that death was only one of many rungs in a ladder and that every step taken led always in the same direction. Vijaya had not feared death.

Did she fear death herself? Mary was not sure. She had seen it many times, even as a child; it brought grief to those who remained, but rest and peace to those it took. She had screamed when she had seen Vijaya's body; it had not been a scream of terror, but of shock. Then the arms had held her. Petrie Sahib's arms had held her. She had fought them instinctively at first, but then they had given her comfort. No man had ever held her so strongly, not even in play. She wished she could feel them around her now.

That evening, Gerald ate dinner alone. Jack had sent his apologies with the bearer, explaining he did not wish to leave his wife. Later, however, he joined Gerald on the verandah of the bungalow.

'I'm very grateful for what you did.' Jack was a silhouette against the light, but his bamboo chair creaked as he leant forward to replenish his glass. 'In the circumstances, I probably wouldn't have coped too well. God knows what Evelyn would have done. I haven't told her yet.' He took a long drink. 'D'you know, I'd forgotten old Vijaya was still around. Sounds awful, I know, but I don't think she's been out of the servants' compound for years. She was a funny old stick; was devoted to Freddie.' He put the glass quickly to his mouth.

'It was a kind of suttee, I believe,' said Gerald. 'I think she meant it as a compliment.'

'Throwing herself on to the funeral pyre? Yes, perhaps so. They live by symbolism, these people; die by it too, sometimes. But she might have spared a moment to think of Evelyn's feelings. It was a pretty inconsiderate thing to do to your memsah'b at a time like this.'

'It was probably the only time for the aiya.'

Gerald had carried the girl to her own quarters and left her with the wife of the head bearer, then he had supervised the moving of the old woman's body and the cleaning of her room. It had not been a pleasant experience for him, and he knew it would be a long time before he forgot the sight of the body. He had insisted it should be washed before being wrapped in its shroud. It had seemed an important gesture at the time. The head bearer was arranging the funeral, and as the aiya had been a Hindu, the body would be taken away for cremation the following day. There had been a small camphorwood casket in her room, and on it a note, written in a spidery pencil scrawl.

'Did you know she left Mary her money? Apparently, her life savings. A few hundred rupees.'

'I didn't know. But I suppose that would be typical of Vijaya.' Jack sighed: 'Just twenty-four hours, and suddenly your life is changed. And a lot of it wasted. Things just ... disintegrate. I'm damned sorry it all had to happen while you're here. Look, old chap, Evelyn and I won't be hurt if you'd prefer to spend the rest of your leave at the club. I can arrange accommodation for you in a dak bungalow. At least you'd find a few fellows of your own age to drink with. And the place would be a bit more lively for you.'

Only this morning, Gerald would have accepted the way out that Jack Warren was offering. But despite Jack's words, he could sense the man wanted him to stay; perhaps he was afraid to be alone. It might be that Evelyn was so locked into her own grief she was unable to comfort her husband. Perhaps it was something so terrible for them it couldn't be shared. Gerald said: 'If you don't mind, I think I'd rather stay. I'll try and make myself useful around the place.'

Jack Warren's relief was obvious. He took a Senior Service from the 'fifty' tin on the table between them, and lit it slowly as though it were a valuable cigar. 'We didn't want you to go,' he said, eventually. 'It's hard to explain how women think at times like this, but having you around is helping Evelyn, helping both of us. She talked about you this afternoon. Said how she thought you and Freddie would have got along well; gone on shikar together after leopard ... you know the kind of daydreaming.' Jack paused, looked away and said, softly: 'Damn! I was going to give him my rifle next time he came home. Alexander Henry double, .45. He always wanted it. I should have let him have it before; I never use the thing now. Used to shoot a lot once. Took Freddie with me for the first time when he was barely five years old. We used to get a lot of wildfowl then, in a bit of a tributary a few miles downstream. Used to shoot from a boat; too many snakes in the reed beds. Freddie thought it was great sport ... once, when he was only about two and a half years old...'

Gerald topped up his whisky glass, then eased himself into a more comfortable position in his chair. Jack wanted to relive Freddie's life and Gerald knew that the man was trying to remember every minute detail in a desperate attempt to keep some part of his son alive.

CHAPTER TWO

Gerald awoke, still enmeshed in his dream, with reality filtering only slowly back to his mind. He lay naked in his bed. Above him, the mosquito net was a pale mist in the sunlight, swaying gently in the draught of the fan blades. In sleep, the Lushai girl had been beside him and he had enjoyed the softness of her body against his own. He had felt her lips caress his shoulders, and even now could smell the musk of her rich perfume. The dream had been so real he had moved an arm as he awakened, searching for her, but he was alone. His penis was erect, an aching column rising above the lean plain of his stomach. Unable to ignore a schoolboy feeling of guilt, he pulled the bedsheet across his thighs.

In the garden the birds were singing in the palm tops, but when he looked at his watch he found it was only four a.m. and that he had been in bed for less than two hours.

Despite his attempts to smother his thoughts of the Lushai girl his erection persisted. He could remember exactly how Mary had felt in his arms when he had carried her from the dead aiya's room. She had seemed weightless, but the feminine warmth of her body had sprung through her flimsy clothing to meet his touch with unexpected sexuality, and her perfume had drowned the harsh iron scent of blood in his nostrils. Once she had stopped resisting him, it was as though the flesh of their bodies had fused together. It was a feeling he had never previously encountered, certainly not in his embraces with Monica.

But it was Monica he should be thinking about now, and having to use her to drive away fantasies of the Lushai girl made him angry with himself. If Monica were here, he reasoned, then he would want her far more than the local girl. The sudden realisation that he had never actually dreamed about Monica disturbed him; it had never occurred to him before. Of course he had experienced erotic dreams, especially when he was younger. Everyone did. In fact, most of the boys at Winchester seemed to have them about the matron, despite the fact she was at least four times their age! But he had never dreamed of Monica.

He wondered why. It was probably a question of respect, he decided. Monica was an accepted part of his future and therefore his mind must have subconsciously chosen to save her for then.

On his last evening in England, she had gazed at him across the table of the pub a few miles from his family home outside Guildford. The pub was busy with servicemen, and Gerald had fought his way to the bar through a crowd of American GIs. A radiogram behind the counter was turned up to full volume and he had been forced to shout his order. It was only by luck Monica had 'bagged' a table, when a pair of Canadians, blue and red 1st Army diamonds on their shoulders, had staggered out to the lavatory.

Conversation had been impossible. He and Monica had sat and looked at each other for an hour before leaving. Outside, it was raining and driving was difficult on unlit roads, with masked headlamps, the wiper blades barely coping with the rain thrashing against the windscreen. He had pulled off the road on to a patch of scrubland near Bagshot, and put his arm around her shoulders.

She had never permitted him to make love to her, not even what Americans described as 'heavy petting', and he had thought that as they were now to be separated for perhaps a couple of years, she might allow him to go further than merely cupping her breasts through the material of her clothing. But it had not been so. She had drawn up her legs beneath her, and stiffened ominously when he had attempted to unbutton the top of her dress. Rather than risk a quarrel on his last night in her company, he had simply kissed her.

Rain had drummed on the MG's roof as the windows misted. The sky outside was totally black, and the two of them could have been in the depths of a damp cavern. She had not asked how long he might be away, and if she was worried for his safety she had not mentioned it. She had only talked about the future; about their lives together when the war ended.

Soon she had drawn his attention to the luminous dial of the dashboard clock; it was twelve-thirty. His train from Euston was at eight a.m.

It had been after two by the time he had driven her home. In the morning it was still raining, and his mother had been silent during the unaccustomed early breakfast. And, just as though her child had been returning to school, the chauffeur had been waiting in the drive with the car already packed with his luggage. Gerald's father had shaken his son's hand beside the car, with the classic soldier's farewell from a parent: 'Take care, old man. Don't try to be a hero.' A cliché. Jack Warren had probably said exactly the same thing to Freddie!

But Freddie Warren had died, and taken his aiya with him. To the old woman, he was not the son of the Memsah'b, but her own, and although she had accepted without complaint the fading part she had played in his later years, with his death she had finally rebelled.

The clattering of an old engine in the bungalow compound grew to mask the bird song and intruded into Gerald's thoughts. He pushed up the mosquito netting, climbed from his bed, and went to the window. Through gaps between the chicks he could see one of the plantation lorries, parked with its engine running near the path leading to the servants' quarters. Its tailboard was down, and several of the servants were clustered nearby. A small procession appeared carrying the wrapped body of the aiya on a rough bier. It was lifted on to the back of the lorry. There were several empty oil drums behind it, and the remains of broken tea cases and a heap of torn hessian sacking. Gerald had the uncomfortable feeling that the body had become merely refuse to be dumped, along with other scrap from the factory, in some festering waste-pit.

Before the tailboard was slammed into place, Mary and the two gardeners climbed into the truck and sat themselves on the drums. The vehicle jerked abruptly as the driver let out the clutch, and then drove noisily down the track towards the road, the remaining servants watching until it became obscured by a veil of dust.

Gerald raised the blind and stared out beyond the trees to the far hills. The birds had begun singing again in the now deserted garden. That was how it was, in India; life as transient as passing through a doorway; death almost unnoticed, with the heat and climate permitting no lying in state, no Irish wake for a body. Here, you were alive, you died, and within hours ceased to exist even as a corpse.

As a child, Gerald had been forbidden to visit the burning ghats, but he had seen them since, passed them on his voyage upriver; most villages had them. Fires drifting their evil-smelling fumes through the trees and across the water. Relatives or friends tending the flames, and poking at the cremating bodies with long sticks. The British soldiers on the steamer had wrinkled their noses and sworn it stank no differently from any army cookhouse.

It was still early as Gerald washed and shaved in cold water in the bowl on the dresser, his mind unable to concentrate and flitting between thoughts like the birds in the fronds of the palms.

He cut himself with the razor, swore, and examined his face in the mirror. Blood was spreading rapidly on the wet skin. He had a brief feeling of panic, that it was somehow an omen, and wiped it desperately with the towel. To his relief the bleeding stopped at once. He stared at his reflection. Monica had once said he was handsome. He doubted if she would think so now; his cheeks were hollowed and jaundiced-looking beneath their tan, and the skin lined by the months of jungle training. His blond hair had aged white in the sun. But he knew his eyes had changed most of all; they were no longer those of a youth.

Gerald rode the daily inspection tour alone, at Jack's suggestion, but took his horse further than usual; to the boundaries where the neat rows of bushes thinned to uncultivated scrub. Thermals shimmered the distant hills and lifted circling kites and vultures on motionless wings until they were lost from sight high above him. Lizards sunned themselves on the hot sand of the track, darting from beneath the legs of the horse only when it seemed certain they would be crushed; crickets scattered explosively from dry clumps of grass as they were disturbed.

From the highest ground of the plantation, he could see the distant river, a brown scar dissecting the jungle, fading to uncertainty in the haze. He dismounted near an outcrop of rock, laced the reins to a tree branch and sat himself on a boulder. The heat of the rock scorched at his thighs.

The only sound was the electric hum of insects.

He stripped off his shirt, used it to wipe sweat from his chest, then draped it over the rock behind him. He pulled his bush hat forward to shield his eyes, then lay back. They said the sun never set on the British Empire, he thought. Somewhere it was always eleven a.m., or two, or midnight. Somewhere, someone was always being born, or dying. Here, he was resting in the sun; somewhere else was a man, stomach down in mud, or snow, with shells bursting around him, shrapnel screaming overhead, while he tried to press himself even more protectively into the earth. Friends Gerald had known at school had already died; one killed during RAF training, another in Sicily in the Armoured Corps. He wondered what they had ever achieved, if achievement was important, if it was enough simply to die for a cause. They had all wanted to fight. None had ever really considered dying; other people died, Freddie Warren for instance. But at least he was older than the rest of us, older than me, thought Gerald, and Freddie must have lived just a little before his death.

Gerald had overheard a conversation between his mother and father, during his embarkation leave. 'One thing we can be thankful for is that Gerald was accepted by the Assam Regiment,' his father had said. 'The Japs are stuck behind the Chindwin, and that's as far as they're likely to get. The Assam Regiment is just an extension of the State Police. It's probable he won't see any action, thank God. It's not as though he'll have to fight in Europe.'

For a while his father's words had made him feel like a coward. It was only when he joined his regiment in India that he realised his father had been reassuring his mother with a lie; they didn't waste time training men in jungle warfare unless they intended to use them to fight. The regiment had already served in Burma. He knew he would probably see action; and now he realised he too might die, just as Freddie Warren had died. It could all end, even before it had begun. Monica was an example; he had never made love to her. He had never made love to anyone! Twenty years old, and still a virgin. The thought made him feel uncomfortable. The expression was usually applied to women ... by men. Male virgins were the butt of army jokes, even amongst his own friends; he would never have made the admission to them.

Had Freddie died a virgin? It was unlikely, at twenty-eight or nine. Damn, it wasn't important, anyway. It had never seemed important with Monica. He had seen her naked, though, he mused. Well, almost naked: by accident. They had been swimming together and he had been teasing her about her swimming costume, calling her a banana split, because the costume had been bright yellow and divided up each side, with the front held to the back with thin strips of material. They had wrestled, and he had accidentally caught his hand in the costume, ripping a strap. For a moment, one of her breasts had been bared. She had never worn the costume again. It had been during the year they first met; he had been fifteen then, and she just three months younger. There had been no other girlfriends.

When he had arrived in India, Jason Wilde, one of his fellow lieutenants, had said: 'You'll like it here, Gerald. Great social life. Plenty of booze. Even a bit of polo at the depot; tennis, anything. And girls are no problem.'

No problem! There were enough notices around the camp to suggest they were the biggest problem of all. VD, warned the posters, in huge black lettering. And if they weren't enough proof, then there was always the sight of the queue outside the MO's surgery after every leave period. If you had any sense, Gerald had told himself, then you kept yourself to yourself out here. The MO had said as much in his lecture shortly after their arrival at the depot. 'Five per cent of the female population here suffers from venereal disease. And any girl who lets you go to bed with her, you can be absolutely certain, is part of that five per cent. How do we know? Because virginity is essential out here if a girl wants to make a good marriage. Therefore, any girl who parts with it has made a positive decision as to the type of life she intends to lead afterwards. Well, lads, we might be able to cure certain forms of VD, but we can't cure all the varieties you can catch in India. So remember, there are some kinds of souvenirs you won't be wanting to take home to your wives and girlfriends...'

Some men gambled. Others didn't.

Jack Warren had driven into Gauhati by the time Gerald returned to the bungalow, so he lunched with Evelyn. She looked pale, tired and very much older. She made no mention of her son, but kept the conversation to the difficulties of running the plantation and factory in wartime. She and Jack, she told Gerald, had come to a decision. They were going to retire as soon as the war ended, and return to England. Running a plantation was work for younger people. She had family in Suffolk, and they would look for a house nearby. Gerald suspected the decision to leave India was hers alone and she was telling him of their plans in order to commit her husband, who might not be quite so enthusiastic about the idea. He decided not to mention it in his report, if he ever got around to writing it.

The lorry which had carried the aiya's body had returned to the factory before noon. Gerald had seen it as he gave his horse to the waiting groom. There had been no sign of Mary, but on his ride he had decided he would try to see her again that day. However, as he walked down the track leading to the glade around the plantation reservoir that afternoon, he grew progressively less certain of his reasons for seeking her.

Inexplicably, Mary had known Petrie Sahib would seek her company. In sadness their minds had somehow reached out tendrils and found each other. She sensed he would never again view her as a servant, but as a woman. It was easy to allow herself to be lifted and carried by the gusty winds of romantic emotions, to permit herself the indulgences of daydreams in which a love between herself and Petrie Sahib blossomed to the heights of those of the Hindu literature she had always enjoyed, the loves of gods and their chosen maidens. She knew in reality it was never so. But reality, today, was too harsh, too cruel for her to dwell on; reality was the sombre silence of her mistress's bungalow, the smoking ashes of sandalwood on a funeral pyre.

She had returned from Vijaya's funeral with her skin, hair and clothing impregnated by the sweet antiseptic smell of the woodsmoke. In the small cubicle of her line-room she had stripped herself naked and washed, head to feet, in the enamel washbasin of tepid water with the thin slivers of perfumed soap she salvaged from Evelyn Warren's bathroom. When she was dry and had tied back her hair in a long, damp plait, she had perfumed herself and dressed carefully in her best sari. She felt clean, refreshed, the skin of her arms and legs more supple where she had rubbed in the perfumed oil which was one of the few luxuries her wages permitted. She hated the reptilian appearance of the skin of the girls who worked the long hours in the sun of the plantation.

She walked slowly to the clearing around the reservoir, confident that if she waited, Petrie Sahib would come to her.

He knew she would be there, almost as much a part of the jungle glade as the vines which clung to the gnarled trees. He deliberately softened his step as he approached, hoping to be able to watch her for a few moments while she was still unaware of his presence. She sat, her back very straight, staring at the dark surface of the pool. She wore the orange sari he had seen on his first day on the plantation, its saffron colour so intense that here in the shade of the trees and bamboo, it glowed like the robe of a Buddhist monk. Again, he felt his scalp prickle. The day before, he had imagined a hidden temple. Now, it seemed close enough to touch. Even had he wanted to call her name, it would have been as difficult as raising his voice in the solemn atmosphere of an English country church.

For the first time, he was able to study her carefully. She was very slender, and childlike, the folds of her sari concealing all the womanly curves of her body. Her hands, clasped on her thighs, were long fingered. Her face was certainly more oriental than that of most Indians he had seen, her nose narrow, slightly *retroussé* and her lips full and sensuous.

She spoke without moving. 'You are making me feel self-conscious, sah'b.'

'I'm sorry. I didn't realise you'd seen me.' Gerald felt like a child caught stealing biscuits.

'I read once that we would not exist today if we had been unable to see out of the corners of our eyes.' The girl turned her head towards him. 'Wild animals would have eaten us all.'

'I suppose so. Do you mind me coming here?'

'Of course not. This place does not belong to me.'

Gerald joined her on the concrete cover and, as he sat next to her, she stared at the pool again. Gerald wanted to put an arm around her; draw her close to him, but was nervous of her reaction. If he frightened her now, or made her angry, he would be left only with the memories of his dreams. He was uncertain how she would react to the approaches of a European, or even how much she might force herself to tolerate them, simply because of her position as a servant in the Warrens' household. He did not want her to feel blackmailed. He folded his arms awkwardly.

'Was this morning bad?' he asked her.

'No, sah'b. Not too bad. I have seen burnings many times. It is usually the way for Hindus.'

'It was generous of the aiya to leave you her money,' he said. 'That should be very helpful for you.'

'How?'

'Well...' He didn't want her to know Jack had discussed her with him. 'Well, it will give you independence.'

Mary laughed. 'Independence. How you British use the word!

With a few hundred rupees a person can buy their independence; but not a country. No matter how wealthy a country may be, it cannot buy such a thing.'

'So you really think we should leave your country?'

'No, I don't think you should leave, sah'b. But I think you should stay as guests rather than conquerors.'

'We're hardly conquerors. Conquering is what the Nazis are trying to do. And the Japanese. You're part of the British Empire.'

'We would rather be part of our own empire, sah'b. We would rather obey our own laws, and dispense our own justice ... even fight our own battles. It will happen, one day. I think perhaps soon.'

'Maybe you're right. And what will you do then? Still work for Warren Sah'b?'

Surprisingly, Mary said: 'No. I shall not work for him.'

'Then who? For an Indian?'

She laughed again. 'I am hoping I may work at a school, sah'b. As a teacher. I have been saving for that purpose. I hope I shall go to Delhi, to a college, and obtain a teaching certificate.'

'That's very ambitious.'

Mary nodded. 'To succeed at anything, one must be so.'

'And then? After you get your certificate, where will you teach?'

'In Assam, of course. Perhaps Shillong.' She stood up, and carefully smoothed her sari.

'Do you have to go?' Gerald asked quickly, and then regretted his question.

'No. But perhaps we can walk a little?'

The bamboo, once they had left the clearing, was high enough to shade the path. In places tall rods arched and met to form green tunnels. Shafts of bright sunlight penetrated the foliage in a theatrical effect. The atmosphere was heavy, moist, beneath the dense canopies. The girl was walking close to Gerald; so close that when the track narrowed their arms touched. They had not spoken for some time and the walk had become a stroll.

Gerald was uncomfortable, the nerves of his stomach feeling like a violin string stretched towards breaking point. This, and the humidity of the surrounding thicket, was making him perspire. He felt boyish and immature. He was supposed to be an officer, he told himself, capable of positive and decisive action. Yet here he was, as diffident as a schoolboy at his first dance and with a servant of one of his father's employees. He was an idiot to risk making a fool of himself with a native girl ... even such an attractive one. He took hold of her hand, half expecting her to resist. Instead, she slipped her fingers between his and held him tightly.

The track opened on to one of the terraced fields and the girl stopped. 'We should go back. I must work again soon.'

Gerald turned her to face him. Her head was level with his chest, but she looked downwards. He lifted her chin, gently. Now there was slight resistance. He let his fingers trace the outline of her jawbone as their eyes met.

'Sah'b, it is not sensible for us.' Her eyes were as dark as the pool in the glade.

'Nothing is sensible anymore. Freddie Warren dying wasn't sensible. The aiya killing herself wasn't sensible. The war isn't sensible. Reality isn't sensible.'

'But we have to live with it, sah'b.'

He felt her body soften a little. 'And calling me sah'b all the time is certainly not sensible.'

'It is the custom ... sah'b.'

'Gerald.'

'Gerald Sah'b.' She tried to move her head aside, but his hand held her firmly, though not fiercely.

Mary could sense his nervousness and beneath it a deeper feeling of fear. 'He is afraid of me,' she thought at first. 'Why should he be afraid?' His deep blue eyes were staring at her. No, it was not her he feared, it was death! The realisation startled her. This man thought he was going to die; thought he was going to be killed! And if he was convinced of this, then he would go to war and not return. She reached her hand up to his cheek and stroked it gently. She felt he was a child, to be drawn close to her until its fear had passed.

She started to say his name, but his lips silenced her. She had not been kissed before, and the intimacy his lips implied almost panicked her for a moment. She could feel her blood pulsing through the veins of her temples. Briefly, she wanted to break away from his arms and run to hide herself in some dark, unknown place, but the feeling passed. She let her body mould itself to his. His arms tightened around her, making it difficult for her to breathe. She knew if he held her much longer, with such passion, she would lose consciousness; her mind was already blurring, her thoughts disjointed and kaleidoscopic.

She pulled her head away. He mistook her action and let his arms drop. She swayed and almost fell. He steadied her, quickly. 'I'm sorry. It was unforgivable of me.'

Mary was silent for a few seconds, knowing that whatever she did or said next could decide the future for both of them. A careless action or word would place a barrier between them he might never again attempt to cross. She could feel him trembling as he held her. She put her arms around him.

This time there was more care and softness in his embrace, and after a little while he moved his kisses to her neck and shoulders and then simply held her close.

'Gerald, the Memsah'b will be wanting me.'

'Damn the Memsah'b!' His arms tightened again.

'I must go. It is my work.' She wriggled, deliberately playful, enjoying the feeling of his body against her own, and the strength of his arms around her.

'What time will you finish tonight?'

'Much too late. Not until the Memsah'b has changed for dinner.'

'We can meet then,' he said.

She wriggled again. 'No, it is impossible. Where would we go? You cannot take me for a walk in the tea at night. There are snakes, and cheetah. You know all that.'

'Tomorrow then?'

'Yes.'

'Here. After tiffin.'

'Yes, Gerald.'

She let him kiss her once more.

Her room was twelve feet square, the floor naked concrete with only a single piece of old carpet beside the bed. The ceiling was corrugated iron, painted dark red, not for decoration but to prevent the metal rusting. In one corner was a wooden cupboard, which served as her wardrobe. A shelf along one white-painted wall held a small collection of domestic pottery. Below it she had pinned a few photographs cut from the pages of Evelyn's discarded magazines: models from *Vogue*, a British village scene from *Country Life*.

There was a solitary window in the room, shuttered outside, and beneath it stood a narrow table upon which burnt a mosquito-coil balanced on a cone of baked clay. There was no fan to disturb the heavy air layered with pungent blue smoke.

Her bed was a bamboo charpoy, sited away from the walls with its feet standing in tinlids full of paraffin, to deter the crawling insects which often found their way under the room's ill-fitting door. Above the bed hung an unshaded light bulb.

The room next door, separated only by a thin wall, had been that of the dead aiya. At night, Mary had listened to her movements; they had often been comforting. But although it was little more than twenty-four hours since the aiya's death in the tiny concrete cell, it was already occupied; now there was the unaccustomed sound of snoring, only feet away.

Mary Sachema lay on her charpoy staring at the crucifix which hung on a nail beyond the foot of her bed. It was her oldest possession, a childhood gift one Christmas from the nuns who had taught her. The solace she found with it was more in its familiarity than the religion into which she had been baptised. Somehow its effect was almost hypnotic, the plaster Christ on its fretwork cross managing to concentrate her thoughts, while isolating her from the stark surrounds of the room.

She had already relived, a dozen times, her last meeting with Gerald Petrie; imagining the touch of his lips, his muscular body pressed against her own, and experiencing the strange intoxication the contact had brought. She knew now she was in love with him, and it was already painful. Protectively, she was attempting to let her thoughts drift and find their way into her dreams; a childhood palliative against anger or hurt. Tonight, her mind refused to co-operate. Love, she had told herself, required the expectation of a future in order to flourish. She could expect nothing other than disappointment. Gerald needed her only briefly, if he needed her at all.

For the past hours she had forced herself to acknowledge every reason for the futility of her love, hoping logic would provide the analeptic she sought. Throughout her life, whenever she had imagined love, it had always been a thing of excitement, happiness and satisfaction. Now she realised despair and hopelessness were also among its attributes.

She sensed this consuming type of love would exist only once in her lifetime. Tearing across her emotions like the edge of a carpenter's rasp, it would forever destroy the keen points of future sentiment, leaving them dull and flattened.

Briefly, she despised herself. Hating the light brown colouring of her skin, the unfeminine slenderness of her figure, her parochial schooling, and even her nationality and background of the hills. She had never visited a city, and yet he had lived in the greatest in the world. Mary felt she could barely comprehend the education he must have experienced, and the knowledge he would have amassed. He knew wealth and its uses, she was ignorant and poor. She had nothing to offer him, nothing with which she could even tempt him.

A moth fluttered against the lightbulb. For a fraction of a second, before the heat scorched its wings and it fell, its shadow brought momentary life to the features of the plaster image on the wall. It was enough to fracture the melancholic line of thought her mind was pursuing, and swing it towards more characteristic determination.

She had met a man whom she now loved, and as her ancestors had fought to hold their precious territories, she must do the same. If he found her attractive, then she must make herself more so. If he required education and worldly experience of her, then she would obtain it. If he wanted a memsah'b, then she would become one. And as far as her colour and physical aspects were concerned, then perhaps they were not, in his eyes, any disadvantage.

Mary turned off the light and lay in the darkness. Soon, his leave would be over and he would return to his unit. She had no idea where this might be – perhaps a thousand miles away. Somehow, she must make herself important to him, make him want to return to her. Would letters be enough? She had not even a photograph of herself to give him.

She did not sleep, that night.

For Gerald, the next two days of his leave passed quickly. In retrospect, it would seem they had been filled entirely by his time spent with Mary. In fact, this was less than three hours each afternoon. He contrived to see her more frequently, deliberately choosing routes through the bungalow complex which might take him near the place where she would be working. He was aware his attention must be obvious to the Warrens, but they said nothing. And his leave, which had at one time seemed interminably long, shortened more rapidly than he would have believed possible. In only another four days he would have to return to his unit, and the war.

He was not thinking of the distant future. To do so meant considering the possibility of his own death. Instead, he concentrated on enjoying the present, attempting to prolong every exciting moment he spent in her company.

Physically, their relationship had progressed little further than kisses, but he recognised subtle changes. She now sought contact with him, finding his hands when she was beside him, holding herself close to him when they sat together.

There was a naivity in her conversation which pleased and relaxed him. There was no feeling of competition, no cleverness. Deliberately he chose subjects he knew would interest her, and of which she would have some understanding. In return, she told him of her childhood in the hills, of tribal customs, insisting he should attempt to learn a few words of Lushai. And it was then her humour first surfaced as she laughed and teased him at his mistakes.

Gerald was considering the possibility he might make love to her before his leave ended. Sometimes, particularly when he was in bed, he found it difficult to think of much else. Since the afternoon when he had first kissed her, he had never once sensed the slightest disapproval of his caresses and felt that there was a secret invitation to him to increase their intimacy. His own resistance was deliberate: just as he was eluding the commitment verbal expressions of his feelings might bring, not perhaps to Mary but to himself, so he was also avoiding that of closer physical contact between them. This reluctance he could barely explain to himself; part was certainly due to his upbringing in a household that valued the pseudo-ethics of the generation of his Victorian grandparents, but other less pleasant aspects he was forced to recognise included his own insecurity, and even the problems, which he despised, of class and race. His family, by the standards of the British aristocracy, were still newcomers, but this in no way lessened the respect the title claimed, and as heir this had been drummed into him from his childhood.

Whatever might have happened during the course of the next few days of Gerald's leave was changed by the arrival at the plantation on the morning of 19 March of a captain of the Intelligence Corps.

The officer, an angular and narrow-faced man in his mid-thirties, and accompanied by an Indian driver, was standing impatiently waiting beside his jeep in the compound when Gerald and Jack arrived back from their morning tour of inspection.

The officer saluted Warren informally with his cane and introduced himself. 'Captain Philip James. Intelligence Corps. Gauhati. Mr Warren? Good.' He stared at Gerald. 'Then, presumably, you are Lieutenant Petrie?' He added, 'Excellent,' when Gerald nodded.

The officer waited while the two men dismounted, then continued. 'Glad to have found you both together. Can kill two birds with one stone.'

Jack handed his reins to the syce and asked: 'Like a drink? Beer? Lemonade?'

The captain shook his head. 'Sorry. Haven't time. Still got a long way to go. Presumably you've heard the news?'

Jack said: 'No. What news?'

'Damned Japs. On the bloody move. Last we heard was that they were in the Kabaw valley. But we know how fast they got through Malaya and Burma. That's why I'm here. Need to talk about evacuation.'

'Evacuation?' Jack looked stunned.

'Possibly. No need to panic, yet.' The captain stared around the compound. 'Just need to discuss a few points. You'll understand, we have to consider every possibility; including them getting as far as the Brahmaputra. Naturally, if we're going to have to fight here then we won't want the responsibility of civilians.'

Jack Warren reacted more violently then Gerald expected. 'What the hell do you expect us to do, just pack our bags and piss off?'

'Not exactly, old chap. I'm not saying we're expecting you to do anything. Just to be prepared. You won't get much notice. And I'm afraid that when you do, you'll not be able to take much with you; a suitcase apiece and no servants. Sorry, but not even a bearer.'

'I'm damned if I'm leaving any of my staff for the Japs to play with,' said Jack angrily.

The captain spoke calmly. 'I don't like it any more than you do, old man. But that's how it is. I'm afraid, unless you care to take the initiative and evacuate yourself now, you'll have to string along with us. There won't be any rail transport, the roads will be full, or closed. So we're keeping our fingers crossed we can find a steamer. And that's if we're lucky.'

'A steamer's a bit vulnerable, isn't it?' asked Gerald.

'If you're thinking of air attack, then a steamer should be all right if we get it away soon enough. It'll take the Japs quite a time to establish a forward airbase.' He faced Jack again. 'I'm afraid a lot of this will have to be destroyed.' He waved the point of his cane in the direction of the factory buildings. 'If we go, we're not leaving them anything.' He saw Jack's stunned look. 'It won't be your responsibility. We'll leave all that to the REs.' He paused. 'Sorry. Nasty war. Do you have any weapons?'

Jack sounded dazed. 'Shotgun, game rifle.'

'Good. Probably won't need them, but I should start carrying 'em around with you. Out in the tea, I mean. Can't see the INA letting this opportunity pass by; could be a bit of trouble, especially at night. Can you trust your chokidar?'

'Explicitly. Been with me fifteen years.'

'Then give him the shotgun. And tell him to use it if he hears anything suspicious. Better warn all your employees to stay indoors after dark. Shouldn't tell them about the evacuation, though; might start a panic. We don't want the kind of refugee problems we got in France.' He hesitated for a moment and then said: 'By the way. You can expect a visit from the Sappers. They like to plan in advance. I think they'll want to have a look at your place from a defence point of view; understand me?'

'Of course.'

'Good.' The captain faced Gerald. 'Ah, yes, Lieutenant Petrie. Young man, I'm afraid your leave is over. Well, almost. Here.' He handed Gerald an envelope. 'Don't bother to read it now. It simply tells you to report to Dimapur tomorrow. All leave has been cancelled.' He spoke to Jack. 'Can you get him down to the RTO's office in Gauhati in the morning by eight ack emma? Save us having to send out transport.'

Jack said: 'Yes.'

'Then I'll be on my way.' The captain turned towards his jeep, then faced them again. 'If I was you, Warren, I'd listen to all the news broadcasts from now on. The war isn't quite so distant any more.'

Jack Warren watched the jeep drive away, then spoke softly. 'I suspect it's been closer to me this week than to him.'

*

He had thought she resembled a fawn, and now, as Mary stared at him, her dark eyes filling with tears, the likeness occurred to him again. He had not expected this reaction. 'You knew I'd have to go in a few days.' He spoke apologetically. 'I'm sorry, Mary.'

She was gripping both his hands tightly. 'But, I thought you would go back to Calcutta.'

He tried to cheer her. 'But Dimapur is much closer. I'll come and visit you.'

'You'll be fighting.'

'Not necessarily. But I'm a soldier, and that is what soldiers are for. But they'll probably put me in charge of captured Japanese or something . . . maybe the cookhouse.' He smiled at her. 'I'll be able to eat all the time. And get myself fat.' The tears were running faster. No one he could remember had ever cried for him before. She pulled herself close to him and he could feel the dampness of her tears against his face. 'It'll all be over one day,' he told her.

'I don't want you to go.' He could feel her breath warm against his neck as she spoke.

'I'm not sure I want to go either. But that's the way it has to be. All good things come to an end.'

'Why must they?'

'I don't know. It's just a saying.'

'A stupid saying. A British saying not an Indian one.' She moved her head slightly, and brought her lips to his. The dream must not be allowed to end so quickly, so incomplete.

It was after eleven p.m. Gerald sat alone on the verandah. Behind him, most of the bungalow lights were out and only a small table-lamp in the lounge shone a yellow beam from the windows into the darkness. He was chain-smoking his cigarettes, lighting each fresh one from the butt of the last.

Above, the sky was bright with stars that appeared too large to be real. Constellations he had known from other times seemed to be within touching distance as he stared at them. Orion, the Hunter, was somehow out of place; once, he had sat on Butser Hill in Hampshire, listening to the scoutmaster describing it. Now, he felt Orion belonged to Butser Hill, not a plantation in Assam. The inconceivable vastness of space was making him feel miniscule and even more vulnerable. He closed his eyes and drew heavily on the cigarette, feeling the hot smoke in his throat, and holding it momentarily in his lungs before releasing it, slowly. Soon, he knew, there would be nights without the comfort of tobacco, nights when the blackness was torn aside by the flame of explosion and propellant, when the only sounds were those of war and death.

He wondered what other soldiers would be thinking tonight; the men pulled back from their leaves, from the bars and clubs of the towns and cities. And those who waited, somewhere, crouched in a trench or foxhole, rifles loaded, watching, listening. Were they, too, afraid? He envied the men who apparently lacked imagination, who faced their war with a detachment which formed a protective casing around them. There were those, a few, who lived for the danger battle would provide; or perhaps the escape.

He knew he was being foolish, allowing his mind to explore subjects he already found sufficiently morbid, but although he had deliberately drunk several large glasses of whisky he was too awake to sleep.

Not far away, he mused, Japanese soldiers would be watching this same night sky. They would be using it, the great compass guiding them through untracked jungle as they moved silently from shadow to shadow. It was said they were animals; it was said they were illiterate and of low intelligence, depending totally on their officers; it was said they were not innovative, that they were incapable of individual action. But despite their critics they had taken much of China, Malaya and Burma and were now on the very frontiers of India. The British propaganda machine became less and less believable. Gerald had spoken to men who had already fought the Japanese. The survivors had told of their unbelievable courage and determination, fanatical disregard of death, and their cruelty towards those they took prisoner. Somewhere between the two opinions, official and experienced, lay the truth. Soon, he would know for himself.

He was suddenly aware of silence. Frogs that had croaked amongst the lilies of the ornamental pool across the lawns, and the crickets in the grass and shrubs, were now stilled. Something had disturbed them, hushed them. He remembered the warning the Intelligence Officer had given to Jack Warren. It might be only the chokidar making his rounds of the gardens. But perhaps it was an intruder, some dacoit or INA guerilla sneaking his way through the groves of rhododendron towards the bungalow? He sat forward in the armchair.

His eyes caught a slight movement in the night shadows.

'Gerald.' Her voice was little more than the whisper of a breeze as she moved from the darkness towards him. Her sari, concealing the movement of her limbs, made her phantom-like against the silhouetted trees.

He stook up quickly. But before he could speak, she placed a finger to her lips and in a second was beside him. She let him kiss her, then said, simply: 'I couldn't sleep. I miss you too much, already.'

'I shall miss you, Mary.'

She remembered the hours of torment that had finally led her, now, to his arms; rebelling against the teaching and codes of her strict upbringing. In the quiet of her room she had clearly heard the voice of a nun at the mission school: 'Fornication is a mortal sin!' Questioned as to the meaning of her words, the nun had blushed as she replied, 'It is animal gratification, outside the sanctity of marriage.' She had forbidden the children to discuss the subject. Although tonight the nun's statement had been the only argument Mary's mind had provided, it had been sufficient to cause her anguish. For a time she had felt herself teetering on the edge of a cliff, over which she might fall to her doom ... to the everlasting pit of demons that was the hell the nun had pictured for her young charges. Strangely, as Mary had visualised it this evening, the faces of the demons had been those of the humans who had warned her of its dangers.

Surely, Mary had desperately rationalised, something given or accepted in a pure and real love could not be sinful, and for Christians to deny the total giving of themselves for love must be wrong; a gift half given or half accepted had no meaning. He will go tomorrow, she had told herself at last. But before he leaves he must know the real strength of my love and understand he is everything to me. For a little while we must both experience the ultimate closeness of a love which will never happen again.

She held him tightly, and her voice was unusually low pitched, serious. 'Gerald. I don't want to leave you tonight.'

For a few seconds he tried to assess the meaning of her words. Her command of English was not perfect. Should he interpret what she had said in its literal sense, or was she offering herself to him? He felt blood flush his cheeks, and made his reply deliberately ambiguous. 'The Warrens. We have to think about them.'

'No. At this time we should think of ourselves. Tomorrow,

Warren Sahib will still be here, but you will be gone. We have only a few hours left. I want us to ...' She hesitated, then continued in a whisper. 'I want us to be together as, as man and woman.'

He experienced a sensation of physical longing more powerful than he had ever known before. He made an attempt to control it, reminding himself of the Warrens' attachment to conventions and how they would view such an indiscretion by a guest.

Mary spoke again: 'Gerald, please.'

He had never felt more wanted, nor such an intense need within himself. The warm length of her body was pressing against him and he was suddenly aware of the stupidity of fighting the desire both of them were experiencing. Damn the Warrens, he thought. And damn the narrow society in which they live. There was no place for outdated customs in wartime; at least, not so far as the young who fought and died were concerned.

He asked, gently: 'Will you come to my room?'

The starlight rippled on her hair, as she nodded.

The crescent of a young moon had risen above the heads of the palms and casuarinas in the gardens, bringing its soft light to his unshuttered room. He started towards the window to close the chicks to ensure their privacy, but she stopped him, fearing darkness might lend anonymity to future memories.

She could feel uncertainty in the hot dampness of his strong hands, and was aware, instinctively, she must not help him. She waited, motionless.

Gerald knew whatever he did she would accept, totally; there would be no resistance, no rejection. Although the thought excited him, it made him cautious; there could be only one first time for them. He took her gently in his arms and kissed her, tasting again the rich oriental fragrance on her skin, enjoying the movement of her body against him. Carefully, she matched her ardour to his, forcing him to lead them both, encouraging him by her response to his caresses.

Often she had imagined kisses from a man she loved, without realising the fullness of emotion she would experience and the manner in which they could detach her mind from any sense of time and reality; soon, the room itself did not exist, no walls surrounded her, the ground beneath her feet no longer supported her. It was as though his lips, and the embrace in which he held her, were carrying her through a maelstrom of overwhelming sensuality.

A moment arrived when she understood the thin layers of clothing separating them were a blasphemy. His hands fumbled awkwardly at her sari, confused by the unfamiliar garment. She wanted to tear it from her, but resisted the urgent desire and prayed silently it would loosen, fall. Fabric slid from her shoulders, but seemed to cling for an eternity before dropping away. Her blouse briefly imprisoned her before he slipped it off her, and she stood, naked.

She expected him to take her in his arms again and hold her close, but instead he stepped back, away from her. Embarrassed, she lowered her head, then felt his eyes exploring her. Perhaps her body would not please him?

Gerald stared at her, fascinated. It seemed to him that mystically he had revealed a goddess. Moonlight turned her skin to the pale, cool, marble of a statue, made her body impossibly delicate and elfin. Her loose hair was a jet veil draping entrancing shoulders and perfect breasts, accentuating the inviting curves of her slim waist.

He wanted to tell her how beautiful she looked, but felt the coarse sound of his voice might dissolve the fragile and entrancing image he needed to retain, forever.

The cry of some hunting nightbird, distant and plaintive, broke the spell of the moment. Gerald was conscious of his own ugly clothing still isolating them. He felt momentary panic. Should he expect her to undress him? He was uncertain. He had been naked many times with other men, in school, or sports, but then the manner of undressing had been unimportant. Mary lifted her head, and her soft, dark eyes watched him, expectantly. There was no way, he decided, in which he could disrobe with elegance; he eased off his tie and shirt, unbuckled his belt, and stepped out of his slacks and underpants. He hoped the poor light concealed the blush he knew was colouring his face and neck; his penis, erect and heavy, was a lever between his thighs.

She had seen naked men before, those who washed themselves at the river, and the youths who swam. But she had never seen the body of a man whom her own body was exciting, nor an erect phallus which stood like an ivory tusk waiting for her, almost threateningly. Gerald was motionless, his only movement the slight rise and fall of his chest. He seemed so self-assured, so confident in his manliness that Mary felt her courage diminishing. She had wanted to behave like a woman, perhaps as a wife, but he must surely now discover she was no more than an unripe girl. She had not realised his penis would bring such a sense of awe to this moment as she anticipated its penetration. The sudden thought he might be misinterpreting her hesitation as disappointment horrified her; his body was beautiful. Instantly her fear was not of him, but that they were separated by even so small a distance.

To Gerald's relief, she came to him and drew him against her, pressing her body against his own, their flesh blending in the embrace.

Neither would remember their move towards the bed; perhaps he carried her, or she had led him. For a long time they lay together, their limbs entwined, each individual cell of their bodies seeking its own erotic contact. In dreams she had underestimated the sexuality of a lover's touch, the inquisitive tongue exciting expectant nerves, the intoxicating provocation of loving hands. His perspiration on her lips now held his identity for her, masculine, salty, no longer alien, generated by the heat of the night and their growing passion.

Momentarily, she felt she had almost failed him, but checked an involuntary tightening of her muscles as his fingers entered the exquisitely secret places of her body, and the hard, bone-like part of him pressed hot against her stomach. To reassure herself, and him, she touched it, grasped it, and held it to her.

Gerald had dreaded the exposure of his own inexperience during this first intimacy, but now his qualms were forgotten. Mary's body responded eagerly to him, encouraging him with its inviting moistness.

He was above her now, lying between her open thighs, his body heavy. She held him, guided him, protectively; the tip of his penis forcing at her. She gasped as it entered her, there was a brief hesitation as he slightly withdrew and then she put both arms around him and drove her hips upwards, accepting him deep within herself, holding him with all her strength, realising that what was now happening was beyond their control. She heard herself gasping, crying. The swirling tumult returned, as new sensations overwhelmed her. Gerald shuddered, groaned; she held him more tightly, at first misunderstanding as he slowed, relaxed, the fierceness of their joining becoming contentment as he gently smoothed her damp hair from her face, and found her parted lips.

The night air, undisturbed by the motionless blades of the fan above them, seemed cool on their bodies.

'Mary,' Gerald whispered between their long kisses, 'Mary, I love you.'

CHAPTER THREE

KOHIMA. SUNDAY, 9 APRIL 1944

Behind the dug-outs and foxholes occupied by the men of the 1st Assam Regiment, the terraced ground rose for a little over four hundred yards to the peak of Garrison Hill. To their east, half a mile away, was the District Commissioner's bungalow in what had been the administrative section of the ruined township. Southwards, each of the more strategically important features of the Kohima Ridge were defended in a series of boxes, the last at Jail Hill, almost a mile from Lieutenant Gerald Petrie's trench. The Naga settlement, which had consisted less than a week ago of scores of thatched-roof dwellings, was already largely demolished by shelling and mortaring; the buildings had little substance, and burnt easily.

The Japanese advance had been terrifyingly swift and determined, their objective the allied railhead at Dimapur, some forty miles to the west. If they could secure it, they would open the gateway to Assam, Bengal and the whole of India. Indeed, the commander of the Japanese 33rd Army had promised himself that for his victory celebrations he would ride through Delhi on a white charger.

The Assam Regiment had been in action for almost two weeks. First, defending an area some thirty-five miles away at Jessami, where they had been surrounded but had managed to break out at night-time and withdraw to their present position reinforcing the Kohima garrison. They had already suffered severe casualties, and only 260 men and officers had survived. The battles had been awesome, with the young and inexperienced sepoys of the regiment firing their weapons until the barrels became red-hot, and the closeness of the attacking enemy had forced them to resort to bayonets, knives and bare fists.

The weather had broken, and low cloud mingled with the smoke of explosions above the hills. The air was humid, dank and stinking, as the bodies of the dead bloated and rotted on the torn ground. Flies tormented the men in daylight, while mosquitoes added to their discomfort as the sun dropped. At present there was no shortage of food, but water was scarce, the only supply tanks being destroyed in the early days of the fighting.

Two days previously, on 7 April, the Japanese had outflanked the Kohima defenders and cut the Dimapur road behind them. Kohima was now under siege.

Lieutenants Gerald Petrie and Stephen Chandler were hunched, side by side, in a narrow trench facing the direction of the last Japanese attack. It had taken place at dawn, less than twenty minutes after 'stand to' had been ordered by the colonel. Its imminence had been signalled by a heavy mortaring, followed by several waves of infantry charges. Despite the machine-guns, Stens and rifles of the defenders, the Japanese had managed to get within grenade-throwing distance of the trenches before being stopped; their bodies were piled, one upon another, thirty yards away, already putrifying in the heat.

Now, some two hours after the attacks had ceased, the regiment's position was being shelled by an infantry gun from the hill beyond the Naga village. It was hardly a bombardment, but at regular five-minute intervals a shell would whistle into the area to explode, showering the men with sticky earth, and stripping the few remaining leaves from the skeletal tree branches and stumps above the terraces of former rice fields.

Chandler held a Sten gun across his knees. His helmet was pulled forward over the upper part of his chubby, boyish face and Gerald thought he was asleep. There had been little opportunity for rest during the night. Any sector commanders who allowed their men to relax soon found them infiltrated by the continuous enemy patrols. There had been several such instances, when guards who had been unable to remain awake had been found with their throats cut and their bodies boobytrapped. Few men in the forward trenches risked sleeping during the hours of darkness.

Another of the shells screamed into the box and exploded

with a dull crump sixty yards away. Chandler moved his head slightly, changed the position of his Sten and found a distorted pack of cigarettes in the breast pocket of his shirt. He patted his pockets, searching for matches. 'Here,' Gerald passed him a box, and took one of the proffered Victory Vs.

'Know what day it is?' asked Chandler, shifting his weight off his cramped buttocks.

'Saturday or Sunday,' said Gerald. Days didn't seem to matter anymore; there were too many of them, and each more uncomfortable than the last. He had been astonished to find that he was unafraid in battle, but always exhausted afterwards. Now, he would have given almost everything he owned to spend a whole day in some peaceful bed. At the moment, he was having difficulty keeping his eyes open.

'Sunday,' said Chandler. 'Easter Sunday.'

Gerald opened the flap of one of his pouches and pulled out a grenade. 'Here.' He tossed it to Chandler. 'Have an Easter Egg.'

Chandler caught it and laughed. A little further along the trench, two of the men, a Khasi naik and a Naga sepoy, turned to watch them, and grinned at the comforting cheerfulness of their officers. 'I'll save that for a Japanese,' Chandler said. He looked closely at Gerald. 'God, you look disgusting. How long since you washed and shaved?'

'A week. And you?'

'The same. But my beard doesn't show. Wish it did. I was hoping to go on my next leave looking like a Chindit; always impresses the ladies. I wonder when we'll get one?'

'A lady or a leave?' asked Gerald. Chandler was the youngest of the regiment's lieutenants and was seldom serious about anything.

Chandler laughed again. 'I was thinking of rest and recreation. Even Dimapur would be acceptable at the moment, though heaven knows the place is indecently crowded and there's sod all to do there.'

'Except drink and sleep. Which is what we both need.'

There was a sudden movement along the trench, the clatter of a bayonet scabbard against a rifle. 'Sah'b.' One of the sepoys was pointing towards the rear of the position. Gerald could see a figure scurrying across the open ground. It dropped out of sight, into a trench.

Chandler was on his knees, pulling back the sliding breech-block of his Sten.

'Calm down,' suggested Gerald. 'One of ours. Probably ammunition.'

'Ammunition? How inconsiderate. I wish it was beer. Or char!'

'Maybe it is.' The thought of a hot mug of tea was pleasant. None had been passed down to the forward positions yet. It had been fourteen hours since their last meal, and that had been meagre, and they had been cold rations. Gerald watched the movement across the furrowed ground. The enemy had seen it as well, and a burst of machine-gun fire followed the man now running for the cover of the trench.

'Come on, you idle bugger,' shouted Chandler.

The man dived the last six feet towards Gerald, slid over the lip of the trench on his stomach and landed in a bundled heap in the soft earth at Gerald's feet. He scrambled into a kneeling position and brushed the filth from his clothing. It was a padre. 'We thought you were the char wallah, sir,' apologised Gerald.

'Sorry if I've disappointed you all.' The padre looked at the two young officers. 'It's Easter Sunday,' he said reverently.

'Yes, sir. We know.' Chandler guessed what the padre was going to suggest next. Prayers always embarrassed him when they were so individual; church parades were reasonably acceptable, but prayers on a man-to-man basis made him uncomfortable.

The padre raised an eyebrow at the tone of Chandler's reply, but made no comment. He pulled a bar of chocolate from his pocket. 'Here, share this between you. Sorry I haven't more.' He waited for a moment until Gerald had placed the precious bar on a ledge of soil and then continued, 'This isn't going to be a full service, you know. But I thought, perhaps you might like communion today.' He looked hard at Chandler again. 'A quick communion, lieutenant?'

Chandler swallowed. There was no mistaking the determination in the padre's stare. 'Yes, sir.'

The padre reached into his pocket, brought out a small box, opened it and placed it on a grubby square of cloth on the floor of the trench. 'Portable altar,' he explained.

'They think of everything, sir,' said Chandler, attempting to lighten the situation.

'Everything,' said the padre, grimly. From another pocket he brought a small pack of wafers and a hip flask, muttered quickly over them, poured a drop of wine into the cap and held it towards Gerald. 'Don't take more than a sip,' warned the padre. 'It has to go round the lot of you out here, and I've only got half a flaskful. Here...' He slipped a biscuit into Gerald's mouth. It was so dry it soaked up what little saliva he had in his mouth and was difficult to swallow. The padre repeated the performance with Chandler, then said a blessing and made the sign of the cross. He began repacking his equipment. 'Any corpses or seriously wounded I should know about?'

'No, sir,' said Gerald. 'Only ones out there are the enemy.'

'Well, I suppose that's something to be thankful for,' said the padre, wrily. He paused for a second. 'Someone ought to do something for them.'

'I wish someone would bury them, sir.' Chandler wrinkled his nose.

'They burnt a lot, with petrol, on Jail Hill.' The padre sighed. 'It's disrespectful, but at least it's hygienic disposal. Perhaps you'll get the chance to do the same here.' He looked at the two men again. 'Which one of you is Lieutenant Petrie? Lieutenant Gerald Petrie?'

'I am, sir.'

'Good,' said the padre, with a brief and disapproving glance at Chandler. 'I've got a message for you; from one of the personnel in the Forward Dressing Station. She just said, would I tell you she was here.'

'She? Ah ha,' grinned Chandler. 'There's no escaping your past, Gerald. Not even in the trenches.'

Gerald ignored him. 'She, sir?'

'Her name's Mary Sachema. A Lushai girl. Came in a few days ago with a group of the Rajputani Rifles, from Jotsoma, wearing Naga clothing; she's been doing a useful job since.'

'Good God!' The thought of Mary here in Kohima stunned Gerald.

The padre coughed. 'I hope that was a benediction, my boy.'

'Is she all right, sir?'

'I suspect you would know that better than I, lieutenant,' said the padre icily. 'But if you mean, is she fit and well? Then she seemed to be, an hour ago.' He made his voice fatherly. 'Look, my boy. I don't know who she is, or what she is to you. But if this were a different time and place, I might have a few words of advice for you.'

'I wouldn't ask for them, sir,' said Gerald firmly.

'But you'd get them anyway.' The padre glanced at his watch. 'I have to be on my way. There's not much of the day left.' He stared at Chandler again. 'Some people actually want communion.'

'Thank you for finding me, sir,' said Gerald. 'And for giving me the message.'

The padre had turned away and was considering the open ground between trenches, plotting the route he would take when he began sprinting from his present cover. He looked back at Gerald. 'Someone always knows where you are, my boy.' He turned his stare on to Chandler. 'Someone always knows.' He pointed a finger upwards: 'Someone. God bless you both.'

His boots dug into the wall of the trench as he heaved himself up with a grunt. Then he was in the open, sprinting, swerving. A tree stump protected him briefly, then like a bolting rabbit he plunged into another dug-out.

'Well, well, well...' said Steve Chandler, knowingly. 'The regimental dark horse surfaces. Suppose you tell Uncle Stevie all about it?'

'She's just a girl I know.' Gerald wanted Chandler to be silent for a while to allow him time to think. How had Mary got here? Good grief, he had worried enough about her safety anyway; even made Jack Warren promise he would see she was evacuated. Damn, it hadn't even been easy explaining to Jack why he was so concerned about the girl. But at least Jack had appeared to adopt a 'man of the world' attitude, and said he would see she was taken out of danger if it became necessary. Why had she come here to the battlefront? Because she wanted to be near him?

'Just a girl you know,' drawled Chandler. 'A Lushai girl? Don't tell me you bribed a sepoy to introduce you to his sister?' He jerked himself backwards as Gerald grabbed the front of his shirt.

Gerald held Chandler's collar tightly, his fist under the startled lieutenant's chin. Chandler saw his friend's face was bloodless with sudden anger, and regretted his joking. 'Don't ever suggest such a thing again,' threatened Gerald. He pushed Chandler away from him roughly.

'I'm sorry,' apologised Chandler. 'I shouldn't have said that.'

'No, you shouldn't.'

'You can hit me, or challenge me to a duel. Either way, I won't fight back.'

'Don't be an idiot.' Gerald's anger was already dying. There had been so much emotion during the past weeks it seemed there was no room for more.

Chandler was silent for a while and then said: 'I gather she means a lot to you, old chap.' Gerald nodded. 'Oh well, then jolly good luck to you. Knew a sergeant once, married an Indian girl. Caused him an awful lot of...'

'Please, Chandler. Please shut up for a while, will you?'

There had seemed little time for the pleasure of memories in the past weeks, still less for tempting providence with the luxury of planning for a future that might not exist. Daydreaming could be fatal and nights were seldom free of the pressures of attacks or patrolling. But although Gerald had attempted to dismiss Mary from his mind, it had been impossible. He could remember the precise moment when he had first told her he loved her, could remember the feminine strength of her arms as she held him and drew him to her lips. Here, even in the battlefield where the stink of death hung in the fetid air, in his imagination he could still enjoy the scent of her perfumed body and feel the soft velvet of her breasts against him.

In Dimapur, waiting for transport to Jessami, he had sent Monica a letter. He had avoided a direct lie, but had not mentioned Mary. War had made life so unsure, so unpredictable, he had written, he could no longer be certain of anything, least of all his own feelings towards permanent relationships. England was so far away, so remote, now so unreal to him, it had become little more than a faded dream. He hoped she would understand that in the circumstances it would be better if she considered herself free of any commitment to him.

He knew Monica would be angry when she received his letter – it would be anger, not hurt. She would certainly telephone his mother; or her mother would telephone. 'Such a shame,' one of them would say. 'They seemed an ideal couple.'

God! What would happen if he told them he loved an Indian girl? His mother would be silent, tight-lipped. It would be something she didn't want to discuss with anyone, either on the telephone or around her bridge tables. She would be horrified. His father would explode: 'Damn you, Gerald! All of us worked out there, every man in the family, and every one of us loved and married decent English women, like your mother. How dare you upset her. How dare you upset us all. How in heaven's name can you command respect in the

Company if you even contemplate marrying an Indian. It's unthinkable.'

Unthinkable! Everything was unthinkable. The blackening corpses of the Japanese a few yards away were unthinkable, the shells which arrived every few minutes around the position were unthinkable, the screams and moans of wounded and dying men were unthinkable.

The only sanity he could find in his thoughts was Mary, and now, somehow, she was here. But was she here, or had the conversation with the padre been only a hallucination brought about by his longing to be with Mary again? How could such a frail and delicate girl find her way into this appalling battlefield?

'Chandler...'

Chandler looked up at him and said, languidly: 'Yes, old chap?'

'Am I going dotty?'

Chandler made a great pretence of examining Gerald. 'Not particularly, I'd say. No more than any of us in this obscene place.'

The Advanced Dressing Station, west of the hospital, had been shelled during the afternoon. One of the doctors had been killed, along with forty of the wounded men. A lot of the medical stores, already in short supply, had been destroyed. For a time, it had been chaos, the cries of the injured mingling with the explosions as shells dropped around them. Part of the wooden structure had caught fire, then smouldered, adding to the dense choking fumes of cordite that fogged the area.

An hour later, there was a cloudburst. Torrential tropical rain sheeted down from low dark clouds, turning the broken ground into swamp, rapidly filling the shell holes with a liquid that stank like sewage, adding to the misery of the wounded, many of whom were without cover.

Mary Sachema had been folding bandages alongside a Scots medical orderly when the first of the shells had landed. The blast had thrown both of them to the ground, but left them only bruised and winded. She had been working in the Dressing Station for the three days since she reached Kohima. It seemed a lifetime.

She had arrived there by accident. One of the Rajputani sepoys had been slightly wounded and the party she accompanied had made their way to the Dressing Station to see that their comrade received medical aid before the remainder reported to the box commander. One of the Rajputanis had attempted to explain her presence to the British doctor who met them; he had not understood the man, who spoke no English.

'You came in with them?' The doctor, a captain with a BBC accent, stared at her in amazement when she introduced herself. 'Why the hell did you come here? All civilians were evacuated a fortnight ago.'

She didn't want to give her real reasons to the man, so said: 'I just want to help.'

'Jesus Christ,' he exclaimed. 'Don't you realise you're just another mouth to feed and water. Another person to get cholera, or be wounded or killed. This isn't a recreation camp, girl. This is a battlefield.'

'I can cook, and I can carry. I can run messages. I can tie up a wound.'

The man stared at her. When he had first seen her, he had thought she was a man, a Naga guide. Her hair was cut short, at neck length, and she was wearing a rough shirt and shorts under a Naga home-weave blanket. Her legs and feet were bare. It was only when she had spoken he had realised she was a woman.

Mary continued, quickly, sensing his indecision. 'I can speak Assamese, Lushai, Naga, Hindi, some Urdu and English. I think you speak no Indian languages.' She indicated towards some of the wounded sepoys lying on the ground outside the Dressing Station. 'I can help you talk to these men.'

The doctor frowned thoughtfully. Someone who could translate the many different languages of the wounded would indeed be useful to him. Few of the Indian orderlies spoke more than a smattering of English, plus their own dialect. This woman might be helpful. 'You've no nursing experience, I suppose?' he asked hopefully.

'We were taught first-aid at school. And hygiene.'

'It's better than nothing. All right, you can stay here. But no complaints, understand. You do what I say, when I say it, without argument. You eat what we eat, when we eat it; and drink what we drink. And if you get hurt, then you've no one to blame but yourself. Better get cleaned up.'

She had discovered the position of the Assam Regiment from one of the wounded brought in to the Dressing Station late that first night. The sepoy was not one of the regiment, so knew none of their officers. It had been another twenty-four hours before she had learnt Gerald Petrie was alive, but although he was less than a mile from her, there seemed no way she could reach him. On Easter Sunday morning, she had overheard the padre explaining he was going to visit their lines and had asked him to take her message. The padre raised his eyebrows at her request, but promised to try to contact the lieutenant. She hoped he had managed.

It had been a long and difficult journey from Gauhati and at times she had despaired of ever finding Gerald. When she had left his bed, just before dawn on their last night together, she had thought all that was necessary was that she should wait for him to return to her. Later, she had stood and watched him leave in Warren Sah'b's car. She had not dared to wave, and he had not seen her standing in the shade of the trees at the side of the bungalow. She had wondered how long it would be before they would be together again.

Later that day, Jack Warren had returned alone from Gauhati and shortly afterwards Evelyn Warren had summoned Mary to her room.

She looked severe. 'I want to know what has been happening between Petrie Sah'b and yourself. And I want the truth.'

Mary had said, innocently: 'We are in love memsah'b.'

Evelyn Warren flushed, and spoke angrily: 'Nonsense, girl. You are not in love. What utter rubbish.'

'I *am* in love with him, memsah'b.'

Evelyn's agitated voice rose. 'You are *not* in love. You are a silly child. You are simply infatuated by a young sah'b; a European. And by his position and rank. He has a fiancée in England.'

'I know that, memsah'b. But he now loves me.'

'Did he tell you that?' She gave Mary no time to answer. 'Of course he didn't. Why should he; you probably gave him everything he wanted anyway. I suppose you let him sleep with you?'

There seemed to be no point in denying it. 'Yes, memsah'b.'

For a moment, Mary thought Evelyn was going to strike her. 'You stupid girl. You stupid, stupid girl. I don't suppose for one moment you know anything at all about contraception? Of course you don't; no Indians do. That's why there are so many chi-chis around the place. I suppose you will say you thought he would marry you?'

'He didn't ask me, memsah'b.' She could feel herself trembling, but knew it was from anger not shame.

'Of course he wouldn't ask you. Petrie Sah'b is the son of a baronet. Do you know what that is, a baronet? A British baronet is more important than a nawab. Would a nawab ask a servant girl to marry him? Do you know who owns this plantation? This house? Many of the plantations in Assam?'

'I know all this, memsah'b. It is his family.'

'And do you think his family would *ever* permit him to marry a Lushai girl? A tribal girl?'

There is no point in me listening to her any more, thought Mary. I am becoming angrier, and she more overbearing. In a few more minutes, I may lose control of myself. She turned and began walking from the room.

'Mary, you have not been dismissed.' Evelyn Warren's voice was furious. 'Come back here, at once. Come back, I say.'

Mary closed the door firmly behind her, went straight to her own room and tied her few belongings in a cotton square. Within ten minutes she was running through the lines of tea bushes, in the direction of Gauhati. She had said goodbye to no one. In a small leather purse in the waistband of her sari she had the money left her by her friend the dead aiya.

She had made up her mind about three important things. The first, that somehow she would find Gerald, and be near him regardless of where he might be. The second, that she would continue to believe completely in his love for her. And thirdly, never again would she ever call a European either memsah'b or sah'b.

On 13 April, following continuous attacks on all the defended positions around Kohima, Mary Sachema was wounded. The main section of the Advanced Dressing Station received a direct hit by a mortar bomb. Two more of the doctors were killed and many of the patients further injured. A piece of the casing of the bomb sliced a fine cut from the left side of Mary's jaw to below her ear; had it been a quarter of an inch deeper, her jugular vein would have been severed. She dressed it herself, holding the edges of the wound together with a broad strip of adhesive tape, and then assisted the remaining doctor and orderlies in attending to the seriously wounded men.

The fighting was bitter, and at very close quarters around the perimeter. Beside the wreckage of the District Commissioner's bungalow, the Japanese and British positions were separated by only the length of the tennis court. The rattle of small arms fire, the thump of mortars and artillery was continuous; the stream of wounded arriving for medical attention neverending.

The only comfort for the weary troops was a message from the garrison commander, congratulating them on their devotion and assuring them a relief force was on its way. Few believed it would arrive before Kohima fell to the enemy.

Two days later, during the afternoon of Saturday the fifteenth, Gerald Petrie, carrying captured Japanese documents to the garrison commander's headquarters, found time to visit the Dressing Station.

The journey from the Assam Regiment's position had taken him over an hour, the thick stinking mud sucking at his feet with every step. It was raining heavily, and the dense grey curtain had temporarily silenced the Japanese artillery. Every yard of the ground inside the perimeter of the defences was cratered. No buildings stood intact for more than three feet above ground level; not a single tree had survived, and the shattered stumps and steaming ground gave an unreal and surrealistic aspect to the panorama. Temporarily, the cleansing rain had laid the stench of rotting death.

He was apprehensive. He had heard nothing of Mary since the padre's message, and now as he approached the Dressing Station it seemed that crater overlapped crater so nothing could possibly have survived the endless bombardment; the dead lay unburied everywhere and it horrified him as he realised Mary could be amongst them. There seemed few signs of life, though he knew hidden beneath the mud and debris, sheltered in foxholes and bunkers, men would be taking advantage of the lull to clean their weapons, reload and rest.

The Advanced Dressing Station consisted of a main pit with side trenches, roofed with corrugated sheeting over baulks of timber. It had been at the rear of the defences when the garrison had first taken up its positions. Now they had been surrounded it was in a fairly exposed hollow amongst the rubble of a number of demolished buildings.

As he approached the ADS, the sight of the wounded lying nearby in slit-trenches, soaked by the heavy downpour, disturbed him. Like all those who were fighting, he had been aware that no matter how serious a wound he might receive, he was unlikely to get more than superficial medical treatment, and any possibility of evacuation to a base hospital was zero. But thinking of wounds in action was like thinking of death, and he had avoided the confrontation. Here, he could no longer escape, and was sickened by it. Men lay silently dying, or groaned and writhed in agony, attended by orderlies who dragged themselves through the swamp-like ground between their patients; wet bandages covered appalling injuries seeping blood and pus, and few drugs were available to ease the pain.

A sepoy stretcher-bearer squatted beside the entrance of the main bunker. The man was exhausted, his arms folded on his knees, and his head on his arms. Rain cascaded from the brim of his helmet on to his clothing and soaked through to his chilled body.

Steps in the ADS bunker's entrance had been cut when the earth was dry. Now, with the rain, they had become a steep, treacherous ramp down which ran a torrent of water, flooding the bunker ankle-deep. A petrol generator thumped noisily a few yards away, beneath a sheet of crumpled tin. The air at the doorway was heavy with the stench of antiseptic and chloroform. Gerald ducked his head, and stood inside, hunched under the low roof, peering into the gloom. There were no beds; the wounded, waiting for attention, lay on their stretchers supported on empty ammunition boxes. The clothing of the orderlies, or doctors – he was unable to distinguish between them – was bloodstained and filthy. They ignored him as he entered.

He felt guilty, as though he were a trespasser in a forbidden place, witnessing some secret rite, so said loudly: 'Excuse me.'

'Gerald!' One of the orderlies called his name. The voice was Mary's, but he failed to recognise her at first. A figure came quickly towards him. 'Gerald.' There were arms clasping him, tightly. He knew her now. Bleak eyes watched them as he led her outside into the rain.

Had he been asked his feelings at this time, Gerald would have been unable to explain the complicated skein of emotions he was experiencing. He was angry she should have exposed herself to so much danger to be near him, yet flattered she had done so. There seemed nothing he could say to her, but to tell her again and again how much he loved her, and to clasp her protectively in his arms. Neither of them felt the heavy tropical rain which beat down upon them.

They were together for less than ten minutes, and as he left her she stood motionless until the mist hid him from her sight.

A few yards away, the sepoy stretcher-bearer puzzled over their long embrace. He doubted if he would be believed by his comrades if he informed them he had seen a British officer kissing a Naga medical orderly in the mud of the battlefield. And moreover, that the reputed head-hunter had seemed to be crying when they parted.

The following day Steve Chandler was killed. A spent bullet ricocheted from the blade of a discarded entrenching tool and struck him in the back of his skull. It was ironic that the regiment's sector was not under attack at the time, and the young lieutenant had removed his helmet whilst resting.

The useless loss of Chandler's life distressed Gerald more than it would have done had he died in battle. It seemed impossible to survive the war. The soldiers talked about the arrival of the relief force, due almost any day, as though they would never have to fight again, but Gerald knew it could not be so. Whatever happened, the fighting would continue; even if the Japanese withdrew, they would have to be followed. And they would resist for every inch of the way, counterattacking with their near unbelievable ferocity, screaming their '*Banzais*', and hurling themselves at their enemy regardless of bullets, bayonets and grenades.

When he had reluctantly left Mary, to trudge his way back to his sector through the waterlogged disorder of the battlefields, it had been with the conviction he would never see her again. Steve Chandler's death appeared to confirm his fears; soon, he too would die. If not here at Kohima, then in some other jungle battle.

He had attempted to conceal his apprehension. The morale of the sepoys of the regiment was still good, but morale, he knew, was an expendable commodity which could easily be diminished. He thought he was succeeding in hiding his feelings, but at the daily briefing in the company commander's field headquarters he discovered that, at least so far as his commander was concerned, he had failed. When the other lieutenants were dismissed, the captain asked him to remain behind.

'All right, Gerald. What's the problem?' Jameson had penetrating pale grey eyes, and now they seemed to dig themselves questioningly into Gerald's brain. It was always impossible to lie to the man.

He shrugged, avoiding an answer.

'Come along now. Was it Steve's death? I know you were friends.' Jameson softened his voice. 'Here, sit down.' He rummaged in a haversack and pulled out a half-bottle of gin. There was a used tea mug on his table and he threw out the dregs, poured gin from the bottle and handed the enamelled mug to Gerald. 'Sorry there's no bitters. I was saving this for our relief.' He eyed the bottle. 'Hopefully, it'll last that long. Grit your teeth and drink up.' He waited as Gerald swallowed the raw alcohol in one swig. 'Suppose you tell me what's wrong.'

Gerald had been intending to tell Steve Chandler all about Mary at the next opportunity. He had felt he must discuss her future safety with someone. Now Chandler was dead, he decided there was nothing to be lost by talking to Captain Jameson. He was normally understanding.

'It's a girl, sir.'

'A girl!' Jameson's eyes widened. 'For Christ's sake, Gerald, everyone else here is worried about the Japs! Is she pregnant or what? It can't be a "Dear John" letter, because we haven't had any mail. Who is she, your fiancée?'

'I don't know, sir.'

'You don't know what?'

'I don't know if she's my fiancée, sir.'

'Well, if that's the only damned problem you've got to worry about, then I suggest you concentrate on the job in hand, and forget about her until this little lot is finished.'

'I'm afraid she's here, sir.'

'Here?' Jameson stared at Gerald with disbelief.

'At the ADS.'

'Good God, man. Now I understand why you look worried.' He paused for a moment. 'I didn't think we had any female nursing staff with us. I thought Pawsey got them all out.'

Gerald explained about Mary Sachema and Jameson let him talk without interruption. When he had finished, Jameson poured him another gin then took a mouthful himself straight from the bottle, wiping a spilled drop of the spirit from the stubble on his chin, before speaking. 'I suppose you know what you're letting yourself in for?' He didn't give Gerald time to answer. 'I've spent all my working life in Assam. I know this country. Know the Brits out here, very well. Not a particularly open-minded lot. Bloody place runs on prejudice.' He stopped himself. 'Not the time for a lecture. But I'll tell you something, my lad. No matter what her background may be, your lady friend must be a very special kind of woman.'

'Yes, sir, she is.'

'They used to follow their own men to war, you know. Damn me ... she did the same.' The captain chuckled, and shook his head. 'Incredible. Followed you into battle.' He became serious again. 'Look, you know there's nothing I can do at the moment to see she stays safe; nothing at all. I can't spare a single man to protect her, least of all yourself. The only thing I can promise is that, come hell or high water, when we're relieved I'll make sure she comes back with us. Does that help?'

'Yes, sir. A lot, sir.'

'Good.' Jameson looked satisfied. 'Well, you'd better run along then. Try and get a bit of rest before you go on patrol tonight. You'll need your wits about you.'

At 22.30 hours, Gerald, accompanied by eight of his platoon and two Naga guides, took advantage of the cloud which obscured the moon to work their way out of the box perimeter for a reconnaissance of the enemy positions on the Dimapur road below the regiment's sector. It had begun raining again.

To the east, only a few hundred yards away, the Royal West Kent Regiment's positions were under heavy attack around the District Commissioner's ruined bungalow. Later, when this had been bloodily repulsed, the Japanese turned their attentions to the area occupied by the Assam Regiment. The attacks were more determined than ever, as the enemy attempted to gain the advantages of the high ground before the relief force arrived.

Gerald's patrol was scheduled to re-enter the perimeter at 01.00 hours. At 04.15, as the sky was beginning to lighten towards the east and the continuous night-time attacks had slowed against the courage of the weary defenders, one solitary Naga survivor of the patrol wriggled in, on his belly, through the shell-holes and piles of fresh corpses, and was taken to Captain Alan Jameson by a havildar. Tied to the Naga's belt was a muddy bundle of cloth that swung heavily at his waist when he stood in front of Jameson. The captain saw it, but ignored it. He could guess its content: an enemy head. Officially, the practice was frowned upon. Today, it seemed appropriate to Jameson.

*

The conversation which had taken place between Alan Jameson and Gerald the previous afternoon was still fresh in the captain's mind, and there had been other casualties for the regiment during the night's attacks. The wounded were already being taken back to the dressing station, and it seemed likely Mary Sachema would question them about Gerald. News of the deaths of regimental officers always spread quickly amongst the men, and the Naga guide would have already been interrogated by the havildar before being brought to the Field Headquarters. Jameson had promised his lieutenant he would take care of the young Lushai girl, and unpleasant though his task might be, he felt it his duty to be the one who informed her Gerald had been killed. It now seemed probable the Second Division, who were reported to be at Zubza, would reach Kohima within the next twenty-four hours, and Jameson determined to arrange for the girl to be evacuated with his own men.

An hour later, he accompanied a party of the walking wounded to the ADS and found Mary.

Captain Jameson had written only a couple of letters to families who had lost men with the regiment. Before Kohima, there had been few casualties, and in any case, when writing he knew his own letters could be cushioned by the official notification the relatives would have already received. Today, he was aware it would be different. He wondered if perhaps he should have asked the padre to do it for him, but dismissed the thought as a form of cowardice; Gerald would have expected him to deal with this matter himself. Jameson hoped it would be like films he had seen where someone appeared, the doctor perhaps, and the anxious relative read his thoughts and said, 'He isn't, is he?' and the doctor simply had to nod his head; that way was easy. He knew it was also unrealistic.

Mary Sachema stood watching him, her hands clasped in front of her, and her eyes meeting his own. She said nothing, her face expressionless. Jameson, who while on his way to the ADS had rehearsed a suitably compassionate manner of informing her, forgot what he had intended to say, knowing that in a moment he would have to destroy her entire world. He began to speak in Hindi, but found it impossible to express himself as sympathetically as he wished, and changed to English.

'I'm very sorry, my dear. I have some very sad news for you. Lieutenant Petrie ... I mean, Gerald. I'm afraid he's been killed.'

CHAPTER FOUR

When Captain Jameson informed Mary of Gerald's death, he had steeled himself for the expression of grief he had so often witnessed in India, the traditional hysteria of public emotion. Instead, the girl's reaction was of complete disbelief, at first calm as he attempted to convince her, and then with growing anger at his persistence.

'I understand your feelings,' he told her, realising there was little more he could say for the present. 'You are very loyal, and very brave. I will do everything I can to help you when we return to Dimapur.' She needed time, he felt, to absorb the news. Some people did, but in his experience, it was more usual for a European than an Indian. He felt sorry for her, alone and without even the impractical hopes of a future with her lover. He wished he could offer her comfort, but could think of none. Only months or years could heal sorrow.

She did not appear to have heard his last words, but asked: 'The Naga, may I speak with him?'

'Of course. I'll arrange for him to come over.'

There had been shock, when Jameson had first spoken; an uncontrollable reflex which exploded as a lightning strike in her mind, cramping the muscles of her stomach and bringing an ice-cold chill to her spine. Jameson had assumed a surprising lack of emotional response to his words, but for an instant she was paralysed, unable even to breathe or think until the crippling white blindness of horror dispersed.

The captain had talked on, offering sympathy, but her mind was already rejecting Gerald's death. She had felt herself so much part of him that she knew she experienced his emotions, living his fears or needs as much as if they were her own. Distance might have separated them over the past weeks, but her conviction that their love was a single entity binding them as surely as a cord had kept her close to him. If Gerald had died, then she would have known without being told; part of her would have died with him. Regardless of what the officer might believe, she was convinced he was still alive, somewhere.

The Angami Naga guide squatted on his haunches a little way from the ADS, and waited for the girl. His tattooed face was expressionless, but he was feeling uneasy. He had been told by the Assam Regiment havildar that a woman wished to speak with him about the lost patrol, but no other explanation had been offered. It occurred to him she might be some kind of government agent, and unless he was cautious he might be punished for allowing the patrol to be ambushed.

    It had been almost two weeks since he had been in the area of the dressing station – now he found it unrecognisable. A short time ago it had been a track bordered by the small houses of the village bazaar; there had been bougainvillaea blossoming against the walls, and bright red bells on the hibiscus bushes that lined the approach. Now there was only desolation.

    The Naga moved his legs into a more comfortable position as the cane rings on his calves dug into his lean muscles. Normally he would have worn only his black loincloth, embroidered with the cowrie shells which denoted his position in his clan, but as he had been employed as army guide, he had been issued with a khaki bush-jacket which he was wearing like a cloak.

    After the patrol had been ambushed, and the grenades exploded amongst them, he had been surprised to find himself still alive. His first inclination had been to run, to escape and find some safe hiding-place in the jungle until the white and yellow men had ceased their fighting and gone away forever. He had lain unmoving in a clump of rotting vegetation beneath a dense thorn, while the Japanese searched the bodies of the dead men. The Naga knew they were dead, for even had they survived the grenades and bullets, the yellow soldiers would have bayoneted them; they always killed the wounded of night patrols they encountered.

    Once the enemy had gone, the Naga had decided to return to

the British lines. It would have been easier for him to make his way through the familiar jungle to the safety of one of the small settlements to the north-west, but he felt he owed a debt to the District Commissioner at Kohima who had moved his family before the Japanese division arrived. There was also the matter of his pay; he earned five rupees a day as a guide.

The head which he collected on his way back to the Assam Regiment position had been a satisfying bonus. It had belonged to a Japanese private who was foolish enough to be modest and excrete alone in the darkness, thirty yards from the safety of his comrades. It was now buried amongst the scattered memorial posts of the Angami cemetery below the regiment's position; in a few days the flesh would have rotted from the bones, and when the fighting was over and the village dwellings rebuilt, it would be displayed amongst the other tropies of the men's house.

The Naga saw the girl appear from the ADS dug-out with the havildar. The sergeant pointed in the direction of the Naga, automatically saluted the girl, and hurried back towards the regiment's sector. The Naga was surprised; he had expected the girl to be European, or at least Bengali. He had difficulty placing her features. She might be a Naga herself, but could as easily be Khasi or Lushai. He knew, however, that she was a town girl; there were no scars on her legs from the harsh jungles of the hills, and as she approached him he saw that although her feet were bare they were not as toughened as those of the women who worked on the terraced land.

'You are the guide?' She squatted, facing him.

He was impressed when she spoke to him in his own language. 'Yes.'

'What is your name?' Her accent had the musical intonation of the Lushai.

'I am Shankok, of the Angami Naga.'

'I want to know about the officer who was with you,' said the girl.

The Naga was cautious. 'I did not know him. It was the first time I had been with him.'

'I understand that. But he was my man.'

The Naga grinned with relief. 'Your man?' So the girl was only a prostitute, a camp-follower of the army. Some of the Naga girls occasionally slept with visiting Europeans. The men gave them gifts for their services, but the youths of the clans teased them afterwards and the women lost status amongst the villagers.

His amusement angered the girl. 'Yes, he is my man. And I want to know what happened to him.'

The Naga shrugged. 'He is dead.' He pulled his dao from its sheath on his belt. He had deliberately not cleaned the blood of the Japanese from the hatchet-shaped blade, and wanted the girl to see it as evidence he had fought. She ignored it.

'How, then, did he die?'

'It was not easy to see in the darkness. There were explosions, bullets. All were killed except myself.'

'You examined the bodies to be certain?'

The Naga did not want to lie positively and attempted an evasive answer. 'Bodies are tossed around by explosions; they are torn to pieces. All were dead.' He slid the dao back into the scabbard and ran his finger around the rows of stone beads at his throat. If she were Naga, he thought, she would show more respect. She would known he was a fierce warrior. The beads indicated the heads he had collected; five in all, not even counting the latest. He coughed, turned his head and spat phlegm, contemptuously, into the mud. 'Your man is dead.'

'You are a liar!' The girl struck him, open-handed across his face. The blow was so unexpected it unbalanced him and he sprawled sideways. 'You are a liar and a coward. You ran and left your friends when they were attacked. You are not fit to call yourself a Naga. When the people of your village learn of this, they will piss on you.' The Naga scrambled to his knees. He had never been struck by a woman before. Only the fact they were alone and unobserved prevented him from retaliating in defence of his pride. He clenched his fists. 'He was fighting for you,' the girl shouted at him. 'For your hills. For our hills. And you deserted him.'

The Naga lowered his head. 'You were not there.'

'But you will take me.'

He looked at her, quickly. 'Take you?' He didn't believe she could be serious, but saw the fire of determination in her eyes. 'You are mad.'

'You are supposed to be a guide.'

'I am a guide for soldiers, not for women who are sick in their heads.'

'Could you find the place where the patrol was attacked again?'

'This is my village. I was born here. I played here as a child. I have hunted all the jungle around here. Ask me if I can find the palm of my own hand.'

'Then take me. This time there will be no danger for you.'

'You are truly insane,' growled the Naga, frowning.

'You have heard the loud voice which the enemy have been using at night to speak to us?' asked the Lushai girl. 'It tells us we should desert the British and join the liberators.'

'I have also been told by the havildar that it lies,' said the Naga.

'It may lie. But it promises safety for those Indian soldiers who leave here.'

'None have gone.'

'No matter. If you are stupid enough to allow the enemy to catch us, you can say to them you are answering the call of the voice. And if you take me, I will pay you.'

The Naga thought for a while. The girl might be correct about the promises of the voice they heard every night, and the money was never easy to obtain in the village. There was seldom a profit from the crops, and work on road building was demeaning for a man. 'How much money?'

'Twenty rupees.'

'There should be two men, myself and my brother. And the money should be forty for each man.'

'Twenty-five each. No more,' said the girl, firmly. 'And be here at dusk.'

'Your madness is catching.' The Naga stood and lazily stretched himself, like an awakening cheetah. 'My brother and I will be here.'

There had been no visible setting of the sun. Hidden by the dark rain clouds, its going was marked only by the fading light in which the flashes of exploding shells, mortar-bombs and phosphorus grenades grew brighter. The artillery bombardment increased; preparation for yet another enemy assault.

For Mary, the afternoon had seemed interminably long as she anticipated nightfall. The stench and overpowering humidity in the dressing station had become unbearable; flies, which bred in the corpses, unburied and rotting, were thick everywhere, dispersing only when the rain showers forced them to seek shelter.

There had been another successful airdrop, which, for a time, had occupied her mind as she sorted the fresh medical equipment with the doctors and orderlies. But now there was a growing sense of anticipation and excitement at the thought of what lay ahead of her. She had barely considered dangers to herself; they were unimportant. Nor had she dared to think of failure. A life without Gerald would be worse than no life at all. For the first time in many weeks, she prayed, concentrating her mind on the crucifix still in her small bundle of possessions. It seemed unnecessary to unwrap it; it would see her and hear her silent prayers through its coverings. She asked only for help.

The Naga guide was late. She worried that he might have been killed during the day's action; without him, she was helpless. She waited at the bunker's entrance, feeling the ground quiver with the explosions that rippled crimson the undersides of the clouds above the ridge of hills. It seemed to her she was experiencing an endless nightmare from which only Gerald could awaken her.

Shadows moved and were turned to silhouettes by distant fire. Moist faces glistened briefly, and the Nagas were beside her. Shankok spoke, but the gunfire drowned most of his words. She heard him say, 'Follow,' and almost lost him as the two men ran, stooping, crouched, past the rubble and on to the sloping, cratered terraces below.

They dropped to the ground near a shattered wall. She joined them. The sounds of battle, behind the ridge, had dulled.

'Wait, now,' the Naga ordered.

'Why?'

He rolled on to his back, wedging himself against the rubble. 'Because there is always a right time to do things, and a wrong time. Now is the wrong time to try to pass through our defences.' He jerked his head towards the other Naga. 'He is my brother, Manwang. He has learnt the right time.'

In the darkness, she could not distinguish Manwang's face, but heard him say: 'We must wait for a patrol, and leave with them. I spoke with my cousin. He says he has been asked to patrol tonight, here. So we must wait. And you must be silent; the yellow men will not be far away.'

She thought the Nagas were asleep, but had it not been for Shankok she would not have heard or seen the patrol. He nudged her hard enough in the ribs to make her gasp. 'Listen.'

There was only silence, but after a few moments she heard a faint metallic rattle twenty yards to their left. There was movement next to her as Manwang slid into the darkness. He returned quickly. 'Come. And say nothing.'

A group of men crouched in a shallow depression below the terrace wall. She heard Shankok whisper to one of them, and felt the rough serge of a sepoy's battledress against her bare arm. She could smell rank sweat and sensed their fear. She recognised the accent of a European speaking Hindi a few feet ahead of her, the man's voice hoarse with apprehension.

A hundred yards to their left a mortar opened fire, to be joined by several others, the hollow explosions of the propellants echoed by the detonating bombs shredding the thin jungle on the lower slopes of the spur. A pair of machine-guns added to the growing thunder, white tracer bullets cutting spectacular paths through the night.

The Naga's breath was warm on her neck, his mouth close to her ear. 'Be ready. Now...'

The men ahead were moving, loping their way across the terraces, dropping over the next of the walls. On either side of her, she saw trenches, black slits in the earth; men waiting, steel glistening on rifles. A parachute flare, fired from some hidden Japanese position, burst into artificial moonlight above the firing mortars, its magnesium flame blinding and revealing. She felt she must drop to the ground, hide herself, but Shankok gripped her arm tightly and held her unmoving; the men of the patrol stood motionless, human debris amongst shattered trees, camouflaged by immobility until the flare faded and died.

On the lower ground, coarse grass and bamboo thicket helped conceal them. They slid now, on their stomachs, dragged by their elbows, each on the track broken by the man ahead, the grass wet and the ground a sponge beneath.

Shankok's hand held her, grasping her wrist. Beside her lay Manwang. The patrol moved on away from them. They lay for several minutes, and then Shankok spoke, softly. 'They have gone. We follow the stream until it is below the banana grove. Then look for the path to Merema.'

Manwang grunted acknowledgement.

There was no longer the smell of battle in the moist air scented by rotting vegetation, but the sounds followed them, and the flashes of explosions still tinted the sky to the south-east. They travelled for an hour, first on a barely distinguishable track through the bamboo thickets, crowded rhododendron and thorn, and then along the shallow, rocky bed of a fast flowing stream, overhung by vines and branches.

At times, the two Nagas were almost casual in the manner they clambered noisily over fallen trees or called directions to each other. At other moments they were cautious, spending long minutes listening or searching the muddy banks for signs of the enemy. The jungle was never silent. Above the sound of the water, frogs croaked in the wet grass and crickets shrilled from beneath the dripping leaves of the trees.

To Mary it seemed impossible that they could find their way in both the darkness and dense forest, but when they left the stream there was no hesitation by the men. Had she been alone, and without purpose in this place, she knew she would have been terrified, imagining each tree the haunt of snakes, each deep shadow beneath the scrub the lair of tiger and leopard. Even her Christianity was proving little more than a veneer to be easily penetrated by devils and demons of the jungle night. And waiting for the two Nagas, that evening, she had realised other dangers; although the Angami had been administered by the British for some years, they still hunted heads when the opportunity arose; it made no difference to them whether the head was from a male or female. If the two Nagas wanted to take their money with as little risk as possible, they could easily kill her and then simply drift away into the jungle; the crime would never be discovered. But if she wished to find Gerald, then she could only place her trust in the two men and her God.

After waiting again while Shankok scouted ahead, they crossed a broad track and entered a plantation of banana trees. They skirted the burnt remains of a group of thatched huts, the damp ashes pungent in the still air. A mist was building in the valleys, as moist as light rain and condensing on the palm leaves.

Beyond the small area of cultivated ground, Shankok stopped. With horror, Mary realised she could identify the familiar stench of stale explosive and putrifying flesh.

The Naga turned to her. 'It was here. Somewhere close by. I told you, they are all dead. You can smell them dead.'

She had been wrong, she thought. Wrong to assume Gerald was still alive, wrong to insist she should be brought out here to find him. In seconds she would be shown rotting pieces of his body. The pleasant memories of him would be destroyed; she would never be able to forget the sight of his corpse. Perhaps she had indeed been insane. She was thankful for the darkness which might somehow protect her senses now.

Manwang was searching the area, sniffing like a dog on the scent of a hare, moving aside torn palm leaves and scrub. He came towards her holding some dark object. She stared at it, at first curiously and then with sickening realisation. It was a gaitered boot, still containing a foot and ankle, the bone splintered and white above the bloodstained canvas. She dropped to her knees and retched.

The Naga tossed the boot aside. 'It is Indian,' he said, contemptuously. 'Not that of a British officer. We will search some more.'

The ground seemed to hold her. She knelt, her hands clutching at the soft earth. Her stomach heaved uncontrollably. The distant sounds of battle grew and enveloped her, adding to the pounding of the blood in her head. The recent wound in her neck throbbed as though it were bursting open.

One of the Nagas shook her by her shoulders. She ignored the man. He shook her more violently. 'You must come now. We have found him.'

'Leave me.' She was begging. 'Leave me here and go back.' She would kill herself when they had gone, when she was alone in the night.

The Naga dragged her to her feet. Her strength had left her and she was unable to resist him. He pulled her with him until they reached an overgrown nullah, its banks thickly reeded. Deep mud squelched beneath their feet. He pushed the reeds aside with his arm.

'You asked to be taken to your man; he is here.' He released her.

She stood, trembling, unable to look down at the corpse she knew was at her feet.

'Are the Lushai afraid of death, then?' Shankok was remembering her insults earlier that day.

She squatted, slowly, feeling her limbs quivering. Her breathing was shallow, painful. She lowered her head. Gerald's hair was bright against the dark, flattened reeds; he seemed to be sleeping.

Mud scarred the pale cheeks. His body was a shadow in the undergrowth.

'Am I a liar?' asked Shankok, coldly. His brother, Manwang, joined them, kneeling beside Gerald. 'I have shown her the Naga are not liars,' Shankok told him. 'Here is her man.'

Manwang leant close to the body and stared at Gerald's neck. He reached forward and tugged gently at something. 'A leech,' he said.

'A leech?' Shankok echoed his brother's words.

Mary sat back on her heels. She felt tears swell at her eyes, her throat tighten with grief.

Manwang spoke again: 'Leeches do not drink the blood of the dead, only the living.'

Mary, locked in her own emotions, did not hear him. 'It is possible your man is alive,' said Shankok almost regretfully. 'But only a little alive.'

'Alive?' She thought she must have misheard him.

'A leech. Look, it sucks at his neck. Blood must still be flowing.'

Alive! She touched the blond hair with her fingertips, then ran them over his cheeks, feeling the soft stubble of his beard. There was a faint warmth to the skin, a living resilience in the flesh. 'He is alive,' she said, as though it were her own discovery. 'Yes, alive.' She bent and gently took his face in her hands, and kissed the still lips.

CHAPTER FIVE

DIMAPUR. 28 MAY 1944

Named after the ancient Kachari capital, 'City of the River People', which had been abandoned to the jungle in the fifteenth century, the modern town of Dimapur had none of its ancestor's powerful architecture. It had grown around a railway station, the new settlement sprawling as it expanded. But even as late as the beginning of the war it had been nothing much more than an insignificant wayside halt and police depot.

Its importance as a railhead to supply and reinforce the armies who fought in Burma had led to rapid, if temporary, wartime growth. It was now a vast military encampment fed by river, road, rail and air. The few European inhabitants, the government's administrators, District Commissioners and Assam police officers, mining engineers, planters, and their ladies had, like the original Kacharis, been overwhelmed and eclipsed. Acres of khaki tentage and camouflaged corrugated-iron Nissen huts ate their way into the surrounding agricultural land and jungle. Barbed wire created a maze of unnatural paths and roadways.

The small civilian hospital, a whitewashed building with a red-painted iron roof, had been filled long before the casualties of the Kohima and Imphal battles began to arrive. The barracks of the Assam police had been requisitioned, but as the numbers of wounded grew they overflowed to fill even more canvas tents and hastily erected marquees, so that from the air it seemed the entire countryside was being prepared to celebrate the crazily extravagant durbar of some millionaire prince.

It was here that Gerald Petrie had been brought unconscious on a bloody stretcher in the back of a military ambulance. The exhausted driver had been barely able to handle his vehicle after unbroken days and nights of circular trips between base and frontline.

More fortunate than other wounded passengers, Gerald felt nothing during the lurching agonising drive on the broken cutcha road. He was unaware of the painful waiting for the queues of injured men at the canvas surgeries, or of his many operations. The grenade which had exploded behind him had pierced him with a dozen jagged lumps of steel, hurled him against the unyielding trunk of a massive tree, spun him away broken into the reed bed. He was unconscious for sixteen days before spells of semi-delirious awareness grew towards normality.

Malaria complicated his recovery. At first he believed he was still in the malignant forest, alone, threatened and helpless. Its oppressive cloak enveloped him with stifling heat, shadows persecuted him and gave no sanctuary. Strange sounds and experiences assailed his senses, while there was pain, always pain, twisting and tormenting his mind and body.

Only gradually did he realise the green canopy of the imagined jungle was the canvas above his bed, its shadows the silhouettes of doctors and medical orderlies who helped him and fed him drugs to contain his agony, and the confused sounds he heard were those of the hospital area in which he lay, now safe from the enemy.

In his insanity, he had shouted and screamed Mary's name, his mind seeking the physical comfort of her body, losing itself in memory when reality became too terrifying to admit. Now, with his lucidity, came the sickening awareness he had no knowledge of either her whereabouts or safety.

He was only one of many hundreds of casualties who had arrived and were still arriving at Dimapur. The battles had not yet ended at Kohima, although the siege itself had been broken; the Japanese were still holding determinedly to the hills and defying the growing Allied forces' attempt to push them back.

The medical orderlies Gerald desperately questioned were unable to help him. The one on duty now, a gnarled Cockney, barely paused while straightening the sheet that seemed to bind Gerald to the camp bed. 'Look mate, er, sir. I'd like to bleedin' help you, but I don't know where anybody's unit is. I ain't even got a spare minute to shit, let alone go runnin' errands. You ain't the only one in 'ere, beggin' your pardon, sir.' He stepped back and surveyed the bed. 'You just take it easy, now. You're comin' along a real treat. Surgeon will be in shortly to 'ave a chat.' He softened the tone of his voice. 'I'll get you a nice cuppa as soon as he's gone.'

Gerald begged: 'Orderly, you have to try to find out for me. It's important.' He was praying Mary would be with them, safe, somewhere.

The orderly sighed. 'I'll ask when I goes to the cookhouse for grub. Maybe there's a few more of your blokes around.' He pointed a finger at Gerald. 'But what's really important, sir, is you keeping your 'air on, and getting yourself better.'

The canvas roof of the marquee in which Gerald lay trapped the sun's heat and drew moisture from the exposed ground beneath the beds, so the temperature and humidity exceeded that outside. The canvas walls were rolled up during the day, but each marquee was sited so close to its neighbour that the air was stagnant and fetid, stinking of antiseptic, gangrene, excreta and urine. The camp beds were crowded together, four rows of twenty to each marquee and separated only by the width of a small locker which held the few personal possessions or pieces of uniform the wounded had managed to retain. There was a monotonous background noise of conversation, punctuated by sounds of pain or yelps of agony as dressings were removed and changed, but rarely laughter.

The surgeon, a colonel of the Medical Corps and past retirement age had it been peacetime, arrived in the camouflaged marquee accompanied by a sister of the Queen Alexander's Nursing Corp, a sergeant medical orderly and a small retinue of clerks. The marquee hushed as he began his rounds. It was half an hour before he reached Gerald's bed.

The colonel, his face heavily lined and grey with fatigue, and wearing a white coat which accentuated the thinness of his legs below his concealed shorts, examined the record board he was handed by the sergeant. He stared at Gerald as though attempting to remember him from amongst the hundreds he had operated on in the past few weeks, then read the board again. 'Ah yes, Lieutenant Petrie. I see you're progressing satisfactorily.' He tapped his head with a slender finger. 'Depressed fracture; took out a piece of shrapnel.' He turned one of the sheets of paper clipped to the board.

'Quite a few pieces, I see.' His eyes caught Gerald's. 'How are you feeling?'

'Not too bad, sir. But I don't seem to be able to move very much.'

The sergeant orderly stepped between Gerald and the surgeon, and whispered softly in the officer's ear. The surgeon nodded and said, 'Hmm,' before speaking again. 'Better get it over with, then.' He paused again, handed the board back to the sergeant and put his hands in his coat pockets. 'I'm afraid the news isn't good, lieutenant.' Gerald noticed the sister of the Queen Alexander's Nursing Corp was staring uncomfortably at her feet as the surgeon spoke. 'You're lucky to be alive, my boy. The shrapnel did a lot of damage; some of it superficial ... most of it. We've mended your head, and your sight and hearing are unimpaired.'

Gerald was experiencing a growing feeling of terror, knowing the surgeon was leading his conversation towards some inconceivable conclusion.

The surgeon's voice was deceptively gentle, attempting reassurance but giving none. 'It's your spine, old fellow. A bit of Japanese metal ended up between two of your thoracic vertebrae.' He allowed Gerald to digest the information for a few moments. 'Took it out, of course. Wish we could do something about the damage it did, but we can't. I'm afraid no one can. One day, perhaps. But neurosurgery just isn't sufficiently advanced to repair a severed spinal cord.'

The numbness which Gerald experienced in his body felt as though it were spreading to his brain. The surgeon was telling him he would never walk again, that he would always be a helpless invalid.

'I think I've said enough for now.' The surgeon tried to smile, but looked like a benign schoolteacher who had regretfully ordered a pupil a hundred lines for playing an amusing practical joke. 'Naturally, you've got yourself a blighty; the war is over for you. You'll be going home as soon as you're fit to travel. There'll be plenty of time for us to chat before then.'

The surgeon stared hard at Gerald for a few moments as though attempting to judge his reaction to the news, then left the cubicle with his retinue. The cockney ward orderly who had been waiting behind the sergeant came over to Gerald's bed and stood awkwardly beside it. 'Sorry about that, sir. Course I knew, but I wasn't allowed to say anything. The colonel likes to tell you blokes himself.' He grimaced sympathetically. 'Look, sir, I know you think it's bad, well maybe it is, but it could be bloody worse. You'll get about, you wait and see. There are plenty of blokes I could show you in 'ere who ain't going anywhere, ever. There's a poor sod in B Ward who's lost all his limbs, his eardrums, and his bleedin' eyesight; he'd change places with you like a shot. You just keep your chin up while I go and get you that cup of tea I promised.'

As the orderly left, Gerald experienced a desperate feeling of loneliness and despair. It would have been better to have died, like Steve Chandler, than to have been sentenced to a lifetime of surely what must be endless misery, totally dependent on others for even the most simple acts. It seemed so unreasonable, so unfair, after only a few weeks in action. He wondered briefly if the surgeon could be mistaken, but knew such hopes were unrealistic. Earlier, when Gerald had tried to move his body in the bed, he had thought that for some medical reason it had been pinioned and was being held in place by pillows, perhaps as part of his treatment. Now he realised he had no real control over the lower portion of it. His arms, although one was bandaged, were the only part of him still mobile. He slowly raised a hand to study it, but tears blurred his vision. He bit his lip. Tears! He couldn't remember when he had last cried, and was ashamed at the realisation that it was with self-pity.

In desperation he attempted to move his feet, willing life into them; the wire cage over his trunk and legs prevented him from seeing the result but he knew it was negative. He put his hands under the sheet and carefully felt his body, pinching the skin to test its sensitivity. Bandages layered it from his chest downwards, further than he could reach, but when he prodded himself with his fingers there was only numbness below his navel and the feeling his body no longer belonged to him.

Half dead! He would be better off completely dead than spending years as some obscene form of centaur, the living upper part of him attached to a corpse. Perhaps there were some pain-killers, even a bottle of aspirin, he could take to end it all now? Almost hopefully he looked at the locker top next to him; it was empty apart from a towel and a beer bottle of water.

The surgeon had left the marquee before the orderly returned with a mug of tea and placed it on Gerald's locker. Gerald was silent as the man rolled the canvas wall a little higher behind his head. 'There now, sir. That'll make you a bit more confortable.' The man's voice was artificially cheerful. He sat himself on the edge of the bed and held the mug towards Gerald's mouth. 'It's not too hot; in fact I think they make it by standing a pot of cold water in the sun. Try a mouthful; do you good.'

The tea was as sweet as thin syrup, but took the dryness from Gerald's mouth. 'Can you get me something for a headache?' He made his request as casual as possible.

The orderly nodded. 'In half a tick.' When Gerald had finished the tea he stood, but before he could move away Gerald spoke again.

'If you left a bottle of aspirin here, I wouldn't need to keep bothering you.'

The orderly sat heavily on Gerald's bed again with a look of resignation on his face. 'Look, sir, I know what you're asking me, and the answer's no. I ain't helpin' you to kill yourself. And you're bloody wrong to be thinking about it. I've been in since 1939; almost five years. I've seen a lot of you blokes; you all think the same at first. Your life ain't over just 'cus you've lost your bleedin' legs, or got yourself a bit paralysed. I don't know what you did for a living but I bet it wasn't manual. Well, what's the difference between sitting at a desk in a posh armchair or sitting at it in a wheelchair? You'll be able to earn your crust, you'll be able to get yourself around your garden, around almost anywhere.'

The orderly smiled and made his voice more friendly. 'You know what I did before it all started? I was a sewerman. I hated it. I was bloody pleased when I got called up. Now, all I want to do is to get back to it. I know a lovely little sewer at the bottom end of Green Park, a sort of grotto where the lake overflows; you wouldn't think a sewer could be pretty but this one is, and that's where I want to be when this lot's over. Well, I can't see you planning to work in sewers, but you've got to understand there's a right place for all of us. Perhaps yours isn't going to be what you originally planned back in Blighty but you'll still find it, somewhere. If you'll take a tip from me, sir, you'll buck yourself up and stop thinking like a bloody idiot.'

Three days passed following Gerald's conversation with the surgeon, and although much of his time was spent sleeping, sedated by drugs, his waking hours were the most miserable he had ever experienced. Despite the orderly's advice, had the opportunity to kill himself arisen he would certainly have taken it. He could see no glimmer of hope for happiness in the future. Mary was gone, and he had no idea where she might be or even if she was still alive. And if she was, then he could no longer offer her any reasonable kind of life; he was useless to any woman as a husband.

In late afternoon, he drifted into yet another disturbed sleep where the nightmares he experienced while awake followed him to torment him further. In it voices summoned him, disregarding his pleas to allow his exhausted mind to fade into oblivion.

The calling of his name was insistent, dragging him gradually back to awareness.

'Gerald. Gerald, wake up, my lad.'

Gerald opened his eyes and tried to focus them on the silhouetted figure above his bed.

'Well, that's better.' The voice became recognisable. Alan Jameson, his company commander, stood grinning down at him, the triangle of a white sling across his chest.

Gerald felt a sense of relief. At last there was a face he recognised, a feeling of friendship. 'Hello, sir.'

'Bugger the sir bit,' said Alan Jameson. 'I gather we're both about to become civilians again, so you may as well begin calling me Alan now. How are you feeling?'

'Not too bad,' lied Gerald. He found himself staring at the sling around the captain's neck. It didn't seem possible a broken wrist or arm would get him a discharge.

Alan Jameson followed Gerald's eyes. 'Oh, this?' He shook the white triangle like a wing. 'Bit of my flipper's gone. A neat amputation, courtesy of our Nip friends. Raised my bloody arm to signal deploy, felt a bit of a thump like catching a ball in the slips, and when I looked my damned hand had gone. Don't know what the hell took it off, but it hurt less than having a tooth out. Anyway, what about yourself?'

'Spine,' said Gerald, wryly.

'Yes, I heard. Had a chat with one of your doctors as I came in. Bad luck. Still, we were all very relieved when we heard you were alive; surprised, too. Thought we'd lost you on that patrol. Only your Naga got back.'

'Sir, do you know what's happened to Mary?'

Alan Jameson looked surprised at Gerald's question. 'She's here in Dimapur.'

'Thank God.' Gerald felt intense relief.

'Don't you remember anything?' Alan asked.

Gerald shook his head. He was experiencing an unaccustomed flood of euphoria. He wanted to shout, laugh ... cry.

'Don't worry yourself, old lad. She's all right. Quite safe. I spoke to her yesterday. Found her before I found you. She's in the civvy hospital; nothing very serious; septicaemia in that neck wound of hers, a touch of malaria and a bit of a female problem. But everything is being sorted out. She was afraid you might be worried about her, but until I came along there was no way in which she could get in touch. The military wouldn't give her any information about you; not even which hospital you were in. She thought you might already be in Calcutta.'

Alone, Gerald might have wept with his relief. Publicly, his upbringing forbade it. His stemmed emotions made it difficult for him to speak. 'Thank you, sir ... thank you for getting her out.'

'Great heavens, old chap, I didn't do anything,' Alan said awkwardly. He took a battered silver cigarette case from his breast pocket and fumbled to open it on the edge of the bed before offering it to Gerald. 'Want one?' Gerald shook his head. 'Was never much good with my left hand,' continued Alan, searching for a lighter and then thumbing its wheel to provide a smoky flame that stank of petrol. He lit his cigarette then spoke with sudden realisation: 'Of course, how stupid of me! You don't know what Mary did ... did for you. It was Mary who brought you in.'

'Brought me in?' Gerald echoed Alan's words, with surprise.

Alan smiled at him. 'I told you in Kohima she was something special, remember? I didn't know what the hell happened at the time, only learnt of it when I came back through the Queens' lines. One of their lads said you'd been brought in to them by a couple of Nagas and a local girl who spoke English. It was easy enough to put two and two together. Seems Mary was pretty sick by the time she got you back, so one of the Queens' MOs arranged to get her treatment. It was just a matter of a bit of detective work for me once they decided I could get out and about a little.'

'How did she do it?' Gerald spoke in little more than a whisper. It was a question to himself rather than to Alan Jameson, but Alan answered.

'She won't say much about it. I'd guess she bribed the Naga scout to take her to where you'd been ambushed. After that, they carried you back; avoided Jap patrols, lay up in daylight and travelled at night. Took them three days, I gather. Nearly got themselves shot by our own troops; might have been if Mary hadn't shouted to them in English. What do you plan to do about her?'

'Plan?' Gerald spoke bitterly. 'I don't have any plans. I can't have plans. Look at me, I'm no use to man nor beast.'

'No use? What a pathetic load of rubbish.'

'It's not pathetic to be realistic, especially for Mary's sake.'

'You're not being realistic.' Alan sounded as angry as if he were addressing a defaulter. 'You're taking the easy way out. You're considering only yourself and how you feel about things, not how Mary may feel; dammit, does feel. Good God, I never thought I'd hear myself telling a British officer he should do the right thing with an Indian girl, but I'm damn well telling you. Do you love her?'

'Of course I love her.'

'Then if she'll have you, marry the girl.'

Alan Jameson became the runner between Mary and Gerald. For the next few days while she was still confined to her bed he carried messages between the two hospitals. At last, one morning a week later, following the daily ward inspection, he arrived with a mysterious look on his face. 'No letter for you today, I'm afraid,' he said, after his usual cheery greeting. 'But no need to look so crestfallen, I've got something better: the real thing. Mary's outside, waiting to see you. Don't suppose you'll want me around for the next half hour so I'll push off.' He gave a thumbs-up sign. 'Lucky chap.'

Gerald watched her walk towards him along the length of the marquee. She had seemed frail and delicate on the night when they had first made love, but now she seemed even more fragile. Whereas she had previously been slender she was now thin and her cheekbones more pronounced. Her neck was bandaged, a broad collar of white above the patterned blouse and sari she was wearing. She had been hesitant as she entered the long tent with its rows of beds, each occupied by prone figures, but once she recognised Gerald her steps became more sure and quickened. He had been afraid he would see pity in her eyes but could see none, only happiness.

She did not speak even when they had kissed, but took his hands and held them tightly.

Gerald stared into her dark, concerned eyes. 'Alan told me what you did for me. Thank you.' He felt hypocritical. Several times during the past days he had wished he had died out in the jungle; he would have faced none of the problems which now confronted him. But the feeling passed as she smiled down at him.

'You would have done the same for me?' He nodded. 'Then, it is no longer important. We are here together.' She kissed him again. 'And you still love me?'

'You don't need to ask me.'

'But I want to hear you say it.'

'Yes, I still love you, Mary.'

They talked for half an hour, the strangeness of their surroundings and the barrier which seemed to have been built by Gerald's injuries gradually dissolving until it was as though they had never been apart. Eventually, Mary lifted Gerald's hands and placed them between her own, on her lap. He could feel the warmth of her thighs. 'Alan has told me he said to you we should be married.'

'Yes, he said that.' Gerald realised he had reached the moment he had been dreading when he must force her to realise there was no future for her with him. He had hoped it would not be during this first meeting, but to mislead her now would only add to the cruelty later. 'Alan was wrong.' Her moist eyes filled and Gerald wanted to take her in his arms and hold her close to him. 'You must understand, Mary. I'm never going to be able to walk again. You need a proper man, not half of one; not some helpless cripple who won't even be able to crawl out of bed without help.'

'But I want to help you, and I know all about your wounds. I spoke to the doctors at my own hospital. They told me what it means. It doesn't matter to me. I just want you as my husband; as my man.'

Gerald turned his head away from her. 'I can't be your man, Mary. Not any more. I'm not a proper man. You could never have children with me.'

Her voice was very soft, drawing his eyes back to her own. 'You are wrong, Gerald.' She lifted his hands and placed the palms flat against the gentle roundness of her stomach. 'We already have our child. It is here, inside me.'

It was becoming more difficult in their growing friendship for Gerald ever to picture Alan as the once stern company commander with the reputation of being bomb-proof and impossible to deceive. His uniform and rank appeared no more than shells within which was concealed a man with a mischievous sense of humour and strong sense of loyalty towards those he liked. The ten years' difference in their ages no longer seemed important and Gerald looked forward to his visits almost as much as those of Mary. Normally, Alan kept out of their way when they were together, knowing their need at such time was simply the company and physical touch of each other. Occasionally, when Gerald or Mary insisted, he would accompany her. Today, he was alone.

Gerald, his head and shoulders propped by a pillow, smiled. 'We're getting married.'

'You've been telling me that for a week. And it was my suggestion anyway. Tell me something less boring.' He stifled an imaginary yawn with the back of his hand.

'We'd like to get married right away.'

'Right away?' Alan raised his thick eyebrows.

'The orderly says there's a chapel in the barracks. So, all we need is a padre.'

'Steady on, old chap, you'll want a few more things than that. For instance you're under twenty-one and in theory still on active service. You need your CO's permission.'

'Don't tell me you don't agree.'

'Of course I agree, but I'm not your CO. It'll be the senior administrator here. And it has to go through the books. And there's bound to be civil requirements if you want things tied up and legal. It'll take some time to arrange.'

'Will you arrange it for us?'

Alan laughed. 'Well, I've got nothing better to do, so why not?'

'And I want to take my discharge out here in India.'

Alan frowned. 'Is that wise? You'll probably get better medical treatment back in the UK. And there's your family to consider.'

'I've decided I'm only considering Mary,' Gerald said, firmly. 'What would happen to her if I'm shipped back to England? It might be two or three years before she could join me there. Besides, I'd rather we spent a little time together here as man and wife before I take her home. As far as my parents are concerned I know damn well what they'll think, but it's my life and I'm the one who's going to make the decisions about how I live it.' Gerald paused. 'Besides, medical treatment isn't going to make that much difference to me. I know what I'm stuck with.'

The administration officer, a major attached to the Royal Army Medical Corps, did not bother to stand when Alan Jameson escorted Mary into his office. He did not even raise his eyes from the sheaf of requisition forms he was examining when his clerk, a diminutive Indian civilian in a baggy dhoti, introduced them. 'Major sah'b. Here are Miss Sachema and Captain Jameson.'

'Won't keep them a minute. Must wait their turn, babu.' The major drawled his words with a plummy Home Counties accent, and made the Hindu term for an educated man sound condescending. After two or three minutes during which Alan Jameson forced himself to control his growing anger at the man's boorishness, the major closed the folder on the documents, then looked over the pair of half-lenses he was wearing. 'Ah yes, you're the application for permission to marry.' He pushed himself back in the sprung office chair, and interlaced his fingers across his waist. 'I suppose you got her pregnant?'

Alan Jameson felt the blood drain from his face in fury, but kept his voice calm. 'You suppose incorrectly. I happen to be the applicant's company commander. Lieutenant Petrie has been seriously wounded. I am acting on his behalf ... sir.' Damn the man, he thought, he was probably something like an assistant bank manager in civvy life who had managed to wangle himself a cushy military number with a King's Commission.

'And this is the woman involved?' asked the major laconically. 'I mean to say, I'm not dealing with her sister, or her aunt, or cousin? Does she understand English?'

'Perfectly,' answered Alan, coldly.

'Most don't.' The major uncoupled his hands, allowed his chair to swing forward and picked up the letter which Gerald had dictated and signed. 'I get a dozen of these things every day ... a dozen. Ridiculous! What the men don't realise is that every little whore is prepared to pretend she's fallen in love with a British soldier so's she can escape from the stinking hole she's living in and get herself a warrant to the land of plenty. Well, part of my job is to see it doesn't happen.'

'Now just a minute...' began Alan.

The major sat upright, abruptly. 'No, captain, I will not "just a minute"! You come out here still wet behind the ears. You don't know India and you don't know Indians outside the army and the sepoys you meet. You don't understand them.'

'And you do, sir.' Alan emphasised the formal title.

'I should hope so after four years, captain.'

'I happen to have been born here, sir,' said Alan, tersely. 'As was Lieutenant Petrie. And had you worked here as a civilian, sir, you would know his family own half of Assam and a goodly portion of the transport system you probably commandeer. And as both our families have worked in India for the best part of a hundred years you are speaking somewhat out of place ... sir.'

The major pivoted his chair so his back was to Alan and Mary, and stared out into the vehicle-crowded barracks compound beyond his window.

Mary looked desperately at Alan, attempting to question him with her eyes. He shook his head at her quickly, silencing her before she could speak. This application is madness, she thought. Gerald was a man who had already risked his life for his country and paid a terrible penalty for his bravery, yet here sat this officer, this cold, insulting Englishman, ignoring what should have been merely a formality. If a man was old enough to fight and perhaps die, then he was certainly of an age when he could choose his wife.

The major spun his chair around to face them again. 'There are, of course, exceptions. Rare, but occasional.' He examined Gerald's letter again. 'I see the lieutenant is almost twenty-one.'

'In two months' time.'

'If he was to wait until he was repatriated, he could marry without official sanction.'

'Both he and I are taking our discharge in India,' said Alan.

The major raised his eyebrows. 'Captain, will you please leave yourself out of Lieutenant Petrie's application. I am really not interested in your future, merely his.'

'As am I, sir.' Alan's voice rose angrily. 'Lieutenant Petrie will be a permanent invalid. He wishes to marry this young lady not only because he happens to love her dearly, but also to assure her future.'

'Has he informed his family?'

'He's written, of course. But you know quite well what the mail situation is at the moment. It can take months to get a letter to the UK, and as long to get an answer back. By which time, he ...'

'Would be twenty-one, anyway,' concluded the major. He removed his half-lenses and polished them with a piece of pink blotting paper. 'Very well. In this case I am prepared to acquiesce to circumstances. Lieutenant Petrie will receive official notification of my decision. Good day, captain.'

The corridors of the barracks, even its mess hall, had become makeshift wards, crowded with the beds, charpoys and straw-filled palliasses of the wounded. It was as crowded as a market place, noisy with the hubbub of conversation and busy with the hundreds of medical orderlies who had been transported in to cope with the swelling numbers of wounded. Gerald, in one of the marquees, was obviously receiving slightly better treatment than most, for even in these circumstances the military was managing to separate its officers from other ranks. There was a squalid untidiness to the place. On a wall beside the administration block entrance doors, which had been wedged open to accommodate yet another couple of palliasses, someone had scrawled a huge chalk drawing of a turbanned head peering over a wall and the words, 'Chad Sahib is watching you'.

Conversation between Alan and Mary was impossible until they reached the main gate and walked out on to the road beyond the guards.

Dimapur frightened Mary. Its teeming population of soldiers of a dozen nationalities crowded the streets, their arrogance forcing the civilians into narrow doorways or the gutter as they passed. The heavy transport lorries and fighting vehicles moving from the station to the battlefront along the narrow, dusty roads shook the buildings and swirled dust and filth amongst the cowering pedestrians and traders.

Mary felt despondent. She had not understood the major's last words, and the anger in Alan's face concealed the outcome of the meeting. At last they reached a small teashop beside an Indian hotel. There was a vacant table and Alan steered her towards it. A young khidmutgar, little more than twelve years old, dusted the chair for them and then stood nearby.

'Tea?' said Alan, then looked quizzically at Mary. She nodded. 'For both of us,' he told the boy.

'Biscuit, sah'b?'

'No, thank you.'

The boy hurried away into the darkness at the back of the teashop. Across the roadway a group of Gurkha soldiers were playing pitch and toss with coins against the wall of a shop. In the gutter by their feet was the fresh corpse of a pi dog which had just been run down by a passing truck.

'Well, now.' Alan reached over the table and took Mary's hand. 'I think, young lady, that's the worst of the official bit done with.'

'The officer refused us permission?'

Alan frowned, then grinned at her. 'So that's what you thought? I wondered why you were looking so miserable. The man said yes. Not in a word, but yes was what he meant.' He squeezed her hand, then released it as the boy appeared with an enamelled pot of tea and two fine porcelain cups and saucers that were out of place on the bare wood of the warped table top. 'Sugar and milk?' asked Alan.

'Sorry, sah'b. No sugar. No milk. Biscuits?'

'Positively no biscuits.' Alan turned back to Mary. 'I'm sorry that damned officer was so boorish. If it had been my own application I'd have told him where he could stick it; but I had to bite my tongue. If I'd been too rude to the blighter he might have thrown us out.'

Mary smiled at him. 'Thank you, Alan.' She hesitated, then said: 'You know what was so strange? It is me who is getting married, who is wanting to get married. Yet that man, the officer, he did not speak a word to me. He did not even look at me. For him, I was no more important than that thing.' She pointed across the road at the corpse of the dog.

'I'm afraid you've got a lot to learn about the Brits. And not all of it is going to be pleasant.' He grimaced. 'This place doesn't bring out the best in all of us. We have a somewhat inflated view of our own importance at the best of times; here, it can get even more out of proportion. Everyone who isn't white and British by birth becomes a savage to be tamed, or converted, or pitied; or simply ignored. We like to think we're the most cultured nation in Europe, but we forget our own culture is only a few hundred years old and countries like India can count theirs in thousands. And we judge things by the wrong standards. We're even brought up and educated to judge by the wrong standards.'

'Surely not all of you?'

Alan laughed. 'Thank God, no. A few of us think for ourselves. Not many, mind you. And the wise ones keep their thoughts to themselves in the company of other Brits.'

'Then why are you helping Gerald and me?'

Alan smiled again. 'Because I like him and I like you, Mary. I think you've both got guts ... spirit. And I think there's something in Gerald that is going to make men like him important soon here.' His face became serious, wistful. 'And, of course, there's Angharad.'

'Angharad?'

'My wife. She would have appreciated your difficulties.'

Mary sensed loss. 'She is in England?'

'She died five years ago. Cholera. We were upcountry and I couldn't do a thing to help her. I met her when I was at university in Cardiff. I was studying engineering and she was a secretary in the college. We married as soon as I got my degree, and came back out here. The Brits didn't like her.'

'But she was English.'

'Welsh.' Alan smiled at unrevealed memories. 'And that caused her a lot of trouble. The Brits couldn't distinguish between her accent and a Bombay Welsh accent. And she was dark complexioned, with black hair. They thought she was Anglo-Indian. But they didn't bargain for a Celtic temper and socialist views. She fought a lot of battles, and generally won them. She would have loved putting our friend the major in his place. And she would have wanted me to help you.'

Officialdom was more concerned with war and its problems than marriage, and even the hospital padre was more occupied by death and pain in the present than wedded bliss in the future. Consequently, the following three weeks which led towards her wedding seemed the longest and most uncertain of Mary's life.

She felt constantly restless and frustrated. Many girls she had known in the past had married, but for them the time before their weddings had been busy with preparation, filled by chatter, teasing and advice. And what fears they might have had were dulled by the thoughts that once they had been taken to their future homes, and the new relationships established with their husband's mother and family, they would be able to settle into a regulated and usually secure marriage.

Here in Dimapur, now that Mary had left the civilian hospital, she was virtually alone, and her accommodation a grubby room she was forced to share with three middle-aged dancing girls who augmented their small income by prostitution. Alan had tried to find her something more pleasant, but it had been impossible. The railhead town of Dimapur was not only crowded by the continuous incoming flood of troops but infested by avaricious traders, thieves, pimps, prostitutes and camp-followers, all preying on the susceptible army.

Apart from Mary's love for Gerald it seemed to her that the one certain thing in her life was the child she carried. Its significance and importance to Gerald awed her. His own love for her was unquestionable, but this precious germinating seed was the last of its species. The responsibility gave her subtly changing feelings, confidence, honour, sometimes fear, and often sadness with her knowledge that it must remain unique and solitary.

Gerald's wounds were now healing swiftly. It seemed impossible to Mary he would never walk again, though she was not so foolish as to doubt the surgeon's prediction. When she had first discovered Gerald lying in the swampy reed bed, she and the two Nagas had stripped him and examined his body. She had carried dressings with her and used them on his wounds. At the time it had seemed the injury to his head was the most serious. The others, mainly small tears and punctures, were scattered across his shoulders and back. She could remember the one nearest his spine, less than half an inch in length and looking like nothing more than a deep scratch; yet it was this tiny wound that had most severely injured him. A piece of metal no bigger than the crescent of one of her fingernails had sliced through his spinal cord. She hid her grief, concealing it beneath her feelings of love.

Alan interpreted her outwardly controlled emotion wrongly, believing the apparent acceptance of Gerald's crippling disability was the Eastern acknowledgement of fate, almost genetic in its nature and ability to over-ride Western teachings. He saw, though, how in some feminine and ingenious manner she was providing her man with a future through the promises of her own body, so that his physical and mental healing quickened as though determined to match the pace of the developing child inside her. Alan recognised, too, how she was giving to Gerald at cost to herself; the infected wound in her neck still required regular dressing and although she had been discharged from the hospital she was still weak.

*

Leaving Gerald at the end of her visit was the hardest part of her days. They were permitted to be together between two and four p.m., times when those who were strong and mobile enough were allowed to walk or sit in narrow paths between the crowded tents. Mornings were reserved for the rounds of the doctors, evenings for the preparations for the patients' nights. She hated the marquee, loathed the stench of antiseptic and chloroform which impregnated even the tea and biscuits the orderly sometimes brought during her visits. She could recognise death in some of the faces that watched her; camp beds containing familiar figures would be surrounded by screens on one visit, occupied by yet another pain-filled body on the next. She had learnt, too, that a man's chances of survival could be judged by the closeness of his bed to the marquee entrance; every day she felt relief when she found Gerald's bed unmoved, or further from the menacing canvas door. One Christmas Eve as a small child she had hidden in the bushes of a garden surrounding a planter's house; the guests were gambling on horseracing, a bearer tossing a huge dice while players moved plywood horses along a chequered track. The movement of the beds in the marquee had revived the memory of the horserace, so she felt that somewhere a cruel die was being cast, turning the tragedy of the war into a grotesque and monstrous game.

Each afternoon Gerald would hold her hand tightly, delaying her going until they were prompted by the orderly. The orderly knew her now and called her his 'love bird', winking at her knowingly, addressing her as 'love' as he escorted her from the marquee. Today, he stopped her just outside the entrance.

'Wait a bit, love. The Guv'nor wants a word with you.'

'The Guv'nor?' The word was unfamiliar.

'Yeah. The Guv. The surgeon.' The orderly saw the concern on her face. 'Don't worry. I don't think it's bad news or anything. I'd guess it's about your wedding. Won't be long now, eh? Better come this way.' He led her to the barrack block and to a small building that might once have been a guard-room. The orderly knocked softly before entering. The surgeon was examining an X-ray plate at the window.

'Lieutenant Petrie's lady, sir,' said the orderly, who then smiled reassuringly at Mary before leaving the room.

The surgeon slid the X-ray into a large brown envelope. 'Please sit down.' He indicated a chair in front of his desk. Mary sat nervously on its edge.

The surgeon stared at her for a few moments before speaking, and then said: 'Captain Jameson has been telling me all about you, as has your fiancé. In fact I'm quite sure he would rather talk about you than his wounds.' He paused and sat himself down opposite her. 'I thought we ought to meet and have a little talk. When are you getting married?'

'I think in one week.' She knew her voice was tremulous.

The surgeon leant back in his chair. 'I'm not going to eat you, young lady.' He reminded her of an elderly cardinal who had once visited the mission school; the nuns had appeared terrified by the man's presence and relieved when he had left, though he had seemed kindly enough to the children. She felt herself relax. 'That's better.' The surgeon, balding and with a fringe of grey hair above his temples, clasped his hands in front of him. 'Now then. I want to discuss Lieutenant Petrie. I gather you speak perfect English so we have no communication problems.' She nodded at him. 'Good. So you quite understand the full extent of his injuries.'

'Yes.'

'That's what Captain Jameson said, but I want to be quite certain.' The surgeon had a gentle, friendly voice; now he leant forward and rested his elbows on his desk. 'Do you really know what you're letting yourself in for, child?' He saw her eyes harden slightly. 'No, don't misunderstand me, I'm not trying to dissuade you from marrying him. But I don't want either of you hurt through misunderstandings. Petrie is young and tough. He obviously kept himself in good shape and there is no reason why he shouldn't have a long and healthy life. Now, I stress that word "long", because what you are taking on is likely to be a lifetime's occupation, not something that will end in a couple of months.'

'I quite understand.' For some reason she added: 'Sir.'

'I've got a daughter about your age; I wonder if she would be so brave and determined in these circumstances.' He paused. 'I'm told you're pregnant; well, it happens, especially in wartime. You realise, of course, Lieutenant Petrie will probably not be able to have any more children? And, I'm afraid, my dear, he won't be able to lead what we call a normal sex life. That can be important when you're young; as you get older, well, other things may take its place. You are going to have to look for them earlier than most.' The surgeon opened his desk drawer and pulled out a file, examining it before he spoke again. 'Hmm! He's progressing very well indeed. I think, with luck, we can start trying to get him into a wheelchair in a few days. Perhaps in time for your wedding. I gather from Jameson that your fiancé is a fairly wealthy young man. That will obviously help you later. I see he wants his discharge here in India. That being the case, it would be sensible for you to employ a nurse for him.' He chuckled. 'Better not call him a nurse, though. I'll tell him I think he should have a valet! It will ease things for you quite considerably, and if he agrees, I'll make sure the man has some nursing experience. Now then, what about you?'

She was uncertain how to answer him. 'What about me?'

'Your health, young lady. You look somewhat peaky.' The surgeon stood, walked round his desk and bent forward to stare into her eyes. 'Hmm. Malaria?'

'Yes.'

'And your neck? I know it was caused by shrapnel but how is it? Let me take off the dressing.' He undid the bandage carefully, and probed with his fingertips. 'Can't have our officers' fiancées being neglected. Yes, I think we'll give it a little more treatment. Good.' He stepped back and pointed at her stomach. 'And how about this?'

'I think it's fine.'

'How long has it been?'

'Nearly three months.'

'Early days; it's a miracle you've still got it. You'll have to take more care if you don't want to risk losing it. Try and get plenty of rest, and don't start trying to heave the lieutenant around yourself. If he ever needs lifting, then get a man to do it. I'll get you some vitamin tablets.' He spent several minutes dressing her neck wound, then scribbled a note on a scrap of paper. 'Here, take this to Lieutenant Petrie's ward orderly. He'll get you the vitamins, and he'll dress your wound each time you visit.' He held his hand towards her, and she took it. His grip was strong, and positive. 'Good luck, young lady.'

Although the days leading towards her marriage were difficult ones for Mary, she had been able to keep herself busy and occupied during them; her visits to Gerald filled much of her time, and there had been many pleasant hours in Alan's company. Gerald, however, was imprisoned in his bed and there were periods when, with nothing to distract him, his mind dwelt on the many problems he knew would face them in their future life together. Some would have been difficult enough without his disability; with it, he sometimes wondered if it were possible for their marriage to survive.

There was never any doubt he loved her and she him, and this was the one undeniable fact which gave him courage. He was not fearful for himself, but for her. How would she be able to adapt to a complete change in her manner of living unless he was always at her side to support and advise her? There would be no allowances made for her by most of the British she must certainly meet; they would always be watching for signs of her background, for the mistakes and *faux pas* she might make without his help. Surely it was impossible to expect her to learn to cope with a husband who was little more than a useless carcass, unable to protect her from the smallest danger, while at the same time she must adjust to the sophistication the marriage would demand and the unaccustomed wealth and authority it would provide?

His tortured mind led him through a thousand imagined situations, and he knew the hurt she might experience would be more painful to him than his own wounds. But despite his fears he understood now there could be no parting for them, a life which did not contain her was inconceivable, too bleak and lonely to accept; without her there was no compensation for what he had already lost.

On 6 June 1944, Gerald and Mary were married in the small chapel at the rear of the barracks. Gerald was awkwardly propped in a wheelchair, wearing a borrowed battledress blouse on which Alan had changed the insignia to those of the Assam Regiment. Mary, beside him, seemed unusually pale in a black sari decorated with silver embroidery which had been a wedding gift from Gerald. The chapel smelt no less of antiseptic than the hospital marquees, and half of its length was occupied by piled boxes of medical stores and equipment. The place was hot and unventilated, and bare walls echoed the chaplain's words like an empty theatre. There were only a dozen guests at the small celebration Alan had arranged in the officers' mess tent. There was no wedding cake to cut and no champagne, but miraculously he had found several bottles of sherry for the traditional toasts.

An hour later, just as the guest of honour, the surgeon, was insisting Gerald should be returned to the serenity of his marquee, an excited orderly burst into the mess and interrupted him. 'Sir. Hope you don't mind, gentlemen. Thought you'd all like to know; the

Second Front's started. Came through on the wireless a few minutes ago. We've just landed in Normandy.'

It was dusk when Alan walked Mary back to her dingy accommodation. The streets of Dimapur were even more crowded than usual; groups of excited soldiers celebrating the news of the Allied invasion of Europe occupied every small café and bar, or gathered in noisy parties around stalls which sold tepid and questionable bottled beer. It was as though they had all forgotten they were merely in transit towards a battleground and perhaps their own deaths; their peace was still a dangerously long time away.

Mary was glad of Alan's company. The return to the squalor of the Indian guesthouse was already a disappointing anticlimax to her wedding, and she was experiencing a depressing sense of unreality as though the happy occasion had never occurred. He offered to buy her a drink in one of the noisy bars but she declined. He left her at the guesthouse door with the words: 'Goodnight, Mrs Mary Petrie.'

She slowly climbed the stairs to her room which overlooked the street. To her relief, the girls who shared it with her were out, but their beds were untidy and unmade and the room stank of stale perspiration. She attempted to open the window but it jammed after only a couple of inches, so she carried a chair to it and sat staring down into the busy street.

Flares were already being lit above the stalls in the untidy market place which had grown at the junction of a crossroads thirty yards to her left. There was a juggler, a tall Punjabi, accompanied by a small boy and girl, who was tossing different fruits into the air and catching them on his forehead; a small crowd watched him. Tampura music from a wireless, turned to full volume in a room opposite, competed with a gramophone on one of the stalls. Voices argued, bargained, few words distinguishable above the hubbub.

Today, Mary knew, had been both an end and a beginning.

'Mrs Mary Petrie.' She said the words aloud. They sounded as though she were introducing a guest to her former memsah'b. I am a memsah'b now, she thought. No, I am not a memsah'b. A memsah'b was not something she wanted to be. I am Mrs Mary Petrie, the wife of Lieutenant Gerald Petrie. I am Mrs Gerald Petrie.

But what exactly did that mean? To be the wife of an Indian meant cooking, washing, mending clothes. But if the Indian was a man of wealth, then servants did the manual work; Gerald was certainly a wealthy man. She knew his family owned the tea plantations and Alan had said there would be no need for her to ever worry about financial problems, even if Gerald never worked. How much was a lot of money? she wondered. Gerald had said they would buy a house once he left the army. He had said it might be in Calcutta or upcountry, and they would decide once the doctors had finished with him. He would surely expect her to help him entertain; his friends would be British. She must never let him down in front of them, that would be disaster. She attempted to remember the things Evelyn Warren had always insisted were important when she entertained. Flowers! Lots of flowers in bowls and vases. Everything spotless; the servants in white, those serving at the table wearing immaculate gloves. Whisky or pink gin for the male guests when they arrived, and sherry or cocktails for the ladies. Cocktails! How did you make a cocktail? Surely any good bearer would know?

Furniture! She would have to buy furniture if Gerald bought a house. Perhaps British houses were sold with furniture in them? She would need furniture and linen; she would need towels. Bath towels, the large ones she had placed daily in Evelyn Warren's bathroom. A bathroom! She had always enjoyed the scent of perfumed water, it had always seemed so luxurious. She had never bathed in a European bath, never lain in deep scented water. Evelyn Warren had spent a lot of time in her bathroom; she had bathed twice a day. Mary remembered her own bath, the small galvanised iron tub which she shared with the other servants. It was barely large enough to sit in, and the water was never more than luke-warm and only three or four inches in depth. There had been a bath in the hospital, but it was stained brown and chipped with age and misuse, and the water had been cold. Were baths sold with houses, or did you also have to buy them?

I am so ignorant, Gerald will think I am a fool, she thought. His friends will laugh at all my mistakes and condemn him for marrying me. They will not understand our love. And if I make him seem foolish, then perhaps he will stop loving me, stop wanting me to be with him. He might even send me away. I wish he were here with me now; no, not here, but in some more pleasant place.

She looked down at her black sari. The room was now almost dark but the silver embroidery traced fine lines on the silk. I am not yet married, she decided. I am almost his wife, but not really his wife. I will become his wife when we are together again, when I can lie beside him at night and know that he is there to touch, when I can hear him breathing as he sleeps beside me. For the moment, I am still Mary Sachema, and I am sad and lonely, and perhaps I am a little lost.

It was the same feeling she had experienced a long time before on the day when the nuns had taken her from her mother's house. She had been five years old then. She could remember the day clearly; her mother had been in mourning after her father's death. Her sister, so young she was still unable to walk, cried continuously in echo of her mother's distress. The nuns had come, two of them, white robed and serious faced. Her mother had wept even more loudly. An aunt had led Mary from the small house with its whitewashed mud walls and thatched roof. Mary had not known why she was being given to the nuns; it would be much better for her, her aunt had promised. The nuns would treat her kindly, give her plenty of good food and teach her to read and write.

That day, too, had been an end and a beginning.

There were sounds in the corridor outside her room, soft talk, and then male laughter. The door latch rattled, and the single electric light bulb was switched on harshly, filling the room with its brightness. One of the dancing girls stood inside the doorway with a man at her side; Mary could smell alcohol. The girl seemed surprised to find the room occupied.

'Who is this man?' Mary asked in Hindi. She thought it was unlikely the girl even knew his name. The man was a soldier, a Madrasi by the dark colouring of his skin; a client the girl was attempting to smuggle to her bed.

The girl giggled, then said: 'Why don't you go out for a while.' She turned to the man. 'It's only one of my sisters.'

'I am not her sister,' Mary reacted angrily. 'We share the room, because there is nowhere else to stay. And I am not a whore like her.' She glared at the girl. 'Take him out, take him away.'

The man pulled a small bottle from his pocket and held it towards Mary, grinning. 'Have a drink. You'll feel more friendly.'

The man's round dark face was shiny with sweat, and the whites of his eyes were already bloodshot with the drink he had consumed in the past hours. He lurched forward holding a small bottle towards Mary. 'Here, woman. Have a drink with us; you'll feel happier. I'll give you two rupees as well, you might be worth it. We can all have fun together.' He made a playful grab at her.

He was so close to her she could smell his breath, cheap rum and biris, the hand-rolled local cigarettes. She pushed him as hard as she could with both hands. 'Get out. Get out.'

Her blow staggered the man backwards, smashing him against the doorframe, the rum bottle hurtling across the room and spraying its contents over the bedding. He regained his balance and took a threatening step towards her but frowned suddenly, doubled forward and was sick. Thin vomit seemed to erupt from his mouth, splattering yellow liquid on to the linoleum and Mary's feet and sari.

She screamed so loudly that for a moment it silenced the conversations in the street below her room. The dancing girl was pale with fright. She grabbed the man who was still retching. 'We are going,' she said, quickly. She half supported the man from the room, his vomit dribbling from his chin down the front of his khaki shirt.

'You are an Assamese bitch,' he slurred at Mary as the girl helped him through the doorway.

Mary heard them stagger down the stairs and a shouted argument begin with the proprietor of the house in its narrow entrance hall.

The room stank from the vomit and rum. Mary loosened her stained sari and rolled it into a ball, then she sat on the edge of her bed and wept.

CHAPTER SIX

CALCUTTA. AUGUST 1944

It was raining as the train, carrying three hundred wounded troops and a few privileged civilian passengers from Dimapur, slowly clanked its way across the complicated web of lines and points into Howrah Junction Station. The journey to Calcutta had taken two and a half tedious days, during which the weather had become increasingly humid and uncomfortable as the train lumbered its way southwards on to the low-lying plain bordering the Bay of Bengal. Many of the passengers, especially the wounded on their stretchers, had developed prickly heat, an irritating rash that soon even those able to move around were unable to avoid.

The temperature outside the carriages was 106 degrees and ten higher in the small compartments; the moist atmosphere and the smell of wounded men and their medication was stifling and oppressive.

Tidy lines of ambulances waited on the station platform, their crews stripped to the waist in the suffocating heat. Military policemen, incongruous in their near-nakedness, ranks worn as armbands on tanned biceps, were deployed amongst the vehicles, their bright red hats as distinctive as poppies in fields of ripe corn. Beyond the ambulances, policemen, porters, station staff and steel-mesh barriers, a mass of Indians jostled each other for a better view of the wounded as they disembarked; had it not been for the police, many tradesmen and foodstuff sellers would have risked scaling the barrier to reach the potential customers.

Steam roared from the valves of the engine's boilers, shaking the dense air, drowning shouted conversations; everywhere there was the stench of burning coal, sulphur-tainted fumes, stale food, antiseptic and sweat.

Rai, the retired Gurkha hamildar now employed as Gerald's bearer, watched the scene with expressionless black eyes. He knew there was no point in hurrying, no point in attempting to move his sahib's wheelchair until the crush thinned. Thirty years in the King's service had taught him the British army moved slowly when there were clerks involved. In appearance he was typical of his race, a short and stocky Nepalese, his round face creased by the sun and his years. His hair, once black, was now grey, as was the moustache which dropped low on both sides of his wide mouth. His hair colouring and wrinkled skin gave him an initially deceptive appearance of great age; in fact, he was just fifty-six and still powerful, capable of swinging Gerald's heavy leather suitcase easily on to his shoulder with one hand.

Rai was proud of the job he had held for less than a fortnight. He had been discharged from the army eight months previously when arthritis from a wound in his ankle, received in France in 1917, had become impossible to ignore. He had delayed returning to Nepal, preferring the atmosphere of a garrison town, and had found work as a porter in the military hospital. The pay had been very low, and the position without prestige, but his pension helped him a little. He was not married, and had no family alive. To his surprise, he had been asked by one of the hospital doctors if he would like the position of bearer and nurse for a wounded British officer, and had been delighted when he was interviewed and then employed. He had been told that if he was satisfactory the position would be permanent. Only one thing disturbed him: the British officer was married to an Assamese woman. It could lead, he thought, to problems. He had always preferred taking orders from Europeans ... and never from women.

For the first ten days of his employment, he had worked under the instructions of a medical orderly in the Dimapur military hospital; there had been a great deal to learn in such a short time. In many ways the wounded officer was like a small child. It was necessary to help him from his bed and into his chair, then assist him to bathe, and then dress him with the cumbersome rubberised canvas bag that hung attached to a thick condom in the crotch of his trousers in daytime. But had it been a child the Gurkha was expected to help he would have refused the job; looking after children was women's work. A wounded British officer was different.

They had already argued. The young officer was fiercely independent and hated the indignities his wound forced him to accept. Rai had been warned this might happen, and had been told by the doctor he must be firm for the good of his sahib. In time the officer would be able to do much more for himself, but the steps of progress must be taken slowly.

The first argument had been about shaving.

'It is my work, sah'b, to shave you.' It was Rai's first day with the lieutenant.

'Nonsense, I've shaved myself for the past month.'

'It's not necessary to shave yourself, sah'b. I am quite experienced.'

'Damn your experience. Give me the razor.'

The ward orderly had watched amused, then winked at Rai. Rai shrugged, and handed the safety razor to the red-faced officer. He wondered for a few minutes if he was going to be sacked. Then the officer had said: 'Don't just stand there, man. I've got soap in my eyes. For God's sake, pass me a towel.' Rai had laughed with relief, and to his pleasure Lieutenant Petrie had laughed with him. After that, the small arguments they had were tempered by their liking for each other.

But the Lushai girl, the Sahib's wife?

Rai had met her only during her visits to the hospital, and sensed her jealousy when he attended the needs of her husband. Her jealousy was never expressed, never very obvious, but if he lifted the Sahib into a more comfortable position in his bed or adjusted his seating in the wheelchair, then he noticed the faintest glint of resentment in her eyes or a subtle change in the tone of her voice. He knew very little about her, only that she had saved the Sahib's life by carrying him back to the lines when he had been wounded. The Sahib always mentioned it as though it were a miracle; Rai allowed himself no judgement, as yet.

It was two hours before Rai and one of the orderlies lifted Gerald's wheelchair from the train and set it on the platform; Mary followed them. The wounded on stretchers were neatly laid in rows, clerks checking the documents pinned to their chests. The injured who were mobile had already been loaded into trucks, most of which had been driven away. More vehicles were arriving; these with fit, unwounded men on their way to Dimapur and the battlefront which was already being pressed deeper into Burma. A new engine had been coupled to the train, with a fresh crew, and within a very short time it would be making its way back across the plains, towards the distant hills.

'Sir!' An MP sergeant snapped to attention in front of Gerald's wheelchair. 'Lost our documentation, have we, sir?' He pointed towards the lapel of Gerald's tunic.

'On leave, sergeant.' Gerald felt in his breast pocket and found his leave pass and identification. The sergeant read them carefully before giving them back.

'Very good, sir.' He indicated Rai. 'Your bearer, sir?'

'Yes. And this lady is my wife. They are both on my warrant.'

The MP studied Mary with obvious interest. 'Of course, sir.' Mary could read curiosity in his gaze and felt herself colouring. To her relief the man faced Gerald again. 'Where will you be staying, sir?'

'The Grand Hotel.'

The sergeant looked thoughtful. 'Well, you'll be wanting a taxi, not one of our ambulances.' He glanced over his shoulder towards the still crowded barrier. 'You'll have to fight your way through that lot.' He hesitated. 'Are you sick, or wounded, sir.'

Rai had the old soldier's typical dislike of red-caps and was beginning to feel protective towards his sahib. The MP was of the same rank he had held himself for several years, so he saw no reason for any special respect. He spoke fiercely. 'The Sah'b was wounded in the Kohima battle.'

The MP looked sharply at Rai. 'Was he now, Johnny?' He relaxed and grinned. 'Right then, if that's the case, you'd better leave this to me.' He turned towards an MP private twenty feet away. 'Wilkins,' he shouted, his voice echoing in the noisy station. 'Wilkins . . . over here, lad.' He waited until Private Wilkins was at attention in front of him, then continued: 'Accompany this group, will you. See 'em through that revolting lot out there, and get 'em a taxi.' He turned to Gerald and saluted him again. 'Good luck, sir. Have a good leave. You too, Johnny.'

Mary was silent on the journey to the hotel as the decrepit taxi bounced and jolted over the pot-holed road, jerking violently whenever its wheels caught in the tramlines that were polished iron traps in its cobbled surface. It was a drive which brought her feelings of amazement and horror; the sheer size of the city was overwhelming, its teeming crowds frightening, its squalor unbelievable. In a few thousand yards she saw more people and vehicles than she had seen in all her previous lifetime; buffalo carts, their six-foot diameter wheels crunching over the granite sets, competed for road space with horse and donkey vehicles of every shape and size. Hordes of bicycles swerved between vehicles and pedestrians, coolies jogged along the gutters, their shoulders bowed beneath the weight of the goods they were carrying on their backs, shoulders, carrying poles or heads. Stalls lined almost every road, and small markets overflowed from narrow alleys and passages between ramshackle buildings. Every small patch of open ground was disfigured by sprawling shacks built of sheets of iron, pieces of tea chests, corrugated paper and sacking, amongst which wandered scavenging pariah dogs and huge white sacred cows, their horns decorated with long strands of coloured ribbon or wool.

Deeper within the city the buildings grew in size, improved in quality. She saw gleaming marble domes, the castellated walls of some palace or government building, a massive white marble statue of the British Queen Victoria glowering disapprovingly at the fruit and vegetable vendors selling their wares at her feet, spitting the red juice of their pan and betelnut over her stained plinth.

The taxi followed the edge of a maidan, its large open parkland dotted with warped banyan and pepal trees, interspaced by ugly dark reservoirs where buffalo were wallowing in the mud at their edges, and then turned on to the main thoroughfare of Chowringhee.

Tyres screeched on the drying road surface as the driver turned dangerously across the flow of traffic to find a parking space outside a long arcade of shops masking the hotel entrance.

An urchin carrying a small square box raced the hotel doorman to open the taxi door. 'Shoe shine, sah'b?' The child ducked as the angry doorman swung a fist at his head and shouted angrily. An instant crowd gathered to watch. Sweetmeat vendors hovered.

Mary felt Gerald's acute embarrassment as Rai and the doorman assisted him into his wheelchair in front of the audience, and there were beads of sweat on his forehead as he was wheeled to the hotel. A European couple stood helpfully aside but stared at him as he passed, pity obvious on the woman's face. Mary was angry, wanted to tell them he was no curiosity to be examined as though he were some strange animal, but she hurried her steps to be beside him as he was pushed down the long entrance hall towards the reception desk.

The desk clerk, a short Bengali with a round face and a pair of large gold-rimmed spectacles, leant forward over the desk and smiled patronisingly down at Gerald as though he were a dwarf. 'Yes, sir?'

'I have a suite booked. And accommodation for my bearer.'

The clerk looked at the lieutenant's pips on Gerald's shoulders with obvious disbelief. Lieutenants never, in the clerk's experience, booked anything other than single rooms, and then smuggled their girlfriends inside after bribing the night porters. 'Name, sir?' He began examining his booking chart.

'Lieutenant Petrie.'

'Ah,' said the clerk. To his astonishment he found the name in the day's bookings.

'It is for an indefinite period,' said Gerald, tersely. 'But, if there are any difficulties, I'm quite sure the Queen's Hotel will be happy to ....'

'No difficulties, sir,' interrupted the clerk hastily. 'None whatsoever, sir. I have it written in here. Begging your pardon, sir, but I am wondering if by any chance you are being a member of the family of Petrie India?'

'Yes, I am.'

'Indeed! That is explaining everything, sir.' The clerk smiled broadly, gold teeth glistening. 'Then you are very welcome, sir. I have been personally acquainted with the Baronet Petrie when he was a guest here in 1939.' The clerk wagged his head from side to side with the satisfaction of his good memory.

'My father,' Gerald admitted wearily.

'My goodness me!' The clerk hurried round from behind his desk and offered Gerald his hand, then bowed when Gerald took it. 'This is a very pleasurable honour, sir. I will naturally be at your service whenever you wish.'

He is treating him like a rajah, like a prince, thought Mary. Is this how they will all treat him in Calcutta? She had not realised he might be so important. How would they treat her as his wife?

The clerk remembered his register. 'Perhaps, sir, you will be so kind as to ... ah, I see a difficulty. One moment.' He lifted the register from the counter and held it in front of Gerald as though it were an oversized autograph book.

Mary saw Gerald stiffen slightly. 'I could have reached it.'

'Of course, sir. But it is no trouble for me.' Gerald took the proffered pen and scribbled his name. The clerk bowed, and returned behind his desk, lifting the suite keys from their rack with a flourish and handing them to a liveried bellboy. 'When you are finished with your bearer, sir, he may return here to me. I will have a room for him, with a telephone connection to your own, of course. The lady, I imagine, sir, will ...'

'The lady,' said Gerald, with defensive haste, 'happens to be Mrs Gerald Petrie, my wife.'

Mary saw the clerk wince. 'I naturally understood, sir.' He bowed himself towards Mary. 'Good afternoon, Mrs Petrie, madam. I hope you will be enjoying your stay with us.'

The hotel suite consisted of three rooms and a balcony overlooking the maidan. The street sounds were ever present through its open windows, but were fortunately dulled by the roof of the arcade below the balcony, which acted as a baffle. The room fans were already turning and the air fresher than at street level.

Rai stood quietly near the door waiting for instructions.

The rooms of the suite were carpeted in pastel green, matching the curtains and the upholstery of the chairs and sofa. Mary could feel the richness of the carpet beneath her chapplis, thicker even than the rugs of the Warrens' bedrooms. She had a childish desire to kick off her chapplis and explore the apartment barefooted, but knew it would expose her inexperience; it was hard to realise the luxuries she could see were there for her use. As casually as possible, she examined the bathroom. It was enormous, the walls plated with veined marble, Edwardian chrome fittings gleaming.

Gerald was watching her. He smiled. 'Civilisation, at last.'

She wanted to tell him to send Rai away, remind him how long it had been since they had been truly alone together, but she momentarily lacked the confidence to do so. She knew he was already very dependent on the Gurkha and trusted him in tasks he denied her, at least for the present. 'You should bathe, and then rest,' she said.

'You're right, I stink.' He called over his shoulder. 'Rai, come and fill the bath, will you please.'

'I could do it ...' she began.

The Gurkha was already in the room, his eyes quickly assessing its confusing equipment.

'Nonsense. It's Rai's job. I'll tell you what, though. Go and telephone room service, ask them to send us up a bottle of whisky and some iced water ... and a couple of glasses. Lemonade for yourself if you'd prefer it. A sandwich if you want one, but not for me.'

The bath water was running, the bath beginning to steam. Rai manipulated the chair, half turning Gerald away from her, and began to loosen his tunic.

'Gerald, I could stay and ...'

'If they haven't got whisky then ask for gin, but we'll need some bitters as well. Run along now, there's a good girl.' He blew her a kiss.

She sat in the lounge facing the ivory pedestal of the telephone on the polished mahogany desk on which was arrayed a leather blotting pad and a selection of hotel stationery.

This is ridiculous, she thought. I am being forced to act like his bearer while the bearer is behaving like his wife. I have been sent for drinks, but it is I who should be bathing my husband. It should be my hands caressing his skin, my hands soaping and relaxing him.

Gerald's voice came from the bathroom: 'Having trouble?'

'No,' she answered sharply. She stared at the telephone. It was the first time she had ever used one. Angrily, she read the service numbers on the card beside the instrument then dialled them, but when she picked up the earpiece there was no sound. It took several attempts with her impatience growing, before she realised the earpiece and its pivoting rest acted as a switch and the dial did not operate until the earpiece was removed. At last she heard a voice and repeated Gerald's instructions; the room service bearer sounded metallic and unreal, so once he had hung up she telephoned again to ensure he had correctly heard her order. The room service bearer sounded affronted.

The desk was beside the window and she stared beyond the balcony at the street below, her mind still occupied by Gerald, so that even the dancing monkeys with their drummer attendants failed to draw her attention.

There was a sound behind her in the room. Rai began unpacking Gerald's suitcase. He spoke to her in Hindi. 'The master is resting in his bath.'

She replied quickly in English, a sudden uncontrolled outburst that twisted her grammar. 'Never in my house you will speak Hindi, only British language. And you must be calling me mistress.'

The Gurkha was startled but controlled his feelings, his face expressionless. 'If you wish so.' He busied himself with the clothes, draping one of Gerald's uniforms across his arms.

'That is my wish ... my orders.' She watched him for a few seconds. 'And you may leave my husband's clothes in his suitcase; I will unpack them myself for him.'

Rai nodded, placed the clothes on the suitcase and made his way back to the bathroom.

Mary picked up the uniform and smoothed it down. It was Gerald's mess kit, sent down from the regimental depot only a fortnight before. It looked smart, elegant, a neat jacket, a cummerbund and tapered trousers with a broad stripe down their sides. She knew it was unlikely to be worn again.

Her conscience was already beginning to nag her. There had been no reason for her to lose her temper with Rai. The bearer had always been polite to her, always respectful. He did only what Gerald requested, and only what he had been instructed to do at the hospital. But it is me who should be unpacking our suitcases, she argued with herself. I should put away our clothing. I may not be strong enough to carry my husband, but everything else is my work. It would even give me pleasure to cook his food, wash his clothing, and clean our rooms for him. Her conscience was unconvinced.

She called the bearer: 'Rai.'

The Gurkha appeared in the doorway, a towel in his hands.

'You are drying him?' She deliberately softened the tone of her voice.

Rai shook his head. 'He rests in the bath, mistress.'

Mary switched to Hindi. 'I wish to say I am sorry, Rai, for my rudeness.'

'I did not notice any rudeness, mistress.' Rai replied in English.

'It was stupid of me to forbid you to use Hindi.'

The Gurkha came a little further into the room. His black eyes studied her face. 'It does not matter. Hindi is not my tongue, nor is

British. Both are the same to me. I see you are tired; you should rest, also. The fan is on in the bedroom and I have removed the bedcover.'

Again she felt the slight pangs of resentment, and Rai noticed the change in her eyes and again sensed her jealousy. If he had married and had a girl child, she would probably be no older than this girl. He knew very little about Mary, but thought he understood her feelings. Sooner or later it must all be sorted out, and perhaps now was the time to try. He said: 'You are a lucky woman. You carry the Sahib's child, and you have his love. Many Indian girls will have the children of British soldiers but few of them will marry the fathers. Your husband is an honest and good man.' Mary nodded, wondering where Rai was leading the conversation. It was the first time he had spoken so many words to her. 'You owe his honesty a debt,' continued Rai, watching her face closely. 'You must produce him a strong child, a son. And to do so you must be prepared to sacrifice a little. You must give some of your husband to me.'

'Give?' She widened her eyes, surprised.

'Yes, give. I was told at the hospital it is probable he will father no more children. This makes the one which you are carrying a rare diamond, as valuable as the greatest gem that has ever been found.'

'I know this.'

'So, while you bear the child I must be permitted to bear the father. The Sahib's child and his child's child and all their descendants, are in your belly. You have more than enough responsibility.' He smiled at her; the first time he had smiled at her. His face was warm and friendly. 'I am not stealing your man from you, daughter. I am ensuring you give him the most precious gift in his world. I am not only the Sahib's bearer, but the bearer of my sahib's household.'

Gerald's voice interrupted the Gurkha: 'Rai!'

Rai noticed as he left Mary that there was no longer resentment in her eyes.

The room service bearer had arrived by the time Rai wheeled Gerald back into the lounge. The heat of the bath had pinkened his face and given it a smooth, childlike look. He pulled her towards him and kissed her, then poured himself a whisky.

'A quick bath, young lady, then, if you feel up to it, out.'

'Out? I don't need rest, I'm too excited. But you are tired.'

'Nonsense.' He grinned at her. 'Shopping is more important.'

'Shopping? Must we buy food to cook in this place?'

Gerald laughed. 'I think our friend the booking clerk might object if we lit a fire in his suite. No, we are shopping for clothes, for luxuries. If I'm going to be a civilian then I need civilian clothes; a dinner jacket, too. There are good tailors in Chowringhee; isn't that right, Rai?'

'Yes, sah'b. Very good tailors.'

'And Rai can't go wandering around looking like something that's escaped from an army surplus store; he has to have a decent outfit. And yourself, darling. You need all sorts of things.'

'Gerald, I have two saris. Two is enough . . . one for washing, one for wearing.'

Gerald laughed, this time loudly. 'Here in Calcutta, you'll need at least three a day! One for morning, one for afternoon, and one for evening; this damned heat is so sticky you'll be soaked half the time. That makes three for washing and three for wearing, at a push. I think you'll need a lot more. And all the other things women need.'

'When I worked,' said Mary reprovingly, 'then I must save for two months to buy one cotton sari.'

'Times have changed.' Gerald drained his glass and began refilling it.

She did not dare calculate the amount of money Gerald had drawn from his account in the Bank of India and then spent in the past four hours. She only knew it was far more than she had ever earned in her life or would have earned for the next several years. It had been like a visit to the mythical Aladdin's cave she had read about at school; they had visited shops she had never dreamed could exist, where beautifully dressed attendants hurried to serve them, sprayed a dozen different perfumes on her wrists and hands, offered her creams and skin tonics and unheard-of luxuries.

The shop girls had appeared so attractive and sophisticated to Mary she had difficulty in accepting that they were there to help and serve her, and in one dressing-room she realised she had made a mistake when she addressed a girl, in Hindi, with too much familiarity. The girl, who had already appraised the inexpensive cotton sari Mary was wearing, had smiled knowingly and Mary had blushed when she realised the shop girl, speaking of her own intimate relationships with British soldiers, had decided she was Gerald's mistress. To Gerald's surprise, Mary had hurried him from that particular shop without making a single purchase. She was relieved he had not understood the conversation.

Gerald had enjoyed watching her bemusement at the arrays of saris, silk blouses, exotic – and to her, impractical – underwear. He had not attempted to guide her and had made only one comment, that he did not want her to wear European dresses. 'You are beautiful in saris,' he told her. 'As long as we are in India I want you looking like yourself, not someone else.' She had been briefly disappointed, but afterwards decided he was probably right.

The selection of saris had been overwhelming. Mary had never realised before that there could be so many colourful designs, so many wonderful materials. When she had shopped in the bazaars of Gauhati or Shillong, her choice of sari had been governed by her small savings, and in any case the traders' wares reflected the lack of wealth of their average customers and there were few expensive garments. Here it was quite different; there were evening saris of the finest silks, so light and transparent they were like cobwebs, embroidered in gold and silk threads, decorated with gemstones and pearls. Gerald was patient, and seemed as enthralled as herself when she tried them on and twirled in front of the shop mirrors, unable to believe it was possible for her to buy any of them.

By the time they had returned to the hotel, all but the last of their purchases had already been delivered and were stacked in their suite. It had taken her half an hour to decide what she should wear for dinner that evening, and she would gladly have foregone her food for the pleasure of simply sitting and examining her new clothes and then arranging them carefully in the bedroom wardrobes.

She knew the excitement was not over. Gerald had insisted on booking her an appointment at the hairdressers in the hotel foyer for the next morning. She had never seen a hairdressing salon before, but was looking forward to the experience. Her hair, which she had cut short when she had first travelled to Kohima, was now tied back in a bun.

The hotel restaurant was the largest room she had ever been inside. Domed ceilings kept it cool, while fluted columns gave it an impression of palatial grandeur. The khidmutgars were impeccably dressed and at the moment outnumbered the guests they served, standing attentively a little way from the tables but moving silently and instantly forward whenever a plate had been emptied or another course brought to the table.

Mary had not understood most of the menu she had been offered. A lot of the dishes were described in French, a custom, Gerald had told her, of many restaurants the British used, even in India. She had found this an intriguing and strange idea. The table's cutlery had given her momentary concern; its quantity rather than unfamiliarity. Old Vijaya had taught her their use, and had been as conscientious in her instruction to the young hill girl as she had been with the Warrens' son when he had been a child. But Vijaya had used only one knife and fork in her lessons, and here there seemed to be an extraordinary number of items even by the standards of the Warrens' own table. She had watched Gerald closely and used whatever he had selected; as he had made no criticism she assumed she had acted correctly.

Her entrance to the restaurant had caused her much amusement, and it was only with difficulty that she had prevented herself from bursting into a fit of giggles once she and Gerald had reached the table. The eyes of every guest in the room had followed them, examining them both, silently questioning the relationship between the young man in the wheelchair, and the exotic Assamese girl who walked at his side. When she had seated herself there had been murmured conversations, kept to an abnormally low level that hinted that they were about the new arrivals. She was aware, too, that she was watched as she ate her meal, and she was uncertain as to whether this was because of her choice of food or the manner in which she tackled each of the dishes. She was relieved when the meal ended and she sat waiting as Gerald finished his pudding and a khidmutgar poured their coffee.

At least I have not shamed him, she thought. It would have been a disaster had she spilt something, knocked over a glass, dropped food. She knew she had been curt with the khidmutgars but had been afraid, since the incident in the shop, of appearing too friendly. In time, she knew it would all become easier; Gerald would help her.

She felt warm, comfortable. She had eaten a little too much, and had been forced to leave some of the food; it had made her feel guilty, though she doubted if it would be wasted. There would bound to be beggars waiting at the kitchen door for any food scraps. Perhaps, by leaving some food, she was actually being charitable. The thought comforted her a little.

Gerald! She was unable to prevent herself staring at him, even as he finished his dinner. She was pleased there had been no wounds on his face, not that they would have prevented her from loving him. She watched him now, enjoying recognising the finest details, the way his eyebrows met above his nose to make a fine blonde line across his forehead, the soft flat curve of his lower eyelids, so typically British, and the deep blue of his pupils. His skin was perfect, unblemished by the pockmarks that scarred so many Indians; like that of a child. She looked at his hands and remembered how soft but strong they had felt when he had made love to her. She wanted him now, wanted him to stand and carry her to their room. It might shock the guests at the other tables but it would thrill her. She wanted his arms around her, wanted him exploring her again, wanted to feel him inside her.

There was a sudden twisting movement in her stomach, so unexpected and unfamiliar it made her gasp.

Gerald looked at her, quickly and concerned. 'Something wrong, darling?' She was sitting upright in her chair, her face pallid. He spun his chair and wheeled himself to her side. 'Khidmutgar!' He called one of the waiters.

She stopped him. 'I think I'm all right.' There was a sudden but sharper movement. She looked at him and smiled. 'It moved. I felt it moving.' She took his hand and placed it on her stomach. 'Can you feel it?'

For a moment, there was nothing, then she felt it again.

Gerald grinned at her. 'My God, yes. I felt it, too.' He leant forward and kissed her. Watching eyes widened.

'Sah'b?' The khidmutgar waited beside them, anxious; aware some emergency had arisen.

'Champagne,' said Gerald, loudly and happily. 'A good bottle. And make sure it's well chilled.'

The only light in the room was a table lamp beside the large bed. The mosquito net had already been unrolled and tucked in on one side, so the bed seemed to be floating inside a fragile tent of white silk. Gerald lay back on the pillows, waiting for her. It had been so different the last time they had shared a bed, so long ago it was only a dream. It had been reality, then. He remembered the heat, the moistness of their bodies together, the feel of her breasts against him, the incredible burst of pleasure he had experienced as his penis entered her firm body. Now there could be nothing. He still loved her; more than even before. But did she understand how much? And was the incomplete and unmanly kind of love he could offer her enough? For either of them?

There was still pleasure, though. The afternoon's shopping! He smiled, remembering her consternation when he had taken her into the first of the many shops. It had been like taking a child to buy a Christmas present ... to buy its first Christmas present. He had enjoyed watching her try on all the clothes, her eyes meeting his and seeking his approval. She had been almost mesmerised by the foyer jeweller's with its vast array of pearls and gemstones, the rings with their huge diamonds. He would buy her a ring, tomorrow, he decided. She had never received an engagement ring.

Her movement now, as she undressed, caught his eye. She folded her sari and put it in one of the dresser drawers. He felt pleased she had lost the thinness that had so startled him when he had first seen her in Dimapur. The child was altering her figure; her breasts were fuller and her stomach no longer flat, but now rounded. She was very beautiful, he thought.

She caught his eyes and smiled. 'Tonight is our wedding night.'

He nodded. 'Our first night alone together.'

She climbed into the bed beside him, resting on her elbow so her breasts touched his chest as she leant over him. He felt their warmth as he put his arms around her. Her lips moved across his face, finding his eyelids, cheeks, mouth.

A steel band seemed to clamp itself across his brain, some inner voice reminding him his limits would soon be reached, without any satisfaction for either of them. He wanted to shout, scream with frustration and anger. Her lips kept him silent, but the sounds were inside his mind, smothering his feelings.

He felt he was in a deep, dark cavern; quicksand enveloped him, pressing at his limbs, imprisoning him, deadening senses, smothering him. He struggled wildly, his lungs gasping for air, while his arms thrust her body from him.

Her eyes were wide, frightened. 'Gerald?'

He turned away from her, silent and ashamed. He realised he had hurt her, deeply; rejected her. For the first time in his life, he experienced real fear, and did not understand it.

*

She could feel the heat of his body near her, but they were not touching. For a long time he lay silent and she had turned off the light to allow him the comfort of the darkness, hoping he would speak to her, explain what had happened. But he said nothing, and after a while his breathing changed to that of sleep.

She wept inwardly, tearlessly, with anguish and self-pity, feeling she had been cheated and his professed love for her was nothing more than words. Perhaps, if she was not carrying his child and he had not been wounded, he would never have married her at all? Or perhaps it was not her he wanted but only his child?

For a time she wished they had never met. Without him, she would still be in the security of the Warrens' household in the familiarity of her narrow world where her daydreams as she sat each afternoon by the peaceful lake had given her so much pleasure. There she had created her fantasies of a world and life that was only love and happiness, and which she now believed could not exist outside her own mind.

She felt empty, a strange hollowness as though everything important in her life had been taken away from her, leaving her nothing more than an empty and valueless husk, like the discarded chrysalis of a moth. She had expected so much and there was nothing.

As though comforting her the child moved inside her, this time gently, reassuringly. She put her hands flat on the curve of her stomach, attempting even closer contact, wanting the child born and available to her arms, to her love. Love! She had accepted her life with Gerald might not hold all the physical pleasure she had previously identified with marriage, but the compensation had been in the knowledge that their love was so strong, so powerful, it had been capable of providing its own special ecstasies. It had failed her.

Unconsciously, she moved her hands lower on her body until they rested on her inner thighs, the tips of her slender fingers smoothing the soft flesh, comforting her with gentle rhythmic movement. Without direction they found the moist opening of her body as she let herself drift in a mindless, dark, protective sea. The movement of her hips responding to the touch brought her to guilty reality and for a moment she hesitated, but Gerald lay beside her, his breathing still soft, relaxed. She felt momentary bitterness towards him; it was his hands that should be comforting her. His loss was not one he bore alone, but was shared equally by herself. More deliberately, she found the places where delicate nerves responded to the sensual encouragement of her fingertips, until the overwhelming fusion of orgasm devoured her.

There was no expected feeling of solace as she lay experiencing the brief candescence of emotional and physical pleasure. Instead, a childlike sense of confessional guilt nagged her; guilt not only encompassing her attempt at self-gratification, but also her easy condemnation of Gerald's action. She had blamed him, but now in retrospect she was no longer certain the blame was deserved. Perhaps, in reality, it was she who had somehow failed?

She thought of Alan, still in Dimapur. They had become close friends and now she missed the friendship and comfort he had always given. He had expected to be discharged, but the Army had asked him to accept an administrative post at the regimental depot. She knew of no other person with whom she could discuss the present tragedy. Alan would have understood and helped her; helped Gerald, somehow.

Calcutta for all its millions of inhabitants, seemed empty.

She found no sleep that night. As the sky lightened, she slid from the bed and, using its coverlet as a robe, stood barefooted on the chilled tiles of the balcony above the silent emptiness of the deserted street.

She witnessed her first Calcutta dawn, the rising sun awakening a momentary but fleeting beauty as its first clean rays turned dust to gold on the leaves and parched grass of the maidan. Briefly, the muddied tanks and reservoirs were liquid brass, reflecting the humped cattle who stood motionless enjoying the cool undisturbed air, only their jaws cudding slowly.

The city awakened reluctantly; a distant bylee-wallah steered an overladen oxcart toward some hidden market; an untidy heap of cardboard boxes wedged in a doorway discharged a crippled beggar who urinated where he rose, his starved voice beginning its endless mantra, the repetitive plea for baksheesh. A line of rickshaws grew beside the maidan, their labourers lathe-thin, squatting beside the wheels to share pan or biris; hopeful for early fares amongst the khansamas seeking the freshest vegetables for their kitchens, or clerks facing long sweaty days at their cramped desks. Cleaners began their relentless and stooped sweeping of steps, pavements, gutters with jarool handbrooms.

Gerald slept. She watched him, attempting to penetrate his unconscious mind. His face was peaceful, but she knew the deceptive mask hid a terrible and unexplained agony which threatened to destroy them both. She had almost succumbed to its violence, almost been defeated by its unexpectedness. But now she began to identify it, recognise it as some distorted and warped demon somehow to be exorcised.

Until his rejection of her she had not realised such an enemy existed. Perhaps its self-betrayal was to her advantage? A demon had revealed itself, but by doing so had unwittingly given itself substance and could therefore be fought. The battlefield lay within herself or Gerald. How she would fight, she did not yet know.

Later she heard a discreet knock on the door of the lounge and found a bearer laying the small table for chota hazri. When he had left she stirred the pot of tea and poured a cup, then carried it to the bedroom.

She awakened Gerald gently, but could see by his expression that memories of the previous night had not left him.

As their eyes met she knew the first of her weapons: her love for him. Despite the long frightening hours it was as strong as ever, a devotion and yearning to touch and hold him forever. She read his momentary fear, and knew that just as she had felt he was lost to her he was experiencing the same dread feeling. She leant and kissed his cheek, then smiled.

'Chota hazri, sah'b.'

Gerald struggled to pull himself more upright, digging his elbows into the mattress behind him, an awkward, whale-like movement. She wanted desperately to help him, cradle him in her arms, but stood patiently. When he had settled himself, she handed him the cup.

He stared down at it, avoiding her gaze. 'I'm sorry ... about last night. I made a terrible ...'

She interrupted him quickly. 'Don't speak. Just drink your tea.'

'But ...' His eyes sought hers, questioningly.

She smiled again, offering him reassurance, then shook her head. 'What happened yesterday is already past.'

'I hurt you.'

'Do you love me?' She sat on the edge of the bed beside him.

'I promise you will never need to ask again.'

She persisted. 'But do you love me now, at this very second?'

He twisted his body to put the cup on the bedside table, then took her in his arms and drew her towards him. 'Yes. I love you this very second.'

'I ask, because there is an Indian saying that the past begins in an instant and cannot be changed. The future is always just ahead, and is unknown. Only the present is our concern, and the present is so small a piece of time it cannot be measured. But it is only there we live. And if you can love me for that moment, it is all I want.'

She felt his arms tighten around her reassuringly, and knew her strength had returned.

She had been looking forward to her visit to the hairdressing salon but when she arrived there she was already impatient. She had arranged to meet Gerald at one p.m. at Firpos, a little further along Chowringhee, and felt there was barely enough time for the secret trip she planned. There might not be another opportunity for several days.

It had been the dome of a distant temple reflecting the dawn sunlight that had brought her inspiration, a place to find advice. Mary had first considered seeking a priest; although she did not know the whereabouts of a Catholic church, she had no doubt there would be one of importance within the city. However, she was uncertain if a priest without some personal experience of marriage would be able to assist her. At the mission school it had always seemed there was some impassable barrier between the sexes, and the visit of a priest had somehow strengthened this idea in the pupils' minds until they often came to resent his weekly arrival and associate it with penances and lengthy tests of their catechisms. And nuns, Mary was certain, would never understand the problem and might even resent her longing for a marriage with more physical contact. But a mahant, and one who served the goddess of fertility, would surely have an answer.

In the hairdressing salon, the terrible problems which had arisen the previous night filled her mind and left little room for the pleasures she had anticipated. An attentive girl suggested a perm, but as Mary was uncertain what this was or how long it might take, she refused. Even so it was over an hour before the girl had completed washing, trimming and setting her hair in gentle waves and a soft roll which curved in towards her neck. Mary found the hairdrier noisy and frightening at first—under its hood the hot air seemed to scorch the tender skin of her neck—but afterwards, when the girl had brushed out her dry hair, it looked softer and had more sheen than Mary had ever noticed before. She knew that in less urgent circumstances a visit to the salon would be enjoyable.

Her conversations with the hairdresser had, however, provided her with the information she needed to find the temple. There was a complex of them, she was told, near the burning ghat at Alipore. She could reach them easily by taxi.

There were no problems with the taxi; the hotel doorman found one for her in a few minutes. Alipore was a common fare, being both the Royal Air Force base and also a popular tourist attraction. The driver, a talkative gold-toothed Sikh, spotted her Assamese accent and began an unofficial tourist-guide commentary in an attempt to improve the amount of baksheesh he assumed he would receive from his passenger. He got little further than explaining how Chowringhee, the route to the holy temples at Alipore, was named after a devout Hindu who built a road to protect pilgrims from tigers, before she silenced him, wanting to spend the time concentrating her mind on her problem. The Sikh, one arm resting on the back of the front passenger seat, felt resentful; if information failed to impress his preoccupied fare, then perhaps speed would. He accelerated through the dense traffic, and by the time he reached the iron bridge over the tributary of the sacred Ganges, Mary was feeling carsick.

She left the taxi driver unpaid, knowing it would force him to wait for her no matter how long she might be absent. The Sikh, again thinking of his baksheesh, condescended with theatrical reluctance.

The area was crowded with stalls selling a mixture of souvenirs to catch the eye of British or foreign servicemen, replicas of holy relics for pilgrims or mourners bringing their dead to the burning ghat, and fruit, vegetables, fly-infested meat and domestic utensils for those who lived in the vicinity or worked locally. On the pavement beside one end of the bridge played a small orchestra, a street singer droning accompaniment to the instruments but ignored by the passers-by. Beyond the bridge, and set on the river's muddy banks, was a temple to Shiva, and before it broad steps where pilgrims were immersing themselves in the brown holy waters.

She passed the woodsellers and the burning ghat protected by the brick outer walls of the temple, and entered a narrow, rubbish-filled street. There, she questioned a saffron-robed priest, and was directed past the tomb tablets of ancient royalty towards the temple of Kali. The street narrowed to an alley, down the centre of which ran a thin stream of oily sewage; on one side were more holy relic traders, and on the other, shrines to the gods and goddesses. She reached a gnarled and twisted tree, blackened and polished with the touch of countless hands, its distorted branches decorated with small pebbles hung there by those who sought the goddess's blessing of children, and tufts of children's hair from those who had received it. In front of the tree stood two red-painted vertical stones signifying womanhood.

Beside the shrine squatted the petitioners for the goddess's favours, a small group of women, the onus of their own or their husband's infertility imprinted on solemn, anxious faces. The air stank of the fly-blown meat of offerings made each day to Kali in the nearby courtyard. A solitary sadhu, wearing only a small loincloth, his body covered by grey ash and with the mark of Kali on his forehead, leant on his spear-like trident in silent vigil.

Mary hesitated, feeling self-conscious, before speaking to the nearest of the squatting women, a small Bengali girl no more than fifteen years old, her childlike face already aged by the fear her husband would reject her if she continued to fail him and so shame both their families. 'Where is the mahant?'

The girl jerked herself from a daydream in which she was bearing twin sons. Mary repeated her question. The girl's voice was as shrill as the sound of a frightened bird. 'The priests will not see us until nightfall. They will come then, if you have given money to the temple. Go inside and they will receive an offering, but they will want more later.'

Mary nodded. She understood what the girl meant. For an amount the priests considered suitable they would fertilise the women themselves; that way, both goddess and families' honour would be satisfied.

She entered the courtyard, the stench of the corpses of the morning's living sacrifices tightening the muscles of her stomach as it carried her mind back to the horrific battlefield at Kohima. She had not yet fully recovered from the swaying, bouncing taxi ride and only with difficulty prevented herself from retching. A temple attendant was hunched on the steps, his face blank with habitual boredom.

'I wish to see the mahant,' she informed him.

'Not possible. But I can take your donation.' The way in which the attendant eyed and mentally valued her expensive clothing was an indication of his expectations.

'If you look at my belly, you will see I am already pregnant,' Mary informed him.

'Then I can receive your donation in respect of your gratitude. I am the collector of all donations.' He had no other work to do for the present, so was quite happy to continue the conversation for as long as the visitor wished. The woman was very attractive, and he wondered if it was her husband who had served her or one of the priests. Which one? 'When did you come here?' he asked, thinking he could check the rota on the temple calendar.

'I have not been before. And I only wish to speak with the mahant. Here, is this what you want?' She opened her purse and gave him ten rupees.

The attendant took the money and placed it in a small leather bag at his waist. He wagged his head from side to side and smiled, his teeth so stained and blackened by betelnut juice that most seemed to be missing. 'The mahant will positively not be disturbed at this time of day. He has many religious duties to perform.'

Mary opened her purse again. In it was the remainder of the money she had inherited from the aiya. The attendant watched as she counted it and kept enough back to pay the taxi driver. She held a thin wad of notes towards the man. 'One hundred and fifty rupees. One hundred for the temple, and fifty for your kindness ... if it is possible for me to see the mahant.' The man reached out his hand. 'Afterwards,' she told him firmly, folding her fingers over the notes.

The man pushed himself upright. His legs, cramped and arthritic by years of squatting at the temple doorway, didn't straighten fully, so he walked with a strange, simian, bent-kneed gait into the darkness of the temple complex. It was several minutes before he returned. 'Give me my baksheesh now, and I will take you to the mahant.' He was not prepared to risk her changing her mind if the mahant failed to satisfy her, or if he were sent on some errand while she was inside the mahant's private quarters.

She paid the fifty rupees and followed him. The interiors of Hindu temples were not unfamiliar to her. Many of her early friends had been Hindu, and with a child's curiosity she had accompanied them to view their worship. Sometimes it had seemed such a terrible sin she had not dared to confess it to the priest, but did so to her own crucifix in the darkness of the dormitory. And as she never actually prayed in the temples she had doubted if her own God would really be too angry.

Poor as the Alipore temple had appeared outside, inside it displayed its wealth with gold-encrusted and lacquered idols to its goddess. Incense burnt in brass holders perfuming the still air, and the bare feet of the attendant padded on a delicately patterned marble floor. There was a sense of oppressiveness as though the structure of the building leant in on itself, compressing everything inside, even those who entered, diminishing them to silence.

The attendant ushered Mary through an arched doorway and across a courtyard to a narrow corridor beneath one wing of the temple. It led to a painted door on which the goddess danced amongst a collection of ferocious demons. The attendant knocked. A resonant voice bade them enter.

The floor was carpeted, the room little more than fifteen feet square, its walls hung with rugs. There was a couch at one end, and a small but heavily carved table on which rested a large, open book. As in the temple itself, incense burned in an alcove; a fine red ember in the gloom. The only window was set high in the walls and was protected by ornamental iron bars. From the ceiling, to one side of the window, hung a large old-fashioned oil lamp.

Mahant Surendranath, a heavily built, jowl-cheeked man, wearing thick-lensed glasses, his head close shaven, was seated on the sofa. Its legs creaked as he moved his weight slightly. She glanced towards the attendant but the man had already gone. She heard the door close behind her.

Unexpectedly, the mahant spoke to her in English. 'Good morning.'

Why not Hindi? For a moment it puzzled her. English was widely spoken, often mingled with Hindi in a single sentence, but this was a Hindu temple where she might expect only pure Hindi to be used. She decided the man was indicating his education, or testing her own.

She replied: 'Good morning.'

The man continued in the same language. 'I am told you have offered our temple quite a lot of money so you may speak with me. One hundred rupees. And I imagine you gave Aloke baksheesh. One day I may forget my position and beat that dacoit.' He smiled at her, the band of loose fat below his chin reminding her of an ill-fitting priest's collar. 'I must warn you, however, I an unable to tell you the sex of the child you carry, and I do not tell fortunes.' She knew he was teasing her and felt relief she had found a man with a sense of humour. 'Come and sit near me, child.' He indicated a small stool beside the carved table.

'I have a personal problem,' she began when she had seated herself.

'Our world is built on personal problems. They are the gods' toys. Do you have a husband?'

'Yes.'

'Then you have one less problem than some girls who seek my help.' He chuckled at his own joke and again the sofa echoed his movement. His face became serious, a questioning dark moon. 'Tell me.'

Mahant Surendranath was silent until she had finished, then eased himself back in the sofa. 'You are not of this faith?'

'I was baptised in a Christian mission school.'

He shook his head slowly. 'I think you will understand, now, that a religion as old as our own is not so easily lost.' He raised a hand quickly. 'Don't misunderstand me. The god, or gods, are the same single being regardless of how they are worshipped. But the needs of the people differ in every culture and every strata within it. What is your husband named?' She was silent. She had said he was British, but felt somehow she might belittle Gerald by naming him. 'Come now, child, I am no village gossip.'

'His name is Petrie.'

'Of Petrie India?'

'Yes. The son.'

'My goodness me!' Surendranath stared at her. Does she know what she has done, he wondered. For generations the Petrie family had taken from the country, built a legendary business fortune and personal empire from the sweat of Indian labourers and staff; paying notoriously low wages and carrying their profits back to England to benefit only those of their own blood. It was well known no Indian had ever held a position of any responsibility in their organisation; even the NLA leader, Subhas Chandra Bose, had named them as exploiters in a widely distributed pamphlet, and yet this young Assamese girl had somehow managed to captivate and marry the heir. Inside her was a Petrie child; half Indian! Was this the fates playing their strange games? The girl would need the help of all the gods and goddesses to survive. But if she did? And if the child was male, and grew to full manhood? What then the Petrie empire? 'I will help you in every way possible,' said the mahant. 'Together we will win against your devil. We will have tea as we talk.' He picked up a small hand-bell from the table and rang it, and within a moment the door was opened. He spoke in Hindi to the chela who appeared. 'They work for their knowledge,' he explained smiling at Mary. The tea was brought so quickly it was obvious it had already been brewed in preparation. The novice priest knelt and placed two cups on the table, bowed to the mahant while still kneeling and then left them. The mahant lifted his cup and sipped at the clear, gold liquid. 'Drink, my child.' He paused, then continued, 'Firstly you must realise that much of a man is centred on his lingam.'

She looked at him, questioningly.

The mahant pointed a large finger at his lower belly. 'The lingam.'

She felt herself blush. 'I understand.'

'Of all parts of the male body, it is considered paramount. It has been worshipped for many thousands of years. A normal, healthy young man will think of it twice every hour, in every hour of his waking day. You tell me your husband has been seriously wounded but is otherwise quite well, is not that so?'

'Yes.'

'Then he will think the same as every other man ... and he will think it as often, perhaps even more frequently. And every time he thinks of it, he is reminded of his inability to use it as he wishes.' The mahant drained his cup and placed it on the table.

'But why does that make him hate me? Last night ...'

'You have told me of last night, and I also know how you felt. But he does not hate you. He does not want to reject you. He hates himself. He despises his own body for its new failing. When you offer yourself to him as you did naked in his bed last night, you are demanding he reveals that which he most abhors: his inability to complete the basic sexual act. You demand he reveals to you the loss of his manhood.'

For a moment, the same feeling of sickness which Mary had experienced in the taxi returned. She had wanted to help Gerald, to illustrate her love and need for him, and yet unwittingly she had contributed to his misery; worse, for a while she had blamed him. 'I did not intend to hurt him so,' she said wretchedly.

'Of course not.' Mahant Surendranath leant forward and took her hand, holding it between both his own. 'A woman does not generally think as a man thinks, nor a man like a woman. The gods have created us as two different animals, yet each dependent upon the other.'

'But what must I do? I cannot hide my feelings for him; surely that would be cruel?'

'He needs your love and he needs your reassurance. But only he can heal himself. I could not do it for him, nor can any doctor. However, one thing which you must accept that he does not need, yet, is your body. The human mind is meagre but complex, and it is always protective of its owner; face it with a door through which it must sooner or later pass but which it fears, and it will pretend the door does not exist. Force it to admit the door and it will become more afraid and stubborn. Persist and soon the fear is turned to hatred.'

'Must I go away?' The thought of leaving Gerald horrified her, but if it was necessary then she would sacrifice her own happiness.

'No, of course not. That would surely distress him and he would be even more certain of his imagined failure. Give him everything of you he needs, your love and respect, your help and reassurance. But at the same time, do not offer him your body in the marriage bed. You must be cunning in this, for it must not be obvious. The gods have given women subtle minds and you must use yours. He must not know he is being denied, he must sense no subterfuge. Conceal yourself from him as though he were a stranger, and hopefully he will pass through the door at a time of his own choosing.'

'But if he cannot, ever?'

'To admit the possibility of defeat is to be defeated.' The mahant changed the subject. 'So what do you plan to do, here in Calcutta? Will your husband work with Petrie India?'

'Eventually, I think. He says he must learn the business from the bottom. He loves Assam, and has said perhaps he could work as under-manager on a plantation. He is avoiding decisions until he is finished with the army.'

'And when will that be?'

'He has a medical board in a few weeks time, they will decide.'

Mahant Surendranath questioned her for another quarter of an hour before ending their conversation with assurances that she would always be welcome at the temple, and that if she asked for him by name he would always see her. He refused her offer of the donation to the temple funds. 'Just promise me, you will come again.'

When she had left him, Surendranath thought for a long time before sending for the most discreet of the temple scribes. He dictated a lengthy letter to his brother, Aurobindo Das, a senior member of the Congress Party.

CHAPTER SEVEN

The contrived flamboyance of Gerald's father's handwriting stood out from the pages of buff stationery as distinctively as had they been written in biblical fire on a Hebrew wall; undoubtedly, that was his father's intention. It had been the same with the letters Gerald had received when at boarding school, the style of his father's hand indicative of his mood. In rare praise the writing assumed normal proportions, but in anger there was even a warning in the addressing of the envelope. It was so obvious that eventually even Gerald's house master recognised the significance: 'Letter for Petrie. Where is he? Ah, there you are boy.' The house master would glance at the handwriting. 'What have you been up to this time, eh, Petrie? Looks like you're about to cop it again.'

Gerald had 'copped it' in his father's present letter. He stared at the folded pages in front of him. The chatter of light conversation surrounded him in the Victorian cool of Firpos. It was still early for tiffin but Firpos's tables were filled by the European women who each day used the place as a coffee club where the current gossip and rumour could be exchanged and later relayed to their husbands. The only other male customers in the room were a group of young American master sergeants occupying a table in one of the corners, drinking the expensive bottled beer as they decided how to fill the boring hours between lunchtime and the evening opening of the YWCA dance hall. One of the sergeants' necks was swollen and reddened by the bites of the bed-bugs he had encountered the previous night in one of the Rippon Street brothels. He scratched it incessantly.

Gerald was infuriated by the contents of his father's letter, its tone no different to many he had received as a child. There was virtually no reference to Gerald's incapacitating injuries, only a curt command he should 'come to his senses' and return to England rather than take his discharge in India. The remainder of the five pages was devoted to expressing his parents' horror at his decision to marry an Indian girl, and the kind of welcome he might expect should he be so foolish as to come home undivorced. If he wished to continue as the son and heir of his family, he was to immediately contact the company solicitors in Calcutta and begin annulment proceedings; they would deal with the matter entirely. His father expected confirmation that his orders would be obeyed by return of post.

But Gerald was no longer the schoolboy his father had remembered, and the thought of complying with his instructions did not even occur to him. His anger was at his parents' assumption that he would obey and at their willingness to dislike the woman of his choice purely on grounds of race, without meeting her or even knowing how much she had been prepared to risk in her love for him. Had his father been facing him now, regardless of his own injuries, Gerald was sure he would have struck him.

His father had not actually used the expression that Gerald would be 'disowned', but the implication was scarcely veiled; he could expect no future in the family company, and it would be necessary for his father to reconsider 'financial possibilities'.

Gerald had already begun composing his reply. It would be brief; fourteen words. 'Dear Father, you may stuff the financial possibilities where the monkey stuffed its nuts ...' There had been many hundreds of hours when he had been forced to consider his future, and many of these bitter and disappointed hours he could never have survived but for his knowledge that Mary would share his future with him. His decision to remain in India had not, as his father believed, been made on the spur of the moment. There were obvious medical advantages in England for a man with his disability, but when he had deliberated on every possibility his choice had been final.

He damned his parents. He could picture them both, facing each other across the antique oak dining-table, his mother silent as his father raged on at his absent son's behaviour. His mother would not support her son against his father; she had never done so, even when it had sometimes been blatantly clear that family justice was being miscarried. She was not a particularly intelligent woman, and over her years of marriage had accumulated rather than lost her bigoted views. Gerald could remember an occasion during his final leave when, for no apparent reason, she had stated at the dining-table that she would never tolerate a man who wore suede shoes in her house; and had meant it! Well, he thought, he had expected his parents' unfavourable reaction when he had written to them telling them about Mary. He supposed he should not now be surprised. But if his father believed he could influence Gerald by blackmail, then he had little idea of his son's character.

Regardless of what actions his father might care to take, Gerald was financially secure; his grandfather's will had seen to that. Only recently, at twenty-one, Gerald had inherited a comfortable income as a result of his ancestor's foresight in placing a large amount of money in trust for him. Despite his father's threats, Gerald would always be comfortably well off. He might never become a millionaire, but here, in India, he would certainly be wealthy.

'*Namaste.*' Mary's soft voice was a welcome disruption to his thoughts. Engrossed in his anger he had not seen her enter the restaurant. She smiled at him, shook her neatly cut and set hair and then slightly angled her head waiting for his approval.

Gerald's anger was forgotten. When he had first seen her in Assam her hair had been long, sometimes plaited. At Kohima it had been hacked short, and later as it had grown she had pulled it back into a bun. Now, it fell in soft feminine waves, its movement seductive, romantic. He made an automatic and frustrating attempt to stand before taking her hand and pulling her towards him. 'You look prettier than ever,' he said, realising the words were inadequate to describe his real feelings.

She stooped so he could kiss her. There was a sudden change in tone of conversation at the next table where three British women sat watching them. Gerald had heard them earlier discussing him in stage whispers; words and phrases that were unintentionally hurtful, 'a shame', 'pitiful', 'such a waste'. Now the women were shocked as the object of their concern actually kissed an Indian girl in public.

Mary sat herself next to him. He attempted to ignore the scandalised whispers and made a great show of examining her hairstyle. 'Ahh! Very nice indeed. Did you enjoy it? I suppose you had to spend hours under a wretched hairdrier?'

'It was very interesting.' She was glad he had apparently overestimated the time her appointment would take. She had wondered how she could explain her absence from the place if he asked.

A khidmutgar, elegant and unflurried in a spotless white achkan, changed the china pot on the table and poured Mary a cup of tea. A few yards away the three British ladies watched and listened. Indian girls were not unknown in Firpos, but were seldom seen in the company of British officers. The women were temporarily spellbound by the possibility of scandal. Gerald noticed them. All the anger generated by his father's letter had not yet left him. He rotated his wheelchair a little. 'You may continue your coffees, ladies. My wife and I have no objections.' He saw horror register in their expressions before he turned back to face Mary.

'Gerald!' she admonished.

'Well, they're like damned vultures, sitting on trees and walls waiting for something to drop dead so they can tear it to pieces. I'm sorry, I shouldn't have embarrassed you.'

'You didn't embarrass me,' she said softly. 'You only hurt yourself. Those ladies are of no consequence to me. You forget. I am an expert on British memsahibs.'

'I suppose so.' He smiled at her, requesting forgiveness, but saw none was needed. Her apparent innocence was deceptive, he thought. Behind it lay a strength both of them would surely need at times. It was comforting to know it was always there.

Mary glanced at the letters. She had received only one herself in her entire lifetime and that had been written by a stranger, a professional scribe, on behalf of her sister. It had been half a page in length. 'From my father,' Gerald explained quickly. He wished he had destroyed the letter before she had arrived. He did not want her to read it. She was already aware of prejudices but he felt it would be better if those of his own family were concealed, at least for the present. He folded the letter casually and tucked it into his pocket. 'The usual sort of family news. All very boring.'

'You went to the company office?' Her warm, gentle eyes were an assurance of her need for him.

He shook his head. 'No. I telephoned from the hotel. Howard Everson is away for a week or so, but his secretary said that there were letters for me. I sent Rai. He brought them back here a few minutes ago.'

'And your parents are well?' There was genuine concern in her question, as though his mother and father were her close friends.

'Yes, undoubtedly so.' Gerald deliberately made his voice cheerful. 'And there's a letter here from sister Jane. I haven't read it yet.' He examined the date stamp on the envelope. 'Posted just three weeks ago; mail is getting a little faster, so we're obviously winning the war.' He picked up his sister's letter and slit the envelope with a tableknife. At least Jane's letter wouldn't be full of harsh criticism and threats. He could picture her writing it, chewing the end of her pen as she did so. Jane's pens, and anyone else's she chose to use while she was home, were always chewed. Her writing was scrawly, almost masculine, undisciplined, but her outward carelessness disguised intense sentimental feelings. She was two years older than himself, but throughout all his childhood years he had felt she was the one friend and confidante he could always rely upon. There would be only good wishes in this letter and perhaps they would help erase the emotions raised by his father. He unfolded the pages.

Dearest Gee,
For the first time in my life I realise my education has been totally inadequate. I should have gone on to Oxford and read English so at least I would be able to compose a coherent letter with all the right words in the correct places. As it is, I can't even get my true feelings down on paper. I don't even know where to begin.

The world seems to be falling to pieces, at least, what has been left of it by the two aitches (Hitler and Hirohito). I was absolutely devastated by the War Office telegram which said you had been wounded. It didn't say if it was serious, or slight. For weeks I prayed, really prayed. So much for being a professed Communist!

Now I'm sad my prayers weren't answered completely, but thank God you are alive and getting yourself fit again. You'll see, it won't be as bad as you think; nothing ever is. I can't wait to meet Mary, she sounds marvellous.

This is the bit of the letter I've been dreading writing. A telegram would have been quicker, but I know from experience far too impersonal. I'm afraid there is bad news. Father has been killed. God, how harsh that looks when you have to write it down! It happened last night. There has to be a Coroner's Inquest so we'll know all the details when it takes place next week. The police say the car skidded on wet cobbles in Northumberland Avenue and crashed into a tram before it caught fire. Small comfort, but they assured me Father's death was instantaneous. The car exploded like a bomb. The chauffeur died too, and several other people were badly injured.

Mother is still under sedation and . . .

Mary watched the change occur in Gerald's face, his expression of pleasure as he had begun his sister's letter now that of blank disbelief as he strove to absorb some disturbing piece of news. She saw his eyes move again to the top of the page to reread the information. She leant forward and put her hand on his arm. 'What has happened?'

He shook his head slowly. 'An accident, my father has been killed.'

Why, she wondered, were the gods or God so cruel to this one man? Her man. They only seemed to give him suffering and anguish as though they were jealous of all he had possessed. It was the way with gods, it seemed. For some humans, the few, there was happiness and contentment, for others only pain. Now, she thought, there must be mourning and sorrow; he must understand she shared it with him. But how did the British mourn? Her only experience had been the death of the Warrens' son. Was it customary, as had happened with Evelyn Warren, for the woman to shut herself away in her room for a while? If there had been tears then she as a servant had not been allowed to see them. The British often concealed their feelings, interred them with their dead deep inside themselves; only anger or joy were allowed to be shown, and then usually with restraint unless they had been drinking. How could she tell Gerald she wanted to share his grief? Perhaps he would understand that when she had accepted him she had accepted his family as her own? She must be certain that somehow she would manage to diminish his sorrow, not compound it. Again she thought of Alan, how he would have advised her, and wished he were still with them.

'Well, I suppose that's that,' said Gerald. He pressed his lips tightly together and shrugged his shoulders. 'Here,' he passed her Jane's letter. 'You can read it.'

The uneven, sloping writing wandering across the pages was difficult for Mary to decipher. The nuns had always insisted their pupils wrote their lessons in copperplate style, every letter perfectly formed and legible, so that often it had been difficult to distinguish one pupil's work from another. Jane's writing would have been cuttingly described, before an entire class, as scribble. But the words were kind and thoughtful. Mary felt she would like this woman. It was a pity she was not here. 'What must a son do now?' she asked.

To her surprise, Gerald's face showed no emotion. If there was any sense of loss at the death of his father he was concealing it perfectly. Perhaps this was the customary manner? 'There'll be quite a few formalities,' he said. 'It'll take time, of course. The family solicitors in London will send various documents over here. There will be papers to sign, shares to transfer ... deeds.'

'Your mother?'

'Jane will see to things at home. She's very capable. I'll telegram mother first, then write.' He looked at the date on the envelope. 'No point in trying to arrange flowers. It'll all be over by now.'

Suddenly she understood. 'I hadn't realised.'

'Realised what?'

'You hated him.' She was surprised to feel shocked.

'Hate? No, I didn't actually hate the old man. But I'm afraid I didn't like him very much either. He never allowed me to get to know him.'

'That is sad.'

'It used to be sad.' Gerald's tone was defensive, but his eyes held hers. 'It was sad when I used to come home from school for my holidays and find neither of my parents waiting for me. For a long time I believed it was business that kept them away, but then, when I was older, I found they spent most of the vacation in Biarritz and Nice. Mother, it seemed, found it difficult to cope with children, and father wasn't interested. Once, just before I joined up, I calculated how much time we'd spent together as a family. Apart from the period we were in Assam, it came to just over one year. One year! And I didn't deduct the time spent sleeping, or playing alone, or when my father was genuinely away on business or in the House of Lords, or mother attending one of her potty garden parties.' Gerald grimaced. 'I didn't hate him, only his ideals and the way he tried to impose them on other people; me in particular. But I can't be expected to miss him now when I gave up missing him years ago.'

The sun had already settled below the roofs of the neighbouring old John Company bungalows of the residential area. Their white walls, still retaining the past heat of the day, were shading to flamingo. The grass in the gardens was lush, trimmed as short as bowling greens, between bright shrubberies and flower beds, which if neglected for only a short time in the tropical humidity would have returned to jungle; the work of the malis at this time of year was to prevent rather than encourage the growth of vegetation.

In the still air of early evening the sound of playing children's voices, high-pitched and sharp, carried across the boundaries and tree-lined streets. In a short while the gardens would be silent, until the guests at some dinner party spilled into the cool night to drink their burra-pegs beneath the exaggerated stars.

Shadows were departing with the fading sunlight as a bearer led Gopal Bannerjee to the steps beneath the bungalow's french windows, and indicated Aurobindo Das sitting, cross-legged as though in meditation, on a rug at the far end of the rectangular lawn. Das's hands rested on his knees, light-skinned palms upwards, lean fingers relaxed. His eyes were closed so Bannerjee wondered for a moment whether he should disturb him, then decided to cough to announce his arrival. He did so.

Das opened his eyes with a slowness that indicated he had been aware of Bannerjee's presence, then raised his hands and placed them together in greeting. Bannerjee duplicated the movement, envying Das's habitual calmness. Das was always calm, seldom showed anger, and always considered everything at length before he acted. His quick mind enjoyed the analysis of political chicanery; of all the Congress Party members, he was one of the most reliable thinkers, planners. He unfolded himself from the rug like an opening jack-knife, his lean body some six feet in height and several inches taller than the average Indian. He smoothed creases from his cream jacket. He was wearing the small peakless cap made popular in the party by its leader, Gandhi.

Das smiled a greeting. 'I'm glad you could come at such short notice.'

'We are friends. It is a pleasure.' Bannerjee was conscious of his own ungainliness, his sagging belly that made elegant movement impossible. Height and slenderness were something he envied but could not attain. He had been short and muscular as a young man, a good wrestler at university and a member of the national team; once he had entered his family's trading company the muscle had turned to fat, and his dark hair had thinned until it was now only a fringe around his scalp.

Unlike Bannerjee, who wore heavy gold rings on the third fingers of both hands, a broad-banded gold wristwatch and a thick chain with a medallion of similar metal around his creased neck, Aurobindo Das had no personal adornment. Although the proprietor of one of the most successful Hindu newspapers, he chose not to show his wealth other than in his careful dress.

'Shall we sit there?' He nodded towards a wooden garden seat at the edge of the gravelled path.

'That would be pleasant.'

'*Nimbu pani?*' Das offered lemonade.

Bannerjee shook his head. 'No, thank you.' He knew a cool drink would encourage him to perspire even more; it was a penalty of his grossness, and in order to appear neat and fresh at this meeting he had changed his clothing only half an hour beforehand.

'Well, what has Mahatma Gandhi decided?' Das asked, once they had settled themselves on the seat.

Uncertain of his friend's reaction, Bannerjee kept the expression on his face neutral. 'He is still insisting he should have a meeting with Jinnah.'

Das frowned. 'Gandhi is wrong about this.'

Bannerjee shrugged. 'Jinnah is the leader of the Muslim League. It is natural Gandhi should meet him.'

'I imagine it is a move the Viceroy is encouraging,' said Das.

Bannerjee hesitated before answering, then nodded. 'Lord Wavell is nobody's fool.'

'But *we* may prove to be someone's. I fear the meeting will be a mistake. I hoped Gandhi would understand this. Jinnah's support has been weakened here in Bengal, the famine of last year saw to that. He has also lost face in the North-west Frontier Province and the Punjab, because of his refusal to negotiate with us last year. For Gandhi to agree to a meeting now is an error. The meeting with Gandhi will bolster Jinnah's prestige and reinstate him in the eyes of the Muslim League. It will surely encourage the British to listen to Jinnah's demands.'

'But the Rajagopalachari formula has to be discussed.'

'Discussed? Perhaps. But certainly not with Jinnah. It is foolish to seriously wound an enemy on the battlefield, then pick him up, restore him to good health and put a sword back in his hands. Remember Lahore in April? Jinnah went there to replace President Khizar Hayat Khan. And what happened?' Das raised his hands questioningly. 'Instead of the thousands he expected to turn out to cheer him, Jinnah stood almost alone. And now Gandhi is offering him a chance to regain his power.' Das sighed. 'Be assured it will cost us a million square miles of territory, perhaps more.'

'I suppose you are right,' said Bannerjee, using his past experience of Das's reasoning to formulate his own opinion.

'I don't agree with Rajagopalachari, for a start. Once you agree in theory that something exists, then a major step has been taken towards its physical existence. For years we have been rejecting the idea of Pakistan as a separate state from a united India. Rajagopalachari suggests we agree with its existence in theory in order to satisfy British demands. It is too dangerous to agree to such a thing.'

'But the British will not consider leaving here until we do agree.' It is the old argument again, thought Bannerjee, the circling carousel: eternal stalemate between the Hindu and Muslim parties, both aiming at freedom, but the Hindus looking for national unity, the Muslim for total independence. 'Islam in danger' was the rival leader's battlecry.

'The British will agree to quit if we present them with an undivided front,' said Das positively. 'We have lived as one nation under their rule for over two hundred years. We can do it under our own rule. And later, if it ever becomes necessary to consider drastic changes, then they can be decided upon without the pressures influencing our decisions today.' He sighed again. 'We have a better opportunity now than ever before. The Viceroy is a soldier and a comparatively simple and uncomplicated man. He supports us. His attitude is one of realism. It doesn't take a soothsayer to know what is likely to happen here once the war is over. There are thousands upon thousands of Indian men in the army; they will come home, wanting jobs. The wartime industries will end, and there will be even greater unemployment. There is already unrest and civil disobedience, so what then? The British will have fought their own war and they will be tired, completely exhausted. Not only will their people be overspent, but also their finances. They will not be able to afford India. Lord Wavell understands all this.'

'You will be speaking to Congress again regarding the Gandhi–Jinnah meeting?'

'Myself and everyone else will be speaking ... as usual, Gopal. One thing the British have managed to do during their occupation is to turn us into a nation of loquacious lawyers. Words have become the only permitted and legal weapons we are allowed to carry, so we use and practise them too often. We play with them, seek new devices. Sometimes I am convinced it is our own obsession with speech that subjugates us, rather than a foreign oppressor.'

Gopal Bannerjee laughed. 'Perhaps.'

'However,' said Das, 'I have a small item of news to exchange for your own. Small, but interesting. Yesterday evening I received a letter from my brother.'

'The priest?'

'The priest, Surendranath.' He reached inside his jacket and pulled out an envelope which he passed to Bannerjee. 'Here, read it for yourself.' He folded his arms and leant back against the seat.

After a few minutes Bannerjee handed back the letter. 'That is most interesting.'

'It is *particularly* interesting in view of Petrie holdings in Assam, and the Governor of Assam's insistence that the Muslim League should form a ministry there despite the fact it is a Hindu majority region.'

'And you believe Petrie India could influence the Governor, if they so wished?'

'Tea is a labour-intensive industry, is it not? There are very many Petrie India employees in Assam. Influence in the right place could determine what happens to Assam if the worst comes to the worst.'

'The worst?'

'Partition. If Jinnah gets his wish, his Pakistan, its size will naturally depend on the territories he can influence before it is formed. He wants Assam, therefore anything which can be used to prevent him obtaining it is of importance to us.'

'But one pregnant woman is hardly ...' began Bannerjee.

'Pregnant women, Gopal, are always the forerunners of empires,' interrupted Aurobindo Das. 'Before such men as Alexander the Great and the Emperor Napoleon, there were pregnant women ... their mothers. Never underestimate them, my friend.'

Ten days after the news of his father's death, Gerald received a dinner invitation from Howard Everson. The note was waiting for him at the hotel reception desk when they returned from the Calcutta Military Hospital where Gerald had undergone his daily hour of physiotherapy. Everson's note was apologetic. He had only that morning returned to the office and learnt that Gerald was in Calcutta. He had immediately visited the hotel in the hope of finding him but had failed to do so. However, he looked forward to seeing him that evening if possible; the dinner party had been arranged some weeks earlier by his wife to celebrate their wedding anniversary. Everson suggested it was an opportunity for Gerald to meet executives of companies with whom Petrie India did business. He hoped the short notice would be excused and Gerald would be able to attend. A few formal words of condolence indicated Everson was aware of his chairman's demise.

Gerald could see the nervousness in Mary's eyes as she read Everson's brief letter. He smiled at her, reassuringly. 'They won't eat you. I think we should go along.' The past days had already changed his plans for his future with the company. He had wanted time; time, he had been forced to recognise, to hide himself away like an injured fox to lick his wounds until they healed. An under-manager's job on a plantation would have given him this. He could, perhaps, have been allowed to come to terms with his disability slowly and without pressure. It was a luxury that was no longer possible. Short of abandoning all future responsibility with the company, he knew now he would be expected to serve on its board of directors. There was no convenient hideaway to be used until he gained confidence and experience, and he was uncomfortably aware he would be pitchforked into a senior position with less business knowledge than the company's most junior clerk. It would not only be difficult for himself, but also for Mary. They might as well both begin now, together.

'I met Everson before I went up to Assam. He's a bit wet, but nothing to be afraid of.' He noticed her hands were trembling. 'Come here.' He took the note from her and tossed it on the sofa, then held both her hands and forced her eyes to meet his. 'What did you think the first time a Jap shell exploded near you?'

Her fingers tightened slightly in his own. 'I thought I would die.'

'Me too; but we didn't, did we?' She shook her head. 'Well, going to a dinner party is a damned sight easier than facing a Japanese battalion. You must have seen dinner parties at the Warrens.'

'I never went to one. They stand and talk, and drink. But I don't know how to talk to the British.'

'You talk to me ... and you talked to Alan.'

'That is different. I suppose I must learn.'

Gerald nodded. ''Fraid so.' He grinned at her. 'You'll knock the men's eyes out.'

'If you were a woman, husband, you would know that that is not necessarily a good idea.'

She was as nervous as an inexperienced actress preparing for a first-night performance. Mary's stomach fluttered at the thought of the evening ahead of her, the first important social function she had ever attended as Gerald's wife. For the first time she was to be the guest of a British woman, a woman whom only a short while ago she would have been expected to address as memsah'b. Now, she must meet the woman as an equal, behave as an equal. She knew it would be difficult. She prayed it would not be impossible.

She knew there was no escape, no excuse for her to remain behind in the hotel that would be acceptable. And even if there were one, then she was only delaying the inevitable: sooner or later they would receive another invitation. Besides, she reminded herself, Gerald needed her with him. Perhaps their need tonight was shared equally between them? Perhaps his need for her on this first social occasion since his wounds was even greater than her need for him? The thought that this might be so comforted her a little.

'Are you ready, darling?' She heard Gerald's questioning voice as she stared critically at herself in the long mirror of the hotel bedroom. Other than kohl around her eyes as a child she had never worn make-up before. Make-up had been forbidden at the mission school even had its pupils been able to afford any. There had never been any need for her to wear it at the Warrens and it was unlikely Evelyn Warren would have encouraged its use by a servant girl.

It had been Gerald's suggestion and resulted in yet another visit to the foyer salon where the salon's beauty specialist had spent more than an hour creaming, shading and powdering Mary's skin. Now, as she examined herself, she was barely able to recognise the woman who returned her gaze as herself. This was no longer the Lushai servant girl.

The make-up had retained her youth but added an elegance she had never before experienced. Somehow it was giving her a feeling of confidence, as though it were a mask capable of disguising her feelings of apprehension. The subtle hand of the beauty specialist drew attention to the finest points of her features, accentuating her eyes and high cheekbones, distracting from the long scar which marked her slender neck. She adjusted the folds of her sari across her shoulders.

Gerald's eyes examined her as she joined him, then he whistled softly; the same whistle she had heard American soldiers use when they wanted to attract the attention of one of the local girls in Gauhati. Somehow Gerald made it a compliment. 'Wow!' She had chosen a pale lemon sari, heavily embroidered in gold; it had been the most expensive of those she had purchased and the careful pleating she had used concealed her pregnancy. He made her turn slowly around in front of him as if she were modelling it. 'There's something missing.' Her heart jumped a beat. What had she forgotten? He held a small package towards her and watched as she opened it. A cluster of diamonds caught the room lights and made her gasp; she had seen diamond rings before, on the fingers of the memsahibs who had visited the plantation on festive occasions. None had been so spectacular as this. He took the ring from her and slid it on to her finger. She stared at it, almost hypnotised by the manner in which it seemed alive, its dancing white flames.

'It's beautiful. Thank you.' The ring held her eyes.

'I'm afraid I'm only gilding the lily.' He realised she didn't understand him. 'When someone is so beautiful that they cannot be improved by adding something, then that is called gilding the lily: putting gold on something which doesn't really need it.'

'You don't want me to wear this ring?' There was concern in her eyes.

'I want you to wear it always. It's yours. A kind of thank you, for everything. A love token from me.'

'It is a charm?'

'Yes.' Gerald took her hand, turned it over and kissed the soft palm. 'Yes, it is a charm.'

A military convoy from the docks delayed the traffic, its outriders on raucous Ariel motorcycles pinning the taxis, private cars, carts and wagons against the gutters of Chowringhee as forty seven-ton Bedford trucks lurched ponderously towards the Ordnance Depot at Dum-Dum. By the time the convoy had passed and the road reopened, Gerald and Mary were half an hour late arriving at Howard Everson's house in Theatre Road. Other guests had been more fortunate, for as the taxi drew to a halt in the bungalow drive they could be seen through the tall open windows, already chatting in groups, their cocktail glasses in their hands. The nervousness which Mary believed had gone returned to dry her throat and tauten the muscles of her stomach.

Rai, who had been sitting beside the taxi driver, unstrapped the wheelchair and assisted Gerald from the vehicle. She waited until he had paid the driver before joining him. Gerald said, 'Steady, girl,' as though he was calming a disquieted horse. She put a hand on his shoulder.

Three broad steps led up to the open door, and beyond was a wide entrance hall into which the guests seemed to have overflowed. A bearer carrying a tray noticed them, disappeared briefly and then returned, empty handed, to help them up the steps. The width of the doorway forced Mary behind the wheelchair, away from the comforting touch of Gerald's body. For a moment she stood outside, alone. Memories of her life as a house servant returned to worsen her apprehension. At parties such as this she had been expected to help the bearers or sometimes the cook, laying tables, arranging sweetmeats on plates, carrying trays of drinks if the guests were numerous. 'Make sure your sari is clean, Mary,' Evelyn Warren would order. 'But most important of all, scrub your nails before my guests arrive.' Mary always obeyed, and so conscientiously that her fingers and knuckles were tender for hours afterwards. She had viewed these European parties, so unreal in her own life, from an abstracted viewpoint, as a leopard stretched along the high branch of a jungle tree might watch the distant passing of the steamer on the winding river. Strangers came and laughed too readily, drank too much. The men lost their dignity and women their tempers. Couples flirted, and if the party was particularly large and drunken, they might slip away together into the darkness of the gardens, to return singly and guiltily a few minutes later to seek the company of their cuckolded husband or wife. The servants were ignored as if they were not more than unthinking automatons to be set into motion by a curt word of command or the signalling fingers of hosts or guests.

'Gerald!' The sound of a man's voice exclaiming his name drew her into the present. She stepped through the doorway.

A narrow-jawed European wearing a white dinner jacket, open at his waist to reveal a maroon cummerbund, began a burst of masculine sympathy. 'Good heavens above! My God, old boy, we didn't know! I say, how damned thoughtless of me. I should have telephoned you. But what with the news of your father ... What is it, old boy, a bally leg wound?'

Gerald's voice was flat: 'Spinal cord.'

'Oh my God, that's rotten luck!'

A woman's voice, piercing, overlaying background conversation: 'Poor man, how dreadful. Howard, do bring him inside, he's sitting in a draught.'

Rai was between Mary and the wheelchair which Everson seized. The woman, middle-aged and petite, her face powdered unnaturally white above a long pink satin dinner-gown, raised her voice authoritatively as she spoke to Gerald's bearer. 'You may leave your sahib now.' To Gerald: 'He can stay in the kitchen.' She faced Mary and in same commanding tone she had used on the bearer said: 'And you had better go along ...'

'Mrs Everson ...' Gerald's interruption was so sudden and positive that later Mary realised it must have been spurred by anticipation and his determination to protect her. Now, she was aware only of its timeliness. There was no doubt Mrs Everson had been about to order Mary to follow Rai to the servants' quarters, but Gerald gave Everson's wife no further time to expand on her blunder. 'Janet ... Howard, I'd like to introduce you to my wife.' Janet Everson's neck displayed the quick blush that was hidden on her face by her pancake make-up. 'This is Mary, *Lady* Petrie.'

There was distinct positiveness in the manner in which he emphasised the title, leaving Janet Everson in no doubt as to how he wished Mary to be treated.

Janet Everson's mouth opened slightly, her eyes widening in horror as she realised how close she had come to an insult which might easily have endangered her husband's future with his company. There was a long moment of silence. Mary found herself enjoying Janet Everson's embarrassment, but then experienced small pangs of sympathy; it was an understandable error, perhaps, she decided. She could very well have been mistaken for Gerald's nurse. But, even so, it was pleasant, for the first time in her life, to be so firmly elevated above the position she had been forced to accept as the exclusive right of British memsahibs. She wished it could have been Evelyn Warren who faced her now.

His wife's unnatural muteness momentarily puzzled Howard Everson. He glanced at her and began attempting to translate her expression, then suddenly realised what had taken place. His eyes threatened her.

The silence had now lengthened and become so obvious that a small group of guests a few yards further along the hallway stopped their chatter and watched in curiosity.

Mary relented, and smiled at Howard Everson. 'I am very pleased to meet you.' She turned to Janet Everson. 'I must thank you for kindly inviting us.'

'I say,' said Everson, loudly and with relief. He grinned, showing a crowded mouth of artificial teeth. 'Lady Petrie.' He held out his hand to her, and as she took it, bowed slightly. 'What a very pleasant surprise.' He gave her no time to reply, but spoke to his wife. 'Janet, you must personally take care of Lady Petrie this evening.' It was an order; but then he changed his mind. 'On second thoughts, I shall take care of her.' He was still holding Mary's hand, and as he felt the tension easing, he realised that she was an exceptionally attractive young woman. 'I shall introduce you to everyone!' In the background, conversation resumed.

Janet Everson began smiling weakly as she led her guests towards the conservatory which was the centre of the party; a few minutes later she excused herself, went to her bathroom and was sick.

It was three a.m. The windows of the suite above Chowringhee were open but the night was still, the air so humid it seemed to drag at the blades of the fans as they revolved slowly, their motors humming faintly. A cricket chirruped optimistically in some small crevice in the bathroom, the marble tiles magnifying the sound and the echo giving the hidden insect the encouragement of competition.

Gerald was slightly drunk and in a moment of bravado had dismissed Rai at the ground-floor entrance to the elevator and then wheeled himself to their rooms. He was feeling elated. As he had expected, Mary had drawn the attention of all the men at the party, and he had made a point of telling Howard Everson of her bravery at Kohima: the story had circulated quickly amongst the guests. As a result, there had been no time when it had been necessary for her to search for conversation. From both Mary's point of view and Gerald's, the party had been the successful crossing of a barrier; he knew it might have been only a stile rather than a cliff-face, but nevertheless it had been overcome. And to his relief there had been no dancing, nothing to point up his disability. Everson had avoided discussing work, but had suggested they meet for lunch later that week. Gerald was now feeling the combined inebriation of alcohol and contentment.

He heard Mary in the suite bedroom, soft rustling sounds. She had already bathed. The bed creaked. He knew she had wanted to help him but had tactfully left him alone. He drained his nightcap of neat Scotch, and put the glass on the coffee table, then wheeled himself into the bathroom. The cricket stilled itself at his intrusion as rubber wheels squeaked on the tiled floor. He ran the bath water.

There was a gap between the foot of the huge bath and the wall. He knew it was large enough to contain his chair and manoeuvred himself into it, wedging the chair so that even if it moved as he undressed it would be held in position by the bath. He stripped himself to the waist, supporting himself with the bath taps whenever his body slumped forward. It was slow and frustrating, making him feel uncomfortably like some huge boneless and amoebic lump of flesh, but the past months had strengthened his arms and he was able to wriggle out of his trousers and underpants. He removed the thick condom and its bag, and emptied them.

Sweat ran from his body, dripped from his nose and chin as though he were an athlete racing under a hot sun. The humid air and the steam of the bath had turned the room into a sauna. His heart was pounding, but he was naked. Balancing himself like a gymnast he managed to get his body across the rim of the bath, slipped but saved himself by using all the strength of his hands. He swore loudly, but pulled himself forward, a hand on either side of the bath, his legs dragging behind him. He did not feel them hit the metal of the bath's bottom as they fell, but knew from the altered angle of his body and the surge of the water that he had succeeded. He rolled himself on to his back.

'Gerald?'

He heard Mary's anxious voice.

'I'm in the bath, darling.' He made it sound as casual as possible, concealing the sense of satisfaction he was experiencing. He splashed noisily.

Mary called again: 'Good.' She lay, staring at the mesh of the mosquito net above her. 'Good'! It seemed an inadequate word to commend the effort it must have taken him, and she lay biting her lip to keep herself silent until it became almost too difficult to bear. She had heard the tyres moving on the tiles, listened to the thump of his hands or body against the metal of the bath, felt his pain in her own limbs and sympathised with his curses. She wanted to run into the bathroom, hold him, kiss him, tell him the importance of his achievement.

There was a silence that wrung her tensed nerves, then more splashing, the sound of water running away, more hollow thumping against the bath. It had been over an hour since he entered the bathroom. Tyres squeaked again. Then a sound she mistook for a moan, pulling her upright in the bed; he was singing! She had never heard him sing before; she could not recognise the song. The bathroom door was pushed open. He sat in his chair, a dry towel around his waist, grinning at her like a child who had just won its first egg and spoon race.

'I made it!'

She could feel tears running down her cheeks and wanted to hold him in her arms.

'No.' He stopped her. 'It's got to be all the way, to count.' He spun the chair and propelled it to his own side of the bed, then locked the brake. He had obviously been contemplating the problem because he didn't hesitate. For a moment she thought he would slide to the floor, but with a quick heave he managed to get himself face down on the bed. It was the first time since their marriage that he had left off his pyjamas and she could see the shrapnel scars across his back. She watched the muscles of his powerful shoulders flex determinedly and heard him take a deep breath, then he gripped the bedhead and turned himself. The towel which he had been wearing had been lost in his struggles. To Mary's surprise, perhaps overlooked in his determination for independence or as a result of his light-headedness, he was not wearing his surgical condom but was completely naked. Perspiration glistened on his chest as he lay back against the pillow. 'Now you can congratulate me,' he said, with satisfaction.

'I give you congratulations.' Her body, feeling as though it had experienced all his exertion and frustration, ached with sympathy.

'I would rather you gave me a kiss. A hundred kisses, that's my reward and I claim it from my fairy princess.'

She remembered the advice of the temple priest. 'If you want a reward, then you must come to me to claim it.'

He grabbed her and pulled her against him, gnawing gently at the soft hollow between her neck and shoulder, brushing aside her sleeping robe. 'If you bite me, I shall scream and the hotel will waken.'

'Let them waken. I shall devour you before their startled eyes ... like a woman-eating tiger.'

She knew he wanted her to feel the strength of his arms as he turned her towards him, his hands lifting her easily, holding her against him so powerfully the air was forced from her lungs. She fought him playfully, sensing his satisfaction when she was unable to break his grip as he slid the robe from her body, aware he was testing himself still. Breathless, she surrendered. 'Kali, save your daughter who is being eaten alive.'

He made a fierce snarling noise, but it was his lips that found the soft muscles above her breasts and followed their gentle curve to her responsive nipples. She groaned. 'I am surely being destroyed by this wild beast.' His tongue was bringing yearning, turning play towards passion as his hands caressed her body, drifted over her rounded belly to the warmth of her thighs. Physical anticipation tormented her with thoughts he might suddenly recoil as he had done before. His hand was between her legs, his strong fingers drawing her buttocks towards him, widening her thighs as though he wanted her to completely expose herself to his touch. She lifted her knee above his body, resting her leg across him to allow his hand the freedom it was seeking. His fingers teased her, his touch no more than the caress of a night breeze but magically drawing all sensation to their tender contact. Her body was begging, pleading for satisfaction, forcing itself against him as she tried to will his fingertips to enter her, drive themselves deep into her to satisfy the yearning she had endured for so long.

He was cradling her against his chest, so her breasts now felt the heat of his body. She moved her arm, her hand instinctively seeking the amatory comfort of his masculinity; it was naked and erect!

Realisation took seconds to filter through the excitement of her churning emotions but then her own eroticism was eclipsed as if she had been suddenly plunged into the ice-cold water of a mountain stream. She forced her body to continue its responses to his touch while she considered her discovery. Somehow the paralysis which had stolen the life from his lower body had overlooked this part of him; she gripped it more tightly, then began to understand. This was not a muscle controlled by the vital cord which had been severed, but an organ servant only to his unconscious mind. She knew he did not feel her hand, for the fine sensory nerves which passed back their information were lost; therefore the stimulation which had affected him could only be through his brain, his eyes, his hands, through those parts of him unaffected by the wound.

She could not tell him, for to do so now might break the fragile psychological link that made this miracle possible. Somehow she must help him to maintain his sexual excitement, so that he could discover for himself that his manhood had been returned to him.

She wondered how she might achieve this, then realised that her dreams on the many lonely nights of the past months had been lessons that might prove their value now. In them he had loved her a hundred different ways, and she had given herself to him so unreservedly and with such an abandon that sometimes on waking she had felt herself almost a harlot.

She moaned and exaggerated the movement of her hips to follow the rhythm of his fingers as he slid them inside her, spreading her legs, giving herself to him and knowing he was watching her. Her own physical desire was so great it would have been easy to allow him to satisfy it, but she forced herself to stay above the emotions and senses attempting to overwhelm her. She realised he wanted her orgasm, needed it as substitute for his own, and was leading her towards it with quickening caresses.

Her movement was catlike, natural, the urgency giving her unaccustomed strength. She was astride him, above him. He was inside her and unaware, surprised. She gave him no time to question, smothering him with kisses, taking his hand and directing it to where the strong column of his penis had entered her body. She felt his hand tighten, explore. She pressed her breasts to his lips, forced herself down on to him feeling the full length of his flesh deep inside her. Her orgasm, heightened by the nights of longing, was massive, arching her back, straining at her muscles convulsively, turning her hands into fists, drawing uncontrolled sound from her lips and then weakening her so waves of dizzy ecstasy brought her down to him again. He held her tightly for a long time before releasing her, then he kissed her gently.

She whispered, 'Thank you,' and knew at last her marriage had begun.

Gerald lay silent for a while then chuckled softly. He put his hand gently on her stomach. 'I hope you realise, young lady, you've probably just ruined my chances with the assessment board. They'll claim a man who can do that can't be a hundred per cent disabled.' He smiled at her, happily.

'And is he?'

He laughed, a deep genuine laugh of pleasure. 'They can stick their pension on the wall. Good Heavens!' He moved his hand slightly and Mary could feel the child inside her. 'It's hopping about like a jumping-bean. Is it upset? Have we hurt it?' There was concern in his voice.

'We've made it happy because it knows we love each other. But it's not an "it", it's a "he" ... your son.'

'You can't know that.'

She kissed his cheek, feeling the roughness of the day's stubble, and enjoying an unexpected sense of proprietary encompassing both man and unborn child. 'I know it, husband.'

CHAPTER EIGHT

KIMBERLEY VILLA, CALCUTTA. DECEMBER 1944

The Hooghly had its own distinctive smell, neither of mud, sewage nor of decaying matter, not even the scent of the coal-burning paddle-steamers, the ocean-going cargo vessels, bum-boats, country boats, or the people who washed their bodies and clothing on the steps along its banks. Somehow the river retained its own smell, sieving it through the narrow spears of the reed beds and allowing it to wander across gardens where it captured the fresh perfume of camelia, hybiscus and a hundred varieties of flowers.

It brought with it the few sounds which might disturb the villa's occupants; the deep thud of triple-expansion engines, turning paddle-wheels, the throb of diesels and the conversational shouts of seamen or the European malim sahibs dispensing orders to their crews in contracted Urdu. Sometimes, but only rarely because of the distance from the city, a bottley-wallah collecting glass or a trader selling produce might raise a cry outside the high protective walls until a chokidar ordered him away.

Kimberley Villa, named after the Secretary of State for India during 1886, the year in which it had been built, faced the Botanical Gardens on the far bank of the river, the arboretum giving the impression of a civilised and well-ordered forest. The villa, like most of its neighbours, could not be called either a bungalow or a house, nor was it by design a mansion. An architect from Europe might have described it as a Victorian colonial structure designed to accommodate a large family and its servants in spacious comfort. There had been several owners over the years, each modernising to the standards of his day, so that Victorian proportions had occasionally been corrupted or disguised. The villa, impressive but neither ugly nor beautiful, had any starkness of its form softened by the shade trees, now so established in its grounds it seemed impossible that little more than sixty years before the site had been raw jungle and swamp where incoming tides disturbed hordes of scarlet land crabs.

Since its purchase three months previously, Kimberley Villa had been the property of Sir Gerald and Lady Petrie.

It was furnished in an expensive but curious mixture of Indian and European taste which somehow worked, giving it a grander and more opulent feeling than many of the normal British residences. Mary was fascinated by colour and liked gilded and heavily carved woodwork, an abundance of mirrors and ornate, bright materials; to her, modern furniture was graceless and flimsy.

It had not been too difficult finding the type of furnishing she admired. There were specialist shops where it was possible to buy the beautiful Afghan, Persian and Indian rugs and carpets which covered all the floors, and the approach of the end of the war and the probability of independence for India had convinced many Europeans that they should prepare to leave for home as soon as passages were available. As a result, there had been many auctions where the grander type of furniture, too difficult and expensive to ship back to England, could be obtained.

Mary had not found it easy to come to terms with the number of rooms which were hers to fill and use as she pleased. Initally she would have been happier with a smaller house; it had seemed extravagant to have space that was idle, but Gerald had liked Kimberley from the moment he had seen it, enjoying its peaceful location near the river, and the gardens where he knew eventually his child would play. Now, however, Mary loved the villa. She and Gerald had chosen even the smallest item within it; they had begun with nothing, and everything she could see or touch provided memories of pleasure.

Now in the late stages of her pregnancy, she understood she had built for herself and their future child an exotic nest, safe and comfortable. And each day she felt and enjoyed a sense of security she had never previously experienced in her lifetime.

It was early evening and all but two of the garden party guests had left. Watching the malis clearing the lawn of cigarette ends, cigar butts and paper napkins, Gerald was amazed at the quantity of debris so small a number of people had managed to create. From the open-sided marquee which had been erected to one side of the garden came the clink of glasses and bottles where the khidmutgar and his boy assisted Rai. In the kitchen, the khansama, his wife and daughter washed plates and cutlery.

'Sir Gerald.' Aurobindo Das drew Gerald's attention and smiled as their eyes met. Gerald liked the man and despite the difference in age they had become friends. Having a conversation with Aurobindo was often like playing a chess game and forced Gerald to keep his mind sharp. They had met when the Hindu newspaper had run an obituary of his father and Aurobindo Das had interviewed Gerald. For Gerald, Das was a useful man to know with a wide circle of acquaintances and contacts, and a store of information on the members of both the Indian and European community. Today, Aurobindo was immaculately dressed as usual in pale fawn achkan and white trouseres, his grey hair military short, his skin pale olive. 'Your party has been a success, I believe.' Das's eyes never left Gerald's.

'You're very formal today, Aurobindo.'

'Formal?' Aurobindo Das moved a garden chair closer to Gerald and sat down. His movement was always as elegant as his dress.

'Sir Gerald.'

Aurobindo laughed. 'I have been listening to people all afternoon. They are very impressed by you. I don't think there are too many titled British gentlemen in Calcutta at the moment ... and you have momentarily elevated your guests to a higher stratum.' Aurobindo saw Gerald raise his eyebrows, so continued, 'It has been said that whenever twelve Englishmen find themselves together they form themselves into a club. That may be true. But if there are more than twelve, then they form themselves into a structured social society; at the head, a Royal Family and their aristocrats, then the financially successful businessmen of the middle-class, and below them as many lesser workers of their own nationality as possible to act as the foundations of the pyramid which they have built. Calcutta is a very fine example of this. At the top of your British society is the Viceroy. Normally, his senior aides and the highest of the military officers form the most superior level, or at least would consider themselves as such. There may be a certain amount of social mingling between that layer and the one beneath it, consisting of the most wealthy and established commercial families, but each will secretly recognise their correct place.'

'So what have I done today?' questioned Gerald, realising Aurobindo was mildly teasing him.

'You have stirred the soup. Some of your guests hold quite minor posts in your company, I believe.'

'It was an opportunity to meet them all. A pre-Christmas celebration.'

'True. But today they have been guests of a titled gentleman, and now they will certainly find those who would like to shake the hand which has shaken the hand. Also there were, I noticed, several government officials and a few military officers, some junior and some senior. That, Gerald, is stirred soup in Calcutta.'

'Stirred soup may bring a better flavour to the top,' said Gerald, playing Aurobindo's game.

'But also bones!' Aurobindo paused. 'Do you have an objection to me raising a matter of business at this time?'

'Of course not. Good God, I think business has been the main topic of conversation today, with the possible exception of the war.'

Aurobindo leant forward confidentially. 'It is a matter of your policy, the policy of Petrie India. May I be so bold as to give you a small piece of advice.'

'Please do.' Gerald already knew advice from Aurobindo Das was always worth consideration.

'I hope you don't mind, but in the course of the preparation of a report for a Congress committee I have been investigating the proportion of Indian citizens employed at senior levels in most of the larger business organisations in our country. I can assure you its meagreness is most disturbing, and something which I know Congress will undoubtedly change as soon as possible. Our Independence is now a foregone conclusion, it is only a question of when and how. And assuredly not all of our party members wish to see continued British involvement in our national development.'

'They want to throw us out. At least, that's what I've been told a couple of dozen times this afternoon.'

'Some might like that, but not all of us. Those who have sound business experience do not wish for such a thing. But Independence will be a very difficult time for the British as well as for ourselves. Certain British companies will be favoured, others will lose their footing in the Indian sub-continent. It will be a time of sharp knives and revenge. However, you can avoid many difficulties if you are prepared to act, and act speedily.'

'Act, how?'

'I hope I will not be speaking out of place, but it is in friendship.'

'Of course. Please continue.'

'Well.' Aurobindo hesitated and ran a finger down the slim bridge of his nose, thoughtfully. 'Firstly, it could be possible for your tea gardens to have Indian under-managers. They would be training for the position of manager when it becomes available. Naturally, you cannot be expected to retire and pay compensation to all your existing managers, and their experience is also invaluable at this time. But a start could be made in a conciliatory direction. Remember, the British have been here two hundred years, but I can assure you they have not yet learned to trust us; they must begin to do so if they wish to continue business in India.'

'I can certainly understand that.'

'Wait, you see there are other things to be done. You would gain enormous support if you were to transfer your head office from London to Calcutta.'

'Good heavens!'

'Listen to me, my friend. What I am telling you will protect your company, and your family. Petrie India must become India Petrie ... not a simple change in the order of the names, but more importantly a change in the minds of those who serve her, and in the minds of those outside the company who watch her. India must appear to be first, and Petrie second. Your head office should be here in India, not in the UK. Such a relocation would be an obvious act of faith at this time. And it is really only a paper transaction for you; there is no need to purchase or sell the buildings themselves, simply to alter the order of importance.'

'It would mean considerable staff changes.'

'Of course that is so. But there are very many qualified men here, to fill any situations which may become available.' Aurobindo leant back in the chair and watched Gerald's reaction; at least, he thought, it was not one of horror, which some of the British he knew would have shown.

'Do I sense that you are making me an offer? My future in India, in return for the company?'

'No, not exactly that, my friend. And not officially from Congress, you understand. Perhaps I can put it this way? Those who show themselves to be friends *for* our future will be treated by us as friends in our future.' He stood up quickly. 'Anyway, I have said quite enough for the present. You must have time to think about my suggestions.' He held out his hand to Gerald. 'That was a very pleasant party indeed. And now I must say goodbye to Lady Mary.'

'She insists her friends should simply call her Mary, Aurobindo.'

Aurobindo smiled. 'Perhaps, and I am also aware that I do not use her title with strict accuracy. But she is becoming well-known throughout Calcutta as Lady Mary, for we Indians. And I personally believe that is how she should be called.'

Aurobindo had just said his goodbye, excused himself and left. Alan Jameson was sitting opposite Mary, staring into her eyes with an embarrassing earnestness. He had arrived from Assam that morning to spend his three weeks' leave and Christmas as a house guest at Kimberley Villa. It was the first time since his arrival that the two of them had been alone together. He shook his head slowly. 'I can't get over it. Six months and you've changed from a beautiful, if stubborn, young girl to an exotic and sophisticated woman.'

She laughed. 'A stubborn fat woman, Alan. And I shall pop any minute.'

'A Christmas baby?'

'I doubt it very much. I don't know exactly when it's due, and the doctor isn't much help. But the baby kicks so strongly now I know he wants to be out playing in the fresh air.'

'Gerald tells me you're convinced it will be a boy.'

'I'm not just convinced, Alan, I know it will be.' She placed her hands on both sides of her swollen stomach. 'Here is my son; Gerald's son.'

'Gerald is a very lucky man.' Alan wondered if she realised how sincerely he meant the compliment. He had spent a lot of time at Digboi, thinking about her; too much time. But it had been like the oriental poem he had once read: 'Trying not to think of you, is still thinking of you.' For a while he had even considered refusing Gerald's invitation to spend this leave with them, but had then told himself he was being foolish. It was stupid to believe he had fallen in love with her, it was surely only her youth that attracted him; there was almost twelve years' difference in their ages, and she was the wife of a friend. It must be only his present loneliness that made him want her. It would pass, perhaps when the war ended and he got back to his normal work and circle of friends again.

Gerald wheeled himself to the side of their table and spun his chair to face them.

Alan said, 'Good party,' and felt momentarily hypocritical. He had been enjoying Mary's exclusive company and briefly resented Gerald's intrusion. Both his sense of guilt and resentment passed almost instantly. 'Can I get either of you a drink?'

'I've had more than enough for the time being.' Gerald tapped the pockets of his jacket. 'I'll scrounge one of your cigarettes, if I may?'

Alan offered his cigarette case, flicking it open with his thumb, then vigorously firing the lighter inside it. His ability to cope with only one hand had greatly improved since the time in Dimapur. His arm ended in a stump he kept concealed in his sleeve, but he had been promised an artificial hand as soon as a suitable one became available.

Gerald drew a long mouthful of smoke from the cigarette, then said to Mary: 'Did you have a chat with Aurobindo?'

'Just a small one.'

'He seems quite a decent chap,' observed Alan.

Mary answered. 'A very nice man. Very kind and thoughtful.'

'He's also very useful, and I think he's honest with us. We've known him a few months now.' Gerald brushed a small bullet of cigarette ash from his lap. 'Has Mary told you he suggested she goes to university?'

'University!' Alan's eyes widened. He looked quickly at Mary.

'It's nonsense, of course. I don't have the brains, or a matriculation. And in any case, I must be looking after our son.'

'I don't think it's such a bad idea,' said Gerald. 'We've already employed an aiya and if she needs help we can get her an assistant. Aurobindo has said there would be no trouble about Mary's acceptance, and I think it would broaden her interests . . . the lectures, debates, and so on.'

'And I think it would be impossible,' Mary said, but without conviction, as though she was hoping to be persuaded by her husband's arguments.

There were still moments, Alan realised, when she needed Gerald's reassurance. Her confidence was far stronger than it had been, but was not yet total. 'What would you read?' he asked.

Gerald answered for Mary: 'Aurobindo has suggested Economics and Indian History.'

Alan whistled through his teeth. 'Good Lord!'

Mary smiled. 'I told you it is a very silly idea.'

Gerald banged his knee with his fist, the movement jolting the wheelchair on its springs. 'Dammit, woman, you spend hours every day with your books as it is.' He turned to Alan. 'I married a bookworm! I thought she would come to the city and discover clothes shops, shoe shops, jeweller's shops ...'

Mary interrupted him: 'I did.'

Gerald continued. 'But she also discovered the library, and the booksellers. You've seen all the bookcases we have scattered all about the house? Well, they're filled with her books, not mine. I've never known anyone consume books as quickly as she does.' The tone of his voice made it obvious he was proud of her new obsession. He turned to face her. 'What did you finish yesterday?'

'*Emma*.'

'Jane Austen,' said Gerald, with unnecessary emphasis.

'I prefer Mukhopadhyay,' admitted Mary. 'Not only because it is in Hindi, you must understand, but I think his prose is better.'

Alan laughed. 'I have to admit I haven't read either of them.'

Gerald stubbed out his cigarette. 'And do you know, she remembers every word of every book she reads?'

Mary made a pushing gesture towards him with her hand. 'Go away, you are exaggerating.' She looked at Alan. 'I do not remember every word. I remember some, of course, if they are important. But it is only a trick. At mission school it was obligatory to learn the Bible . . . and so I developed a certain way of remembering, to please my teachers.'

'She even reads Mrs Beeton.'

Mary spoke in mock anger: 'Gerald, you must stop this stupid talk.' And then to Alan: 'It is necessary for a Lushai wife to learn how to feed a British husband.' She became serious. 'What did Aurobindo have to say to you?'

Gerald repeated their conversation and when he had finished, Alan said quietly: 'I can see his point, but it would be a damn big step to take.'

'I'm not even certain I can take it, even if I want to,' Gerald frowned, 'certainly not the transfer of head office. For a start, regardless of the proportion of shares I own, I'm still very much the new boy.'

'I doubt if you'll be able to do very much until we get the war over. But that shouldn't be too long now. The Americans are near the Rhine and the Russians at Warsaw. Spring should see it over in Europe. Presumably you'll go back to England for a while?'

Gerald shook his head firmly. 'No, it's not what I want. It's not even necessary. My uncle is MD, and the company isn't going to drop to pieces because I choose to stay in India ... in fact they'll hardly notice I'm here. Of course, I suppose I'll have to make a trip back to the UK one day, but it'll be a short one; I'd be way out of my depth in London.' He paused thoughtfully, his forehead creased with a frown. 'You know, this is the easy end of the business. Here it virtually runs itself just so long as you keep an eye on things. There are very few decisions to be made. It's more accountancy than anything else ... watching expenditures, keeping an eye on warehouse stocks and shipping arrangements. I don't know a damn thing about the marketing end. I can just see what the family shareholders might say if I tell them we ought to move the major decision-making to Calcutta. My shares certainly put me in a majority position but I don't have the experience to enforce my authority. At least, not yet.'

'But you could make the staff changes over here,' suggested Mary. 'Employ more Indians; especially in Assam. Didn't you tell me that the Warrens are planning to leave?'

'That's true,' mused Gerald. 'It might be possible to replace Jack with a suitably qualified Indian manager. Yes, quite possible indeed.'

It was late evening. Beyond the windows the reflections of the lights of a small coaster moored in the reach were jostled on the surface of the water by the eddies and ripples, so that the dark silhouette of the vessel appeared to be surrounded by a dancing swarm of fireflies. The dying embers of an oil-drum brazier glowed dull red in front of the Botanical Gardens on the far bank where several country boats had been beached as the tide receded, their crews grouped in the warmth. A light breeze brought the faint sound of drumming to the open windows of the villa.

It had been almost ten o'clock by the time dinner had ended, and Mary had dismissed the servants as soon as the table had been cleared. It had been a long and tiring day for them, beginning shortly after dawn with the preparations for the afternoon's party. Even Rai, normally stoical, had looked exhausted by nightfall.

Now, Alan and Gerald were playing snooker, and Mary was watching them. The billiard room was not an addition to the villa but had been incorporated in the original plan, a large annexe to the first sahib's study. The room was only sparsely furnished and its bare walls echoed with the sharp click of the ivory balls. Both men had been wearing dinner jackets, but these had now been discarded and they played in their shirt-sleeves, drinking their whiskies between shots, moving the indicators on the scoreboard with the chalked tips of their cues.

Mary watched them in the square pool of light cast by the reflectors above the table. Two men, both disabled by the same horrible war, Gerald expertly propelling himself in his wheelchair to examine or take his shots, Alan with a brass cue-rest beneath his handless arm as though he were carrying a gun. If they ever mentioned their wounds it was to make rough jokes at each other's expense in a manner no outsider would ever understand.

She watched them, knowing for the first time that they both loved her. She had realised it during dinner, catching Alan's grey eyes unexpectedly, reading his feelings when he spoke to her across the table; but neither Alan nor Gerald knew what she had discovered. At first it had frightened her, appearing a threat to her happiness, a destructive element she had not anticipated. Later, she knew all was safe; only for a short while had Alan allowed his shield to drop, and then he had recovered it. She had seen from his expression he would never allow it to happen again. He did not know she had noticed.

She was fond of him, too, she thought, but quite differently from Gerald. As a sister might be fond of an older brother; no, a stronger feeling than that... more trusting, an affection strengthened by the warmth of true friendship. Experimentally she attempted to reverse the two men's roles in her life; her mind would not permit it.

The sudden contraction, like a severe pre-menstrual cramp within her stomach, startled her, made her gasp loudly. It coincided with a burst of laughter from Gerald as Alan missed an easy shot, and she was grateful they had not heard her. The mai had told her it might take many hours and she was not to fear the first slow movements. She glanced at the brass clock on the mantelpiece. It was eleven-thirty p.m. The midwife had said it might be twelve or fourteen hours from this first sign, perhaps longer, until the child was born. There was plenty of time. She felt glad it was happening at last. Soon, she thought, she would be able to hold their son in her arms; they would both be able to hold him. He would be part of them both. So much had happened to her since she had conceived she felt she had been carrying the child for a lifetime, that she had never lived without it. But she had no fear of its birth and felt contented that it had begun.

She excused herself and left the two men to their game and their drinks. She did not want to sleep and knew it might soon become impossible anyway, but she wanted to be alone to compose herself and to enjoy all the experiences she knew lay ahead.

The next contraction came as she was undressing, fifteen minutes after the first; a pain that increased then faded as her muscles tensed and relaxed. She showered carefully and unhurriedly. This was one of the most important events of her life, she had told herself. Every second of it was to be savoured. She was glad she was alone so for the moment it need not be shared, even with Gerald.

Naked, she stood for a while before the dressing mirror and studied her body. Lately Gerald had found it slightly amusing, not realising his humour might hurt her. He had told her she looked like a ripe pear; it had been intended as a joke. She had become cross with him: 'I look like a woman, not a fruit. I look like a woman who has a man who loves her, and who is about to give him his child. A pear does not look like a woman and a woman does not look like a pear ... nor a fig, nor a pomegranate.' He had laughed at her outburst, but then held her close and kissed her.

She tried to picture the child inside her. The mai had told her it lay with its head downwards, resting in her pelvis. How it suddenly decided it should be born, no one knew; perhaps it didn't decide for itself, but the gods decided. The mai was a devout Hindu who, although she had studied midwifery at the European hospital, was quite certain the gods had far more to do with conception and birth than British doctors might admit. 'A moment will arrive when baby and mother know the gods have decided the time is right for the birth,' she had said, with conviction. 'Sometimes there is a false start, but usually it will progress. Do nothing but accept it as happening and that it must happen. Do not anticipate, do not even attempt to use your mind. Let your brain sleep and your body do its natural work in its own way.'

The hills! For a few moments she remembered them and felt sad. It would have been better if her child, their child, could have been born in the hills. They were all she missed of her earlier life. Every day, since her own birth until she and Gerald had travelled from Dimapur, she had seen the hills. Gerald had replaced the security their presence gave to her, but she missed their lonely beauty. Even at Kohima where they had been scarred and polluted by the terrible battles, she had known that once men left, the hills would rejuvenate themselves; the rains would soften the craters, rot away the steel and bones, smooth the savaged earth; and the seeds of the jungle would germinate in the damp warmth and cloak the hills' obscenely exposed flesh.

'You will love the hills, too,' she told the unborn child. 'Your father and I will take you to them. Perhaps we will take you to the place where your father almost died for them. By the time you are old enough it will be beautiful again. You will stand with us, and look out over the valleys full of jungle, and the terraced fields of rice, and see the villages on the high ridges and the streams and waterfalls. And you will love the hills as we love them, and the hills will love you in return.'

Another contraction pulled at the lower muscles of her abdomen, forcing her to sit on the edge of the bed. She swung her feet up and lay on her side. The contraction had been more powerful, more positive, the pain a little sharper. It diminished slowly, like the uncoiling of a spring that had tightened on her swollen womb.

On the wall beyond the foot of the bed hung her crucifix. It had been the only personal possession she had brought from Kohima, and when she had left the dressing station to search for Gerald she had stuffed it into the small gunny-bag of medical equipment and field dressings she had taken. The wooden cross had been broken somewhere on the long journey through the jungle; the plaster figure had lost its feet and its paint was discoloured. She had repaired it with a strip of surgical plaster in the Dimapur hospital. Gerald had looked at her a little strangely when she had asked him to have it hung on the wall of their bedroom, but he had made no objection. Perhaps, she had thought, he would have preferred a new crucifix, a silver or brass one which might have blended in more attractively with the bedroom furnishings. But a new one would have been an insult to the original which had comforted her for so long.

She looked at it now, knowing the dark stain on one of the arms of the cross was blood; there had been others it had comforted, at Kohima.

'I must not think of death,' she told herself. 'I must think of life; think of the future.' University? Perhaps it was not too silly an idea. Perhaps it was a good idea, all of Aurobindo's ideas seemed good. He had insisted on her joining the Congress Party and she had met a lot of his friends at the few meetings she had been able to attend. It had enlarged their number of acquaintances in Calcutta, and even if Gerald hadn't, or didn't, want to actually participate in Indian politics, he never objected to her taking part. Perhaps when she was stronger again and had a little time to spare, she might also agree to Aurobindo's suggestion that she might like to serve on a committee formed to discuss the future of Assam and the Naga territories.

'It will all depend on you,' she said to her child. 'When you need me I will always be at your side. I promise you, you will never call my name and find yourself alone.'

The sheets on the bed were fresh, still crisp beneath her body and smelling faintly of the lavender water the dhobi-wallah sprayed on them once they had been bleached and dried in the sun. She stretched herself luxuriously. The pillows were soft beneath her head and shoulders. She was always conscious, sometimes with a feeling of guilt, of the luxury of the world in which she now lived. The Europeans seemed to be able to ignore the poverty surrounding them, or were so horrified by it that they blamed those who were suffering for its effect on their consciences. But she had been close to it. She had never starved perhaps, and she had never been forced to accept that an empty stomach and the hard ground for a bed were a normal part of her life. But she knew she had avoided it by the merest chance. She had watched the young prostitutes in Calcutta, shared a room with the dancing girls at Dimapur, and been aware that it was not a life they lived by choice. If they were lucky they worked for a dowry then went to some district where they were unknown and found themselves a husband; most didn't, either the madam of the brothel in which they worked kept them poor deliberately so that she might not lose their services, or they became ill and diseased and soon begged in the gutters.

'One day, my son, I will take you to my village, and you will sleep in my mamoon's basha, on a charpoy,' she told the child. 'It will smell of the paraffin that stops the bed-bugs from climbing the legs of the charpoy. But you may still get bitten by the ones which sometimes fall from the roof. And perhaps we will squat together in the doorway, and watch my aunt grinding corn for chapatti. We may even have a supper of curried eggs, and wash it down with a tin cup of goat's milk. I think it might do you good to know how so many of our people live. You may even enjoy it, for a while. Your father will stay in the Dak bungalow, with Rai to look after him; he will drink his whisky and tell you your mother is mad. But we might do it together, you and I.'

It was gone three a.m. when Alan potted pink then black and asked Gerald: 'Enough?'

Gerald grinned. '*Pax*. Five games to three. I'll get my revenge tomorrow evening.'

'This evening.' Alan said, looking at the clock. He followed Gerald out into the lounge. 'Mary will think you've deserted her.'

'Deserted her! You should know by now, if I deserted Mary she'd follow me to the ends of the earth.'

'Like a devoted dog.' Alan sounded displeased by Gerald's boast.

'God, no! I didn't mean it like that. Cigar?' He held a box towards Alan.

Alan took one, examined the tip and then sliced it with the cutter on the coffee table. 'You and I will kill ourselves with cigars and whisky at three in the morning.' He lit the cigar and then sat opposite Gerald. 'Well, old son, what's it been like?'

'Marriage, my wound, business?'

'All three.'

Gerald pondered for a while. 'If it hadn't been for Mary, everything would have been rotten. She's a brick as far as I'm concerned. Seems to be able to cope with anything, or anybody. It's almost uncanny; she senses things. Gets things correct that she's never done before. Puts up with a hell of a lot from me. I think I was pretty beastly to her for a while, only thought of myself, my damned back.'

'We knew it wouldn't be easy.'

'Easier for me than for her, though she'd never admit it.'

'I suppose you've had the usual problem with the Brits? Especially the women.'

Gerald nodded. 'Just as you warned. Some of them act like a pack of cats; nice enough when you face them, unpleasant when your back is turned. At first I thought Mary didn't notice, but she does. But she's got the best protection she could have ... a distinct indifference to them if they choose to behave like that. Her friends are people who like her, know her; she doesn't bother about the others. Anyway, we get more social invitations than we can accept, from Indians as well as the British. Hell, I should have warned you, we've got drinks tomorrow evening with the Viceroy's ADC. You're invited.'

'Thanks, that's the kind of relaxation I need after months upcountry. What about the back?' Alan blew a smoke ring and watched it swirl out of existence in the draught of the electric punkahs.

'Physiotherapy is down to twice a week. I'm supposed to do exercises every day, but I don't seem to find time. One thing you can say about it, it's pretty painless; just damned annoying. I got a hundred per cent from the Board as you'd expect; Christ, it's worth about a bottle of Scotch a week. It makes no difference to me, but how the hell they expect one of the lads to live on it back home God knows!' He nodded towards Alan's arm. 'Yours?'

Alan waved the stump. 'Think I'll get a hook rather than a wooden hand. Then if I can't find a bed for the night I can hang myself up in someone's wardrobe.' He laughed. 'Actually, you know they say you can still feel them when they're gone. Well, I get a pain in one of my missing fingers. It's damned aggravating when you can't rub it. And if I'm not careful I can still try to pick something up with the hand which isn't there; old habits die hard, and you can look a bit of a fool making vague passes at a whisky glass a few inches from the end of your wrist.' He laughed again. 'I think it's time we hit the sack, old chap.'

Gerald said: 'I'll put my feet up here. Wedge myself on the chesterfield.'

Alan looked concerned. 'Why? What on earth's the matter with your own bed?'

Gerald smiled. 'We had a cat once, Jane and I, when we were kids. It used to produce batches of kittens with zealous regularity. But whenever it was going to give birth it got a strange look in its eyes and went and found a spot where it wouldn't be disturbed. Mary's eyes had that same look this evening; distracted, dreamy. I won't sleep tonight ... I suppose I'm excited, too. I'll pop in every now and again and make sure she's all right, but I'll stay here.'

Alan grinned. 'That being the case, I'll keep you company.' He looked around. 'Better get the decanter, I suppose.'

James Nlamo Petrie was born at nine-fifteen a.m. on the seventeenth of December 1944. He received his christening three days later. His second name was that of Mary's late father.

CHAPTER NINE

CALCUTTA. JULY 1953

The second great war had ended eight years previously, in victory for the Allies. British India no longer existed. On 15 August 1947, and following the terrible religious killings of 1946 when five thousand men, women and children were massacred in Calcutta alone, India and Pakistan had become independent countries. Whether the latter could be claimed as a victory by anyone was a matter of opinion.

The Company, Petrie India, flourished. With the end of wartime constrictions on shipping, and wartime rationing, the business had expanded far beyond its pre-war capacity. Few of the Britons who had worked with the company prior to September 1939 now remained in its employ. Natural wastage, plus the exit of those who had decided they were unable to live in a country where they were no longer privileged citizens, had reduced British executive staff to less than a handful. Most of the major plantations were now managed by Indian nationals, and managed well and profitably. Only the tea plantation workers themselves resented the change; although former British managers would have found it hard to believe, the Indians proved far harder taskmasters to their own countrymen and women than their predecessors.

National disasters still occurred. The great Bengal famine of 1943 had fortunately not repeated itself, although people still starved. Droughts, cyclones and floods still devastated parts of the country. The latest horrific calamity had been the earthquake, epicentred in northern Assam; an estimated fifty thousand had died, some buried in the villages beneath the mountains which had been shaken down upon them, others of the cholera and plagues which followed.

None of the audience who listened to the speakers in Paramahamsa Hall in Calcutta had felt the tremors or witnessed the appalling carnage. The slides which they had seen projected on to the twelve-foot square screen were sepia-coloured and unable to reproduce either the crimson blood-soaked debris which had lain over the crushed bodies, or the terrible stink of death which pervaded the ruins of such villages as had escaped complete burial.

One speaker was a ten-year-old girl who had lost her parents, brothers and sisters, and every one of her known relatives. Her world had literally crumbled around her, leaving her unhurt beneath the fallen concrete blocks of her school until rescuers found her three days later. The other was a senior clerk of an upriver office of the Brahmaputra River Transport Company who had been visiting his elderly father in the stricken region. His father's village had been situated on a tributary of the river. He had felt the ground begin to vibrate beneath his feet, heard the terrible roar of rending earth, and seen the calm surface of the river begin to leap upwards in sharp pointed waves as though its bed were being struck from below by some gigantic steam-hammer. Great crevices had appeared in the earth to envelop those unfortunate enough to be caught by them; the structures of the village had collapsed, walls on inmates, thatched roofs on to cooking fires; dogs went insane, birds fell silent. The few bashas of the village which survived the earthquake were destroyed by the fires which blazed in its wake.

The remaining six speakers appealed to the audience for charity, for the charity of their organisations to swell the meagre funds available to help those who needed them so urgently. The last speaker had been Lady Petrie, Chairwoman of the Assam Educational Trust. She had spoken for twenty minutes, confidently and with a sincerity and concern that had brought the immediate promise of assistance from members of the audience. The hall was emptying now and Gerald waited for her at the steps leading from the platform.

One of the other speakers, an aide of the Minister of Internal Affairs, a good-looking Bengali of about forty years of age, intercepted her. 'That was excellent, Lady Mary, may I congratulate you on your oratory. It was very passionate. I felt myself reaching for my cheque book.'

Mary smiled innocently at him. 'If you care to get it out of your pocket, Mr Naoroji, I will be happy to receive your personal donation on behalf of the fund. None of us are exempted.'

Gerald coughed behind his hand to conceal his grin.

The aide, Motilal Naoroji, was confused. 'I meant it figuratively speaking, you understand. But naturally I will be pressing your case most forcefully with the Minister.'

'You may inform him I shall be pressing it myself, with the utmost determination. And I don't expect it to be passed from committee to committee before anything is done.'

The aide retreated, bowing. Mary joined Gerald.

'Well done.' Gerald pivoted his chair and matched its speed to her walk. 'If the audience reaction was anything to go by then you should get some of the help you need.'

'You know what we're like,' she told him. 'It will be proposed, amended, then amended again, argued and debated over, challenged and eventually agreed. In the meantime, ten thousand people will have died of hunger or sickness. All I can say is, perhaps in the end another ten thousand will be saved.'

Aurobindo Das and one of his senior reporters, a youthful, moustachioed man wearing European clothing and carrying his notebook, joined them near the doorway. Aurobindo took Mary's arm. 'Thank you.' He spoke to Gerald: 'And thank you, too.'

'I've done nothing. It's been Mary's show.'

'A hundred-thousand-rupee donation is hardly nothing, my friend,' said Aurobindo. 'And although you have claimed it was from Petrie India, I suspect that is not the truth. Such a donation would require the approval of your entire board, and you have not had the time ...'

Mary interrupted him. 'Gift horses, Aurobindo,' she said with mock severity.

Aurobindo laughed. 'Oh, I am not looking in his mouth, Lady Mary. It is more than I would dare. But, talking of mouths, I wonder if you would care to join me for dinner? I have a table booked at the Grand.'

Mary said to Gerald: 'I could telephone the house and ask Renana to put James to bed.'

'I promised him another chapter of *The Jungle Book*,' Gerald reminded her.

Mary smiled, knowing Gerald was voicing his own disappointment as much as anticipating that of James. He loved his son dearly, and enjoyed every moment of his company. Despite the fact that James could now read competently, the nightly half-hour story was a ritual Gerald hated missing. When James had been smaller, he had always listened, enthralled, on his father's knee, his eyes wide and sparkling. Now, the pair of them sat together in the lounge, and it was a time when Mary left them both alone. 'I think he will forgive you tonight.'

'I suppose so,' agreed Gerald. 'I'll ask Rai to speak to Renana and then Sekander can pick us up later; say at eleven.'

'We'd love to come then,' Mary told Aurobindo. 'We haven't eaten there for ages. We heard they have a new chef.'

At the hall doorway Rai saluted at Gerald's arrival, then eased his wheelchair down the two steps to the pavement. Sekander, at the wheel of the elderly but immaculate Bentley, was waiting at the kerbside.

The Grand itself had changed little since the first time Mary and Gerald had stayed there in 1944. Every now and then it had a new coat of paint, but structurally it was unaltered. Even the plants in their pots on the tall stands in the foyer seemed to be the same ones that had been there almost eight years before. The desk clerk in the reception was the same man; but older, balder, stouter and even more obsequious to those he knew.

'My lord ...' His voice pierced the flight-weary chatter of the group of exhausted American tourists waiting to book in at his desk. The clerk had broken his conversation to one of them in mid-word as he recognised Gerald and hurried around the desk to greet him. The Americans' eyes followed him. 'My lord,' said the clerk again when he was a yard away from Gerald, 'you will be wanting our best suite, of course, my lord.'

'I'm afraid that tonight we are requiring only your restaurant, Mr De,' Gerald said.

The clerk was unabashed and delighted Gerald had used his name. His smile broadened. 'Never mind, my lord. The hotel is always at your very welcome disposal. I am sincerely hoping that yourself and Lady Mary will be enjoying your repast.' He made a low sweeping bow as Gerald wheeled the chair towards the restaurant doors. As the clerk returned to his desk Gerald heard him speaking loudly for the benefit of the tourists: 'A most extremely important man. A British lord. And with him is Lady Mary, a very titled Indian lady who is most famous here in Calcutta.'

'I wish to God he wouldn't do that,' grunted Gerald.

'He's only trying to be polite,' explained Mary.

'But I'm not a lord.'

'He doesn't know that. To him a baronet is a lord. And it really doesn't matter.' She paused inside the restaurant doors as the head waiter came towards them. 'Ah, there's Aurobindo. He's beaten us here.' She led Gerald towards Aurobindo's table, the head waiter fussing beside them.

Eyes watched them as they made their way past the other tables. Times had certainly changed, Gerald thought. Once the eyes would have been those of British women, questioning, disapproving their arrival. Now there were more Indians in the place than Europeans, and most of those were tourists. Many of the Indians knew Mary and greeted her courteously as she passed them, smiling her own recognition and pausing briefly to speak to those who were her friends.

Accompanying Mary, Gerald felt immense satisfaction. He was proud of the confidence she had developed, and the subtle elegance she had added to her beauty. To please him she had grown her hair long again so that now it fell below her shoulder blades. Today, because the afternoon had been a formal occasion, she wore it in a broad plait which drew the hair from her forehead, but Gerald preferred it when it hung loose, sweeping her shoulders and framing the fine lines of her face, presenting, he felt, a softer, more real image of her character.

Aurobindo stood while the head waiter settled Mary in her seat and then removed a chair to make room for Gerald. When he had spun his wheelchair into place she took his hand and held it on her lap. He was conscious of the warmth of her thighs through the cloth of her sari. Even after years of marriage the touch of her body gave him a thrill of pleasure.

She spoke to Aurobindo. 'He is cross.'

Aurobindo said: 'I expect he is tired.'

Gerald smiled. 'I wish you two wouldn't talk about me as though I'm deaf.' Mary leant towards him and kissed his cheek. 'That's better.'

'Lady Mary tells me you are thinking of going home for a visit,' said Aurobindo. Somehow, during their friendship, he had managed to make the title he insisted on using sound part of her name so that it had now become informal.

'England's not home, Aurobindo,' corrected Gerald. 'It's just where I lived during my school and college days. Yes, I think we have to make the trip. I've avoided it long enough. Counting the war, I've been out here ten years.'

'And his mother is getting old,' Mary added.

'That's not the reason for the visit. Dammit, if I dropped dead tomorrow Mother wouldn't pause in her game of bridge to say Amen! From what Jane told us when she was over here, my name is taboo. I never get a reply to my letters or invitations and the only communication is an annual Christmas card with a five pound note in it to young James, from his loving Grandma.'

The conversation paused momentarily as they gave their orders to the khidmutgar, then Mary said: 'We're not going immediately. I couldn't anyway, not with my present commitments. We're leaving in mid-August, flying back by Super Constellation. James is very excited at the prospect of a flight; I shall be terrified.'

'James will be staying in the UK for his schooling?' questioned Aurobindo.

'I hope you're not going to make a big story of a Petrie India director taking his child away from India for his education?' Gerald thought he had seen a quick look of disapproval in Aurobindo's eyes when he had spoken.

'Of course not. You are quite correct to send him to school there. The British education is undoubtedly better than ours at present. But, perhaps things will be different by the time James has a son of his own. I certainly hope so. You will miss him,' he said to Mary.

'Yes, I will miss him.' More than anyone will ever know, she thought. 'But Gerald will miss him, too. Very much. They spend so much time together. Cricket ...'

'One-handed, and with one of our malis doing my running for me,' interjected Gerald.

'And tennis ...'

'Just so long as he keeps hitting the ball straight back at me.'

Aurobindo laughed. 'Children can keep you very occupied.'

'You keep my wife occupied,' said Gerald with mock seriousness. 'You and your committees, Aurobindo, and your debates.'

'I have only showed her the way. She occupies herself.' Aurobindo was momentarily defensive. 'Anyway, my friend, you can hardly blame Congress for making use of her. In this country we have many workers, and quite a few intellectuals. But a combination of the two, an intellectual who is actually prepared to work, is rare indeed.'

'Intellectual is a stupid word.' Mary wrinkled her nose disgustedly. 'Everyone is an intellectual of one kind or another. It means nothing more than the ability to receive and comprehend information ...'

'As distinct from merely experiencing,' interrupted Aurobindo. 'You reason, Lady Mary, and you understand.'

'And you flatter too much.'

Dinner in Aurobindo's company always had a disquieting effect on Mary's mind, stirring around ideas and forcing it to a state of activity from which it took hours to return.

Her mind was too awakened now to sleep. Gerald had already bathed and retired to bed. The interior of the villa was silent. In the trees beyond the new tennis court an owl was calling for a mate, shrill whistling cries that pierced the still night air and brought answers from the forest canopy across the river. Behind the shrubbery the chokidar's paraffin lantern glowed as he made his hourly rounds of the walls, talking to himself as he did so. He would have claimed the one-sided conversation was necessary because he lacked companionship in his lonely occupation, but both Mary and Gerald suspected the chokidar feared stumbling on some knife-carrying hur who might have decided to attempt to rob their villa. Crime had greatly increased since Partition and night prowlers were a common hazard in the residential areas.

She searched the bookshelves for a favourite novel which might hurry her mind to the calmness sleep required, then sat near a solitary table lamp reading the book's familiar words. They failed to penetrate her mind.

Once, she had thought, perhaps Aurobindo's plan was to draw her away from her family for his obscure reason, but this she had realised was not so. Whatever it was he planned included them all, even James ... perhaps the latter more than Gerald and herself. He had shown a close interest in the boy since the day of his birth, almost as if he had been a relative of his own family, a fond nephew.

Since the day of his birth ... her mind repeated her unspoken words. Almost nine years ago! Nine years since she had lain waiting in her bed; waiting for so long, and with such absorption she had delayed calling for the mai until it was almost too late. The midwife had arrived only minutes before James had thrust himself eagerly into the world. Almost nine years.

It seemed impossible that the girl she could remember from before then had been herself. She had thought herself so educated at Gauhati; only the aiya, the khansama and herself had been able to read and write more than their own names, and the other servants and their wives had been envious. What would they think of her now, she wondered? Many would never have heard of a university. University! That too had been Aurobindo's idea; she had laughed the first time he suggested it. She resisted until James had been two years old, when she had realised his future education could be assisted by her own. Even then, she had thought university an impossibility, but encouragement from Gerald and the help of several private tutors had eventually enabled her to matriculate and apply for a place; she suspected Aurobindo's influence might have been used, but he had denied it when she questioned him. She had found the study hard but enjoyed the lectures and the reading. She had been proud when she received her degree.

For nearly a decade, Gerald had been crippled. But since the night when he had first managed to bathe himself, the important night when he had first made love to her as her husband, he had never once admitted either pain or frustration. To him, climbing into his wheelchair was no different from someone else putting on their shoes before going out, or so he claimed. But sometimes, as he watched James playing in the garden, she knew by his eyes he dearly wanted to be running beside him, chasing him, kicking his football between imaginary goal posts, enjoying a greater share of his son's childhood.

Nine years. And Gerald had worked hard, too; visiting factories and go-downs, spending long hours at the office with the head clerks of the departments, memorising procedures and documents until he was able to accept that his title of India Director had been earned. He now spoke Hindi fluently. Everson had left, retired to England, as had the Warrens, and many of the British India hands had gone.

Mary chuckled to herself at the memory of the Warrens' last

evening in India. Gerald had insisted they should come to dinner and though Evelyn Warren had been obviously embarrassed by the suggestion, they were forced to accept. Mary and Gerald had concocted a small joke together; the dinner which was served was totally Indian, with the table prepared without a single piece of cutlery and the food extremely hot and heavily spiced. Evelyn Warren had spent her last night in India red-faced and unable to maintain her dignity; Jack Warren had got drunk, enjoyed himself and not bothered to try.

Those British who came to work in India now did so with a different attitude to their former colonialist relations. In a few places the old attitudes still persisted, but they were quickly dying as those who sought vainly to maintain them retired or were replaced.

Nine years. Years of loving Gerald, and being loved in return. Nine years of dividing her affections between her husband and son; so like his father in many ways, even if there was little resemblance in looks. She had hoped he would be tall and blond, blue-eyed; he was slender and would be as tall as his father, perhaps taller, but his eyes and colouring were hers, and his hair as jet as her own; a determined, strong-willed boy who played every one of his games as though his life depended on its outcome. She would miss him terribly when he stayed in England at school.

'Daughter.' It was Rai's voice, soft, interrupting her thoughts. He used the name only when they were alone together, when he sensed she might appreciate this small sign of his affection for her. He never used it publicly, never within Gerald's earshot. It was something only they shared, and others might not understand. He put a cup and saucer on the table at her side. 'I saw by the light you were not sleeping, and thought you would like cocoa.'

She said: 'Thank you, Rai.'

He stood for a moment, hesitatingly. 'I listened at the hall tonight. What you said was good. More people should hear what you say, not only the important ones.' He paused. 'Once, a very long time ago, I thought you were a Lushai monkey trying to be a memsah'b. I discovered quickly I was wrong. Tonight, when I heard you say the Brahmins, Khattriyas, Vaisyas and Sudras must throw aside their castes and act together to help others raise themselves, I knew you had been born a strong woman.'

*

The next day was Saturday. By mid-morning the July heat was already uncomfortably oppressive as the sun sucked the moisture of the delta swamps into the laden air above Calcutta and its suburbs. As Gerald remarked to James at breakfast, he would not have been surprised to see flying-fish amongst the exhausted birds in the garden treetops. James giggled at the idea.

They had planned the day to please James, knowing that soon they would miss the sound of his laughter, his exuberant company. He had chosen first to visit Chowringhee market where, a friend had told him, one of the stall holders had a tame tiger cub for sale; he was optimistic but not hopeful of his chances of persuading his father to purchase it. In the afternoon there was to be a picnic while watching a match between a Marwari team and the local players at the polo ground where he was learning to ride, and the day would be rounded off by a visit to the Swimming Club before returning home.

As James had correctly surmised, he failed to convince his father of the need to own a rapidly growing carnivore of doubtful temperament; the stall owner had several recent scars on his arms and was prepared to sell the tiger cub for a ridiculously low sum of money, following them for forty or fifty yards through the market and dropping his price with every couple of paces. It had been difficult to dissuade the persistent trader. Later Gerald had bought James a tuck-box, the strength of which had been demonstrated by its vendor leaping up and down on the lid; a sales technique which went someway towards compensating James for his failure to acquire a tiger. Mary made several domestic purchases, leaving Gerald and James to wander through the market area followed by a hamal with James's new box on his head.

They lunched at the Queens, enjoying the cool air-conditioned atmosphere and the peace of its restaurant after the crowded bedlam of the market. Even James was reluctant to leave the comfort of the hotel for the humidity outside, and seemed happy to allow his parents to prolong tiffin through the hottest time of the day and take their coffee in the spacious lounge afterwards.

By the time they reached the polo ground a few miles west of Dum-Dum, it was three-thirty and the first chukka had begun. The game was an important one of the cup series and had drawn a good crowd of spectators, Indian and European. The ground itself was in a pleasant rural situation, bordered on three sides by agricultural plantations with natural hedges of dense bamboo, and on the fourth by a stretch of overgrown woodland, the property of the club.

The clubhouse and bar, open to members of the public for the duration of the match, was a two-storey bungalow; its private enclosure large enough to permit spectators to sit in comfort and view the matches while attended by the bar stewards. Backing it, and the narrow gardens which surrounded the building, was the woodland; greener and less dusty looking than any near the city.

The stabling, medical tent and training area were a hundred yards away to the left of the building, and included the practice nets where players could sit on artificial wooden horses and hit polo balls which were returned to them by the surrounding net and the slope of the concrete. A few sweetmeat vendors were permitted in the grounds, under the watchful eyes of a number of Sikh policemen carrying shotguns by their slings around their shoulders. Since the riots of Partition the police were always armed when they were expected to deal with crowds.

Sekander drove the car as close as possible to the cutcha path leading to the clubhouse, then unloaded Gerald's wheelchair and assisted him into it. When all his passengers had dismounted and were making their way towards the building, the chauffeur reversed the vehicle and drove it across the grass of a paddock to the shade of the trees where several other cars were parked. He knew it would be at least an hour and a half before his master and mistress would be requiring their picnic, so he strolled across to the side of the ground to watch the progress of the game.

There were a number of tables set on the enclosure lawn below the clubhouse verandah and Mary and Gerald decided to sit at one of these. James, activated by his lunch and the excitement of the spectators, begged to be permitted to wander off on his own. Gerald warned him not to get in the way of the ponies as they came from the ground, and to stay within sight, and then let him go.

A bearer waited silently until the boy had run towards the edge of the field near the goal posts, and then asked: 'Drinks, sah'b?'

Mary fanned herself with her hand. 'Lemonade, please.'

'And a beer. Heineken. Make sure it's cold if possible.'

The bearer nodded.

There was perspiration running down Gerald's face with the exertion of propelling his wheelchair. The front of his cotton shirt was stained by his sweat. He pulled it away from his skin and flapped it. 'I think we should go to the hills in future in July or August. It's too damned hot here.'

'To Assam?'

'Why not? I have to make fairly regular visits, it's just a matter of timing them differently. It would be a lot cooler up there.'

'It would be nice to go together, to see it again. I was thinking last night, we must take James.'

'There would be time during his Easter holidays,' Gerald said. 'We could fly up to Gauhati and drive from there.'

'Would you want to visit Kohima?' Mary asked, uncertain as to her own feelings and curious about Gerald's.

'It wouldn't mean much to James.' Gerald's reply was evasive.

'It might. He knows quite a lot about it. But that wasn't what I asked you.'

'Sometimes, I still dream about the place. I suppose we'll never forget. Perhaps I should go back, to lay ghosts.'

Mary frowned. 'That would be wrong.' She quoted Edmonds's lines that were cut into the stone of the British memorial at the battleground cemetery. '"When you go home, Tell them of us and say, For their tomorrow We gave our today." Lord Mountbatten said it was the most important battle of the Far East war. It would be wrong to lay the ghosts of the men who died in it. That will happen soon enough without our seeking it.'

The bearer put glasses on the table and handed Gerald a chit to sign. Gerald did so, and as the bearer began to leave put his hand in the breast pocket of his shirt and then said: 'Damn!' He called to the bearer. 'Can you get me some cigarettes?'

The bearer shook his head apologetically. 'I am sorry, sah'b. So many people here, we have no cigarettes.' His face brightened. 'We have cigar, sah'b. Being made in Holland. Tasting very nice indeed.'

'No thanks.'

'Very good, sah'b.'

'I thought you filled your case before we came out,' said Mary.

'I did. Left the damn thing in the glove compartment of the car.'

The crowd of spectators were loudly cheering the dash of a home player, forcing Mary to raise her voice. 'When James returns, you can ask him to fetch it for you.'

Gerald took a quick swig of the iced beer and then wiped the thin line of froth from his lips. The swell of noise fell as a Marwari intercepted the ball and home team player and then galloped the ball upfield. 'I'll trundle over and get them myself.' He released the wheelchair brake and pushed against the wheel. 'Back shortly.' A couple of yards from the table he stopped the chair, spun it to face Mary and rolled it to her side. He leant forward and kissed her.

'What have I done to deserve that?'

'I always kiss you when I leave you.' He grinned at her, with a foolish schoolboy expression on his face.

'That is poor compensation for showing you prefer your cigarettes to my company,' said Mary, jokingly. 'I shall find myself a more caring gentleman while you are gone.'

Gerald laughed, turned his chair again and began wheeling it towards the Bentley two hundred yards away beneath the shade trees.

Mary watched him go, knowing once he left the comparative smoothness of the pathway it would be difficult for him, but that even if Sekander noticed him and attempted to help, the chauffeur would be rebuffed. Gerald was fiercely independent and only prepared to accept assistance when it was totally impossible for him to manage on his own. She could see the powerful muscles of his arms rippling as he pushed at the wheels to move the chair from the path to the grass of the paddock.

She searched her handbag to find her sunglasses, then leant back in her chair and closed her eyes. She had slept little the previous night. The sounds of the crowd were like waves on the beach where they had holidayed the previous year. It had been the first time she had seen the full magnificence of the ocean and she had spent hours just staring across its vast azure surface towards an unknown horizon. Its mysteries had frightened her but the sound it made had been soporific. She dozed now.

'Mummy.' James's voice beside her, too close to her ear, jarred her fully awake. 'Can I have a drink, please? Where's Daddy?' He gave her no time to answer either question. 'The game's super. When the bell rang for the second chukka, Mr Mukkerjee's pony stopped dead and tossed him over its neck.' He threw himself on to the chair beside her. 'I'm very thirsty. Mr Mukkerjee said a very rude word. I think if there hadn't been so many people watching he might have hit the pony. Is Daddy in the club?'

'He went to fetch his cigarettes,' answered Mary. She looked at James, his shirt was soaked with perspiration and his face florid with the heat. She brushed damp hair from his eyes and persisted as he turned his head away from her hand. 'Sit quietly and cool down. When the bearer comes, I'll ask him to get you a lemonade.'

'An orange, please.' He let his shoulders sag. 'Phew! Everything is so hot today. The ponies have got foam all over them. Daddy's a long time.'

'No, I don't think ...' How long had she dozed, she wondered? She tried to see Gerald but a section of the crowd had moved and obscured her view of the parking area. She glanced at her watch, it was four-thirty. Gerald had probably been gone for half an hour! That was too long a time for a short trip to the car. Perhaps he was talking to a friend. She felt suddenly uneasy.

James climbed on to the seat of his chair and peered over the crowd.

'James, please get down. Seats aren't made for feet.'

James pointed. 'I can see Daddy. He's just a little way from the car.'

'Is he coming back?'

'He's flopping.'

'Flopping?'

'And sort of waving his arms in a funny way. Mummy ...'

Mary was already on her feet. The feeling of uneasiness had become one of dread. 'Stay where you are,' she ordered James. He knew by the tone of her command not to argue. 'Wait for us here.' She hurried past the edge of the crowd of spectators, her eyes searching the paddock and the line of cars. Then she saw Gerald. He was some thirty yards from the Bentley, slumped sideways in the wheelchair, his left arm dangling and moving feebly. She began running. When she was closer she called his name, at first hopefully and then with desperation. The crowd nearest to her turned to watch in astonishment as she tripped, sprawled her full length in the grass, then stumbled to her feet to continue wildly towards him.

One of the Sikh policemen on the outskirts of the crowd followed her with his eyes, then saw the wheelchair and its occupant. He ran a diagonal path to her own to arrive at the wheelchair only a moment behind her.

Gerald's body was held in the chair by the padded arm. His chin was on his chest and a dribble of saliva ran from his lips. His right arm twitched, hanging beside the wheel.

'Gerald!' She said his name loudly, and tried to sit him upright in the chair, but he was too heavy for her to move. He made no response.

The Sikh spoke in Hindi. 'It may be his heart.' He took hold of Gerald's shoulders, lifted him from the wheelchair and laid him on the grass. The chair tilted and fell on its side. There was a youth nearby with a tray of cakes he was fanning with a piece of palm leaf to keep off flies. The policeman called to him. 'You. Go and fetch the doctor.'

The boy shrugged. The Sikh was instantly angry. 'Put your tray down. Go at once. The doctor is in the tent beside the stables.' He glowered furiously. 'No one will steal your cakes. Run quickly.' Mary was cradling Gerald's head on her lap as she knelt beside him.

She could feel the cold dampness of his skin against her hands. His lips were a strange blue. His breathing was irregular, frightening; his body jerking as it fought to drag the heavy air into his chest with deep gasping convulsions.

'My darling, my darling . . .' She was repeating the words over and over again, rocking the upper part of her body backwards and forwards just as she had comforted James in her arms during his childhood sicknesses. Gerald's eyes were open but she knew he could not see her. His heart? Perhaps the Sikh was correct; the heat and the exertion.

The Sikh asked: 'Is he always ill?'

She understood it as a reference to the wheelchair, and shook her head. 'He is very strong. But he was wounded during the war.'

The Sikh, with a row of campaign ribbons on his uniform, nodded. 'Perhaps then it is his wound. It sometimes happens afterwards; after many years.' A crowd was gathering around them, curious. The Sikh shouted at them. 'Move back. This man is sick.'

Mary heard someone say in English: 'Good heavens, it's Sir Gerald Petrie; looks as though the fellow's had a stroke.'

Sekander pushed his way through and dropped to his knees beside her. 'Ma'am, what is wrong? Oh dear! I will get the motorcar and we will take him to the hospital.' He stood, expecting her confirmation.

'Wait.' The Sikh spoke to him. 'The doctor has been sent for. He will decide what should be done.' The policeman unbuttoned the lower part of Gerald's shirt and put his ear to his chest for a few moments, but said nothing when he straightened again.

There was more movement at the rim of the growing crowd, and then a European's voice. 'Let me get through, you idiots.' The voice changed to Hindi. 'Make way, quickly.' A lightly built man, his tanned skin contrasting sharply with the whiteness of his shirt and shorts, placed a medical bag beside Gerald and then squatted by Mary. She recognised him as Stefan Poulis, a Greek doctor who was a member of the polo club and acted as their medical officer. Poulis saw the look of fear in her eyes. 'Don't worry, Lady Petrie. It may just be heat exhaustion.' His calm voice comforted her. He leant forward and examined Gerald's eyes, moving the lids higher with his thumb. Then he opened his medical bag and pulled out a stethoscope, clipping it to his ears and listening to Gerald's heartbeat. He frowned. 'What happened?'

Mary answered him, her voice thin, tremulous. 'I don't know. He went to the car to get cigarettes. We just saw him, slumped in his wheelchair!'

Poulis was holding Gerald's wrist in his hand. 'Do you have a rug in your car?'

Mary said: 'I think so.'

'I will get it, doctor sah'b,' Sekander volunteered quickly, happy to be able to do something helpful.

'What is the matter with him?' Mary questioned.

Poulis shook his head. 'It looks like a collapse of the central nervous system. Sir Gerald was wounded in the spine, I believe. It may be something to do with that ... but it seems more cerebral ...'

A horrified shout interrupted him. Sekander's voice, wild, terrified, in Hindi. 'Snake, snake. There is a big snake.'

The crowd scattered sharply, backing away from Sekander who was twenty yards from them near the front of the Bentley. He was staring at something writhing in the long grass. The Sikh policeman swung his shotgun from his shoulder and ran to Sekander loading the gun with cartridges from his bandolier as he did so. He aimed the gun downwards; there were two sudden, loud explosions and a cloud of brown dust kicked up from the grass.

Doctor Poulis exclaimed: 'Snakebite; that's it!' He examined Gerald's legs, pulling his trousers above his calves. On his left leg, above the thin anklebone, the wasted muscle was punctured and torn where long fangs had chewed.

The Sikh policeman dragged a twisting headless carcass through the horrified crowd and dropped it a few feet away.

'Cobra. Its back was broken. I think the chair wheel must have run over it.'

Mary grabbed at Gerald's leg, trying to get her mouth over the seeping wound. Poulis stopped her, pushing his arm across her chest. 'No. That's no good. It chewed very deep; I imagine with his paralysis, he didn't feel the attack. Didn't defend himself.' He pulled a tourniquet from his bag and wound it tightly around Gerald's thigh as he continued talking. 'We must get him to hospital as fast as possible. Perhaps it is a good thing he is paralysed, any movement of his limbs would speed the flow of venom in the veins. It may save his life.'

May save his life ... the words terrified Mary. Only, may save? Dear God, she prayed, don't let him die. Don't take him away from me. She bit her knuckles. 'Gerald ... Gerald.'

'Mummy.' James's arms were around her shoulders as she knelt.

Doctor Poulis spoke to Sekander and the policeman. 'Help me get him to the car. And be careful how you lift him, keep his head and chest higher than his legs.'

She heard James's voice, pitched higher than usual with his concern. 'What's the matter with Daddy?'

The journey to the hospital was a nightmare, the time exaggerated by urgency. Sekander drove fiercely, the heavy Bentley lurching and bouncing over the pot-holed road, its tyres screeching on the hot tarmac of the bends, scattering gravel. Traffic in the suburbs slowed them only little as he wove through it, the twin horns blaring.

The vehicle was a stinking oven. Doctor Poulis crouched uncomfortably on the floor in the back, holding Gerald near-upright on the seat. Mary was in the front, kneeling and facing backwards. She had heard James retch beside her and was unable to help him.

Porters at the hospital, encouraged to haste by the doctor's commands, lifted Gerald on to a stretcher and hurried him into the building. Mary, James dragging at her sari and still carsick, followed them.

In the casualty emergency room a Bengali houseman was already filling a syringe from a bottle he had taken from the refrigerator, holding the instrument upright close to his eyes. He handed it to Poulis who had been cleaning Gerald's forearm with cotton wool and surgical spirit. Poulis ran the needle deep into a flattened vein and injected the fluid, then turned slowly to face Mary, his shoulders slumping as he relaxed. 'Now all we can do is wait and hope.' He dropped the syringe into a kidney bowl and took her arm. 'Don't stay in here. It does no good. Come and sit outside in the waiting room, I'll get us all cups of tea. And I think, perhaps, you should have some Codeine tablets.'

A young nurse was undressing Gerald while the houseman wiped the perspiration and spittle from his face. He is so pale, thought Mary. So very white that even his tan seems to have gone. She resented Poulis's insistent grip on her arm but allowed him to lead her from the room. She looked back over her shoulder. Gerald's face was calm, as though he merely slept.

'Snakes are horrible. I hate them. But Daddy will be all right.' James's statement, she knew, was reassurance for himself.

Snakebite! A danger she seldom considered. Some Europeans were almost obsessed by their fear of the reptiles, but if you grew up in a country which had so many of them then you accepted them; you respected them and disliked them, but the precautions you took were natural, almost inherited. If you lived in a basha, it was automatic to look beneath your charpoy and shake out your bedclothes before sleeping; and to step from the bed each morning so your feet weren't placed within reach of a krait that might have slipped in during the night and was lying hidden beneath the charpoy. It was natural to keep a sharp look-out if you walked through long grass, especially near wet ditches or the damp roots of trees or bamboos. And you never picked anything up from the ground without making certain nothing lay concealed beneath it. But Gerald, and in his wheelchair, had probably not even noticed the snake. As the doctor had said, with his paralysis he would not have even felt its bite, not known the cause of the sickness that had suddenly overwhelmed him, preventing him from shouting for help. 'Oh, Gerald,' her mind gently admonished him. 'You never like us to help you, but you need us so much. If Rai had been with us he could have gone for your cigarettes. Even had you allowed Sekander to push you, he would have probably seen the cobra; we Indians have a kind of sixth sense which warns us about snakes. Perhaps we instinctively know the places where we are most likely to encounter them.'

A student nurse, a dark-skinned Madrasi girl, brought them mugs of tea, so sweetened with cane sugar that it was almost syrup. The waiting area was briefly noisy with the arrival of a stonemason who had been knocked from his bicycle by a passing lorry which had failed to stop. The man's wrist was badly broken; probably a calamity which would affect the lives of his entire family for weeks to come. It was set and plastered in a nearby cubicle and they heard the man's moans fade, muffled, beneath the anaesthetic gas.

'Will Daddy have to stay in here?' asked James. She heard the worry in his voice; a child's genuine concern.

'For a little while, I expect. Until he's well again.' Please, for not too long, she prayed. The villa was always empty without him, the bed in their room seeming to treble in size making her feel small and lonely at night. She tried to remember how long it might take to get over snakebite, and with a sudden horror realised she knew of no one in her village in Assam who had ever survived the bite of a large cobra. The thought that there had been no serum available for them helped quieten her disturbed mind.

'The positive elements of mentation are constructive,' one of her professors had once said. 'The negative, destructive.' He had been a deeply religious man. 'It makes no difference whether you are Hindu, Muslim or Christian, prayer is by its very nature positive because it is based on total trust of an almighty being.' She remembered his words now, and those of the Twenty-third Psalm: 'Yeah though I walk through the valley of the shadow of death ...'

'What did you say, Mummy?'

She had not realised she had begun reciting the psalm aloud, and caught James's wide brown eyes watching her. 'I was just talking to God,' she explained softly.

'Shall I talk to Him as well?'

'If you like.'

'What shall I say?'

'Ask Him to make Daddy better, quickly.' She remembered how she had prayed when she and the Nagas had found Gerald in the jungle. God had been kind, then.

She saw the face of the young houseman at the oval window in the emergency room door and attempted to interpret his expression. He beckoned to Poulis. The doctor disappeared inside for a short while, and then returned. Mary stood as the door opened and her heart sank as the doctor came towards her; there was no reassuring smile.

'Lady Petrie, I'm very sorry ... I'm afraid we lost him.'

I'm afraid we lost him! Lost him ... lost him ... she felt the strength leaving her legs, a darkness clouding her brain, the room tilting, swaying. Doctor Poulis's arms steadied her, helped her back into the hard wooden seat.

James's voice. 'Mummy, where is Daddy lost?' The room steadied. She put her arms around him and held him very close.

Stefan Poulis said gently: 'We really didn't have a chance, it was just too late for the serum. I think it would be sensible for you to go home now. I'll come along with you.'

'I have to see him.' Her voice sounded foreign to her own ears.

'I understand. The boy can wait with me, here.' Stefan Poulis took James from her. James struggled to follow her, but Doctor Poulis held him firmly. 'She'll be back in a minute, James. You have to help her now. She'll need you, do you understand?' James shook his head tearfully.

Mary walked slowly to the operating table where Gerald lay. His body had been covered to his neck with a white sheet which hung almost to the floor on either side. The nurse and houseman stood, silent, motionless. Tears ran down the young nurse's face, darkening the neck of her starched uniform where they fell from her chin. She made no attempt to stem them.

'We have lost him ...' the doctor had said. I have lost him, Mary thought. I have lost the most precious thing in my life; I would gladly have died for him a hundred times.

She smoothed his blond hair with her fingers, feeling its softness, then let her hand run gently down his cheek. The skin was already unnaturally cold. His mouth was slightly open and she could see his white, even teeth. She stooped and kissed his forehead.

Can you feel my lips? she asked him silently. Are you watching me from somewhere, sharing and understanding my sorrow? Are you beside me now, feeling the terrible yearning of my love for you?

She heard his voice, distantly as though carried from afar by the wind, but distinct. 'And I love you, my darling. I love you.'

Somehow she controlled her grief until the silent aiya put James to bed that night, then she wept.

PART II

CHAPTER TEN

CALCUTTA/LONDON. OCTOBER 1953

The baroque and rodomontade architecture of the Victorian tombs gave the northern end of Park Street Burial Ground the appearance of a horror movie set. Unlike the cemeteries of British towns and cities where the poor outnumber the rich and even the most outrageous extravagances of the wealthy are compensated by the meagre graves of their workers, in nineteenth-century Calcutta there had been few impoverished Europeans and their mausoleums were a final ostentatious indication of the status their families believed they had attained; the bodies of their inferiors did not share the same hallowed ground but had been drifted down the river as ash or fed to the vultures in the bone-heaped funeral towers, some to be further exploited by being shipped to England as rearticulated skeletons for medical students or ground into dust with the bones of animals and used as fertiliser on rosebeds.

As the power and wealth of the Victorians had diminished so had the size of their tombs, and the old section of the churchyard seemed to tumble towards the modern where more austere but acceptable tombstones and graves dissected the sward beneath the shade of the pepals and neems. Between old and new stood the church, built in replica of the Norman edifice in a Suffolk village so that its expatriate congregation could, at least on their Sabbaths, imagine they were gentlefolk celebrating the Lord's Day in the distant civilisation of their homeland.

Sekander had switched off the engine of the Bentley and it was parked outside the gates, protected from the heat of the mid-day sun by the shadows of the trees lining the road. It rocked gently on its springs as James fidgeted, kneeling on the seat and watching through the rear window of the car. He could not see his father's grave, but saw his mother a hundred and fifty yards away pause, then stoop until she was hidden by the uneven walls of headstones. He had anticipated the boredom and discomfort of waiting in the overheated car when Mary had refused to allow him to accompany her. He had not really understood her reasons for wanting to be alone in the cemetery. It was not as though his father was really there, not as though you could touch him; it was just a piece of uninteresting ground and a grey polished slab of marble. He had felt cross for a few moments but Alan had distracted him by reminding him that in only two hours he would be in an aircraft and on his way to England.

The boy rested his elbows on the windowledge and made faces at his reflection in the glass. He yawned, deliberately loudly, then said: 'Mummy looks like an angel.'

'Yes, she does.' Alan had watched her walk away from the car, her white sari giving her a look of biblical purity, but he knew the outward serenity concealed her true feelings from her son, and this further parting from Gerald was almost as much as she could bear. There had been many times in the past ten weeks since Gerald's death when Alan had wanted to take her in his arms to comfort her; when he had wanted to tell her: 'Begin again with me, I understand how much you loved him, understand I can never replace him but please accept my love for what it is. At least it is here, available and very real.' He knew if he had spoken she would have rebuffed him, perhaps have been deeply hurt by what she might consider a disloyalty to his dead friend, even if she accepted his sincerity. He had remembered his own feelings after Angharad's death, the depth of misery which had flooded his life when she had lain unmoving, her pale face resting on his chest. He had tried to will life back to her through the pulse of his own heartbeats and had cursed a god so cruel as to take away from him the only being he held dear. He knew he too would have resented anyone's attempt to replace her and her memory in any way; it had been three or four years before even purely sexual desire had occurred, and he had never expected to feel anything more than friendship or regard for another woman. Time, he knew, healed the wound, dimmed the memories, replaced them by need; the old love remained, and was loyal and eternal, but time made room in a human soul for new love.

The sound of Mary's voice when she had telephoned him the morning after Gerald's death was still fresh enough to haunt him. It had been the voice of a desolate child, a voice so emptied of its character by the wretchedness of those first heartsick hours that it had been unrecognisable. He had flown down to Calcutta immediately, arriving at Kimberley that evening. Despite her invitation to stay in the house and his own longing to be close to her, he had booked himself into the Grand; somehow it had seemed more respectful to Gerald's memory. He had returned to Assam a few days after the funeral, feeling for the first time that instead of going back to his home, he was leaving it. He had arranged to take his accumulated leave a month later and for the past five weeks had been in Calcutta with most of his time spent in Mary's company. Slowly her burden of sadness was diminishing, but even though Gerald was dead, she was keeping as much of him alive as she was able, treasuring his wishes, the plans they had made together, as a jilted bride might treasure the mummifying petals of her bouquet while dreaming of a future that no longer existed. Alan knew, had she been alone and without her son's love and need for her, perhaps without his own affection, like the lover's rose she would have faded, crumbled to dust.

Alan had used James as a weapon to protect her. It was through him, he had insisted, she would survive, must survive. The future which she assumed lost was now James's future, owed to Gerald.

Her mind had seized on the idea as though it were a lifebelt tossed to a drowning man in a wild sea. Over the past weeks her son's future had become an obsession, her mind seeking and analysing long-past conversations she had held with Gerald about James, questioning even her definitions of Gerald's wishes so that there might be no doubt she would fulfil them as he would have done himself, overlooking nothing.

It was not exactly as Alan had hoped when he had first introduced the subject. He had not realised she would attempt such a precise and literal translation of Gerald's ideas. James must go to England as they had once planned, despite the fact that it had never been Gerald's intention to isolate her from the last remaining family love. Kimberley would be a lonely place for her for many long months of the years ahead.

James interrupted Alan's thoughts. 'Will Mummy always wear a white sari now?'

'For as long as she's in mourning for your father.'

'Will that be for ever?'

'I hope not.' Alan answered the boy truthfully. Mary had been wearing the traditional white for two months and it was not unknown for Indian widows to wear it for the remainder of their lives, despite the possibility they might be quite young at the time of their husband's death. It was an indication of their continuing sorrow and allegiance. Alan had asked himself James's question many times during the past weeks; it had been impossible to answer. Mary's love for Gerald had been so powerful while he was alive that Alan was uncertain whether even death could diminish it. Few people loved as Mary loved, an animal love, uncomplicated and unconditional, the kind of love that made a swan starve itself to death when its mate died. A swan! With a feeling of dismay Alan wondered if James had wrongly described his mother's appearance. Perhaps it was a swan she resembled in her white sari? Silently he prayed it was not so.

She was squatting beside the grave, a position which a European would have found uncomfortable but which she had used since her childhood. It brought her as close as possible to Gerald; by reaching out her hand she could touch the pale grey marble chippings around the foot of the headstone. If she pushed the tips of her fingers beneath the sharp pebbles, she could feel the warm earth which held him. In her mind she saw him only as he had been in life, as he had been when she had first met and loved him: strong, tall, vital.

She rocked herself forward until she was kneeling and then spoke silently, only her mind forming the words she knew he would hear: 'Alan is in the car, darling, with James, we're on our way to the airport. The flight is at two-thirty.' She picked up a handful of the hot marble chippings and let them fall through her fingers as though she were counting the beads on a rosary. 'Alan has been marvellous, he arranged absolutely everything, even our passports. And James is feeling very important because he has one of his own. He's very excited but underneath I think he's frightened; not of the flying like me, simply of all the strange things he has to face. Alan has been very good, keeping him happy and telling him of all the things he will be able to do at school in England. Alan goes back to Assam tomorrow, so you will be alone for a while; please don't mind too much.

'I cabled Jane and asked her to meet us at the airport. It will all be so strange for us. I cabled Uncle Simon, too, and told him we were coming to England. I'll speak to him as soon as we arrive. I need his help with James's schooling. A man's opinion is important; he'll be able to advise me. I'd like him in the background for James's peace of mind; someone he can meet when he's lonely, a man's company. A boy needs a man, darling.

'Don't be angry, but I've written to your mother. James will need her as well. He has to have family around him in a strange country. You'll see, she'll love him just as much as we do.

'I'm hoping I haven't forgotten anything. I made lists and then ticked things off as I went along, but I'm still sure I'll forget something important.

'Rai is quite confident he can manage Kimberley while we are away, and I've kept on all the staff, including Renana. I know James won't really need an aiya any more, but she's been with us so long I couldn't part with her. She's so willing I know she'll make a place for herself. And Rai has promised to keep an eye on the malis and see that they don't neglect your garden or let the weeds grow in the tennis court. The storm last night loosened a lot of creeper and damaged the river wall, but it is being cleared and repaired. I shall miss Kimberley, miss everything, just as I miss you.

'I said James was frightened. I'm frightened too. Remember, darling, I used to want to visit London with you? Now, I can't imagine what it will be like.'

She closed her eyes so she could picture him more clearly. His arms were reaching out to her. She imagined the touch of his lips on her cheek. She gave the assurance she knew he would have needed in life. 'I'll take care, darling. I'll be back soon, I promise.'

Karachi, Beirut, Zurich. The nerve-tearing moments of the Constellation's first take-off had become tedium, with sleep imposed by the hypnotic drone of engines between the interruptions for meals and refuelling stops. Time ceased to exist in the noisome limbo of the flight. Even in memory there was only confusion; was it at Karachi or Beirut where James had seen the camels and shouted 'Oont' so loudly the passenger in front of him had spilled his breakfast tray in his lap? Was it Beirut or Zurich where the cold air that had taken her breath away had been sucked into the aircraft as the doors were opened? Which mountains or storm had rocked and shaken the aircraft so violently that they had been forced to wear and tighten their seatbelts? For the past two hours there had been nothing below but frothy mountains of rose-hued cumulus, unbroken, a panorama already familiar. James was sleeping when the seatbelt warning light came on; she awakened him as the aircraft's nose dipped towards the cloud.

The pilot's voice, unnaturally high-pitched as it competed with the roar of the engines, cut through the dry smoky air of the passenger deck. 'Ladies and gentlemen, we will be landing at London Airport in seven minutes. Will you please extinguish any cigarettes, cigars or pipes and fasten your seatbelts. Please keep your seatbelts fastened until the aircraft is stationary. Visibility at London Airport is twelve hundred yards, and unfortunately it is raining. We trust you have enjoyed your flight ...'

Rain, driven and chilled by a south-westerly gale already touched by autumn, swept across the glistening black tarmac of London Airport and formed rippled lakes beneath the wings of stationary aircraft. Clothing which unknowing passengers had thought suitable for cooler climates when it had been purchased in tropical heat, became tissue-thin as they disembarked and ran the long few yards to their waiting transport. Wind snatched at hats, scarves, recently brushed hair. There were frustrating delays for them at baggage collection points, shuffling queues at both Customs and Immigration, while their rain-wet clothing exaggerated the odours of lengthy flights. At last they were ejected into the real world where once again their own volition was recognisable.

Mary experienced panic as she followed the porter with their baggage through the swing doors. She hesitated. The porter continued through the waiting crowd. Where was James? By her side. She could not see Jane in the crush of people. Where was the porter and the luggage? Voices were shouting excited welcomes; not to her. Her eyes searched desperately.

'Mary ...' Jane's voice, and then Jane herself a few feet away, her blonde hair beneath a hat tied back in a ponytail, a grey cape swinging from her shoulders over a matching grey suit; eyes like Gerald's, her face more square, feminine, handsome rather than pretty. 'Mary, how wonderful to see you here.' The blue eyes smiling genuine pleasure. 'And you, James. My goodness, you've become quite a young man.' Kisses for both of them.

Jane was talking as she drove, but Mary's mind was unable to focus on her words. This was England, London, Gerald's country, Gerald's city, but there was no feeling of him having belonged here; orderly red brick or pebble-dashed rows of suburban houses seen through rain-splashed windows, and white-faced people bowed against the weather beneath umbrellas as they sheltered waiting for transport or hurried between shops, bore no relationship to the England she had pictured whenever Gerald had spoken of it. He had told of green fields and woodland, and she had seen none apart from small market gardens near the airport and smaller parks as they drove towards the heart of the city. Everything seemed to be concrete, brick, sombre, miserable. Gerald could never have belonged here, he belonged to warmth, to tropical lushness, to clear skies and open countryside; to the hills. She understood now why he had delayed his return to England for so long.

The car heater was blowing warm air against her legs, its heat artificial, the air only momentarily comfortable and misting the windows with condensation.

I would die here, she thought. Is this the place the British so proudly call 'home'? Am I doing the right thing bringing James here to such an unpleasant climate?

James, wedged by suitcases in a corner of the rear seat, talked excitedly. 'I've just seen an Austin Atlantic. I saw an advertisement for them in Daddy's *Picture Post* and I've just seen a real one; a red one. There are lots of good motorcars here, Aunt Jane. And lots of cinemas and things.' He spelled out the name on a building. 'C H I S W I C K. Chis-wick Empire. What's a Chis-wick Empire, Aunt Jane?' He rubbed moisture from the side window and stared across the open triangle of the grass of Chiswick Green as trafficlights momentarily held the car. 'Why are there no animals on their maidan, Aunt Jane?'

Jane was laughing. James was right though, thought Mary, there seemed to be no animals, only a few dogs imprisoned on leads and she had seen no birds. She remembered the photographs she had seen in magazines; there *was* countryside in England and there *was* sun, but not here and not today, only this strange city of thousands upon thousands of houses, oddly characterless and drab, and all the time packed closer and closer together, becoming older, taller, more smoke-stained, more threatening.

'Of course I haven't booked you a hotel,' Jane had protested. 'You must stay with me. My little house is quite big enough for us all and it's very near to the shops, near everything; I'm sure you'll like it.

It's much more sensible than a hotel and you can come and go as you please.'

I must bath, thought Mary. She was sticky and uncomfortable. It would be good to lie in warm scented water and relax. Jane would certainly allow her bearer to hang up her clothes and press a sari for her. It would be pleasant to be human once again, to feel clean and refreshed. And she must sleep, a real undisturbed sleep.

The buildings were becoming grander, more impressive, but stood tall on either side of the road like the waiting jaws of a vice, adding a touch of claustrophobia to the mingled feelings Mary was experiencing.

Jane turned the car unexpectedly to the left through a narrow archway into a lane between terraces of small houses, Ebury Mews. She stopped close to an old terraced house, parking within three feet of its door and switched off the engine. 'Here we are. It's not the Ritz, but it's my home. Yours too, for as long as you want.'

James scowled and pressed his face against the damp window. 'You live here, Aunt Jane?' There was horrified disbelief in his voice.

The interior of the mews house was dark, necessitating the use of an electric light even though it was not yet five p.m. A narrow hallway contained a staircase to the upper floor; to the left of the only entrance was a living-room, neither dining-room nor lounge but a combination of both and only some twelve feet square. At the far end of the hallway were steps down to a tiny kitchen. On the upper floor, two small bedrooms and a combined bathroom and lavatory which smelled of recent redecoration.

'I thought you were rich,' said James tactlessly, when he had spent a few minutes critically examining the accommodation, his dark eyes holding Jane's reprovingly.

Jane laughed. 'Wait until you decide to buy a house of your own in London, young man, you'll find out how rich you need to be then.' She made herself sound apologetic. 'I'm what's known as a career woman and I try to live within my earnings. That's hard enough here, even in a place as small as this.'

'But we've got millions and millions of rupees,' persisted James.

Mary tried to stop him. 'Rupees aren't pounds, James. And this is London not Calcutta. It's far more expensive here.'

Jane grimaced. 'And I'm afraid it's the Petrie sons who inherit the money, not the daughters. Grandfather expected us all to find rich husbands. He didn't anticipate bachelor girls.'

'But where does your khansama live and your bearer?'

'I'm afraid, James, I don't have any servants. Not many people do in England any more.' Jane's eyes twinkled. 'We make our own beds and do our own cooking and cleaning.'

James said, 'Gosh,' dispiritedly.

A street light in the mews created stars from the rain drops on the strip of window visible between the curtains and cast a meagre yellow beam across the ceiling of the bedroom. There was a distant background hum of traffic and the occasional sound of aircraft passing above and the sky beyond the window was not night-black but dull red, as though the city burnt.

There were two single beds in the room and an arm's length away from Mary, James slept, his breathing shallow, even. As usual, he had been active and full of energy one moment, exhausted the next, and asleep even before she had kissed him goodnight.

Afterwards she and Jane had talked, sad, awkward conversations about her bereavement that had been avoided in James's company, about the happenings of the past and then her plans, until at last she had been unable to stave off her own exhaustion. But now in her bed, sleep ignored her.

The bedroom, featureless apart from an antique embroidered sampler on one wall and a dressing table and wardrobe against another, reminded her uncomfortably of her cell in the line-rooms of the plantation and brought back memories which seemed to belong to another life, another woman.

The unfamiliar blankets and quilt on the bed were heavy, their weight compressing her, but without them she knew she would be cold. Jane had said it was fifty-eight degrees during the day, but it had been close to a hundred in Calcutta before they had left, and although the air cooled at night there, it only became pleasant, seldom uncomfortable; here the chill stiffened Mary's limbs, and this was still, Jane warned, only late autumn. Could James survive winter? Tomorrow, Mary decided, she must buy both of them thicker clothing. Jane would help her. She would know the shopkeepers who were honest in their bargaining and sold the best quality goods.

Jane! It had been amusing for Mary in the early days of her

marriage to think she had British relatives. True they were only relatives by marriage, but even that had been quite inconceivable in her childhood when she had watched the planters and their wives. But Jane had made her feel like a real sister, a blood sister, and Jane's affection for Gerald had cemented the girls' relationship and made them kin. Mary wondered what her own sister, Elaben, was doing now. Since being taken by the nuns, Mary had met her only four or five times, the last just before she went to work for the Warrens over ten years ago! Elaben had been fourteen then, and already promised in marriage to the son of a farmer, and had been so different from Mary there had been no feeling of kinship; she had been sparely educated and was unable to read or write. Their mother had died a few years before and at the last meeting of the sisters they had found nothing in common.

Mother! Gerald's mother! Soon she would meet her. It might be an ordeal, but it was important James should know his grandmother. He had already inherited his father's title, now he must learn everything about the background of his family, the kind of things only a grandmother could tell a child.

Mary remembered how Gerald had protected her during the first years of their marriage, dismissing the rift between his mother and himself as nothing more than a family squabble. It was only as the confidence in their love had grown that he had admitted the truth to Mary, and then only a little at a time so that it might not hurt her. It had not hurt, but it had made her angry at his mother and given her even more pride in Gerald when she had understood that he had chosen to marry her even though by doing so he had lost the love of his parents.

Jane's reaction had bemused her when they had discussed the situation once they had become friends. 'Mother! Good heavens, Mary, you mustn't take any notice of her. She gets bees in her bonnet. When we had the first General Election at the end of the war she wanted to vote Conservative, so she voted for a Colonel somebody-or-other. He turned out to be the Labour candidate, the Conservative was an ex-sergeant, a builder's foreman. Mother was infuriated. She wrote to Clement Atlee accusing him of using underhanded methods to gain votes; wanted the entire General Election declared null and void. She must have written hundreds of letters. She even wrote to the King.'

Mary found it hard to picture this strange woman who felt

her own views so important she could write to her King. There had been no photographs in India to give her any idea of how she might look. Was she tall and fair like Jane and Gerald, or had they both resembled their father? What little Mary knew of her tended to create the image of a woman, a giant, sour-faced, grim and unbending in her views, as arrogant as the worst of the memsah'bs she had met in her youth; in her mind, when she had thought about them in her plantation cell they had always seemed bigger and more threatening than they became in reality. Perhaps this would be so with Margaret Petrie?

And there was Simon Petrie to meet in London. She would telephone him tomorrow and arrange to visit his office the following day. She felt she needed a little time to compose herself in preparation for the favours she would ask him. She smiled to herself remembering the first occasion she had called Simon Petrie uncle. It had been Gerald's suggestion: 'He's my uncle, so of course you must call him that.' She had laughed at the idea, but when Simon Petrie had visited Calcutta and they had been introduced by Gerald, she had called him Uncle Simon in greeting him. The look of incredulity on his face at such an unexpected familiarity by an Indian girl had amused her so much she had been forced to disguise her giggles in an exaggerated fit of coughing.

Over the years he had stayed with them twice, the strong odour of his pipe tobacco lingering for days after he had returned to England. He had often seemed unfriendly and distant, his mind always occupied by the purposes of his visits to India. She had learnt that his working day began when he wakened, and ended when he slept; dinner parties for his benefit were a disaster. Simon Petrie's food was only the fuel his engine needed to run efficiently and frivolous conversations were intrusions into the time he allocated for his trips to Calcutta. But she was quite confident now that family loyalties would guarantee her his help. It was a comforting thought and eased her exhausted mind towards the sleep she so badly needed.

The old Mincing Lane office of Petrie India had been bombed in 1941. Now, in its place stood a modern block, two storeys higher than the original and, although more practical, out of place amongst the ancient buildings which had survived. Like many of the tea companies it was sited close to the London auction rooms where the buyers and sellers confronted each other on Mondays through the medium of their brokers.

The office block was shared by three separate firms of tea merchants and shippers, whose co-operation was limited to the division of the salaries of the two Royal Corps of Commissionaires' doormen who guarded the glass-enclosed portals and foyer and directed visitors to the appropriate floors. The entire building was owned by Petrie India, the other two companies were their tenants.

Simon Petrie's office was on the ground floor. When the building had been rebuilt he had considered using the top floor; the view across London, which included the impressive façade and dome of St Paul's Cathedral, had been only momentarily inviting. He had chosen the first two floors for Petrie India as they seemed more prestigious and implied occupation of an indeterminate number of floors above. However, as a result of his decision there was no view whatsoever for either himself or his staff on the ground floor; traffic noise and the hubbub of pedestrians on the narrow and busy street had forced the architects to raise the lower sill of the windows above eye level. Even if the clerks or typists stood on chairs to peer outside, as the younger ones sometimes did, they saw only the heads of pedestrians, passing traffic, and beyond that the equally imprisoning walls of the offices on the far side of the roadway. The sun barely reach the windows in the height of midsummer and a few days later was gone until the following year.

The entrance hall of the pre-Blitz Petrie India building had contained a lifesize portrait of the Company's founder, David Langley Petrie. Below had stood an enormous brass lion, the gift of a Rajah, polished by generations of London's cleaners until it had shone like a temple god. The bomb and subsequent fire had reduced the portrait to ashes and the lion to a blackened plaque of metal, for which one of the demolition labourers had received seven shillings and sixpence from a scrap merchant. The new foyer, neutral ground for all the tea companies of the block, was purely functional, the walls decorated only by black and white photographs of tea gardens, tea factories, tea warehouses, and a Royal tea party at Buckingham Palace, to which Gerald's father had been invited in 1938. He could be seen in the photograph shaking hands with His Majesty King George the Sixth, whose Coronation he had also attended as a minor peer of the realm.

At the far end of the foyer, beyond the two aluminium-fronted elevators which served the upper floors, was the 'tube', a narrow corridor running the length of the building and nicknamed by Petrie India employees after the London Underground because of its resemblance to the characterless passages which linked the sub-city railway platforms.

Simon Petrie's office could be approached from two different doors in the left-hand wall of the 'tube'. The first entrance, the only one ever used by the staff, was through the protective office of his private secretary. The alternative entrance, forbidden except to fellow members of the board of directors, was through the boardroom itself further along the corridor.

The chairman's secretary, Elizabeth Willoughby, guarded his privacy in a small annexe, a glass-panelled door separating her cramped cubicle from the spacious grandeur of Simon Petrie's office. She was thirty-five years old, with ginger hair and nondescript features; she was easily lost in the smallest crowd. Her softly spoken manner was deceptive and concealed a quick and inventive mind. Her mother had been Dutch, and Elizabeth Willoughby was bilingual; as a former commander in the ATS she had been a member of the Special Operations Executive and had worked for three years in occupied Holland where she had proved herself capable of loyalty to the point of death if she decided a cause was just. It was a rare quality which Simon Petrie had foolishly failed to appreciate or foster. An emergent post-war feminist, she resented his belief that women were little more than extensions of the keys of a typewriter; she was denied the right of the smallest and most insignificant decisions; Simon Petrie made a point of calling any of his male employees by the commissioned rank they had attained in the wartime army, Captain Edwards in Accounts and Colonel Nicols in Sales, but Commander Elizabeth Willoughby he referred to simply as Miss Willoughby. She did not want to be addressed by her former rank, but it was his pointed male chauvinism she had begun to dislike wholeheartedly.

The glass panel of the chairman's door acted like the diaphragm of a telephone earpiece, and rather than muffling his conversations it amplified them. It was an architectural failure of which he was unaware. Elizabeth listened to the conversations which took place in his office from the habits of her SOE training rather than curiosity. Simon Petrie was talking now, his voice deep and roughened by a lifetime's use of the harsh pipe tobacco whose fumes tainted the resentful Elizabeth's clothing and pervaded every room in the building. His son, William, promoted only recently to managing director, had entered his father's office through Elizabeth's annexe only a few moments previously. William Petrie had all of his father's mannerisms but few of his talents.

She heard Simon Petrie ask his son: 'Have they all arrived?'

Elizabeth frowned. The question was an example of Simon Petrie's doubting of her ability to cope with the most minor task. As each member of the board of directors had arrived she had welcomed them to the boardroom, seen they were seated and served with a cup of coffee by one of the office juniors, and then personally reported their arrival to Simon Petrie. When the last of them had taken their place at the long mahogany table she had informed him of the fact.

It was Elizabeth's third year with Petrie India; she had decided there would not be another. The only thing keeping her there for the past eighteen months had been her father's advice when she had first left school and taken a job: 'Never leave a position under less than three years.' He had been assistant manager in a bank until a doodlebug had terminated his life and career while he waited for a train at Waterloo Station. 'Under three years implies unreliability,' he had told her. 'If you find you've made a mistake, grit your teeth and stick it out. In the long run, it pays.'

Her thoughts had distracted her, but William Petrie's voice drew her attention again. 'All this trouble because of one damn fool.' She realised he was talking about his cousin Gerald, the baronet who had died of snakebite. The late baronet was the reason for the present board meeting; the reason for the several board meetings which had taken place over the past few weeks, the innumerable letters between board members and chairman, and countless telephone calls and visits from Bronowski, the Company's legal advisor.

Simon Petrie made no comment and William Petrie continued peevishly. 'I've never known a punctual Indian.' Elizabeth could picture him scrutinising his watch with a characteristic look of annoyance. William Petrie was perpetually annoyed and suffered from indigestion as a result of his aggravations. One of his own secretary's daily tasks was to ensure a constant supply of Rennies in the otherwise empty cigarette box on his desk. 'She's fifteen minutes late, and I have a lunch appointment at twelve-thirty.'

She! Although William Petrie called her 'she', Elizabeth knew he meant Mary Lady Petrie. It had become quite obvious during the conversations she had overheard that William Petrie hated her. It wasn't simply that Lady Petrie was coloured, had been a servant on one of the company plantations and held the precious shares. It was something else, something that had puzzled Elizabeth until her mind had decoded the various comments he made. William Petrie, she realised, was jealous of the son which Lady Petrie had produced for her late husband. And he was jealous of other things. His cousin the late Sir Gerald Petrie *might* have died in the war. If so, when his father had been killed in the road accident the title would have passed to Simon Petrie and eventually to William. Sir Gerald's survival of the war and his begetting of a son frustrated William's secret longing. Elizabeth had heard Simon Petrie describe to William how Sir Gerald had told him his life had been saved by this Indian woman; that had been over two years previously when the chairman had returned from a trip to India. William Petrie's hatred of Lady Petrie seemed to stem from that date, though it had not been so obvious when his cousin Gerald had been alive.

'Mary Lady Petrie.' Elizabeth said the name and title aloud. What she knew of the woman intrigued her; an Indian Mata Hari who had ended up with more than fifty per cent of the voting shares of a conservative British company ... a Conservative with a large 'C' male-orientated British company! It appealed to Elizabeth's sense of justice. How jolly tough for them! An outsider, a woman, with voting shares! Well, two fingers to the dying old guard of the British Raj, thought Elizabeth. It was interesting to see how they were rallying to save their flag, interesting to learn how every generation was expected to perpetuate the retention of power and wealth within the original family, give or take a few cousins and approved in-laws. Petrie India shares were never 'sold' beyond the family, Elizabeth had learned. They were jealously protected, each owner simply considering himself the privileged guardian of them until such time as they were willed or donated to another appropriate holder ... always male.

By good fortune, it seemed to Elizabeth, or simply the fortuitous lack of foresight by the late baronet's father in overlooking, probably because the present situation was quite inconceivable, the need to place his willed shares in trust for the future generations of Petries, Lady Petrie had inherited those shares and also the shares of her husband without the usual legal strings attached!

Elizabeth had attended all the hurried board meetings to record the minutes in her impeccable shorthand, and had heard the wordy discourses of Bronowski, the company solicitor, as the various options were debated. It had become clear to her, as merely an interested bystander, that much of Bronowski's advice was coloured by his awareness of the delicacy of the situation, which could easily result in a change of power within Petrie India, and might in turn lead to a change of legal representation. He had ended his speech at the last board meeting with the somewhat fatuous suggestion that there was no need to panic.

Panic! If anyone in the Petrie India board of directors was panicking it was the managing director, William Petrie, and it was his overt nervousness which affected the remainder of the board of directors. Elizabeth had already noted that William Petrie was a weakling; he could never have reached his present position without his father's influence. William hated uncertainty but also hated decisions, hated anything which might rock the stability of his boat. He was forty-five years old, comfortably off and interested only in his golf club at Richmond. His daughter was happily married to a young merchant banker, and his wife fully occupied working with the WRVS. Nothing had disturbed the nicely programmed pattern of William's life until the death of Sir Gerald Petrie; now there was an intolerable uncertainty within it.

Unlike his son, Simon Petrie's only interest was Petrie India. He was already past retirement age and would be sixty-seven in a few weeks' time. Elizabeth had heard him proclaim his intention of 'dying in the saddle'. She found him a cold and unfeeling man whose dedication to Petrie India appeared to be a substitute for the affection he was unable to give to people. She had learned quite a lot about him in the years she had served as his secretary, the information gleaned from words of his older staff and the conversations between the members of the board while they relaxed over their coffee cups or their gin and tonics or malt whiskies after shareholders' meetings. Simon had been the second son of a Petrie title-holder, and had grown up with no expectations other than of a reasonable post in the Company if he could prove his worth. His own father's time and interest had been entirely spent on his older brother who would inherit the title and the chairmanship of the family company. Simon Petrie had worked hard, the drive being his determination to establish in his father's mind that even though his older brother might be the heir he was the better man. He had reached the post of managing director and then been frustrated until the unexpected wartime road accident had removed the barrier to his remaining ambition. He had readily assumed the role of chairman and quickly established a total autocracy; none of the board of directors had been strong enough to defend themselves.

Once, he might have been a handsome man, Elizabeth had thought, but his eyes reminded her of the dead eyes of cod lying on the marble slab of a fishmonger's stall; they were emotionless and empty. Occasionally he smiled, but his eyes indicated nothing. He had been tall, but was now stooped. A grey moustache was trimmed in a neat line above his upper lip, its centre stained by the smoke of his pipe. His hair was also grey, but his eyebrows dark and heavy. His face was long, his jaw narrow and pronounced, and as he drew on his pipe his cheeks hollowed, reminding her of a portrait she had once seen of a youthful and unbearded Abraham Lincoln.

The glass panel of the inner office door was momentarily shadowed, giving Elizabeth time to appear involved in searching the pages of a telephone directory before it was opened. William Petrie paused in the doorway and spoke back into his father's office. 'I'll go and keep the others happy.' She heard Simon Petrie grunt, his normal acknowledgement, before William closed the door and spoke brusquely to her. 'I'll be in the boardroom. Damned woman's late.'

Elizabeth smiled as William Petrie left her office, then put her tongue out at the closing door. She had no sooner put a cylinder on the dictaphone and begun to adjust her earphones than the intercom on her desk buzzed. She flicked a switch. 'Reception here, Miss Willoughby. Lady Petrie for Mr Petrie. For Mr Simon Petrie.'

Elizabeth said, 'Thanks George,' then took her mirror from her handbag, checked her make-up and patted her hair into place before leaving her desk. She knocked on Simon Petrie's door before opening it. 'I believe Lady Petrie has arrived, sir.'

Simon Petrie was standing in front of his teak bookcase, filling his pipe. He tucked it back into his breast pocket. 'Bring her in here first.'

To Mary's surprise, she had been unable to barter for any of the clothes she had purchased for James and herself the previous day at the famous Harrods store. To buy without bargaining had seemed foolish; shopkeepers always allowed themselves more than sufficient profit, and an Indian wife's skill as a housekeeper could be judged on her ability to buy at a keen price. An Indian shopkeeper would have no respect for a customer who accepted the first price he gave, and even when the British system had been explained to Mary by Jane, she felt certain she would have been able to obtain some kind of a reduction had she been permitted; no shopkeeper, even the owner of such an affluent store as Harrods, would wish to miss good sales for the sake of a few pounds or even shillings.

The shopping had been difficult. It was easy enough to find suitable clothes for James. In fact, in a week or two he would need a school uniform anyway; in the meantime vests, sweaters and an overcoat would keep him warm. But buying for herself presented problems she had not anticipated. Had she been prepared to wear British clothes it would have been easier, but the promise she had made to Gerald that she would always wear saris was a promise she intended never to break.

The visit to the lingerie department had been the most amusing part of her shopping, for both herself and Jane. Very little European underwear was suitable for wearing beneath a sari, especially if the wearer's prime concern was her warmth. French knickers and full length slips made the sari too bulky and the thought of woollen winter vests worn under a light blouse had both the women almost hysterical. Mary had eventually bought warm knickers, stockings and suspender belts, and it had been necessary for Jane to show her later the order in which they were worn and how they were fastened. They had felt restrictive and uncomfortable at first but she had appreciated them later in the chill air. Jane had warned her how delicately the stockings needed to be handled if ladders were to be avoided.

Cardigans did not look attractive with saris, but Mary found there were light sweaters that might perhaps be worn in place of a blouse providing they were sufficiently well-fitting and decorative. The wool, however, irritated her skin; she had never before worn anything other than either cotton, or since her marriage, silk. Coats were an even greater problem; the present 'New Look' mid-calf length coats were quite out of place above a sari making it appear that no matter what the time of the day she was dressed in a ballgown. The only alternative had been a fur cape that swung open enough to allow the full sari to be seen. To Mary it had seemed an almost inexcusable extravagance even though she was used to the wealth Gerald had provided. But the beauty of the silver fox fur and its incredible softness had finally convinced her. The Harrods saleswoman had draped the cloak around Mary's shoulders, and once Mary had seen it in place in the long mirrors she had been unable to remove it. Even later, back at Jane's house, she had stood for a long time in front of the wardrobe mirror enjoying the heavy pull of the furs as they swung away from her shoulders when she turned to admire it.

She had telephoned both Simon Petrie and the home of Gerald's mother that afternoon, and had been surprised when Simon Petrie suggested she should visit the Petrie India offices the following day. Her conversation with him had been brief, but she had learned from his stay in Kimberley to expect little more from him. His stiffness she interpreted as no more than an elderly Englishman's reaction to a private telephone call at his place of business; there had been times when she had telephoned Gerald at his Calcutta office and found his reaction uncharacteristically curt, an indication that his mind was fully occupied by his work. She was convinced, however, that Simon Petrie, as James's great-uncle and the male head of the Petrie family, would help her in every way he could.

Her call to the home of Gerald's mother had been less fruitful. A housekeeper had apologised for her mistress's absence but had promised a message would be given and perhaps Margaret Petrie would return the call. Mary hoped this would be the case as it would be an indication that Gerald's mother was, after all, prepared to offer friendship if only in memory of her dead son.

Just as her first use of make-up so many years before had given her confidence when she attended her first European dinner party, so her silver fox cape added to it now in the unfamiliar surroundings of the cold new city. Jane was taking James to Whipsnade for the day in her car, and so Mary had used a taxi to reach the Petrie India office. She had noticed the cab driver's quick appraisal of the value of the fur, and the speed with which he had hurried to open the door of his vehicle; British taxi drivers, it seemed, were no different from their Indian counterparts when it came to the assessment of the quantity of baksheesh they might receive.

For the first time since her arrival in England, the sun was shining, but its rays were devoid of warmth, and the chill wind remained in the city streets. However, the tiredness which had followed the long flight had gone, and Mary felt a sense of growing optimism. This morning she knew she was looking her best. She dispelled what nervousness she felt at the thought of meeting Simon Petrie again by continually reminding herself he was one of her own family, James's family, and this meeting was for James's benefit, for his future. When her son, Gerald's son, remained in England, he must feel there were members of his family near him, close at hand and concerned for his welfare. He would certainly spend quite a lot of time with Jane, but as a male he must also have the company of a man. She felt Simon Petrie would understand this and help her. James was the most important thing in her life now, and until all the necessary arrangements had been made for his future and his peace of mind so far from his home and her love, she could concern herself with little else.

The London offices of Petrie India were smaller than she had expected; those in Calcutta occupied an enormous and impressive building overlooking Delhousy Square and were richly decorated by fluted columns and sculpted figures above the red stone canopy of the ornate entrance. The front of the London building was of plain brick and its doors of glass, not heavy wood embossed with wrought iron. She gave her name to the uniformed commissionaire and waited while he telephoned Simon Petrie's office. In the Calcutta office she would have been ushered to a waiting lounge, here there was only a padded bench seat beside the commissionaire's desk.

The foyer was busy. Messengers and office workers came and went as she waited, their voices as drab and colourless as their style of dress. She felt disappointed. She had not known what to expect in British business houses, but had believed they would be somehow grander in every way than those in India, even noisier, places where the British conducted their affairs with the impossible hurry, dash and efficiency they seemed to expect from their Indian workers. Indian offices were full of noise, the babble of conversation, argument, discussion; in the background somewhere, even if it only drifted in through the windows from the streets, would be distant music, someone singing. Here there was a sombre funereal atmosphere she found depressing. She had thought she understood the English, believed the years she had spent as the wife of one of them had prepared her for the visit to their country. She realised now she knew very little about them, that their homeland was as alien as if it existed on another planet.

'Lady Petrie?' She had not noticed the arrival of the woman who questioned her and the unexpected voice startled her. The woman noticed her reaction. 'I'm sorry, I didn't mean to creep up on you but these carpets muffle footsteps.' Elizabeth had already examined Mary as she approached her, had decided she was enviably attractive and thought the sari and the fur cape extremely elegant. It was the kind of impossibly exotic image she would have liked to present herself, perhaps on the few occasions when she received theatre invitations. Mentally she sighed and shrugged; her own hair was not red enough to be startling, and her freckled complexion had been the bane of her life since childhood. The years in army-issue flat shoes made her walk clumsily and she had no illusions about her plumpening figure; she felt she was becoming matronly, physically and mentally. 'I'll take you to Mr Petrie's office.'

Mary had attended enough lectures and listened to a sufficient number of speakers to be conscious of the difference between a carefully rehearsed speech and one which was made with the sincerity of spontaneous emotion. To her amazement, she found her mind classifying Simon Petrie's welcome as unctuous and shallow; the correct words were being spoken but something barely visible in his manner contaminated them and made them worthless.

He had kissed her cheek when it had been offered but she had not felt his lips, only the stiff bristles of his moustache against her skin. His eyes held hers but seemed to look through her, beyond her.

'We were terribly sorry to learn of Gerald's tragic death, my dear. Dreadful thing for you ... for everyone, of course.' He seemed embarrassed. Was this the normal British reaction when expressing sympathy? Was her mind misjudging him? 'I gather you are staying at Jane's. Sensible. London hotels are exorbitant. Difficult trip, I suppose. Very tiring.'

Is he going to keep me standing, wondered Mary. There was an armchair beside Simon Petrie's desk, perhaps she should make a pointed move towards it? 'I wanted to see you to discuss James. He is coming here to school.'

'Yes, I remember Gerald saying something about that. A wise decision; you can't better the British education system.'

'I've brought him with me.' There was a vagueness to Simon Petrie's attitude Mary was finding bewildering. The man's mind was not on her or on what she was saying, but on something else.

Simon Petrie said: 'Yes, of course ...'

'I have to find him what you call a preparatory school, and also make whatever arrangements necessary for the remainder of his education. That is the purpose of my visit here. I need advice.'

'I see.' Simon Petrie paused, then said more brightly, 'Well, my dear, I think I should introduce you to the board of directors. They've been kept waiting rather a long time.'

Elizabeth who had been deliberately hovering in the doorway with her notepad and minute book saw Mary's eyes widen. 'The old blighter,' she thought. 'He hasn't heard a word the woman said. She's not interested in his precious company, only her son. She wants his help and he's throwing her to the lions.' Simon Petrie nodded his head towards the boardroom and Elizabeth understood it as a silent order for her to open the door for himself and the guest. She wished she could have been able to whisper some word of encouragement to the unsuspecting victim; had she anticipated this innocence she would have been tempted to warn her before bringing her to Simon Petrie's office. Damn Simon Petrie, and Petrie India!

The boardroom was some thirty feet in length, an oblong and unattractive room dominated by its enormous mahogany table around which were scattered the eight members of the board of directors. Some of them had arrived more than half an hour previously and the air was already thick with cigarette and cigar smoke. There were empty coffee cups and biscuit crumbs beside the papers in front of each of them. They had been talking as the door was opened; now there was silence and every head turned to watch Mary enter. Automatically, the men rose to their feet. Eyes that had already formed opinions examined her critically. It was a situation contained in nightmares, nakedness before a hostile and vindictive crowd. Elizabeth felt and understood Mary's dismay.

Once, Elizabeth had shot a man, an SS-Sturmann of the Freiwilligen Legion Niederlande who had unexpectedly entered the cellar where she and her small group of resistance workers were operating an illegal printing press. She had reacted protectively then, without conscious thought; she did so again now, in defence of the obviously embarrassed woman. A tray holding a coffee-pot, hot milk jug and bowl of brown sugar protruded slightly over the edge of the boardroom table by her side. Elizabeth leant on it, catapulting its contents on to the floor at her feet, adding to the noise of the breaking china with a cry of dismay at her own clumsiness. Warm coffee splattered her silk stockings and Simon Petrie's trousers and shoes, and sugar began dissolving in the pile of the wet carpet.

The confusion drew the board members' attention from Mary as Elizabeth loudly apologised to Simon Petrie and began attempting to collect the shattered remains of the coffee service.

Simon Petrie brushed his trousers with his handkerchief and spoke testily. 'Just leave it, Miss Willoughby.' A hubbub of conversation swelled.

Elizabeth straightened herself and replaced the tray on the table. As she did so, her eyes met Mary's.

Elizabeth winked. 'I hope I didn't splash you,' she said, with the faintest hint of a smile.

'No,' replied Mary. 'I'm sorry you have ruined your stockings.' She realised now that the secretary had caused the diversion for her benefit, and was grateful. The unexpected confrontation with the board members had been frightening. Now she had been given the opportunity to compose herself.

'It'll wash out,' said Elizabeth lightly.

'Gentlemen, gentlemen.' Simon Petrie was trying to bring some order to his meeting. Gradually the noise subsided. The faces of the men were no longer cold and examining, the papers on the long table had been scattered by their startled movements; they began rearranging the disturbed documents into neat piles. Simon Petrie walked quickly to his seat at the head of the table and raised his voice again. 'Gentlemen please, I would like to introduce you to our major shareholder, Mary Lady Petrie.'

Simon Petrie had asked Elizabeth to seat Mary at the far end of the table to himself but Elizabeth now realised it placed Lady Petrie in much the same position as a victim at an inquisition. With determination, she led Mary to Simon Petrie's side and sat her next to him. It immediately put him at a disadvantage; once seated, he would have to turn almost sideways in his own chair to speak to her. Furthermore, it placed Lady Petrie within intimate proximity of the chairman, and Elizabeth was confident that by now all the board members would have become aware of the exotic appearance of their fellow shareholder, and the heady perfume she was wearing.

Simon Petrie scowled at Elizabeth and then said to Mary: 'I'd better make individual introductions.' He began indicating the board members clockwise. 'My son, William; of course you know he is our managing director. And Julian Petrie, another cousin, my sister Claudette's son. Mark Harben and Frederick Harben; our company solicitor, Mr Bronowski...' He reeled off the remaining names while the members of the board muttered customary platitudes and settled, still fidgeting, in their leather-padded chairs. It was interesting, thought Mary, that none of them had managed to regain the calculated attitudes of superiority they had shown on her initial entrance to the room. If the opportunity arose later, she would thank the secretary.

Simon Petrie cleared his throat, then spoke again: 'I am quite sure I can welcome Lady Petrie to this meeting on behalf of all the board.' He found himself in the difficult position of attempting to be formal with his fellow directors, while considering he should be less formal with the woman sitting close beside him. 'I have naturally given her our condolences on her husband's, my nephew Gerald's ... our India director's unfortunate and untimely death of which you are all aware. We are all, I know, very conscious of the unique situation which has arisen as a result of his demise.' He turned and looked down at Mary. 'It's a matter of the shares, Mary.' Her wide dark eyes stared up at him blankly. She reminded him of a child, of one of the misty sentimental watercolours of angels Victorians liked to hang above their bedheads. Simon Petrie could remember such a painting in his mother's room. 'Your husband's shares ... your shares,' he explained with an unaccustomed feeling of discomfort. Damn, he thought, this was exactly why women should never be involved in business; they were incapable of understanding it, too capable of distraction. He paused for a moment and then said: 'You do realise, of course, you hold a high percentage of the available shares in Petrie India?'

Mary nodded. 'I know I have been left some shares in Gerald's will.' Simon Petrie's conversation was puzzling her. The unexpected sight of the board members, confronting her like hungry animals waiting to be fed when the boardroom door had been opened, had momentarily unnerved her, but she had then thought this simply an unusual way of introducing her to them. Why, though, was Simon Petrie now asking her if she knew about the shares? Gerald's will! It had been little more than a scrawled note. She had not even know of its existence until Alan had produced it. It had been written while Gerald was in hospital, the day after they had been married; witnessed by the surgeon and the sergeant orderly. It had said simply: 'In the event of my death I leave all my worldly possessions to my wife Mary.' It named Alan as Gerald's executor, and it was Alan who had dealt with all the legal aspects of the transfer of bank account and capital, the ownership of Kimberley and the Petrie India shares to Mary's name after Gerald's death and during the sad days when only her love of James and her knowledge of his need for her prevented her from taking her life.

'Your solicitors must obviously have advised you,' persisted Simon Petrie.

'Solicitors? What about?'

This was ridiculous, he thought. He had never experienced such naivity in business. He was aware all the members of the board were watching him, their faces deliberately expressionless as though they were attempting to disassociate themselves from the painful situation that was obviously developing. Simon Petrie returned their stares, silently demanding their assistance; for once, none was offered. He spoke impatiently. 'My dear Mary, someone must have advised you of the value of the family shares, and the position in which your husband's death and the manner in which he disposed of his holdings has placed us all?'

What does he want me to say, wondered Mary. I can't answer him because I don't understand his question. I have family shares in Petrie India, but so do all the others here. Have I done something wrong? Was there something an Englishwoman would have done on her husband's death I have neglected to do? Surely Alan would have advised me if that were so?

To Simon Petrie's relief, Copel Bronowski, a heavily jowled man whose suit fitted tightly across his broad shoulders and showed his muscles when he moved, leant forward, his heavy elbows on the table. He peered at Mary through thick-lensed glasses with gold rims, and clasped his stubby fingers. A broad gold ring caught the light. 'Who is acting on your behalf? ...' He added, 'My lady,' in almost a whisper. There was a slight mid-European accent in his speech. He sat back in his chair and drew his clasped hands to his stomach, then said: 'Your legal behalf.' Bronowski had quit Russia in 1936 and although he had a strong hatred of Communism, was sufficiently socialist to dislike the use of titles.

Mary was still bewildered. He must mean who had helped her when Gerald had died. She answered: 'Captain Alan Jameson.'

Bronowski raised his eyebrows and then said, with satisfaction: 'Ah. Then Captain Jameson is your solicitor.'

Mary shook her head. 'No. He was my husband's commander. A friend.'

'You have no solicitor?' Bronowski blinked like a surprised owl.

'Not here in Britain. Why should I?' Her disarming wide-eyed expression sapped Bronowski's confidence.

'It is normal to have a solicitor,' he said weakly. 'Even I sometimes seek the advice of a colleague.' Damn, he thought to himself, I was brought here with the expectation of having to act as legal referee in a family battle for company control. This rather charming young woman doesn't even understand what the shares mean to her. He caught Simon Petrie's eyes. 'I think one of us ought to give Lady Petrie an explanation of our concern.'

Simon Petrie visibly squirmed. 'Yes. Yes, it would seem appropriate.'

Frederick Harben, a cousin by the marriage of Simon Petrie's aunt, said 'Hear, hear' loudly, and ignored Simon Petrie's frown in his direction.

Simon Petrie brushed a strand of creamed hair from his forehead, and wished he could sit back in his chair and light his pipe. It was something he did whenever he needed time to think. The situation did not allow him that luxury now. 'You see, Mary, due to omissions in both my brother's will, and that of your husband, Gerald, over fifty per cent of Petrie India shares have been left to you without any legal stipulations as to their future disposal.'

Ah, thought Mary, so there was something that should have been done; perhaps by Gerald. As his widow, there must be some obligation I have not fulfilled. It dismayed her to think in some way after his death she had failed Gerald despite her efforts during his lifetime never to do so. She felt tears of shame well up in her eyes and tried to fight them back. She spoke tremulously: 'I accept all the responsibility. I ... I haven't bothered very much about his business during the past few weeks. I should have known there were things to do about it.'

Bronowski decided there was an opportunity to exploit. He spoke reassuringly. 'There is absolutely no blame attached to yourself, Lady Petrie. None whatsoever.' He was pleased to see relief in her eyes; it would make her more amenable to what he would shortly suggest. 'We obtained a copy of your late husband's will through the Company solicitors in Calcutta. We were surprised to find it so ... so simple. However, normally Petrie family shares are protected by willing them in trust to future heirs, with the present holder benefitting from the profits declared annually by the company. In this manner, the shares always remain within the family.'

Mary said: 'I see.' She wondered what should be done now, but waited for Bronowski to continue.

He opened a file which lay on the desk in front of him. Mary became conscious that the members of the board around her were sitting rigidly, focussing their attention on Bronowski in tense anticipation. She experienced the terrifying feeling that a trap was about to be sprung, a trap the others were expecting and in which she was to be the prey. 'I have a proposition for you, Lady Petrie.' He drew out a sheet of paper and studied it for a few seconds. Mary was suddenly aware that this would prove to be the bait. She felt vulnerable, threatened. Bronowski raised his eyes and for a moment tried to stare her out. He failed, coughed, and then stared down at the paper. 'The proposal is, from the board of directors, that your shares should be purchased from you for a sum of money which will place you in a financially secure position for the remainder of your life.' He continued hurriedly, as though to prevent any interruption before the trap was completely set. 'We have calculated the value of your shares at one hundred and thirty-five thousand pounds.' He scrutinised figures. 'That represents in your own money, two million one hundred and sixty thousand rupees.' He lifted his head and smiled at her. 'A very substantial amount, Lady Petrie.'

Mary felt emptiness inside her, the cold bleak void of loneliness. Even when she had learnt of the displeasure of Gerald's mother at his marriage she had still considered herself part of the Petrie family. There had been pride in seeing the Petrie name on the Calcutta offices, or stencilled on the cases of the tea the steamers brought downriver to the ghats and company go-downs. Meeting Simon Petrie in Calcutta and having him stay as a guest in her home had seemed to confirm the sense of belonging which she enjoyed. Now she realised that she had never been accepted. To the Petries she was no more than an intruder to be rid of as soon as they were able. They were neither interested in her, nor her son. Nor her son! The words repeated themselves in her mind. Gerald's son! He was *their* flesh and *their* blood, and they wanted no part of him. They wanted her to sell them his future, his heritage. The chill of hurt distilled towards anger.

William Petrie had been silent during the meeting, but decided now was an opportune moment for him to make, as managing director, some observation which would be recorded in the minutes and indicate to absent shareholders that he had been closely involved in the negotiations. He smiled at her gratuitously. 'I am quite sure our offer is most generous in the circumstances.'

The speed and force of her reply momentarily shocked him. 'In what circumstances, William?' Her use of his Christian name, implying her relationship, added impetus to her words. Her brown eyes, previously soft, were diamond hard, adding to his discomfort. 'In the circumstances that my skin is darker than your own, William? In the circumstances that I was born an Indian national? In the circumstances that I am a woman? In what circumstances exactly are you suggesting, William?'

Sitting at her small desk beyond the board table, Elizabeth stabbed a full-stop in her notepad and breathed a silent 'hurrah'.

William Petrie reddened. 'We know very little about you.' He tried to make it sound like a reasonable excuse.

'I am quite sure you will have been informed I was a Company memsah'b's servant,' said Mary, fiercely. 'And you will know from what you have always been told, servants are quite dishonest and untrustworthy. Are they some of your circumstances?' Her eyes refused to release him. 'There are other things you should know, William. Although I was born an Indian, I am British by marriage. Furthermore, I am a Petrie, and a Petrie by choice. And whether you enjoy the fact or not, my son James is not only a Petrie but the present Baronet Petrie; Sir James Nlamo Petrie.'

'Bullseye,' said Elizabeth softly.

Bronowski adjusted his spectacles by pushing them further up the wide bridge of his nose with his forefinger. 'Gentlemen, Lady Petrie.' He held his hands apart, palm upwards, in an appeal. 'There is no need for anyone to become heated. This matter can be resolved quite simply, by legal intermediaries representing both parties.'

'I am my own representative,' said Mary firmly. These men had insulted not only her, but her son and the memory of her late husband. The British might not consider it normal to bargain in their shops, but they would certainly learn now that it was necessary to bargain in their commerce. She turned her attention to Bronowski. 'I consider the Company's offer to be an insult,' she told him. 'It does not represent even one twentieth of Petrie assets in India alone.' She tried to remember things Gerald had mentioned, things which even the Warrens had talked of so many years ago. 'And there are the estates in Ceylon, the interest in the river transport company, and the

London properties.' She strengthened her position. 'I would also like to remind you, I am already wealthy.'

Inside himself, Simon Petrie smiled with satisfaction. Despite her anger, or perhaps because of it, Mary appeared to have made the first move towards a financial settlement. He had expected her to bargain; not publicly, nor did he intend to allow her to do so, but the stage was being set for the negotiations to begin. It had not been pleasant, but he had attended worse meetings in his lifetime. It would have been less emotional dealing with a man. He said: 'I think you should understand, Mary, a valuation of voting shares does not necessarily represent the value of the total of company assets. Voting shares are treated rather uniquely.'

He overlooked the clarity of her thoughts when she was concentrating on a subject. She removed the anger from her voice and spoke to him calmly. 'I notice you refer to my shares as voting shares. Are there other kinds?' Simon Petrie cursed himself and avoided answering the question. Mary noted his reluctance and faced Bronowski. 'Will you please explain. I am sure you would not wish there to be any misunderstanding that might cause you professional embarrassment later.'

Bronowski bit his lower lip. Neither his professional nor his personal morals allowed him the dishonesty he realised was necessary to protect his client's interests. Mentally he shrugged. Who were his clients? Petrie India? The major voting shareholder? He took a deep breath and avoided Simon Petrie's stare. 'There are two types of family share, my lady. There are the normal family shares which were originally purchased by shareholders when they were offered to relatives by the founder of Petrie India. And there are one hundred shares known as voting shares. In the case of family shares, holders receive such bonuses from company profits as are deemed disposable on an annual basis, and nothing more.' He paused, but she refused to accept his silence.

'And the one hundred voting shares, Mr Bronowski?'

'Exactly as they are named. A voting share entitles its holder to a vote at shareholders' meetings.'

She persisted. 'One vote for one share?'

'Yes, that is so.'

There was complete silence in the boardroom; the sounds of traffic in the streets outside penetrated only distantly. Mary stood and adjusted the fur cape theatrically around her shoulders, the movement fanning the fragrance of her perfume across the table. The members waited, uncertain of her intentions. She spoke to them collectively: 'Then I think the question of my voting shares in Petrie India should be dealt with at a more appropriate time.' She gathered the cape closer. 'I wish you a good morning, gentlemen.'

There was a hurried movement of chairs and bodies as she strode away from the table, leaving them on their feet and watching her departure.

Elizabeth guided her to the foyer. She was unable to resist saying: 'Well done ... well done.'

In the silent boardroom Simon Petrie pulled the filled briar from his pocket, found his lighter and set the flame thoughtfully to the tobacco. William Petrie put his hand in his pocket for his indigestion tablets, then said loudly: 'Blast. Damn and blast the woman.'

Bronowski gathered up his file, and decided to lunch at the Feathers before returning to his offices. Nothing had happened which he had not anticipated as a possibility. The British always tended to feel superior and secure when dealing with foreigners; it was a national weakness and today's outcome earned them none of his sympathy.

CHAPTER ELEVEN

Mary had heard the British in India comment on the different smells which assailed them, some pleasant, many revolting, when they had first arrived in the sub-continent. She had thought they had exaggerated; at times she was herself aware of the many odours in the villages, the cooking fires, the animals and the scents of the flowers, even of the tea bushes, but they seldom penetrated her consciousness sufficiently to intrude. Here in London, however, she understood how the British had felt during their first days in a strange country; the smells of the unfamiliar city forced themselves upon her, petrol and diesel fumes mingling with the sweet odours the damp weather and rain expelled from the drains in the gutters; wet clothing, damp raincoats, business suits that were infrequently cleaned and which smelt of sour urine and sweat in the moist and humid press of crowded stores. And everywhere the sulphurous air poisoned by the fumes of coal fires. Even the toast which Jane had made for breakfast that morning had tasted of coal gas. It no longer surprised her so many of the British she saw in London streets coughed or sniffed incessantly.

Still nervous in London, she had used a taxi to get from Mincing Lane to Kensington. She knew the mews house would be empty, and although Jane had given her a key she had decided to lunch in the restaurant where Jane had taken James and herself the previous day. She had sought the same table, and deliberately prolonged the meal, finding comfort in the small familiarity of the surroundings.

Although she had been angry in the Petrie India boardroom, and was angry still, the sense of rejection was still strong enough to hurt her. Despite Jane's warning about Simon Petrie, she nevertheless expected him to help her, even if it was only grudgingly at first. It seemed to her now that British family loyalties or ties of blood had no meaning. Almost all of the members of the board of directors had been related to her, if only distantly, by her marriage to Gerald, but they had behaved as though she were a complete outsider.

She was angry with herself, too; angry she had not taken a closer interest in Gerald's legacy after his death. It had not seemed important, then; only death, Gerald's death, had been important at first. And then James's future. Alan had told her about the shares, and the money which had been left to her and which he had arranged with Lloyd and Bannerjee, Gerald's solicitors, to transfer to her name and account. She could remember even the occasion of his conversation, remember him walking with her along the bank of the Hooghly, the evening warm and sultry, the surface of the river undisturbed but for a small flock of water-fowl near the reeds, the surface of the water like liquid brown glass.

Alan had talked earnestly and with concern, and his nearness had been comforting for her, but she had heard only the sound of his voice, not the words he had spoken; she had only been able to think of the times when that same evening walk had been taken with Gerald at her side; James would have been bathed and put to bed by Renana, they would have kissed him goodnight, and then, just before the sun began to set behind the Botanical Gardens on the far side of the river, Gerald would ask: 'Fancy a stroll?'

She would know then that his business day had been strenuous and he was seeking the peace of the riverside in her company. It had always flattered her, always made her feel even closer to him. Gerald would use the word 'stroll' as though he would actually be walking, not propelling himself in the hated wheelchair; he had never let her push it, but she would rest her hand gently on his shoulder as they made their way for a quarter of a mile to the sloping bank where the ferry-boat was beached every evening. The ferrymen knew them and always welcomed them.

As Gerald's Hindi had improved he had chatted with them for a while, joked with them before he and Mary returned to Kimberley. It would be almost dark when they arrived home, the lights of the house bright and welcoming in the dusk.

Memories of all those 'strolls' with Gerald had occupied her mind while Alan had been speaking. Poor Alan, she thought. He was so kind to herself and James, so concerned for both of them, and yet at times she almost ignored him, had certainly ignored his feelings though she had welcomed his support. Did he still love her, she wondered? He had loved her in the past; when Gerald had been alive. There had been that solitary occasion when she had seen it in his eyes as he watched her. Was it his continuing love for her that had brought him so quickly to her side when tragedy had struck her life? Momentarily her thoughts brought her sadness, not for herself but for Alan. No matter how much he might care for her, might even love her still, she could offer him no more than her gratitude and friendship. Regardless of his feelings, her own love, the special love of a woman for a man, was forever enmeshed in memories.

The feeling of slight dominated her thinking; there was no escape from it. The cold businesslike manner in which it had been proposed that she should sell her rights to any connection with Petrie India brought a new and growing anger to her mind. She had been angry before, in the boardroom, but then it had been hot anger; now it was replaced by the chill anger of determination, determination that she would protect her son's future. But how? She knew nothing of British law. Surely she could not be forced to sell the shares? And if they gave her voting power, then how much power? Why was it so important to the Petrie India board of directors that they should buy them from her? Who could she find to advise her, here in England where she was only a foreigner, a woman who could easily be exploited? Who could she trust? Only Jane.

She returned to the mews house, its interior cold and unwelcoming, touched with damp and scented by the dead coals in its fireplace. It seemed more depressing than any other building she had visited in her lifetime. For a long time she was alone, her only company the monotonous and deliberate ticking of a grandfather clock in one corner of the room.

James had chatted his way to bed after the supper of cold meats and salad. His day had been one of excitement, its success judged by the strange animals he had seen, the number of different ice-creams he had eaten in the zoo's kiosks. Jane had quickly noticed Mary's changed mood, but had not questioned her as to the success of her visit. Now, in the living-room, the fire glowing in the grate, she listened until Mary had finished, then spoke softly.

'I don't know how to apologise to you.' She shook her head, avoiding Mary's eyes, and staring at the fire. The spurts of flame from the coals lit her cheeks giving them an artificial blush, moving the shadows of the furniture against the walls. 'You must think we're all a pretty rotten lot.' She paused. 'What will you do now?'

I will bargain, thought Mary. Bargain as hard as I can to protect James's future. And the trick was to walk away from the first offer as though it held no interest at all. It was not always easy to do. She said: 'Nothing for the moment,' then decided Jane deserved more of an answer. 'Gerald used to tell me, always sleep on decisions ...'

'But never on arguments.' Jane completed the quotation. 'Something my father used to say to us when we were children. Quite right, too; a pity that Mother has always ignored it.'

Mother! Mary realised with a sudden pang of dismay that Margaret Petrie was another problem she had almost certainly faced with too much optimism. If the family had planned to remove her from their business, then they would want no part of her or James in their private lives. Her world, which had appeared so large when it had been shared with Gerald, had now diminished until it was little more than a sphere which contained only herself and her son.

Alone, later, her mind sought comfort in the distant familiarity of India. She let it wander through the colourful rooms at Kimberley, the shaded peaceful gardens with their memories of happiness and laughter. Somehow, it was carried to the hills and for a brief few seconds she stood on a flat, green terrace overlooking the river, distant jungle and sandy flood plains. But it was Alan who stood beside her, and his steel-grey eyes caught hers and questioned. A sense of guilt confused and momentarily frightened her. She fought the image until it fragmented and dispersed. She had wanted the reassurance of memories not fantasy; the terrace on which she had stood had not existed in reality nor had the momentary warmth, far more intimate than simple affection, which she had experienced on that strange hillside with Alan.

Perhaps, she decided, she had allowed herself to rely on him far too much in the past months, so that now her mind conjured him to her aid rather than permit her the more painful but necessary independence. But, although she reminded herself that she alone must now make all the decisions for her own and James's future, she was unable totally to banish the recent real memories of Alan which projected themselves; how close he had walked to her through the airport at Dum-Dum, a slim and still military figure even in his lightweight civilian suit as he had collected their tickets at the Air India counter; the lightest of farewell kisses on her cheek and his discernible reluctance to release her arm. How, as she had turned at the aircraft's steps he had been standing, his artificial hand clasped behind his back as though to conceal his disability, but then his sad acknowledgement of her final wave.

Simon Petrie telephoned early the next morning. He was courteous, apologetic. It had been unreasonable of him, he told Mary, to expect a lady, totally unaccustomed to British business procedure, to be faced with such an important matter in so unfamiliar surroundings. It was really unnecessary to involve the other members of his board of directors, and he was quite certain the whole thing could be sorted out in the more pleasant atmosphere of a City luncheon club. Perhaps she would care to join him the following day. His chauffeur would collect her at twelve-thirty.

Mary agreed. She had hoped for a response in some form or another, and his call indicated that Petrie India were prepared to negotiate with her.

Simon Petrie replaced the telephone receiver, leant back in his chair and began filling his pipe. In the past fifty years he had bargained many times with Indians, and he felt he had been correct in his judgement of Mary; she was little different from the others. If anything, she was far more naive than any of the merchants with whom he normally conducted business. And bargaining was a game Simon Petrie enjoyed.

He pressed the intercom button. The set clicked into life.

'Yes, sir.' Elizabeth Willoughby's voice was brusquely efficient.

'Tell Bronowski I want him here at four this afternoon ... Mr William, too. And Mr Julian and the Harbens.'

'Yes, sir.'

'And book me a table at the City Rooms, tomorrow. One o'clock.'

'For how many, sir?' asked Elizabeth.

'Three,' said Simon Petrie. He switched off the intercom, struck a Swan Vesta, and when it had stopped flaring held the flame to his pipe and drew in a deep lungful of the tobacco smoke.

*

The second meeting with Simon Petrie had begun more pleasantly than the first. He was accompanied by Bronowski, but Mary had half-expected this might be the case. Business was not discussed during the lunch, and had it not been for her experience in the Petrie India offices two days previously, Mary would have found Simon Petrie's company surprisingly enjoyable. He seemed warm, and fatherly, genuinely concerned by the problems of James's future with which he assured her he would help in every way. It was difficult to believe that this was the man who had embarrassed and then angered her in the boardroom. By the end of the lunch she was beginning to wonder if she had totally misunderstood him and if perhaps she should have been the one to make amends.

The waiter led them through to the lounge for coffee, but it was not until it had been served that Bronowski raised the question of her shares in Petrie India. At first, she thought Simon Petrie was about to dismiss the matter. He seemed a little annoyed Bronowski should have introduced the subject, as though it were almost ungentlemanly. He was again apologetic.

'I'm sorry, my dear. Business is like a mole which suddenly appears in the middle of your nicest piece of lawn. Still, I suppose we had better allow Mr Bronowski to have his say.' He chuckled. 'After all, that's what we pay him for.'

It was his eyes that warned Mary. His narrow face had showed humour, but the eyes denied the emotion as they watched her. She realised the entire meeting until this moment had been a charade, and his apparent congeniality in the pleasant Dickensian atmosphere of the eating club had almost disarmed her.

'Of course.'

Simon Petrie did not notice the fractional hardening of her voice. He felt confident now that she would accept the new proposals. The first offer from Petrie India had been deliberately low; this would now appear generous, especially if she thought everything was being conducted by him and with her own interests at heart.

Bronowski fumbled in his breast pocket and brought out a folded sheet of paper which he examined. He adjusted his glasses with his forefinger and then cleared his throat. He smiled at her. 'I am quite sure there will be no further problems, Lady Petrie.' He spoke more brightly. 'As you quite correctly pointed out, there were assets which were overlooked when the first suggestions were made.' He deliberately avoided the use of the word 'offer', in an attempt to maintain the sense of friendship he felt had been successfully introduced. 'Nothing more than a careless administrative oversight. Afterwards, we felt extremely foolish.' He spoke more confidentially. 'Your uncle drew it to our attention.'

He cleared his throat again, a habit when he examined legal papers before speaking. 'Your uncle has suggested that a far more suitable figure would be three hundred thousand pounds. I should add that it is somewhat grander than the financial director advised, based on the true value of your present holding. And also, your uncle has suggested that a trust should be formed especially for the benefit of your son James. This would be a further sum of fifty thousand pounds which would be invested, at the discretion of an agreed broker or perhaps bank, and would mature until your son reaches twenty-one.' He paused, attempting to judge her reaction. 'This would, naturally, guarantee your son substance, regardless of anything which might affect your own personal wealth or property.' He folded the paper and handed it to her. 'I took the liberty of putting our proposals in writing ... not a contract, of course. That is a simple matter that can be dealt with at a later date. A matter for lawyers.'

'No wonder you feel uneasy about their offer. I simply don't believe in Petrie generosity.' Jane spoke vehemently, when she had listened to Mary's description of the luncheon that evening. She tightened her lips into a thin line. 'Uncle Simon is a hard old businessman, not a philanthropist. His entire life has been devoted to increasing the profits of Petrie India. He's a typical Petrie, and none of them are charitable when it comes down to the Company. Some disguise it better than others, but underneath they're all the same ... chips off the old Picey Petrie block. It's almost genetic, this fanatical regard for Petrie India. A male Petrie trait; they think there's something mystical about it all, as though they control the key to the western world's trade with the east.' Her voice had risen with sudden anger. 'Even Gerald was the same.'

Mary shook her head. 'No. He was different from them.'

Jane lowered her voice. 'I'm not criticising him, but he was a Petrie, and no one is perfect. You told me he never changed the title of the Company.'

'He wanted to.' Mary felt defensive. She had never heard Jane talk like this before.

'But he didn't. And probably Uncle Simon told him it would be detrimental to the Company. Regardless of the advice of your Indian friend, Gerald would have listened to Uncle Simon. That's the way with them ... Company first, males second, and women of no importance. That's the way Uncle Simon's mind will be working now. He isn't the slightest bit concerned about you. He is acting entirely for the benefit of Petrie India. I'd stake my life on it, Mary, I really would.'

'They've offered me a great deal of money. Far more than I shall ever need. Perhaps it is sensible for me to accept.'

'Sensible? It's nonsense. It's exactly what they hope you will do. Then they'll be rid of you. The money isn't important, but the principle is. It's time the men in the Petrie family were shown it's a changing world, and they have to acknowledge that women share it with them. You must get advice about this. Fight them if necessary.' She paused, 'Lewis!' It was almost an exclamation, spoken explosively as she pushed herself from the chair. 'Lewis Kiernan. He'd be delighted if I asked him.'

Mary watched her pick up the telephone. Jane faced her, the receiver in her hand, a finger poised above the dial. 'Do you mind if I ask him to help us?'

Us! The word brought a touch of warmth to Mary, more comforting than the fire in the living-room grate; it indicated Jane's friendship, implied her involvement. She smiled and said: 'I need help from anyone, I think.'

Jane spun the dial, jamming the handset between her chin and neck while she held the telephone. 'It's about time Lewis earned the suppers he scrounges. A friend,' she explained. 'Not very serious, but he's rather nice. The trouble is he's typically Irish; won't begin to think about settling down until he's forty-five.' Mary could hear the ringing tone softly in the instrument, then the click as it was answered. 'Lewis, Jane here. You busy? ... Lewis, be serious, I need some advice ... very amusing ... well, can you drag yourself away from your book and pop round here? Yes, I've got some whisky ... no, I'm not alone, my sister-in-law is staying with me. No, she won't be going to the cinema; she wants to meet you.' Jane looked at Mary and raised her eyebrows in mock desperation. 'Ten minutes, then. 'Bye now.' She replaced the receiver and shrugged her shoulders. 'I'm afraid you're about to meet the lunatic fringe of the British legal profession.'

*

Mary had met only a few Irishmen in India, though she could recognise their accent. She had always thought of them as one of the British tribes, and by their reputation as fighters they had earned a place in Indian history as soldiers of fortune. They were disreputable in their drinking habits in the lower quarters of Calcutta, according to the more staid, or discreet, English, and originated from some green but desolate isle shaped like a pariah-dog to the west of the main island of Britain. They were quite different from the English; like the Scotsmen who worked in the jute industry, far more of them married Indian girls and accepted the mixed marriages amongst themselves, forming small communities who seldom mingled socially with the English, who regarded them almost as outcasts. Consequently she was unable to picture this Lewis Kiernan whom Jane believed would help her. But he was a friend of Jane's and according to her a solicitor who, although he had only been qualified for a few years, was already making a name for himself in the City.

He arrived at the small mews house like a whirlwind, bursting past Jane into the hallway, trying to grab her with hands that were both already holding bottles of wine. Mary heard her protest: 'Lewis, this isn't a party.'

'A wake then?'

'Lewis.'

The door was pushed open and Lewis Kiernan's huge frame dwarfed the furniture and seemed to occupy half the room. He was one of the biggest men Mary had ever seen and for a moment startled her; Jane had warned her of his exuberance, but not his size. Gerald had been tall, but Lewis Kiernan would have dwarfed him. He was over six feet six inches in height, broad shouldered and barrel-chested. His hands were so large they almost concealed the bottles they held. His neck appeared to be the same width as his head. His hair was black, crinkled wire. He stood, a giant staring down at Mary with amused eyes, and then said in an exaggerated Irish accent: 'Well now, what in the name of all the holy places do I see sitting there in the gloom?'

Jane pushed her way past him with difficulty. 'Lewis, we just aren't in the mood.'

His broad face creased as he smiled. His mouth was wide, his teeth large but even. His eyes, Mary could see now, were quite dark; almost as dark as her own. 'I'll have to change that, then.' He handed Jane the two bottles and took a couple of paces towards Mary. 'And is this the sister-in-law who won't be going to the cinema?' He towered over her.

Jane had mentioned Mary to him during past conversations, but had never described her. Somehow his mind had identified her with the wife of one of the few Indians he had ever met, the owner of a small café near the King George the Fifth docks and whom he had represented in one of his first cases as a newly qualified solicitor. The woman had been fat, taciturn and had smelt of fried fish and chips. Now he experienced an unexpected sense of incredulity, as though he had opened a box thought to be empty but which in fact contained a rare gem. He stared at Mary, fascinated. Her dark skin was flawless, contrasting dramatically with the white silk of her clothing. Her features were incredibly fine, more those of a slender child than a woman. He was aware how clumsy he must seem to her, and was grateful when Jane broke the lengthening silence.

'Mary, this is Lewis. Lewis, Mary.'

His enormous hand reached for Mary's, and totally enveloped it in a powerful yet gentle grip. Mary realised he was probably so strong he could easily crush her, but just as large hounds have the gentlest mouths, he was conscious of his strength and the need to use it carefully. The palm of his hand was warm but dry, and calloused enough to surprise her; she had expected it to be softer. He said 'Mary,' pronouncing the 'r' far more distinctly than would an Englishman, his voice rich and deep, and his eyes sparkled mischievously. 'And would you be named after Bloody Mary, or the Holy Virgin herself whose robes you've obviously borrowed?'

The Irish accent softened as he became serious, until it was barely discernible, but the Irish ability to give a normal sentence literary charm remained; a natural and unaffected gift. He had refused to relax until Jane had given him a large glass of whisky and opened the wine for Mary and herself. Then he sat himself on the sofa, his bulk occupying the space of two people, and his legs so long they seemed unsupported by the narrowness of the piece of furniture. He rested one of his arms along the back of the sofa and listened as Jane explained Mary's dilemma. His face was calm now and only his dark eyes moved, watching Jane as she spoke and flicking towards Mary to judge her reaction. In the half-light of the room, Mary could see how he would age; he would become a gnarled white-haired bear of a man, gentle or fierce as the moment determined; a patriarch to whom people would take their problems. She sensed his future as not in law, but perhaps politics. Something about him, the sheer size of him, generated the warmth of confidence, honesty. He was young as yet, but the signs were there even now.

When Jane had finished, Lewis said, 'Ah ...' He drained his glass but made no sign he wanted another. Jane handed him the whisky bottle and he uncapped it slowly. Whisky splashed his trousers but he ignored it. Jane took the bottle from him just as it seemed his glass was about to overflow.

He spoke as though he were quoting from a book on company law. 'A holder of more than fifty per cent of company voting shares would control the company, subject to the rights of the minorities. And would have power over all but those decisions which would fundamentally change the company.' He looked quickly at Mary and grinned. 'How about that?'

'It sounds fine,' said Jane, 'but perhaps you can explain it for us.'

He laughed, a rich laugh that Mary could hear echoed by the mechanism of the grandfather clock behind her. 'It means exactly what it says. If you own more than half the voting shares, you can do what you like with Petrie India. The rights of the minorities are simply the rights of any shareholder with less than fifty per cent. And fundamental changes would be considered such things as totally changing the business of the company, say from the import of tea to the manufacture of pianos, or something along those lines.' He shook his head and took a deep swig at the whisky. 'There are really no problems at all, ladies. You can lead them a fine jig should you choose to do so.'

Jane said, 'No wonder they were worried.'

'It doesn't excuse the despicable way in which they behaved,' Lewis said firmly. 'I don't like criticising my own profession, but the ethics of whoever advised them are questionable. This kind of thing, the taking advantage of the common man's ignorance,' he caught Mary's eyes reassuringly, 'I mean ignorance of rights in law, Mary, is certainly unethical. There now, how does it feel to know you have your own little kingdom to play with?'

Jane didn't allow Mary to answer him. 'Lewis, you're a typical lawyer. You've only half solved the problems. It's one thing knowing something can be done, but what should be done?'

Lewis said, 'Ah ...' again, and pressed himself back in the

sofa. His face was serious. 'I've been quite happy to inform this pretty young lady of her rights without any thought of recompense. Now, however, we enter a different field; the field of legal advice. The moral code of my profession does not permit me to give advice to clients, unless of course they may be a charity, without a fee.' He pushed out his lower lip slightly. 'You must understand, if it were known that certain members of the legal profession gave their services without fees, then those seeking advice would flock to them, to the detriment of those others in the profession who needs must charge for their services.'

Jane groaned loudly and said, 'Blackmail.'

'Really, Jane, I don't mind ...' Mary began, but Lewis interrupted her.

'My fee will be one meal, to be served this coming Sunday evening. Naturally, I will provide the liquid courses.'

Mary realised he had been teasing them.

'Impossible, Lewis, we can't afford to feed you,' smiled Jane. She turned to Mary. 'This hulking great brute of a man can eat a whole ox at one sitting. They call him Desperate Dan in his office, because he takes a leg of beef with him for lunch and gnaws it down to the bone.'

'If you can find a more worthy solicitor, then do so,' said Lewis airily.

'I think we should buy him his oxen,' Mary said, meeting Lewis's blank gaze.

'But on Saturday night.' Jane softened her voice. 'I know him too well. His idea of an early evening is three o'clock in the morning. Two evenings in Lewis's company and it takes a month to get rid of the bags under my eyes.'

'Saturday is rugby,' said Lewis. 'The London Welsh at Dulwich.' He fingered the slightly crooked bridge of his nose. 'I owe them something from the last game.'

Jane sighed. 'And you'll be drunk by eight o'clock.'

'Hopefully,' Lewis grinned.

'All right, we agree, Sunday evening.'

'Done.' Lewis sat more upright. 'Now let me find out exactly what my client has in mind. Simple revenge? Solicitors aren't really in the retribution business, but their clients often are.'

'I'd like to see the whole damn board out on their necks,' said Jane vehemently.

Lewis put a look of exasperation on his face. 'Which of you ladies am I representing?'

Jane pouted. 'Mary.'

'Then go and put the coffee on, Jane.' He faced Mary again. 'So what would you like to do about Petrie India? Tell me and we'll see if it's possible.'

Mary had been attempting to analyse what Lewis had said. It had sounded as though she had total control over Petrie India, but surely that must be impossible? 'Did you really mean I can do almost anything I want with the Company?'

'Within reasonable limits, yes.'

'Well, the most important thing is to ensure my son's future.' She found it bewildering. All her life, it seemed, she had known of this powerful company. Now it appeared she as good as owned it. Why, she wondered, had Gerald never taken advantage of the power the shares yielded? He had talked of his plans for the Company. Perhaps he was simply biding his time until his knowledge of its workings gave him the confidence of experience.

'There is no trouble about that whatsoever,' said Lewis confidently. 'There are several ways of dealing with it; a contract to enable him to enter the Company at the age of eighteen, later if he wishes, and then an eventual junior directorship. Obviously, he will inherit your shares, and so in time he will have similar control to your own. There are other ways. I'd suggest, however, the most important step to take now must be to establish your own position.'

Jane questioned him from the doorway. 'A shareholders' meeting?'

'Stop taking the wind from my sails. Yes, another shareholders' meeting. Call one at once; better still, I shall do that on your behalf. I think it will show them you mean business.'

Elizabeth Willoughby viewed the developments within the London office of Petrie India with growing interest. She had intended to hand in her resignation at the end of the month, but had become as excitedly involved in witnessing the uncoiling drama as she had with the weekly Saturday afternoon cinema serials of her childhood. She had decided for the moment that the unpleasantness of her job was outweighed by the satisfaction she was receiving from the panic of the Company's directors and shareholders.

It had begun with the delivery of a formal application for an extraordinary shareholders' meeting; that in itself was almost unprecedented in the history of Petrie India. It was as though a time-bomb had been placed in the offices, but whereas for a real bomb the offices could have been evacuated, this one promised to explode amongst the Company's most senior members regardless of their frenzied attempts to escape its consequences; Elizabeth wanted to be present when the explosion occurred. Her feelings had surprised her. She had not realised her character included this odd sadistic streak that for the past few days had made her uncomfortable bus ride to the office pleasurable. She was no different, she thought, to the French women who had sat in the squares of Paris, knitting as victims were brought to the sacrificial guillotines of the Revolution.

The boredom of Elizabeth's office routine had gone; there seemed to be no longer any routine. Company directors came and went, singly, in pairs, in groups. They argued loudly, made inane suggestions, and aroused Simon Petrie to fury. She had never seen him emotional before, but now his moods were always uncertain.

His son William, however, had adopted the haunted look of a man under sentence of death. He had never been a fighter, and unlike his father seemed to have accepted defeat in mid-battle. Elizabeth found her feeling of contempt for the man increase by the hour. She despised male weakness.

Lewis made Mary laugh, teased James until he giggled uncontrollably and became almost hysterical. The first time he had done so, she had felt a twinge of sadness combined with guilt. She had not laughed since before Gerald's death, had not believed there could be laughter in her life again. It was barely three months since Gerald had died, too soon, surely, for laughter? She tried not to be amused by Lewis but it was an impossibility; James encouraged him, reacted to him, wanted the games and the cheerfulness after the sombre weeks. Strangely, the unaccustomed rough-and-tumble male play filled Mary with a wistful sadness; the sights of James being swung high above Lewis's head, shrieking with delight as he was somersaulted or held upside down by Lewis's powerful hands, were destined to become memories which should rightly be of Gerald and his son ... but such memories could never have been. Mary's emotions were continuously confused.

The three weeks leading to the shareholders' meeting had been busy for her, the role which she had planned for Simon Petrie already partly filled by Lewis. He had suggested several preparatory schools which he thought might be suitable for James and had used his office secretary to write for their prospectuses. Although both he and Jane were unobtainable during the daytime, Jane having now returned to her work in the public relations department at Durpril Oil after her week's holiday, Lewis was spending almost all his free hours at the mews house. Mary hired a car and driver to visit the schools who had already replied, and after having talked at length to the headmasters, had made the decision that James would become a pupil at Massendon House near Marlborough at the beginning of the new term after the coming Christmas vacation.

James viewed his future at Massendon House, a huge and rambling early Georgian manor house, with less enthusiasm than his mother. Isolated by its own forty acres of grounds, and surrounded by woodland, despite the cricket and football pitches and the seemingly contented fellow pupils he had seen both at their lessons and games, it had seemed poor exchange for the loss of his mother's company and the familiarity of Kimberley. One attraction, however, was Lewis, who had faithfully promised him he would visit Massendon House at least once a month and collect James to spend the weekend with Jane and himself in London. James was to spend mid-term breaks with them as well, and would fly home to India for all the main holidays.

For Mary, it was impossible for her to reconcile herself with the continuously changing British weather. The heavy cold rain of the first few days of her visit had stopped, but given way to almost a week of evening fog, so dense and heavy that traffic could only move in the London streets guided by handheld flares. The fog killed sound, muffled even speech with its choking, sulphurous fumes, and according to the newspapers she read, was taking a daily toll of the older and more feeble citizens of the capital. For a few hours each day it cleared, but returned in the humid windless atmosphere as soon as the pitiful sun began to drop below the skyline of buildings.

More rain had removed it, rain and strong gales, followed by weather sharper and colder than any she had ever experienced. The skies had cleared and the sun shone, but brought no warmth. Ice coated the pavements and the roads, and unexpectedly brought the discomfort of chilblains and chapped hands and cheeks to both herself and James. Rain returned briefly and brought more comfortable temperatures, but was replaced again within a day by the cold arctic driven frost.

She had still been unable to contact Gerald's mother. Despite several telephone calls and even a letter, Margaret Petrie had not responded. Jane had also attempted to contact her mother, without success. According to her housekeeper, Margaret Petrie was away, visiting friends in the north of England, and had given no indication of when she might return to Ash Park Manor. Although Jane did not believe this was the case, she advised Mary against journeying to her mother's house on the offchance she would meet her. Her mother would certainly view it as an impertinence, and would not see them 'out of bloody-mindedness', she warned. All they could do was to hope Margaret Petrie might change her mind before Mary returned to India; in the meantime, she was obviously determined to have nothing to do with either her own daughter or her daughter-in-law. Strangely, Margaret Petrie's refusal even to see or speak to Jane was a little comforting to Mary; it would have been more hurtful had the refusal been directed only at herself and James. It appeared to indicate a state of mental unbalance rather than hatred.

Twice a year William Petrie visited his Aunt Margaret. He had done so since childhood. From his point of view, it was a purely diplomatic relationship. In his younger days it had been a tactful reminder to her of his birthday, or the approach of Christmas. As he had grown older it had become a habit, two Saturday afternoons a year, when he drove out from Richmond, usually accompanied by his wife Jennifer, to spend three hours in his aunt's company.

Today he had arrived alone, annoyed, apprehensive, and aware that it was less than six months since he had made the same journey.

The sound of Margaret Petrie's voice on the telephone that morning had made him wince. 'What *is* going on, William?' she had demanded stridently. 'No, of course I don't want an explanation over this wretched instrument. Come out at once and see me. No, not tomorrow; today.' It was Saturday and he had planned a round of golf. Worse, it was fine and sunny. He was convinced that by tomorrow it would be raining.

The welcome Margaret Petrie had given him on his arrival at Ash Park Manor had been impatient and cursory. As yet he had not even been offered a cup of coffee to relax him after the tedious journey. She gave him no time to compose himself before she began questioning ... grilling him as though he were on trial and she the prosecuting barrister. The only reaction he received to his answers were the disgusted clickings of her tongue. After an hour, he felt there was nothing more he could explain, and she knew as much as himself.

She had not finished. 'Tell me about this woman,' she demanded. 'What is she like?' The antique armchair in which she was sitting dwarfed her angular frame.

William hesitated. He had never really thought very much about Mary Petrie, only of the threat she posed to the Company and himself. 'Black,' he said.

'Nonsense,' charged his aunt sharply. 'She is from Assam, not Madras.'

William avoided her penetrating blue eyes. 'Well, dark brown then. Indian brown. She's got black hair.'

'Is she attractive?' demanded Margaret Petrie.

'Some of the board thought so, I believe. If you like that sort of thing.' He was reluctant to use any words that might be interpreted as praise for a woman he considered an enemy.

'Beautiful? Some are.'

He was finding her stare discomforting. 'I didn't think so. She's a typical Indian. No different from all the others you see in bazaars. Hard. Very hard and brittle ... probably because of her background. Determined to better herself.'

'And you think that's a fault?'

William realised his aunt's question might be masking a criticism of himself. He became defensive. 'I don't suppose it's a fault, but you know what I mean. Trying to keep up with the Jones's ... trying to prove her education.'

'They can be troublesome,' admitted Margaret Petrie. 'Especially the servant class.' She linked thin fingers on her tweed lap.

'That describes her perfectly,' said William quickly. 'I hadn't thought of it myself. She's servant class. Wears cheap perfume, dresses garishly. I'd agree she is certainly troublesome.'

'A plantation girl,' said his aunt.

William nodded. 'Trying to act above her station.'

It was difficult to remain depressed or saddened for long in Lewis's company, and Mary had begun to realise she was becoming more and more dependent on him; at times she had found herself counting the hours until she would see him again. Somehow he was like the sun above the City, arriving to drive away the mist or frosts that formed in his absence. Problems Mary encountered, or imagined, during the day were usually dissipated by his presence or by a few words of his advice or reassurance. The atmosphere of the mews house changed as he stepped through the door, his body, personality and rich voice filling every minute crevice of its structure.

That Jane and Lewis liked each other was unquestionable, but there was never physical contact, never an endearing word between them. They teased or insulted each other, obviously met and drank or ate together frequently, occasionally visited the theatre or cinema in each other's company, but that seemed to be as far as the friendship went, or might ever go. One evening, unable to contain her curiosity longer, Mary had questioned Jane. Jane had been amused.

'Lewis? Lewis and me?' She had laughed. 'As I said, he's an Irishman. They only get interested in permanent relationships when they're in their dotage. We're just friends really.' There was the slightest hint of regret not quite concealed by her humour, and Mary noticed it and questioned further. 'Lewis is his own man. He won't be tamed any more than the west wind. How he ever went into law I shall never know; he should be an explorer, a big game hunter ... even a tea planter. But law ...!'

'He could be a poet or an author,' Mary had observed.

'A poet!' Jane had laughed almost hysterically at the idea. 'A bricklayer would be nearer the mark. Lewis is just a big-hearted ...' she sought for the words '... a big-hearted Irish rugby-playing, hard drinking child. He hasn't grown up yet. He probably never will. I like him for it, perhaps, but whoever marries him will end up by being his mother not his wife.'

Mary had thought about Jane's description of Lewis; to her it had seemed incorrect, inaccurate, unfair. True, he was boisterous, probably at times impetuous, but he was caring and sensitive. She knew his liking for James was genuine and that had warmed her to him. And if, as Jane had said before Mary had first met Lewis, he was making a name for himself in his profession, then there was a serious side to him as well. He had completely taken over the matter of Petrie India, had exchanged cables with Lloyd and Bannerjee, had contacted the company secretary and the other shareholders, had informed them of the extraordinary meeting, and had completed all the formalities. When she had been nervous of the directors' reactions he had brushed aside her worries and reminded her what it would all mean to herself and James.

On the evening before the meeting, he took her out to dinner alone and spent the three hours they were together bolstering her confidence. Like a doctor advising a patient before an operation, he explained to her what would happen and what she must do. When the taxi dropped them back at the mews house he refused Mary's invitation for a nightcap, but left her at the door. 'You need a little time to yourself,' he explained. 'Time to concentrate your mind; to collect your thoughts. I'll be with you tomorrow, right beside you to jog your elbow if you need it, so no more worrying.' He took both of Mary's hands and the contact itself was comforting to her. 'You just get some sleep. I'll pick you up at nine-thirty.'

That night she lay awake anticipating the events of the next day, considering the dictates Lewis had suggested, the speech she might be required to make when her proposals had been accepted. She had not expected to sleep, but realised she had done so when she was awakened.

It was not a sound that disturbed her nor a movement, but subconscious expectation, the feeling she should be awake.

With a mother's concern, her immediate thoughts were for her child, for James. Perhaps he was ill, needed her comfort? She rolled quickly on to her side. In the light of the street lamps in the mews she could see him, his head dark on the pillow, sleeping peacefully. She reached to touch him, to draw the blanket a little closer around his neck. She let her hand rest there for a while, enjoying the touch of the soft, warm young skin; James would have resisted this feminine indulgence had he been awake. He was already developing the independence of manhood.

Mary was aware sleep might not now return so readily and attempted to force her mind away from the coming day and towards her own solitary return to Calcutta. Jane had warned her that despite the present weather's apparent severity it would get even colder once the year had turned. Calcutta would be far more pleasant. It would be lonely without James, but she determined to fill the hours to their maximum so that the months until his first vacational return to India would pass swiftly. It would not be too difficult, for already the desk in the room in Kimberley which she had converted into a small office for herself would be filling with her committee work. Committees!

She smiled to herself. Aurobindo had cunningly ensnared her. It had begun with the educational committee, and in retrospect she knew it had been merely an introduction. At first she had been nervous, but as her confidence had grown she had assumed greater responsibilities until, to her surprise, she had been elected chairman. The post had enhanced her reputation, as had the level-headed manner in which she approached its many problems. She had the knack of creating a bond between herself and her committee members that turned them from mere fellow-travellers into conscientious workers determined to prove themselves. First one committee and then two. More had followed. Gerald had never objected, and in return for his quiet support she had always ensured that her work never interposed itself between them, or between herself and James.

As her mind conjured back the memories, her grief returned; no longer the wild and sickening torment bleaching and emptying her in the first weeks of mourning, but a gentle sorrow that in many ways was harder to control, with its reminder that the loss and loneliness were forever.

She felt her eyes filling, misting James's face across the dark void between the beds. For a moment she needed the comfort of James's body held against her own, his head nestling her shoulder, the grasp of his hands. She turned away from him and lay staring upwards, her arms outside the blankets, cold in the chill night air.

There was a small alien movement of the bedclothes near her feet, the settling of the eiderdown beneath the weight of a body. It was sufficient to freeze her. Had it been her charpoy in Assam, she might have assumed it were a rat, or worse, a snake. She would have thrown off the blanket in such a manner as to have enveloped it for the seconds it would have taken her to switch on the light and defend herself. There were no snakes, she knew, here in London. There had been no mention of rats. A cat? An open window on the ground floor which had allowed an animal to enter? Her bedroom door was closed; had it been a cat she must surely have seen it.

She needed time to build her courage to raise her head from the pillow.

The shadow near the foot of her bed had little more substance than the night itself.

A dacoit, a hur who had slipped past the chokidar? There was no chokidar in the mews house, no one she could call to aid her. A cold fear gripped her mind, seemed to compress her lungs so even the drawing of a breath was impossible. She was unable to scream.

With an incredible physical effort she pushed herself backwards and upwards, feeling the hard rods of the iron bedhead against her shoulders as she did so. The pain of the contact broke the spell of fear, she drew in a sharp breath but the intended cry died in her throat as her eyes focused. In the artificial dusk created by the street light in the mews, Gerald watched her, his eyes meeting hers with the same depth of emotion she had experienced throughout the years of their marriage.

She sat more upright, supporting herself by her arms, her hands gripping the bedclothes, aware that she might be experiencing only an illusion of her own mind and yet desperately wanting some confirmation that this might not be so.

She said his name softly: 'Gerald . . .' There seemed to be relief in his eyes at her recognition. All logic warned her this was no more than a dream stemming from her need for him. She ignored it. 'Gerald?' She invited a response as she might have done in the past when he lay at her side. He smiled.

Later she was uncertain how long it had been before he moved away from the bed and stood, watching her, until his image blurred and faded and was gone. She remembered only that he had stood, unaided, a tall and upright figure, slender and handsome, as he had been the first day she had seen him waiting on the deck of the paddle-steamer.

Now the room was empty, its shadows only shadows. Had Gerald even been there? She experienced moments of doubt. Her Catholic schooling had never denied spirits, good or evil; in the hill villages their existence was recognised, expected by the ancient religion. But though she had heard many stories of them she had grown to believe they were no more than primitive fantasy. Was she even awake now?

She swung her feet to the floor, walked to the window and drew back the curtain. Frost ferns grew across the edges of the glass panes. There was a faint mist in the mews, softening the harsh glare of the street light. Cobbles glistened. She could see no comforting sign of life. Behind her she heard James breathing steadily, evenly.

She left the room, closing the door softly behind her, then switched on the landing light. The house was night silent, cold, but she welcomed the reality of the chill air on her shoulders. She lit the gas beneath the kettle in the kitchen and made herself coffee from liquid concentrate. Its taste was harsh, iron-like, bitter. She drank it kneeling before the dying embers of the fire in the living-room. The grandfather clock struck three chimes on its mean bell, the voice of a feeble tenor hiding in the frame of a bass.

During those first sad days when Gerald had been taken from her she remembered she had called for him a hundred times; offered her God anything He might choose in return for a little more time with the man she so deeply loved. Why now, she wondered? Why not then? What could his visit mean? Had it become as impossible for him to continue without her as it had almost become for her when he had died?

Almost become? Had the separation been only a test?

Was there another reason for his visit? He had not spoken to her, only smiled. Did his smile mean approval? Approval of what? Of her action with his company?

Had she in fact only imagined his visit? Perhaps she had awakened only as she stepped from the bed, remembering the dream and believing it to be something which had just taken place?

There seemed to be so many questions, so many possibilities; no answers.

An hour later she returned to the bedroom, turned off the landing light and stepped into its darkness. Inside the door she paused as her nostrils caught the scent, a scent the room had never previously held but which had once been part of her life. His scent, as clear and familiar to her as the scent of any animal's mate. It had been there in Kimberley, in his rooms, on his suits and shirts in the wardrobes and dressers, lingering as a painful reminder until common sense had forced her to ask Rai sadly to dispose of the clothing. It had been a day when she had been unable to remain in the house, and afterwards its emptiness had been more pronounced.

The scent, his scent, was in the bedroom of the mews house. When she lay in her bed it was still there, but in the morning it had gone.

The Petrie India boardroom had been rearranged. The long table had been shortened and now stood across the width of the room. Chairs had been added in three rows before it.

Seats around the table were filled by the board members, and in front of them was a scattered audience of men and women.

Lewis had kept Mary out in the street until the last minutes before the opening of the meeting. A taxi had delivered them a quarter of an hour early and Lewis had cursed his poor timing. He did not want Mary subjected to any influences she might encounter prior to the commencement of the meeting in the enmity of the boardroom, and which might erode her present determination. Lewis had anticipated problems with London's traffic, but the taxi ride from the mews had been unusually direct and fast.

When they finally entered the Petrie India building, Mary was feeling even more nervous than on the occasion of her first visit.

One of the commissionaires politely, but formally, directed them to the boardroom where conversations which had been taking place immediately ceased. Heads turned and eyes followed eyes until every face in the room was directed towards Mary in the taut silence. She knew now, without Lewis, she would never have been able to continue against this open hostility. There was no sign of the secretary who had proved to be an ally on her previous visit. For a moment Mary stood, motionless, then Lewis took her arm and led her to a seat. The faces continued to watch her, then as Simon Petrie coughed loudly for attention, turned towards the table.

There was no mistaking the coldness in Simon Petrie's voice as he officially opened the meeting. He made no effort to conceal it and introduced Mary to the shareholders as the one who had called the meeting with obvious sarcasm when he used her title. The other directors sat stiffly and grim-faced as he spoke.

'As shareholders, you are already aware of the financial success of Petrie India since the termination of wartime hostilities. I sincerely doubt if any of you have any cause to be dissatisfied with the hard work of all the members of the board of directors. These are the gentlemen whom *you* have previously chosen to represent your interests on the board, and I am quite certain that regardless of the outcome of this regrettable meeting, they will still have your complete confidence.'

There was a quick and overspontaneous burst of applause, like that of a theatre claque. Simon Petrie acknowledged it with a nod of his head.

'You have all received copies of the agenda for this meeting. It is painfully brief, and I believe totally unjustified. It is a vote of no confidence in the entire board of directors of Petrie India. And as you will have seen, it has been proposed by Lady Petrie.'

There were cries of 'Shame', and a few faces, now angry, turned again to stare at Mary. She felt the blood drain from her face.

To her further embarrassment, Simon Petrie continued, this time his eyes firmly fixed on her, recognising the discomfort he was causing. 'Lady Petrie, as most of you will know, is the widow of our late India director, Sir Gerald Petrie. And in view of the family connections, and because she had, herself, little or no knowledge of the workings of this long established company, either in India or here, generous offers have been made to her ...'

Mary was startled by Lewis rising quickly to his feet. He appeared to tower over the shareholders on the chairs in front of him. His voice cut across that of Simon Petrie, diminishing it with his Irish richness. 'May I suggest, sir, as a point of order, that the proposition be now put before those present.' In explanation, he added: 'I am Lewis Kiernan and represent Lady Petrie, mister chairman.'

Simon Petrie said frostily: 'Indeed.' He read again from the paper. 'The proposition is as follows: That a vote of no confidence be given for all members of the board of directors of Petrie India.'

The cries of 'Shame' were repeated.

Simon Petrie held up a hand. 'The outcome of a vote on this proposal is already quite clear to us all. The proposer, Lady Petrie, is the major shareholder in this company. It would be wasting all of our time to insist on formal declarations. Myself and my fellow directors have discussed the situation at great length and we are left with no alternatives. Very regretfully indeed, we must tender our resignations.'

A man sitting only a little way from Mary spoke deliberately loudly: 'The bitch.'

A small man in a pinstriped business suit stood quickly. 'I want a word first, mister chairman.' He turned to face Mary. 'Who the hell does she think she is? We're family shareholders, we don't even know her; don't want to know her. We're quite satisfied with ...'

Simon Petrie stopped the man. 'The board quite understands your feelings, Andrew. There is nothing that can be done, I assure you. If there had been any way in which this situation could have been avoided, we would have attempted it. We are quite as concerned for the future of Petrie India as yourself.'

Lewis was on his feet again. 'Mr Petrie. In view of the resignation of the board of directors, my client wishes the following proposals to fill the vacant positions to be put before the shareholders ...'

The man in the pinstriped suit said furiously: 'I suppose this is a bloody formality, too. The whole thing is a disgrace; a farce.'

Lewis spoke again before the man could continue his ranting. It was obvious Simon Petrie intended to do nothing to prevent him. 'Mr Petrie, I believe it will be to everyone's advantage if you continue to control the meeting. I am sure the shareholders of Petrie India will find the propositions bearable.' Lewis's deep voice drowned the rising babble of conversation and commanded silence. He said: 'Thank you.'

Simon Petrie returned his stare. 'Perhaps you will put your client's proposition.'

The room was now silent. Lewis opened a file and read from it. 'The position of chairman of Petrie India shall be held jointly by my client Mary Lady Petrie and Mr Simon Petrie.'

Simon Petrie frowned. The proposition he should continue, even as joint chairman, was something he had not expected, certainly not considered. He had devoted his entire life to the Company and had dreaded the likelihood of his enforced retirement. This was an opportunity to continue, but he was being given no time to consider the terms. Just how much was she likely to intererfere? Or, he thought quickly, was this an indication she was prepared to leave the Company in his hands and accept a nominal title to indicate her ability to control Petrie India if she so wished? The latter was a possibility in view of her lack of commercial experience. Simon Petrie had always prided himself on his ability to make a decision cleanly and speedily. He said, deliberately concealing any emotion: 'I would be prepared to accept the position of joint chairman with Lady Petrie.' There was a murmur of surprise. At least, Simon Petrie thought, he would be in a position to keep an eye on things. He spoke again to the shareholders: 'The position as far as casting your votes is concerned remains the same as in the first proposition. You may do so, of course, if you wish, but it is merely a formality regardless of how you may feel.'

'Thank you, mister chairman,' said Lewis, reverting to Simon Petrie's former company title. 'In view of your own acceptance, I am sure the remainder of the shareholders will wish to do the same.' He looked down at them. 'Of course, they may formally abstain if they so wish.'

The man in the pinstriped suit stood again, but this time there was less aggression in his voice. 'I made my point earlier. The purpose of this company is to work efficiently at making a sensible profit. We all know that so far as any proposal Lady Petrie cares to make, we have Hobson's Choice. That being the case, the Company will be more efficient if it can be run amicably. I'll vote rather than abstain. And I'll vote for the joint chairmanship.' There were reluctant murmurs of acceptance.

Simon Petrie said: 'Then I request the proposal be noted as passed.'

'I have three further proposals, mister chairman,' said Lewis. 'The first is that the former members of the board of directors be reinstated en masse, should they be willing to resume their former positions.'

Simon Petrie was unable to conceal his surprise this time. He faced the board members. 'Do you all agree?' It took him only a moment to realise they were as stunned as himself. He made up their minds for them. 'They will be pleased to resume their positions, should that be the wish of the shareholders.'

Pinstripe was on his feet again. 'Damn it, we're acting out a political drama here. If this is what Lady Petrie intended all along, I would like to know the reasons.'

Simon Petrie silenced him with a glare, and then spoke to Lewis. 'You said three further proposals, I believe.'

'Yes. I have a proposal for the addition of a junior director. Lady Petrie proposes that Miss Jane Petrie should be asked to accept a suitable junior directorship.'

Simon Petrie grimaced. 'The board can do nothing but agree. Your final proposition, Mr Kiernan?'

Lewis said: 'Lady Petrie proposes a change of name for that part of the Company operating in India. She proposes that instead of trading on the sub-continent as Petrie India, it should become in future India Petrie.' He paused. 'As you will understand, my client is in the unique position amongst board members of understanding certain aspects of Indian politics. It is her honest belief a change of company title will be, in the long term, to the advantage of the Company.'

Simon Petrie looked thoughtful. He remembered a conversation he had held with Gerald Petrie several years previously. The change of company name had arisen then, but he had refused and Gerald had not pursued the subject. To Mary Petrie, however, it had remained important enough for her to bring it up now. Just how much did she know about the running of Petrie India? Had she been more involved than he was aware or was she merely following the wishes of her dead husband? He said: 'A suggestion was made to this effect some years ago. It has been under consideration since that time. There are no insurmountable problems regarding such a change, so it will be carried through. Do you have any further proposals, Mr Kiernan?' Lewis shook his head. 'That being the case, I feel I should invite Lady Petrie to join me here.' He indicated his son's chair next to him, forcing William to blush but then move his position. The shuffling continued along the line of directors as Mary left her own seat and walked self-consciously to Simon Petrie's side.

When she had seated herself, he spoke: 'There are always milestones in the life of a company, and undoubtedly today is a milestone for Petrie India.' In the minutes since the re-election of the board, Simon Petrie had been concentrating his thoughts on his future part in the Company; his feelings regarding the other propositions had been almost negative, they were only of minor importance. The inclusion of Jane Petrie on the board presented no problems, and the change of title of the Company in India might even be a good thing in the present time of Indian political upheaval. His own position? Mary Petrie could have totally removed the existing board members and replaced them with anyone she chose to select. She had not done so. That being the case, it would be far less complicated to accept her than attempt to fight her openly, at least here and now. It might not be necessary to fight her at all. She had certainly shown spirit, fighting spirit, the kind of spirit Simon admired in a man but which was missing in the character of his own son. He remembered the way her dark eyes had burned with anger, real fury, at the previous board meeting when it had been suggested she sell her shares; later he had admitted to himself he had never seen such a genuine deep anger in his son's eyes.

He continued: 'In some ways it appears to me appropriate that as the Company has, for its entire existence, had such close ties with the sub-continent, we have at last someone of that parentage on our board.' He smiled thinly. 'And for the first time in company history, we have a lady board member, my co-chairman. On behalf of fellow members of the board I welcome her.' He turned slightly, nodded, and then sat down.

He had said very little, Mary realised. There had been no warmth in his welcome, but neither had there been the former sarcasm. He had not enjoyed what had happened, but was prepared to accept it. To protect the Company, or himself, she wondered? The room was silent, and she realised the board members and shareholders were waiting for her to reply. The rows of eyes watched her with cold anticipation, reminding her of the eyes of hyenas at the Calcutta Zoo, waiting hungrily to be fed. Only the owners of these eyes would be far more critical of what they might receive. The room was over-warm, and when she had seated herself next to Simon Petrie she had draped her fur over the back of the chair. Now, as she stood, her sari drew a sharp contrast between its white silk and the pale olive of her skin. Sunlight, reflecting from the glass of the high windows, added lustre to the natural sheen of her hair, framing her delicate face. The shareholders who had watched her entrance with their anger corrupting the image they had seen were now surprised to find her quite beautiful.

She wished she could cough to clear her throat. If my voice squeaks, she thought, I will forget everything I want to say, everything I have rehearsed. But perhaps that would be better.

She smiled and bowed her head towards Simon Petrie: 'Mister chairman.' She made the smile as warm as possible. 'I prefer to use my more normal method of address to you: Uncle Simon.' One of the shareholders laughed, briefly. Simon Petrie's brow furrowed: Was she trying to ridicule him? She looked back towards the shareholders. 'It is very difficult for me to be formal to someone whom I have liked and respected as a relative and friend for the past nine years, so you must all forgive me.

'I had written out, and practised, the small speech I knew I would be required to present to you this morning. Now, somehow, it doesn't seem to be appropriate.' She saw Lewis tilt his head, questioningly. 'One of you gentlemen shareholders asked a little while ago why it was necessary for me to provide what appeared to be political drama. I can assure you I have more than enough political drama in India, and I have no desire or intention of making it part of my personal role in India Petrie, or Petrie India.'

She looked directly at the pinstriped-suited man in the front row. 'What has happened this morning, has happened in order to *protect* our company.' She smiled quickly. 'Not from our directors, or yourselves. But from a change of policy that might have led anywhere.' She became aware Simon Petrie was staring at her with curiosity. 'You British are renowned throughout the world for your traditions; for your fine traditions, and it is my determination to maintain one of those fine traditions which forced today's issues. I wish to ensure that the major shareholding of Petrie India is always held eventually by the titled heir of the founder's family.'

She spoke slowly and carefully, aware her accent might detract from the sense of importance she wished to instil in her words. 'I have taken a great interest in the history of my husband's family. It may surprise a few of you to learn that in many ways I am not unique within it. The wife of the founder of Petrie India, Sir David Langley Petrie, was in fact a German lady.' It had been Lewis's idea to check the family records at Somerset House; by luck there had been a foreigner in the family tree. Almost miraculously, it was the wife of Sir David Petrie. Mary continued, lightening the tone of her voice and aware that German nationality was still anathema to most of the shareholders who retained unpleasant memories of the recent war. 'Anna Leipsiger. And I am quite certain she too would have done everything in *her* power to ensure the satisfactory futures of her descendants. I am sure you will all admit Petrie India did not suffer then because of the influences of a lady of foreign extraction, and I can assure you the situation is no different today.'

There was no longer the open hostility in the eyes watching her now, and the shareholders were listening to her. She felt the tenseness that had been cramping her stomach muscles begin to ease. 'I do not intend to interfere in any way with the working of Petrie India here in London.' She smiled down at Simon Petrie. 'I would not dare to interfere.' This time there was more response to her humour and as she caught Simon Petrie's eyes she could see faint amusement in them. Just as she had sometimes rested her hand on Gerald's shoulder when they had walked together, now she put her hand lightly on Simon Petrie's shoulder. 'I will, however, take a keen interest in India Petrie, and I hope my Uncle Simon will be prepared to give me all the advice and assistance I will undoubtedly need.

'My son, James Nlamo Petrie, is the present baronet. One day, I sincerely hope, he will become chairman of this fine company. When he does so, then I am quite sure the shareholders of his day will find him as conscientious of his responsibilities as have been *all* the line of Petrie men. Uncle Simon, members of the board of directors, and shareholders, I am proud to be a Petrie; proud to be joint chairman of Petrie India and India Petrie.' She was watching Lewis's face. It was serious. Had she said something stupid, something offensive to the British she wondered? She sat down feeling mentally washed out, drained. Lewis's face relaxed into a grin. He clapped her, his large hands bringing sounds like pistol shots into the silence of the room. To her relief he was joined by the shareholders and the board of directors.

Simon Petrie stood, took Mary's hand and drew her to her feet beside him. He continued to hold her hand. 'Gentlemen ...' He waited until they were silent. 'My joint chairman and I declare this meeting closed. Our thanks for your attendance.' He turned to William. 'You'd better open up the bar and see they all have a drink. They'll want to chat awhile.' He faced Mary. 'Well?'

'Well, Uncle Simon?'

He realised he was still holding her hand, released it quickly, then cleared his throat and spoke gruffly. 'I suppose I should take my new joint chairman to lunch.'

Lewis was beside her now, towering above them both. 'Might I suggest the Ritz as appropriate, sir.' Simon Petrie glared up at him, but Lewis grinned mischievously. He spoke to Mary. 'I'll leave you with Mr Petrie.' She wanted Lewis with her but sensed he would refuse, so nodded. 'I'll contact you later.' She knew it would be that evening. He eased himself away past the chairs and through the throng of shareholders, now talking, lighting their cigarettes, cigars, accepting glasses of drink. She felt a little sorrow at his leaving.

'The Ritz it shall be then.' Simon Petrie helped her on with her fur cape. 'My God, it must be twenty-five years since I took a young woman to lunch at the Ritz.' He caught her eye again. 'Anna Leipsiger indeed!'

CHAPTER TWELVE

The letter which invited Jane, Mary and James to visit Margaret Petrie at her Guildford home was as brief as a formal dinner invitation. It said simply: 'The three of you may come to tea at four p.m. on Friday. Mother.' It had been addressed to Jane, and apart from numerical inference, mentioned neither Mary nor James.

Jane opened it at the breakfast table, passed it to Mary and said: 'Wonders never cease; we've been honoured by a royal command.'

James looked up excitedly from his cereal bowl, a dribble of milk on his dark chin. 'The new Queen wants to see us?'

Jane smiled and shook her head. 'The invitation is from your grandmother.'

The excitement remained in James's eyes. 'Grandmother? Good! When are we going to see her?'

'Friday.'

'Tomorrow?'

'Twenty-four hours' notice is as much as anyone can expect from Mother,' Jane observed wryly. 'And heaven help anyone who tries to back out.'

'Must we RSVP, like a party invitation?' James asked.

'Quite unnecessary with Mother. We turn up as ordered or she'll assume we're cutting her dead and cross us off her invitation list forever. I don't really think we want that to happen, do we?'

James shook his head vigorously.

Mary folded the note and smiled at Jane. 'I thought she'd never get in touch with us. I'd given up hope.'

'Hope!' Jane widened her eyes and tightened her lips in a

despairing gesture. 'Don't raise it. We may not be able to change the invitation, but Mother can. A quick last-minute telegram; one word, "Cancel". If you're very lucky, she may add, "Letter follows", or simply "Stop inconvenient". It's happened to me plenty of times.'

'Is Grandmother mad?' asked James, balancing a spoon of cornflakes precariously.

Jane moved it delicately so it was above his bowl. 'Definitely not mad. Eccentric; scatty; and frequently a bitch.' She looked at Mary and grinned. 'Excuse my definition.' She paused, thoughtfully. 'Used up all my holiday, so I'll have to go sick. Damn. Mother always does this to me when I'm looking and feeling at my healthiest! Perhaps I'll have to eat a piece of soap.'

James's eyes widened. 'Eat a piece of soap?'

'A trick we used at school to avoid hockey in the rain.' She saw James's quizzical expression and regretted her words. 'On reflection, I shouldn't have said that. It tastes terrible,' she warned him. 'And if they find out they never believe you again, not even when you're really ill.'

Deep in her own thoughts, Mary had not heard Jane's conversation with James. At last she was going to meet Gerald's mother; Gerald's son, his grandmother. It was the realisation of another ambition, a binding of the important family ties, and gave her the warm internal glow of satisfaction. How sad it had not taken place when Gerald had been alive so that he could have enjoyed the pleasure of the reconciliation. But perhaps he could still enjoy it? Would enjoy it. He had smiled at her the night he had visited her; he would certainly smile again at the sight of James in his grandmother's arms. Perhaps that was why Gerald's spirit was still restless? And the meeting was to take place soon . . . tomorrow! She would know what Margaret Petrie was really like; surely Gerald's mother could not be the ogre she seemed to like to present herself as? She must take Margaret Petrie a gift. Not too large a gift or it would appear she was trying to influence her judgement. It must be something small; something tasteful. But what?

'I must take something,' she said quickly.

'I know how you feel, darling. The aspirin is in the kitchen,' answered Jane.

'I mean tomorrow. A present of some kind.'

'For God's sake, not a peace offering. Mother will dismiss it as obsequiousness. She once sacked a gardener for bringing her baskets of her own apples without her asking for them.' She paused. 'Got it! One flower.'

'One?' Mary looked horrified.

'One,' repeated Jane. 'And not an orchid or something romantic like a red rose. One simple and solitary bloom. Nothing ostentatious. A tea rose in a small bunch of fern would be ideal. You'll get one at the florists at the corner in the morning. He always has those in his displays.'

'But it seems so mean ...'

'Take a tip from an expert at handling her somewhat odd mother, it will be far better received than anything else you might think of giving her.'

It had taken far longer the next day to dress James and make sure he was well washed, tidily dressed, hair neatly brushed into place, than it took Mary to prepare herself. She was far too nervous to eat any lunch and the time until their departure from the mews house dragged slowly by. She was edgy, her temper unusually quick and James, once he was ready, kept out of her way and sat quietly in the living-room looking through the pictures of Jane's magazines.

Although Mary spent a lot of time in her preparations for the visit, Jane was little more than casual. She came home from work at one o'clock, unhurriedly ate a large pork pie and salad, and then changed into a comfortable homeweave dirndl skirt and sweater. She brushed her hair back into a ponytail and wore no make-up.

With the sun already lowering, they drove out of London, diverting into the artificial countryside of Richmond Park with its diminishing Nissen-hutted military camps, to join the Thames for a short while beyond Kingston before reaching the A3 which led them to Guildford.

Although the war had ended several years previously, the need for conscripts to police the troublesome areas of the Middle and Far East still kept the garrison towns filled with khaki. The soldiers had not been so obvious in London; Mary had seen a few in the West End, but they were rare in the City, which offered them little in the way of entertainment. In Guildford, however, there were as many soldiers on the streets as civilians, and the uniforms brought back unpleasant memories. Briefly Mary could picture the shredded remnants of the drab cloth, bloodstained, torn and blackening flesh, once as pale and unblemished as that of the men she now saw.

They passed Stoughton Barracks on the top of Guildford Hill, its guards oddly familiar before its red brick gatehouses, swinging their pickaxe handles as though they expected at any minute to be attacked by a ravaging mob of Guildford citizens. Towards Ash, Jane drove past a straggling column of recruits dressed in blue PT shorts and sleeved vests, their faces crimson with effort as they ran, urged on by tracksuited instructors. To Mary they all seemed so young; so much younger than the men who had died at Kohima, though they must have been the same age. Had Gerald been no older that night he had gone on patrol? No older that day when she had been told by Alan he had been killed? Memories drew her mind away from the reason for the journey, and when Jane turned the vehicle into a gravel drive lined by a neatly cut box hedge, Mary's nervousness returned so suddenly and violently that she was forced to swallow hard to prevent herself from being sick.

The house, rust-coloured brickwork divided by blackened oak timbers, Victorian mock-Tudor, loomed above the skein of autumn branches of elms drifting their few remaining yellowed leaves on to a thick golden carpet beneath. Dense rhododendron bushes, which Mary had not expected to see in England, replaced the box hedge as the drive opened to a turning-circle before the entrance. The last of the failing sunlight filtered through the skeletal elms surrounding the property, but a thin mist was already forming above the damp ground, softening the outline of the house like an old out-of-focus photograph, sepia. By winter moonlight, Ash Park Manor would be ghostly. Three storeys high, with narrow dormer windows in the servants' quarters beneath its roof, it had been built to impress. Slightly to the left were outbuildings, a coach-house with a spired clock and pigeon loft, a weather vane formed as a coach and four, potting sheds, and the moss-stained glass of a long greenhouse sheltered by a south-facing wall which held the naked cordons of fruit trees.

Jane, with relief in her voice at the completion of her drive, said, 'Home.' She parked the car, its wheels crunching the wet gravel, a little beyond the door. The house seemed deserted; no lights glowed in the small-paned windows.

'Gosh!' James stared at the manor, unable to relate it to the small London mews residence where they had lived for the past weeks. This was much closer to the type of building he had expected to find as a Petrie family house in England. It was twice the size of

Kimberley, the rambling grounds and woodland, gardens and outbuildings which he could see inviting his exploration. Mary turned in her seat and tried to brush back his hair; washed only three hours before it was already lank, uncontrollable. His suit, which she had carefully pressed, was creased; her heart sank even more. James looked, she thought, as though she took no trouble at all with his appearance. What would his critical grandmother think?

She said peevishly: 'James, look at you.'

He was already climbing from the car. Mary glanced despairingly at Jane.

'Boys. They're all the same,' Jane grinned. 'Well, brace yourself. Here we go: Geronimo!'

Mary glanced apprehensively towards the house. Behind one of its windows she saw movement; someone watched, and she knew it would be Margaret Petrie. Mary felt as though she was about to walk the last few yards to the gallows.

Jane did not knock at the panelled oak door, but turned its wrought-iron latch and pushed it open, to be met immediately by the housekeeper in the marble-tiled hall which echoed her footsteps. Mary, holding James firmly by the hand, followed her closely as though separation from her friend, by even a yard, would invite disaster. The warmth of the house was scented with woodsmoke. Behind them, the door closed heavily, with an ominous sound of finality.

The housekeeper smiled a welcome. 'Hello, Miss Jane.'

'Hello, Dorothy.' Jane shrugged off her coat.

The housekeeper, obviously aware of the identity of the other visitors, acknowledged them. 'My lady ... and Master James.' She took their coats, folding them carefully over a thick arm. She was in her fifties, a well-built woman with heavy breasts and a ruddy country complexion. Her accent was softer than those to which Mary had become accustomed in London. 'I hope you had a good trip out here.'

'Not too bad.' Jane lowered her voice to a whisper. 'How's the dragon today?'

The housekeeper chuckled. 'Shhh. Really, Miss Jane! Your mother is keeping very well.'

'She always is ... I meant her temper.' Jane indicated the long hall to Mary. 'The mausoleum entrance!' The tiled floor, its surface broken only by a Persian rug, stretched twenty yards into the depths of the house. To the left was a heavy oak staircase six feet in width, angling around the stairwell to the floor above like the minstrel gallery of a medieval castle. The polished oak was oppressive, the massiveness of the structure unnecessarily heavy; it would have supported the weight of a steam train. The newel posts and banisters were carved in church tradition with spirals of fruitful vines, the surface of each carved grape and leaf glowing with the polish of generations of exhausted housemaids. 'It gave me the willies when I was a child; it still does. The only time it seemed friendly was at Christmas when we used to have a tree here, beside the stairs.' She glanced at Dorothy. 'Lead on MacDuff.'

The housekeeper opened a door to a room on the right of the hall, and Mary knew now for certain it had been Margaret Petrie who had been watching their arrival in the car. The room was large, the lower portions of its walls panelled in oak, the ceiling heavily decorated with ornate plasterwork. On the side farthest from the door was a large stone fireplace containing a fire-basket in which logs flared and crackled. The furniture matched the room in size and opulence, more polished oak, side tables holding brass-stemmed table lamps, Morris print covers over enormous armchairs and a chesterfield, oil paintings of rural scenes, and on the marble mantle an elegant boule clock and matching ornaments.

For a moment the room seemed unoccupied, but then Mary heard a woman's voice. 'Jane?' The owner of the voice was hidden by the high back of the chesterfield.

Mary followed Jane as the housekeeper left them. James was staring, fascinated, at an oil painting of a collection of dead game nailed to a barn door. Mary, still holding his hand, was forced to drag him with her.

'Ah, there you are. You're late.' The boule clock showed seven minutes past four. Margaret Petrie was sitting in the far corner of the chesterfield, her shoulders supported partly by one of its arms, partly by its padded back. Although it was quite hot in the room there was a tartan travelling rug draped across her knees, on which rested a copy of *Gone with the Wind*. Mary doubted if she had been reading the book; it seemed more likely that after Margaret Petrie had witnessed their arrival she had returned to the chesterfield and arranged herself in her present pose; it was too contrived, too casual.

Her appearance was not what Mary had expected. Margaret Petrie was blonde; the hair colouring might have once been natural, but now the tinting disguised what Mary suspected was pure white.

She was pale skinned, well made-up and with a bone structure suggesting she had once been a woman of considerable beauty. But she was thin; so thin that Mary was instantly reminded of the elderly beggarwomen who traipsed the Calcutta gutters, their hands skinny, withered, clawing hopefully towards the passers-by. The eyes, which for the moment were ignoring her, were Gerald's eyes; the same rich and hypnotic blue, exaggerated by the transparency of her skin and the light hair. Mary was unable to prevent herself staring at them.

Margaret Petrie ignored her until Jane had stooped and kissed her cheek, then she looked slowly towards Mary with the hesitant reluctance of someone forced to admit the existence of something of which they disapprove. She said nothing for what seemed an age to Mary, but the eyes examined her carefully from head to feet, lingering on her sari.

Mary felt herself blushing. She said: 'Good afternoon. I'm very pleased to meet you.' The words sounded insincere to her own ears, not spoken with the warmth a woman should offer her mother-in-law, even in these strained circumstances. She was conscious she had spoken in an unusually flat tone of voice, and resented the woman's ability, even in her silence, to add to her discomfort.

Margaret Petrie turned her attention to James. The deep blue eyes continued their examination.

James stared back at her, with the innocence of his age. 'Are you my grandmother?' he asked, determinedly. The dark eyes questioned blue.

Margaret Petrie's eyebrows raised a quarter of an inch. There was the hint of a frown of disapproval. 'So you are James.'

James said: 'Yes. Are you my daddy's mother?' Mary felt his hand in her own. It was warm, damp; he too was nervous.

'I have been led to believe so.'

Mary felt herself stiffen with anger. Before she could respond to Margaret Petrie's innuendo, James spoke again. 'Then you must be my grandmother.' He waited for Margaret Petrie's confirmation.

Margaret Petrie, still frowning, tilted her head a little as though considering how she should reply. The child was half-smiling at her, his eyes anxious. She had hoped to see some resemblance to Gerald in his face, but there was none; his skin colour was as dark as his mother's. It was not easy to answer him. Part of her mind demanded a rejection, but she could already see hurt forming in the young eyes. She took a steady, deep breath, and then said: 'Yes, I am your grandmother.'

To both Margaret Petrie's surprise and Mary's, James twisted his hand free of her own, ran the three yards between himself and his grandmother, and placed the small bouquet of fern and the single tea rose on her lap. Mary had forgotten it, but James must have picked it up from the seat beside him when he had climbed from the car. She had not noticed it in his hand.

The older woman jumped as though he had dropped a lizard on to her knees, then she realised what he had given her. She looked at it strangely for a moment, then picked it up, carefully. To Mary's surprise, the woman's face had softened, changed. When she spoke, her voice was different.

'How did you know I liked roses?'

James was already learning the craft of charm, and was determined to give credit to no one for the gift which had obviously pleased his grandmother. 'I just thought it was something you would like.'

'So you chose it yourself?'

James lied: 'Yes.' He looked quickly at Mary, anticipating her disapproval and was relieved to see none.

Jane stood a few yards away, watching, curiously.

'Then it must go into water right away,' said Margaret Petrie. 'Jane, call Dorothy, will you?' She smiled at James, and began removing the silver-paper wrapping which held the bouquet together. 'My son ...' She hesitated for a moment and then corrected herself. 'Your father brought me one, every time he came home, from school or the army. I never thought I would receive another.' She held the rose close to her nose, its immature fragrance carried memories she had forgotten existed; of a young man, still boyish, exerting his masculine independence with an aloofness towards her she had found aggravating at times. The single tea rose, she had always felt, had been the only real indication of his innermost feelings for her.

The housekeeper had entered the room when Jane had pressed the bell-push set in the wall beside the fireplace and now waited beside the chesterfield.

'Ah, Dorothy. Put this in water, will you. And use the silver flute.' Margaret Petrie turned to James. 'I imagine you must be thirsty after the long drive?'

James said, 'Yes,' hopefully.

'I thought as much. Children always get thirsty. Go with Dorothy and she'll find you something to drink ... and a biscuit, no doubt.' She looked towards the housekeeper. 'And then I think we'll have our tea.'

'Yes, my lady.' Dorothy led James from the room.

The atmosphere had softened. The blue eyes met Mary's again. 'For heaven's sake, both of you, don't just stand there. Sit down.' She admonished Jane. 'Not there. Sit where I can see you.'

Mary sat in one of the huge armchairs. It was so deep she was unable to lean against the back. Margaret Petrie watched her. 'That's better. I hate people standing over me.' To Jane: 'Your father always did that; always stood over me. Used to like to talk standing up. He used to give me a headache.' She spoke to Mary. 'You're quite a pretty little thing; I can see how you managed to turn Gerald's head ...'

'Mother!' Jane spoke quickly and defensively. 'That's unfair.'

'Be quiet. I'm not accusing her, merely making an observation. The ability to allow their heads to be turned is a male Petrie weakness.' Margaret Petrie returned her stare to Mary and remembered William's remarks about her clothing. William had been a sneak, and spiteful, since childhood. But he was useful when she wanted information. She said: 'I see you are in mourning still.'

Mary was surprised. Few of the British realised white was the colour of mourning in India; then she remembered Margaret Petrie had lived there for some years. 'Yes.' She had decided for the moment she would let the older woman lead the conversation.

'The colour of snow. So cold, white. We British mourned in white once, but Queen Victoria changed that. Now everyone seems contented with a black armband; soon they won't even bother. Respect is a diminishing courtesy in England.'

Mary remained silent; there seemed nothing to say. 'How is Mr Nehru?' Margaret Petrie asked unexpectedly.

'I ...' began Mary, surprised by the question.

'My brother-in-law Simon informed me you knew him,' said Margaret Petrie, her voice sharpening quickly.

'Well, yes. I've met him a number of times. But it is several months since I last spoke to him. Have you met him?'

'Jawarharlal Nehru? In 1929. He was quite a pushy young man in those days. Yes, that was the year when he became president of the All-India Trade Union Congress. He was a man for playing poor hands for high stakes. We met him in Delhi at one of the Governor's garden parties. Of course, we didn't expect much to come of him, then. Like most colonials, he never knew his place.'

Mary felt the pulse in her temples increase. 'And what do you believe was Pandit Nehru's place?'

The eyes of the two women locked. Mary's question had been a challenge, there was no mistaking it. For Jane it was like watching two men gripping hands to begin arm-wrestling; for a moment she was tempted to distract them, but decided if she did so it would provide only a temporary respite. Sooner or later, one or other of them would offer the challenge again. If there was to be combat at all, it was better over and done with.

Margaret Petrie manoeuvred: 'At that time, young lady, Nehru's place was to support the British Empire, not to attempt to destroy it.'

'Nehru never attempted to destroy the British Empire. It was never his aim. He wanted freedom for India.'

'And he destroyed the Empire in achieving it. It amounts to the same thing. It is an indication of how ignorance breeds sedition.'

'I think that's rubbish!'

The complete dismissal of her views astonished Margaret Petrie beyond the point of anger. It had been many years since she had received even the smallest criticism, let alone one so abrupt.

She said, almost disbelievingly, 'I beg your pardon.'

Mary realised she had passed the point of no return, but the nervousness she had experienced before she had met Margaret Petrie had now left her, and the woman's words had been an intended though indirect insult just like her initial reluctance to accept James. 'The history of India is no less complicated than the history of Britain. I studied it for three years and have only skimmed its surface. You form your views as a spectator, and then present them to others as facts.'

'The destruction of our British Empire is a fact.'

'A fact, yes. But its destruction, as you call it, was coincidental to Jawarharlal Nehru's actions. For years I have listened to you British moaning and complaining of the way we have stolen our country back from you. You blame it on everyone except yourselves, refusing to accept it was never yours to own in the first place, failing to realise your Empire was dying of senile decay; that it was being maintained by false argument and exploitation. You always claim to be benefactors, though it has always been the British who have been the beneficiaries. Even in the very last minutes before our independence, you were still trying to present yourselves as the great international philanthropist, when the truth of the matter was that you could no longer afford the luxury of India.'

To Mary's surprise, Margaret Petrie leant forward on the chesterfield and asked in a concerned manner: 'Do you like cucumber sandwiches?'

Cucumbers? The woman's question was so irrelevant, so unexpected, Mary's mind, tensed by the anxiety she had formerly experienced and by the anger of the past moments, unwound like the broken spring of a clock. She burst into laughter. The question was ridiculous; the woman was ridiculous. She attempted to fight mounting hysteria, feeling tears rising through the collapsing humour, a surge of pent-up but turbulent emotion held in check for all the past weeks. The laughter became sobs and she dropped her head to her lap and held it with her hands.

Jane was furious. She was instantly on her feet and beside Mary, her arms around her hunched shoulders. She glared at her mother. Her voice echoed from the panelled walls. 'You're such a stupid woman. Can't you imagine what she's been through? Don't you know what it's been like for her since Gerald died? Don't you have any feelings at all?' She turned her attention to Mary, comforting her; the sobs were muffled in folds of silk, but her body shuddered with each breath. 'It's all right, Mary. Don't take any notice of her. We'll leave as soon as you're better.' She faced her mother again. 'Don't you know what it's like to lose someone you love? Have you ever loved anyone other than yourself? Haven't you ever needed anyone? Why do you think she even bothered to come to see you? I should have known better than to bring her. You don't deserve her.'

Margaret Petrie's pale face was bloodless. She swayed slightly as though she was about to faint, but steadied herself, pushed the palms of both her hands to her mouth, indecisively, then dropped to her knees in front of Mary. She touched Mary's head. 'I didn't intend to hurt her,' she said defensively to Jane. 'And I most certainly know what it's like to lose the men you love. I've lost a husband and a son.' She softened her voice. 'Come along, my dear. I'm very sorry.' She tried to ease Jane's hands from Mary's shoulders. Jane resisted.

'Mother!'

'Go and help Dorothy with the tea,' said Margaret Petrie mildly.

Jane's voice rose. 'I will not go anywhere. Leave us alone.' She knew she was close to tears herself, now. The visit had been a mistake for which she would never forgive herself. She should have been more aware of the terrible tension which had been building inside Mary since Gerald's death; anticipated that it might be released by her mother's unpredictable and often unreasonable behaviour.

In Mary's mind there were swirling and confused heliographic flashes of her past with Gerald; it was his arms she was feeling around her now, the strength of his hands holding her; tears were the rain of the Kohima battlefield, the crackle of the fire, distant rifle-shots, the voices, his voice. But there was no reality amongst the turmoil of memory, no moment when her mind rested on a single incident she could transfix or grasp to bring coherence and reason.

She felt hands beneath her face, gentle but determined, lifting her towards the light she sought to avoid, from the darkness concealing her. 'Mary...' Her name spoken by the unfamiliar voice. 'Mary... Come to me, dear.' The hands slipped deeper beneath her, between arms and trunk, finding purchase, drawing her upwards, forwards. She had no strength to resist them.

Jane's anger lessened. This aspect of her mother had been hidden from her since early childhood; she remembered it now. The fragrance of perfume as her mother's body drew her close and the slender arms held her, comforting her, driving away tears, fright. Neutralising and dispelling fear or sorrow. How long had it been? Before she had left Assam to begin her schooling—over twenty years! She let her mother ease Mary into the folds of her arms, watched her bury the dark sleek hair close to her breast, her body moving, rocking gently, transmitting the exclusive maternal security of a symbolic womb within which a stricken child might hide.

'My dear... my poor dear...' The voice soft, seductive. A slim hand caressed damp hair, smoothed it.

The struggle for breath between convulsive sobs lessened; images dulled in Mary's mind. She felt tired, exhausted, the soothing voice inviting sleep, which she resisted. They were no longer Gerald's arms which held her, but the arms of another. Not Jane's; the arms of Margaret Petrie! For a fraction of a second she tensed, fearful at the recognition, then as the gentle voice seduced her, she allowed herself to sink deeper against the woman's body.

Margaret Petrie held her for several minutes, only gradually and carefully bringing her voice back to a normal level. At last, with the hint of satisfaction and a wan smile towards Jane, she lifted Mary's head and said: 'There now ...' She took a small lace kerchief from her sleeve and dabbed at the smeared eye make-up on Mary's cheeks before sliding her hands lower until she could hold both Mary's hands. 'What I think we all really need is a nice cup of tea.'

Jane watched them, the two women sitting so close together at the oak table their shoulders touched, soft laughter, the mutual amusement at the early family photographs discovered, rediscovered, in the albums dragged from the musty-smelling leather sea trunk, decorated with shipping labels and hotel stickers, hidden for more than a decade in the dusty recesses of the boxroom.

It was eight p.m. and in the kitchen Dorothy worked to cook an unplanned dinner pestered by James who was enthralled by stories of his father's childhood, just as one day his own children might listen to the tales of his aiya. Dorothy had served two generations of the Petrie family, from a beginning as a fourteen-year-old kitchen maid in a house filled with servants, to the present day when she, a part-time cleaning lady, and a gardener who doubled as chauffeur, were its entire staff. There was lots to be told, and although she was professing vexation, secretly she was enjoying the company of the latest Master Petrie in her usually solitary domain.

Jane's mind was finding only small comfort in the seemingly amiable atmosphere of the dining-room; she knew it was deceptive, encouraged by the release of emotion, the luxury of the room, the warmth cast by the logs burning in the iron fire-basket near her feet. Her mother was totally unpredictable. Her present conciliatory mood might last a minute, a month, a year. At the moment, Jane felt she would be grateful if it lasted only for the length of their visit.

When the break had first occurred between her brother and mother, Jane had prayed it might be nothing more than a temporary form of punishment for him, but as the years had passed and her mother showed no signs of seeking a reconciliation, it had seemed depressingly permanent. Would her mother, she now wondered, have softened had Gerald been present today, or would the enmity between them have inflamed the already difficult situation? It was only possible to guess, and any answer would be hypothetical. Her mother's thoughts, words, deeds, seemed to be controlled by countless secret hair-triggers, so finely set that the lightest touch could fire her in some unexpected and capricious way. To a stranger the present scene would appear one of calm domestic enjoyment, its fragile and perhaps temporary balance concealed.

Margaret Petrie's hand covered Mary's as it rested on the table. It was pale, the fingers long and the nails carefully manicured. It did not hold Mary's hand, but simply maintained contact as they chatted; it seemed to have no weight. They had searched the pages of five albums together in the past two hours, from the first Baronet Petrie's time to Gerald's last photograph, taken the day he had received his King's Commission. He had been trying to look so serious, so much older than his age; stern-faced, with no hint of his humour, a young officer commissioned for war and aware of his responsibilities. It saddened Mary. The only time she had seen his face so stern had been the first time he had spoken to her as he had stepped ashore from the paddle-steamer. Even his voice had been cold then, icy with annoyance at the press of people who surrounded him; she had feared there could be no emotion in him, though on that very evening she had lain on the charpoy and thought of him, later had dreamed of him. In retrospect, girlish silly dreams, but they had been realised, even if only for a little while.

The slim hand tightened a little on her own, seeking her attention. 'I wonder, do you have photographs?' The question was asked with a mild hint of trepidation as though even if Mary possessed them she might deny their existence.

'I brought one or two. I hoped ... I thought you might like to see them.' Mary searched her handbag and produced a wallet. There were only a dozen small prints, but she had chosen them carefully, anticipating this occasion the evening before she had flown from Calcutta. There had been few photographs taken before they had purchased Kimberley and she had deliberately left them in India. When they had been taken she had liked them; there was even one small print given to Gerald by one of the witnesses at their wedding, but now the girl in them seemed too naive, too unsophisticated. Often when she looked at them she could never understand why Gerald had found her even the slightest bit attractive; she was thin, obviously an upcountry tribal girl. The later photographs were more flattering. Gerald, too, had become more handsome as his boyish features had matured to full manhood. She was sorry, though, that she had none when he was unwounded. She passed them to Margaret, and explained them as she laid them in front of her.

She had chosen only those photographs that captured the happiest moments, mostly of them together, the 'snaps' taken by friends, when they were touching, smiling together, with James as a baby, at his christening, at their parties.

Margaret Petrie browsed through them carefully and silently. When she had examined them all, she said, sadly: 'Poor Gerald. They make me feel ashamed. I should have come out to him; come out to you both. How easy it is to regret things when it's too late.'

'It isn't too late. I've seen him ...' Mary stopped herself abruptly. She had decided never to mention to anyone what she believed had happened in her room the previous week. She hoped now Margaret Petrie would misconstrue her words.

'What on earth do you mean, you've seen him?'

With the new relationship established, and she hoped flourishing, Mary found it difficult to lie. She lowered her head and spoke softly. 'I saw him the other night.' She felt foolish.

'A dream?'

Mary shook her head. 'No.'

'What happened?'

Mary told her, avoiding her eyes, and feeling more uncertain as she progressed. It seemed unbelievable when put into words to be heard by another person. If it was movement that had disturbed her, why could she not have touched him? Why had he sat there so silently? How could she even be certain, now, she had been awake? The used cup in the kitchen sink in the morning was proof to her, but could be proof to no one else.

Margaret Petrie, however, expressed no doubt. When Mary had finished, she said: 'That's beautiful, my dear. I think you've been very lucky.' She paused and sighed. 'I tried to contact Harold.' There was exasperation in her voice. 'He would be far too busy to get in touch himself, without a prod. I used a clairvoyant, supposed to be very good. I think she raised everyone from Cardinal Wolsey to King George the Fifth, but not Harold.' The hand gripped Mary's again, this time more tightly. 'I think Gerald and yourself must have been very much in love.' Her blue eyes had moistened.

Mary nodded. 'Very much, Mother.'

Later, when Mary, James and Jane had left, and the lights of their car had been extinguished by the garden shrubs beyond the curve of the manor drive, Margaret Petrie, hugging herself against the east wind that was tearing the last remaining leaves from the elms, returned into the house and closed the door behind her. Without the voices of her guests it seemed empty.

She poked the fire in the dining-room to settle the smouldering logs, and regretted having given Dorothy permission to retire to her small apartment in the attics an hour previously. She knew there would be a vacuum-flask of chocolate beside her bed and a hot-water bottle beneath the sheets, but the thought of the chill corridors and bedroom delayed her. She crouched by the dying embers and rubbed warmth into her thin hands.

She remembered Mary had called her Mother. She had overlooked it at the time, but it seemed presumptuous now ... although, perhaps not. After all, Indians frequently addressed older women as Mother. It was a sign of respect rather than relationship. She was reminded of those British girls who had married dark-skinned American servicemen, and then found themselves a few months later pushing around perambulators containing black babies. Mother indeed! Really! What had Gerald been thinking about when he had married an Indian girl? If it was only sex he had wanted, then goodness knows, he could have had it without marriage. Everyone knew that young men on plantations sometimes took mistresses from amongst the girls who worked in the tea gardens, but Heavens above, they didn't wed them ... or even talk about them.

She pictured the reactions of some of her friends whose bridge parties she occasionally attended. 'Isobel, Louise, Angela, this is my daughter-in-law, Mary ...' Raised eyebrows, overpolite greetings, later gossip. It was a relief to know the girl intended to return to India once her son was at school.

'James.' Margaret Petrie said the name aloud, knowing Gerald must have chosen it. It had been her own father's Christian name, and Gerald had been his favourite grandson; they had been fond of each other. A pity, she thought, that her father had died when Gerald was only seven. His grandfather would have been a good influence on him as he had grown older ... far more of an influence than his father.

Mind you, credit to Gerald and his wife, the boy was charming. Such a pity he was so dark-skinned. A shame he had none of Gerald's fine features. Was he even Gerald's son? The idea shocked her. He could be the son of a houseboy, a gardener! A cold draught on her back brought a shudder that was momentarily appropriate. An Indian bastard the present Baronet Petrie! The thought amused her. If it were true, then old Picey Petrie would be turning in his grave. An Indian Lady Petrie was difficult enough to cope with, as Simon had discovered.

Margaret smiled, remembering her brother-in-law's anger when he had found Gerald had taken no steps to protect the family's interest in his company voting shares. Margaret Petrie had never liked Simon, had recognised that his ambitions frequently threatened her husband; the two of them had barely been friends when they were boys together ... one of them knowing, Simon knowing, that despite his ability he would never be permitted to match his older brother. Jealousy! It was no different between cousins; William had always resented Gerald, even though Gerald was years younger. William had always been a spiteful little cad towards Gerald; still was. 'Black' was how William had described Mary. Well, she certainly wasn't black. Coffee-coloured, perhaps, decided Margaret. And more Burmese than Indian. Somehow, Burmese women were almost socially acceptable; Dutchmen frequently married them. And she was quite beautiful; enviably so.

William was so bitter about Mary that Margaret Petrie decided she would telephone him the following day to tell him how charming she had found her daughter-in-law, and how delightful she found her grandson. William would make quite certain his father learnt her views. Yes, thought Margaret, she would speak to William and tell him James was already showing interest in Petrie India, and was so like Gerald ...

It was gone eleven p.m. by the time Jane had driven them back to London. Mary felt exhausted, both physically and mentally, but the feeling was cushioned by satisfaction; a race won was less tiring for the winner than the loser, and she was experiencing a sense of gratification that more than compensated for her tiredness. She had felt briefly ashamed of her loss of control, the first time it had happened in her entire life, unexpected, total, but somehow it had led to acceptance. Margaret Petrie might not love her as a daughter-in-law, but she no longer rejected her, no longer rejected James, and that was the most important thing of all.

Mary felt she wanted to sleep; not the sleep of a single night, but an eternal sleep justified by the fulfilment of her ambitions, of Gerald's ambitions. It would be easy now to allow herself to drift away from reality, never to return. Gerald's presence in her room was still an invitation and perhaps he had intended it as such; he had stood, upright, strong once more, as though he were waiting for her.

It was only now, when the mental spring had fully unwound itself, that she became aware of the immensity of the problems of the past years. She had accepted them too easily, believed she had overcome them as they had arisen. It had not been so. Each problem had tightened the coil inside her mind, had compressed it, exerted its own secret pressures. For the first time she was able to view them as an outsider, as though her mind had detached itself from her body. She had attempted an impossible task; they had both attempted it. Each difficulty had been a single battle within a war, and it was only today that victory had been achieved. Had Gerald lived, the wars would have continued. It seemed to her he had sacrificed himself for her benefit, for the benefit of his son, and had given her peace at the cost of his own life.

Since his death, she had only felt a deep sense of loss, a yearning for him to be close to her once more. The need had been a spiritual one, almost religious in its requirement. Tonight it was different. Tonight she wanted the warmth of his body against her own, the touch of their flesh as they lay together, his hands caressing her, a physical joining. It was harder to bear than the former longing where there still seemed to be some faint contact between them, the whispered words to him in the garden at Kimberley, at his graveside, in her dreams; the physical desire was a hunger that must only grow.

To her relief the pace of the following days increased. In less than three weeks, in early January, James would begin his schooling and she must return to India. In the meantime there was Christmas to be celebrated, and as she had accepted Margaret Petrie's invitation to spend the holidays at the Manor, there were presents to include amongst her shopping. The knowledge that she was soon to be parted from James for many months had made his company even more important; now almost every day included sight-seeing or a visit to some place of interest to them both.

Jane, reluctantly at first, to Mary's surprise, had accepted the position as a junior director on the Petrie India board. She had enjoyed her present work and the friends it had made her, and pictured her position in the family company as a life sentence of imprisonment. Only after she and Mary had spent many hours with Simon Petrie at his office had Jane begun to warm to the change and look forward to the time when she would join the Company in the New Year.

It was as though Simon Petrie had accepted defeat with a shrug of his shoulders and an implicit acceptance that times had indeed changed and, that being the case, then the best should be made of a bad job. If Jane was to join the Company, a man's world in his opinion, then she would be expected to do a man's job. It suited Jane. Initially, she was to work under the various department directors so that she might gain a thorough experience of the various workings of the Company. If she showed a liking and aptitude to one particular aspect, then she would be allowed to specialise; if not, then the general training would in time permit her to replace a retiring director. She had assessed her opportunities within the Company, measuring abilities and ages, before making a final decision. There may never have been a female junior director before, she eventually decided, but there seemed no reason now why there should not one day be a female managing director, or even sole chairman.

Jane was not in love with Lewis Kiernan, though there had been a time in their relationship when she had thought it a possibility. Love, she now felt, was almost chemical in the reactions it produced and the manner in which it did so. You added acid to water and it exploded. If it didn't, then the combination was not what it appeared. She was quite aware, however, that Lewis had become completely captivated by Mary and it had been obvious from almost their first meeting. But he was being cautious, very cautious. Normally, Jane knew, he would have discussed it with her. He had done so in the past when some particular girl had attracted him. The relationships had invariably been short-lived. He had never mentioned his feelings regarding Mary, but his big lap-dog eyes watched her every movement with fascination, and he treated her with the skill and attention of a master craftsman handling delicate materials.

Mary seemed unaware that Lewis had fallen in love with her, basing her own relationship with him on that established between the two friends. How sad, Jane thought, that it had happened at this time. Both were vulnerable in different ways, and both might be hurt.

If only a few more months had passed before they had met, there might be a different outcome. At the moment it seemed hopeless. She had wondered if she should speak to Lewis, caution him perhaps, but decided not to interfere. They were both adults and must make their own decisions.

Lewis had become a punctuation mark in Mary's day. She rose, bathed, dressed, oversaw James's ablutions and dressing, then breakfasted. Soon afterwards there would be a brief but regular telephone call from Lewis. 'Everything okay, Mary? Anything you want me to do? I'll see you later then.' Only a few words, the need to hear her voice to carry him through the day. Each evening, after supper but before James had gone to bed, Lewis would drop in. The excuse was 'to settle the boy'. It was usually unsettling, ending with Lewis hauling James across one of his shoulders and carrying him noisily up to the bathroom. Sometimes Lewis would take them all out, usually unexpectedly, to the theatre, the cinema, once to the circus.

On Saturdays, James accompanied him to the rugby matches and in return Lewis had foresworn the drinking that normally followed them. They returned together in the early evening, cold, tired, and with Lewis frequently bruised from incidents James would recount with juvenile and bloodthirsty relish.

Short winter days carried them quickly towards Christmas.

It was Christmas Eve, the routine was changed. Lewis had made his daily telephone call knowing he would not see Mary again until the holiday period had past. At lunchtime he would be flying from London to Dublin where he would be spending a few days with his parents. He sounded subdued, as though he was about to tell her something, but then changed his mind. A few minutes after she had replaced the receiver, there was the patter of Christmas mail through the letterbox; a letter from Alan, his third.

James had fetched the mail as keenly as a labrador retriever, anxious to sort through the anticipated Christmas cards from Indian friends. She took Alan's letter from him.

She read it silently, stunned, and hushed James when he questioned her. The letter was quite different from any she had previously received from Alan; even the writing was different, lacking the normally positive crispness of style that was so much part of his character.

'My dear Mary...' The addition of the single word 'My' was a warning to her that the letter might be on a more intimate level than usual. 'India has become empty for me since you left, and it is no use my pretending any longer. While Gerald was alive I had accepted the situation, and God knows I would have done anything to prevent the tragedy. I didn't intend to even attempt to tell you my feelings at this time, but one has little control over circumstance. I am forced to make a decision, and your answer will help me.

'My job here in Assam has come to an abrupt end. Simply policy to replace an ageing Brit with a young national. I suppose I was half-expecting it, but hoped it would hang on for another few years. Unfortunately, people with the kind of admin experience I can offer are two a penny in India and Brits aren't exactly popular – phasing us out is what it's called. I don't blame anyone, it is the right policy.

'However, I have the chance of a good job in Malaya, Singapore. It'll take me right through to retirement in a senior executive position. The "once in a lifetime" job! I have to let them know by late February.

'I love you very dearly, and just how much you mean to me became more obvious when you left. I had become accustomed to the miles separating us in India, but the landmass of Bengal and East Pakistan in no way equals the oceans and continents that have suddenly appeared between us. You have taken my heart with you.

'By now you will have completed the arrangements for James and his future, and with luck everything will have gone well with all the other business. Perhaps you now have time to think of yourself. Calcutta is not really the flower of the sub-continent, and I don't believe it holds much more for you than memories.

'I've never written a marriage proposal before, so please forgive me if it sounds formal. My dearest wish is that you consent to become my wife, and accompany me to Malaya. It is very little more flying time from England, so your separations from James will be no longer. In the meantime we can begin a new life together, sharing everything from the outset.'

James was staring at her as she finished the letter. 'Is Uncle Alan all right?'

She nodded, conscious that her cheeks were burning, that James must see she was shocked by the contents of the letter. She attempted to collect her thoughts and compose herself; wanted to re-read Alan's words.

James held out his hand. Normally she allowed him Alan's letters. She said: 'It's only business this time.' As nonchalantly as possible she stood, walked to her handbag and tucked the letter inside. To her relief, James lost interest. She cleared the table, washed up mechanically, and leaving James to arrange the latest batch of Christmas cards, went up to the bedroom.

She read Alan's letter again, sitting on her bed. She had the odd feeling of guilt, as though she was a child once more in the mission school, reading some forbidden book in the privacy of the dormitory. The contents were so unexpected she found them hard to believe at first. As Alan had written, she had known he was fond of her, but that had been so very long ago ... She had never contemplated him in the role of her husband. But she knew he would have written the letter with total sincerity, and the love for her which he professed was real. Poor Alan, she thought. It would have been so difficult for him. His actions were always deliberate, always considered. He would have spent hours in thought before picking up his pen and committing his plea to her. He would have attempted to understand her feelings as she read his letter, attempted to anticipate every reaction, her reply. He would already have experienced her rejection as well as her acceptance. His exacting thought processes had been part of his greatest strength as a wartime officer; even at Kohima his careful planning had led to less casualties in his company than in many others. But his foresight was often painful to him; he could see his men dying even as he gave them his orders. Others were not so sensitive.

The thought of his need for her was pleasantly reassuring. She glanced at the bedside clock. It would be six p.m. in Assam now; the sun was already dropping below the purple range of evening hills. Alan liked watching sundown; even at Kimberley he would sit on the verandah with a drink and stare far across the river into the unknown distance as the shadows retreated into dusk and the evening colours dimmed. He would be watching now, perhaps seeing the hills darken and the bright stars emerging above the forest.

The image attracted her, invited her. She could smell the blossoms of the garden shrubs, the wood-fires in the compound and on the riverbank, the damp sweet smell of the river, even the blue smoke of Alan's cigarette as it hung motionless in the still air.

She enjoyed the compliment of his proposal; there was a difference in their ages and she had always viewed him as mature, worldly. He had known her when she was no more than a servant girl, who with a naive ignorance had followed her man to war. Now, he wanted that same woman as his wife, to take her with him to a strange country to share their future together.

But could she love Alan? The wound of Gerald's death was still too raw. In a year, perhaps two, it might be different. Gerald still existed for her. She was not prepared to let go of him yet; was too fearful to release the precious memories. If she were to agree to marry Alan now he would be sharing her no less than if she had another lover.

The warmth was replaced by a feeling of sadness. Alan would already know her decision; must know it. The letter was of his hope not his expectation. He would be there, now, in Assam, feeling the same loneliness she felt, but knowing it must continue and she would refuse him. She wished he was with her so that she might hold his hand, read his grey eyes while she told him, explain her reasons to him, could soften his hurt with some small hope for the future. There were tears on her cheeks as she folded the letter. She could only write to him; but not yet, not today.

It was the first truly English Christmas she had experienced, the first without Gerald for many years. There was none of the snow she had seen in Christmas cards, but a heavy white frost coated the trees and the lawns, and chilled the draughty passages and corridors of Ash Park Manor. Beyond the windows orderly white fields stretched towards the long ridge Jane had called the Hog's Back.

In Calcutta, Christmas had always been warm, the weather pleasant, and the social life active. On Christmas Eve there were bagpipers in Chowringhee, and too many parties to accept all the invitations. In Calcutta, on Christmas Day, they breakfasted late, joined friends at the club for lunchtime drinks, returned for a barbecue in Kimberley's gardens. For the past five years, Rai had played Father Christmas, an incongruous and amusing figure, brown-skinned, white-bearded with cotton wool, prancing, gnome-like; appearing theatrically from the bushes with a sack of presents over his shoulder. It was as much an occasion for Rai as for the family, and he spent hours in preparation, his performance watched enviously though critically by the other members of the household. He would dance tantalisingly close to James, teasingly darting away at the last moment until James would be on the edge of his seat, his eyes wide, biting his fingers in desperation. At last all the presents would be handed out by Rai, his clothing damp with his exertions, his wide mouth a broad grin of pleasure. In return, he would solemnly receive his own gift from Gerald; it never varied—a litre bottle of 100° West Indian rum.

In the evening, there was always a party at Kimberley; two parties. One for James and his friends which began in late afternoon and included their tea, and one for their own adult friends and acquaintants. The games room was cleared and used as a bar, and the lounge furniture removed so that there was room for a small dance-band and dancing. It seldom ended before Boxing Day dawn when the guests would breakfast on the damp lawns before returning home exhausted.

Here in Ash Park Manor the day began in silence. The unheated bedroom was cold enough to make Mary's breath visible when she arose, wrapped herself in a thick dressing-gown and searched the house for signs of life. James still lay sleeping, tired by the lateness of the previous evening when they had chatted around the fire in the panelled lounge; he had been allowed a small glass of sherry by his grandmother.

Dorothy was already at work in the kitchen. It was eight-thirty. A twenty-five pound turkey had been in the oven for the past two hours, and she was preparing vegetables for the multi-tiered steamer on the table. Potatoes were peeled and in salted water, and a mound of brussel sprouts lay ready near the old-fashioned kitchen range. She welcomed Mary with a cup of tea.

Mary returned to her room, drank the tea and then bathed in the icy bathroom, the water little more than tepid. James had awakened when she returned.

Presents were opened after breakfast, and the quantity astonished James and herself. She had known there would be gifts for herself and James from Lewis and Jane, but Margaret Petrie, to Mary's embarrassment, had obviously contacted all the family and made her orders clear. There were gifts from relatives Mary had not known existed; she had not even sent a card to one of them.

Lunch was at two o'clock and as formal as might be possible with only the four of them; they were equally spaced around a huge table, and even had Mary stretched out her arm she would have been unable to reach either Jane or James seated on either side of her.

At three o'clock they listened to the Queen's Christmas speech which for the first time in the history of the monarchy had been transmitted from New Zealand. Afterwards, Margaret Petrie dozed in her armchair, while Jane, Mary and James strolled for a couple of miles along the damp lanes. At first the lunch kept them warm, but by the time they returned to the house they were chilled to the marrow.

In the evening they played games with James until his bedtime, then sat before the log fire and talked. The subjects of the conversations were light, unimportant, recollections. A little after ten Margaret Petrie retired to her bed leaving Jane and Mary alone. In the hall, the lights of the Christmas tree beside the staircase threw coloured reflections against the frosting windows. When the sounds of Margaret Petrie's footsteps faded on the carpeting of the landing Jane walked over and closed the drawing-room door.

'I never thought we'd see another one of those in the house.'

'A tree?'

Jane nodded.

'James loved it; the first real Christmas tree he's seen.'

Jane moved from her chair to the chesterfield beside Mary. 'Something has been worrying you all day. Want to talk about it? Is it Mother?'

Mary smiled and shook her head. 'No. It's ... it's Alan.' She had been unable to prevent herself from dwelling on the subject of his letter. Even during lunch she had thought of it, wondered what he might be doing at that moment.

Jane refilled the sherry glasses. 'Have you heard from him again?'

'Yesterday.' Mary saw Jane's brow furrow in concern. 'Oh, he's fine. It's ... well, he is leaving India; going to Singapore.'

Jane said, 'Oh dear.' She was silent for a few moments, and then asked: 'How long is his contract?' She was aware how much Mary had depended on him in the past months.

'I don't think it's a normal contract. It's a permanent position.'

Jane grimaced, and studied the reflection of the fire in her glass, thoughtfully. 'And he's asked you to go with him.'

Mary caught her eyes. 'How did you know?'

'I hardly need to be a clairvoyant. If it were simply a matter of him leaving India you would have mentioned it earlier. It had to be a bigger problem. And is it one?'

'Yes. He's asked me to marry him.'

'And you feel you can't because of loyalties to Gerald.'
'Not only that.'
'You don't love him.'
'I don't know if I can love him.' She sounded exasperated. 'Jane, how can I lie in bed next to someone, wishing it were someone else? Gerald said once I spoke in my sleep ... when I was worried ... what if I spoke about Gerald? What if I called Alan Gerald? They were friends for so long I can't even separate them in my mind. I don't even know if I'm capable of a physical relationship with any man, let alone Alan.'

'He would make a good husband.'

Mary looked miserable. 'He would make a perfect husband. He is considerate, thoughtful, intelligent. I know he would be loving. I'm fond of him; very fond of him, but I don't know where the line is between fondness and love. There must be one. But there was no need for me to look for love with Gerald. It was just there, always there. And it was so strong it was a reality I could almost touch, almost hold in my hands.'

'There are lots of different kinds of love.'

'I only know one kind. I can only judge my feelings by what I have experienced.'

Jane spoke softly, seriously. 'Mary, one day you'll have to make yourself understand that Gerald isn't important to your future any more. It sounds hard, and cruel, but I don't mean it that way. We both loved him, and we've both grieved. But we can't grieve forever. You mustn't. It doesn't matter whether Gerald has been dead for four months, a year, two years ... think very carefully before you reject Alan's love. I rejected someone, once. I've regretted it deeply ever since.'

'You?' Jane had never spoken of love before.

'He was Polish. During the war. I met him when I was helping out at the Union Jack Club. He was a sergeant pilot. Mother never knew, but we lived together. We had a little flat off Queensway where he used to come at weekends; whenever he had leave. He wanted to marry me, and I couldn't make up my mind if I loved him or simply admired him. He was a wild, adventurous kind of man, escaped from the Russians and then the Germans. Walked most of the way to England. He'd been an amateur pilot before.' She dropped her head and stared at the fire. 'He was killed over Folkestone in 1942. I didn't know for a month. He just stopped arriving. I telephoned his base, but they wouldn't tell me anything. In the end, one of his friends remembered me and had the decency to come and let me know what had happened.' She emptied her glass quickly and then caught Mary's eyes and held them with her own. 'I knew I loved him when it was too late. I didn't even have a photograph of him, just his shaving soap and WD razor in a celluloid tube. And this ...' She hooked a finger into the top of her rollneck sweater and drew out a small gold medallion. 'A Saint Christopher. He bought it one afternoon when we were together; I think it cost him a week's pay.'

Mary said: 'I'm sorry, I didn't know.'

'No one knows, only you.' Jane smiled wistfully at the memory. 'There was something horrible, afterwards ... horrible for me. There were some French letters in the drawer of my bedside table. I couldn't bear to touch them, couldn't even look at them. I'd insisted he used them, and when he'd gone I realised what I would have given then to be carrying his child.' She paused again. 'Those were my mistakes, and I've never stopped regretting them.'

Mary cabled Alan on New Year's Eve. There had been few hours during the course of the previous week when she had not thought of his proposal, and of the decision she was unable to make. Her cable was long, written as a letter, punctuated as a telegram, and she wished dearly she could have given him a more positive reply.

> Dear Alan stop deeply touched by your letter stop can only ask for more time stop passage booked home by sea and will arrive Bombay on Celicia on February 4 stop Dum-Dum airport February 5 stop all well here stop fondest love Mary.

CHAPTER THIRTEEN

The day Mary had most dreaded had arrived; the day when she must leave James in the care of strangers, and for the first time in his life without her support. It had been bad enough when he had gone to the British primary school in Calcutta, but her fears then had been lessened by the knowledge that he would return to her within a very few hours; now it would be months.

For the past weeks she had dismissed his growing worry, told him frequently how much he would enjoy his new life, the company of new friends in the pleasant surroundings of Massendon House. Now, she felt she was betraying his trust in her.

Fussily she had packed and repacked his trunk several times to be certain everything he was likely to need had been included. His tuck-box had been extravagantly filled with many of the confectioneries left over from the Christmas and New Year celebrations. His pocket money, probably an unnecessarily large amount, was sealed in an envelope to be given to his house master.

On his last night in the mews house he had only slept from sheer exhaustion. She was aware he had deliberately kept himself awake for as long as possible to enjoy every last prolonged moment of her company. He seemed to have shrunk visibly, to have lost his former confidence and to need the constant reassurance of her touch. He had not cried, but the tears had been close behind the eyes watching her every movement.

She tried to sound cheerful as Jane drove them out past Marlborough and the rolling countryside beyond, where the school was situated. She had hoped for sun on that last day but there was none, only a heavy overcast sky and sleet that melted as soon as it touched the wet earth.

At the main entrance to the school a line of cars queued, their occupants remaining inside their vehicles until the gradual movement brought them to the arched doorway when the boys, their fathers and chauffeurs, unloaded cases and trunks from the boots and hurried them into the building where their mothers awaited them. The hallway was crowded, noisy, smelling of damp clothing and the wax polish of the floor. A porter helped carry James's trunk through the crush and left them in the main assembly hall with its rows and rows of chairs.

It took Mary several minutes to find the house master, harassed and busy with his term's charges. He was in his early forties, clean-shaven, and bespectacled. To his pupils she thought he was perhaps excessively harsh as he ordered them to their dormitories with a near military precision to his speech, but when she introduced herself he softened immediately. 'You must forgive me, Lady Petrie. First day is always chaos and we try to settle them down as quickly as possible.' He saw James standing nervously behind Mary. 'Ah, there you are, Petrie.' He held his hand towards James. 'Welcome to Massendon. I think you'll quite like it here. Do you remember who I am?' They had met on their first visit to the school.

James said reluctantly, 'Mr Carpenter.'

'Well done, Petrie.' He spoke to Mary. 'Would you like to come up and see where he'll be sleeping? Good. No, please don't bother with his trunk. Is it labelled? Ah yes! It'll be brought up later.' He led the way from the hall, up a dimly lit staircase and then along a wide corridor. At last he reached an open door beyond which there was a hubbub of excited noise which stilled as he entered. There were a dozen beds in the room, iron beds separated by either tall lockers or windows. The house master paused inside the doorway and read a list on a notice-board. 'Here we are. Bed three.' He pointed. 'That will be his bed, and there's his locker.'

Mary had toured the school on her previous visit, and although she had not seen this particular dormitory it resembled all the others. She knew at the far end, through the white painted door, were the toilets and washroom. The showers and baths were in the main corridors.

'Parents always like to know where their sons are sleeping,' said the house master. 'You can be assured he will be comfortable and well looked after. Matron will see to that. And, of course, boys of this age make friends very quickly.'

It seemed so bleak, so unwelcoming. The room was pale cream, the curtains lime, and the lockers and woodwork all white. There were no carpets or rugs on the polished teak floor. Like the entrance hall, it smelt of wax polish. Mary felt she was banishing a lap-dog, used to the luxuries of his mistress's boudoir, to the confines of a garden shed; worse. There was still time to change her mind, she thought. Still time to take James away from this place, take him back to India with her. She could feel his nervousness in the hand tightly gripping her own, and when she glanced down at him, could see his face was pale, the olive colouring of his skin unnaturally ashen with fear. She was hating herself, doubting her choice of school, questioning all her decisions about his education.

Mr Carpenter was watching her closely. 'I can see you are concerned. It's quite natural.' He was speaking to her like a doctor to a patient, his rather broad face reassuring. 'Parents of the new boys take longer to accustom themselves than their children. I can promise you, even before you have reached home your son will be over the worst. In a couple of days' time he'll be feeling like an old hand. By next term, he'll be wanting to get back to his friends; it's always like that.'

She met the matron, bustling, busy, self-assured. A woman little taller than herself with a broad Scots accent and red hair, no make-up but the appearance of having recently scrubbed herself with a yard-broom and carbolic soap. 'Lady Petrie, he will have all the attention he needs. He looks healthy, and we seldom experience anything more than the odd cold, occasional measles or chicken pox, and the rare case of mumps. Cuts and bruises, of course, from the games, but nothing more. And their diets are excellent; you will have seen menus for the meals? Naturally the boys complain at times, but all boys do. And if there's something they really can't cope with then we usually manage to find something else.' She peered at James. 'I suppose he is used to curries all the time?'

'Of course not,' replied Mary indignantly. The woman was not making a very good impression. Surely matrons were a kind of substitute mother? This woman was too hard and insensitive.

They served tea and biscuits for the parents in the assembly hall, and Mary sat with Jane and James. Around them newly arrived groups of boys gathered, met their friends, dispersed to their dormitories, the library or games rooms. The first-timers whose parents had already left them wandered aimlessly, looking lost, or were herded by prefects into the bowels of the building.

James neither ate the biscuits nor drank the tea. He just sat dejectedly, his shoulders slumped, his face expressionless.

There was nothing, Mary knew, she could say to comfort him. Even reminding him that in only three months' time he would be flying back to Calcutta for his first holiday did nothing to cheer him. Promises from Jane that she or Lewis would visit him the following weekend were as ineffectual.

His trunk and tuck-box were no longer in the aisle, and the clock above the hall stage was showing a little after four p.m.

'James Petrie? James Petrie?' A half-broken voice was shouting his name. Mary signalled and a young house prefect, his face showing his pride at the responsibility of his position, came over and solemnly shook her hand. 'Pierce ...' he introduced himself. 'Pierce, Marcus. Saint Ellen's House, ma'am.' His accent was impeccable, as was his uniform, the blazer crisp, his trousers sharply creased and his shoes as polished as a guardsman's. He glanced towards the clock. 'I'm rather afraid parents must leave now. But I'll take care of him.' He spoke to James. 'First day is worst day. Hated mine. Do you like stories?' James nodded, uncertain of the question. 'Good. Because Cushy always reads one for first-timers. They're fun ... just before lights out in the dorm. Lets you have a bit of a dorm party, too.' He turned to Mary. 'Cushy's the matron, ma'am.' He looked at James's frightened face. 'I'll take care of you, show you around a bit. Have you said goodbye?' James shook his head. The young prefect remembered his own first day, his reluctance to kiss his mother farewell in front of other boys, despite his need to do so. He smiled at him. 'Tell you what. I'll wait around the corner at the bottom of the stairs. You come along in a minute.' He made a small bow towards Mary, grinned again at James, and left them.

James sniffed loudly, and for a moment Mary thought he was about to cry. Had he done so she knew she would have been unable to leave him. She wanted to gather him in her arms and promise him she would never allow them to be parted from each other, but he seemed to gather himself, stiffen his shoulders a little, an action he had copied from Gerald even as a very small child. To her surprise, unexpectedly, he used one of his father's expressions. 'It'll only get better.' He tried to smile at her.

'Yes, it will only get better,' she assured him. She held out her arms and pulled him to her. 'You won't forget to write?'

He answered with his head buried in her shoulder. 'And you'll write, too? Every week?'

'Every week,' she promised.

Suddenly he was gone, wrenching himself from her arms, running away from her, not looking back, fearful that even a last glance would bring the tears he was attempting to control.

Jane took her hand in both her own. 'In ten minutes' time, he'll be raiding his tuck-box and swapping things with the other boys. He'll be all right ... wait and see. I survived it.'

Mary was silent. She had surived too, survived all those early years in the mission school, survived the separation from her own family. But she could remember the sorrow even across the span of time. Now she was inflicting the same sorrows, the same pain, on her son. Were the advantages worth the anguish for them both, she wondered sadly?

She had determined she would remain in England for as little time as possible once she had been parted from James, and had accordingly booked a passage on a ship leaving Liverpool two days after the Massendon House term began. Had she stayed even a week longer, she knew she would have been unable to resist visiting him, and by doing so would prolong the sadness and loneliness for both of them. James had taken a step towards manhood and she had no right to attempt to draw him back.

To occupy her mind she crammed the remaining hours in London with last-minute shopping, unnecessary presents for friends in Calcutta, a final lunch with Simon Petrie.

It was not until late on the eve of her departure that she found herself alone with Lewis. They had eaten at the Savoy and then returned to the mews house. Jane had used the excuse she was exhausted to leave them. The fire in the living-room was unlit, the house chilly. Lewis was reluctant to leave. The wind in the mews had tousled his wiry mop of hair, making him look even more dishevelled and bear-like than usual.

He had never kissed Mary, never attempted to hold her in his arms. When they had been out together, the most intimate thing he had done was to take her arm and link it with his own ... once, in play with James, he swung her from her feet, but she had felt so delicate, so fragile, in his arms that he had immediately set her gently down again. Now, she realised, he wanted more of her but she was unable to help him, unable to make even the slightest move which could ease his discomfort. He fidgeted awkwardly.

He smiled grimly, then shrugged his wide shoulders. His soft Irish brogue was more obvious since his vacation with his family. 'I'm very bad at this sort of thing.' She looked at him quizzically. 'At telling people my feelings,' he explained. He laughed briefly. 'An Irishman, lost for words! A fine kind of lawyer I am!' He leant towards her. 'Mary, I'm trying to tell you there's no need for you to go back to India. You can stay here in London.'

'I have to go back, Lewis. There's Kimberley and the staff, and the business now; I'll have to devote a lot of my time to that. And there's other work I must do. I can't have a vacation in England forever.'

'Hell!' Lewis ruffled his hair with his hands in mock exasperation. 'I didn't mean stay here on holiday. I meant live here ... for good. Sell everything in India, or bring it with you ... whatever.'

'I can't. Be serious.'

'I am serious.' He jerked his chair forward, its castors dragging the rug so the standard lamp rocked dangerously. He steadied it, then reached and took her hand. 'Mary, you'd make a fine wife.'

'Lewis!' She found herself laughing at him, not in ridicule but at his boyish attempt to add intimacy to the moment by hinting at deeper future involvement.

'Mary, I'm asking you to marry me.' His eyes, sad teddy-bear eyes, caught hers.

Her humour faded with the realisation he was genuinely proposing to her. 'Oh, Lewis, I'm sorry. I thought you were teasing me.' She wished now he had been. Somehow his words seemed to threaten their friendship by presenting her with a bridge to be either crossed or destroyed.

'There's no more time for games.'

'We've only known each other for a few weeks. You can't want to marry me. This isn't me sitting here ... not the real Mary Petrie. She was left behind in India.' Perhaps, Mary thought, the real Mary Petrie no longer existed, eroded to dust by the events of the past months. It gave her a feeling of uncertainty, of unreality, making the room, Lewis, the entire situation, dreamlike and impermanent.

'I'll settle for the Mary Petrie I've met,' said Lewis, softly. 'Though I doubt if the one in India is any different.'

'Oh, Lewis.' Her life, it seemed, consisted only of hurting others.

'Is that a yes, or a no?'

'I'm afraid it's a no. Lewis, it has to be no.'

To her relief, he let go of her hand and sat back in his chair. His eyes twinkled with the mischievous light that had first attracted her. 'The Irish are very persistent. Will you mind?'

She smiled and said: 'No, I won't mind.' He would write, and she knew she would enjoy his letters. If the friendship faded it would fade gradually, almost unnoticed as the years passed.

He stood, straightening himself, stretching casually; the familiar giant of a man. She let him pull her to her feet. She half expected him to kiss her, wondering how her emotions would react when he did so. Instead, he touched her hair lightly, letting his fingers rest for a moment on her cheek. 'You'll take care of yourself until we meet again?'

When would that be, she wondered? It might be many years before she returned to England. 'You take care, too.'

From the doorway she watched him stride the length of the mews. At the street light above the mews arch he turned, waved, and a moment later was lost from her sight in the misty darkness.

It was the first time she had stood on the deck of an ocean liner, though she had seen many cargo ships in Calcutta, and at the end of the war the grey-painted troop-ships which had ferried the men of the British army home to England.

The *Celicia*, she knew, was not one of the famous; Lewis had suggested she would be more comfortable if she waited for the *Chusan* or one of the Peninsular and Orient Line's more comfortable vessels, but it would have meant remaining in England for a further month. The *Celicia*'s sailing date was convenient.

It was a 'one class' ship, built not as a luxury liner, but as a means of transport for those wishing to journey between England, the Far East and Australia. She was neither uncomfortable nor slow, but lacked the glitter and lustre of the cruise ships with their ornate ballrooms, gilded lounges, spacious dining halls and five-star hotel accommodation.

At 12,000 tons *Celicia* was little more than a third their size, and livelier in heavy seas. Like many of the others, she too had served in the war, and now where her white and black paint flaked from her hull or the stanchions of rails and the lifeboat davits, her wartime camouflage showed. Her crew were mainly British, the stewards Goanese.

Moored to the Liverpool wharf, she gave her passengers the comforting feeling of security. For Mary, there had been none of the apprehension she had experienced at the airport, where the aircraft in their parking bays had seemed frail and inadequate.

She had bidden Jane farewell at the London railway station; it had been tearful for both of them. The journey from Euston to Lime Street had taken five hours, then a taxi had delivered her to the quay where porters carried her luggage on board. At the time she had wondered if she would ever see it again, but when she was escorted to her cabin by one of the stewards the suitcases she had labelled 'wanted on board' were already beside her bunk.

At Lewis's suggestion, the cabin was on the port side of the ship. 'Posh,' he had explained.

'Port out, starboard home. The way the wealthy British always travel to and from India. The people who can't afford the more expensive tickets travel in the cabins facing the tropical sun, they become ovens. Most uncomfortable. You'll travel posh.'

He had booked one of the only suites available. It was little more than a double-sized cabin but had a small lounge area with a desk and table, its own shower and toilet and a bed rather than a bunk. She had been pleased to find it spotlessly clean, the linen well ironed and freshly aired.

The activity, the sound of feet on the deckhead above her cabin, and music on the ship's tannoy system, drew her back on deck into the chill greyness of the January afternoon. The Liverpool skyline was familiar from the cruise brochures, dominated as it was by the Liver Building, claimed to be one of the tallest buildings in England. Across the river, and barely visible in a light fog, was the outline of the Wirral peninsular and the Black Rock Fort.

The rail was crowded as passengers waved their goodbyes to those who remained below on the dockside. All visitors to the *Celicia* had been warned ashore half an hour previously. Now, as her mooring cables were unlooped from the bollards on the wharf and drawn back on board, a recording of Jimmy Shand's accordion band began playing 'Will ye no come home again' from the deck speakers, and handkerchiefs which had been used to signal to friends now dabbed eyes or were clasped over noisily blown noses. Mary had not expected so much emotion from the British; it surprised her. Men who would present themselves in India as unfeeling burra-sahibs now stood, staring across the widening gap between ship and quayside, with tears running down their cheeks. Their women sobbed openly. She attempted to compare the drab docks, the grey city beneath its dull pall of industrial smoke, the cold damp weather, with the colourful warmth of their destination. It seemed impossible that anyone should prefer this. She realised she would never understand them. She had visited their country, stayed in their homes, lived with them, but knew little more about them than before.

Fascinated by the new experience, for a time she stood and watched as a bustle of tugs swung the *Celicia* about and turned her bows towards the Liverpool bar.

The light Mersey chop became a swell as the land receded, and by the time Mary found her cabin again in the maze of corridors, decks and companionways, she was already feeling seasick.

The Atlantic gale, bettering force nine in the Irish Sea, met the *Celicia* head-on as she swung on to a more southerly course west of Anglesey six hours later. The deep, long, troughs of the storm-driven waves lifted and dropped her in slow corkscrews, her bow cleaving deep into spume-crested caverns, her hull shivering, shaking as she recovered, forcing herself upwards once more, to be remorselessly beaten down again.

Only three passengers risked the dining saloon that night. Their chairs were chained to the deck, while soup plates, kept on the table by a framework of wood fiddles, swirled their contents like miniature seas. It was an unexpected blessing for the ship's officers who were able to eat their first meal of the voyage undisturbed by the necessity to entertain their new table guests.

A few passengers attempted a meal in the privacy of their cabins, but the ship's movement was exaggerated in the claustrophobic atmosphere of the accommodation. Most lay in their bunks.

Mary, who had never experienced seasickness, genuinely believed she was dying. Each long pitching movement of the ship seemed to terminate with a wrench that churned her intestines. Her slender muscles were already weak with the effort of holding herself in one place on the bed, and now the rolling of the vessel had increased. She had been sick, at first in the bathroom then in a bowl which she had found beneath the wash basin. She had placed it beside the bed. It was no longer there and she had become incapable of reaching it. She had rung for the steward, and after what seemed an interminable length of time, he had knocked and entered, but there was little he could do to help her. He had erected guard rails along the sides of the bed, and these prevented her from being flung on to the floor, and he had supplied her with clean towels. He could not stay with her; most of the passengers in his section of the accommodation were in a similar state.

The storm continued for the next twenty-four hours, salt spume spraying the decks, the rollers increasing in length and depth as the *Celicia* made her way south to the more open waters of the western approaches and across the ill-famed Bay of Biscay.

A few of the passengers had found their sea-legs, but the majority still remained below. For Mary, it was a nightmare.

In the late evening of the second night at sea, the wind dropped and the waves eased. Mary lapsed into exhausted sleep.

She was awakened by the cabin steward. Sunlight flooded the cabin from the windows which overlooked the promenade deck. The *Celicia* seemed motionless, only the sound of her engines throbbed in the oppressive air of the cabin; in the bathroom, glasses rattled in their chrome holders. To Mary's astonishment, her seasickness had gone. She felt weak, and her stomach was sore and tender, but otherwise she felt well. The glass of orange juice and the pot of tea which the steward carefully laid on her table were welcome; sweet tea healing the chafed lining of her throat.

With the tact of his trade, the cabin steward had not looked at her during his visit. She was relieved; she felt filthy, disgusted with her condition. Her hair was matted, the nightdress she had managed to crawl into stained with vomit; the bed-linen was no better. The cabin stank.

Feeling guilty at the mess she had made, and which the cabin steward would otherwise have to clean up, she spent half an hour tidying the place. She would have liked to clean up completely, but there were no cleaning materials in the bathroom, no floorcloth she could use. When it was more reasonable, she showered, washed her hair and dressed. The fresh sari rebuilt her morale. She towelled her hair almost dry, then combed it back off her face. She could feel the heat of the sun through the glass of the cabin windows; it invited her outside. Still a little unsteady, she walked out on to the deck. It was eight-forty a.m.

The Mediterranean sun was bright. A warm breeze scented by the teak of the ship caressed her skin. Two miles away, already slipping from the *Celicia*'s port beam, was Gibraltar, the massive rock spectacular against the clear blue sky; a few hundred yards from the vessel, fishing boats hung on streamed nets, their masts dipping as if in salute as the bow wave and wash reached them.

Mary paid no attention to the figure which moved to the rail at her side. She had noticed other passengers, many looking pale and still ill, taking the sun nearer the bow of the ship. She assumed this was one of them, and if they made a move to be friendly, she would respond. She would, however, much prefer to be left alone until she felt stronger.

'They tell me that no one has ever died of seasickness.' The voice was Lewis's.

She faced him, startled, her mind refusing for an instant to believe it possible. Lewis was in London, in grey, cold England, now behind her. It was impossible to accept him here, on board the ship, standing in the near tropical sunshine.

He saw her astonishment and grinned down at her, sheepishly, the overgrown schoolboy look which had amused her when they had first met. It had seemed so unlike her images of Europeans in their homelands; an exposure of vulnerability. 'I didn't expect me to be here either. When I left you at Jane's, I went home and wondered if I'd ever see you again. Click! I made a decision. Wrote a letter to the firm saying there'd been a family disaster in Ireland and I was using up the remainder of my holidays. Then I caught the milk train to Liverpool and took a chance on a berth. Thanks to the diligence of the booking clerk in the shipping company office, I got a cancellation.' He looked momentarily guilty. 'I was on board by eleven. Got myself sorted out before you arrived. I was watching you ... from up there.' He pointed to the recreation deck behind the bridge. She said nothing, so he continued: 'I know you've been ill ... I wanted to help but I didn't think it was the right time to announce I was around. How are you feeling now?'

She was still dazed by his presence on the ship, and uncertain of her feelings. She was pleased to see him, but felt herself suddenly faced by a problem she had imagined was resolved. She said: 'I feel better, thank you.'

He leant on the rail next to her, close enough for her to feel a slight contact with his shoulder. He stared across the clear blue water. 'There were porpoises jumping in front of the ship earlier. It's beautiful, isn't it?'

She remembered the sombre colours of England. 'Very beautiful.' She was suddenly angry. She turned quickly to face him. 'Lewis, why have you done this to me?'

'I knew you would be furious.' His face was serious, concerned.

'Then why?'

'Because I didn't want to spend the rest of my life cursing myself for lost opportunities. When I was walking home, I thought of all the times when I just might have said something to you ... sort of prepared the ground, instead of springing it on you at the last minute when it was a certainty you would refuse. Good God, you didn't even take me seriously at first. I could have kicked myself.'

'Lewis, you won't make me change my mind.' The wind was catching his hair, ruffling it so he looked like a great shaggy dog. His eyes were demanding her forgiveness. Her anger dissolved in the warmth of the sun.

'But may I try?' His eyes were begging.

'Lewis, Jane was right. You are impossible.' She softened her voice. 'But I am impressed. I've heard of men pursuing women, but I never expected it to happen to me.' She reprimanded him now, as she might have reprimanded James for misbehaviour. 'But it is very irresponsible of you. Everyone will be concerned. You can't just disappear. And it takes over three weeks to Bombay ... you will certainly lose your position.'

He laughed at her, a deep laugh of amusement and relief that carried along the deck, turning the heads of other passengers. 'I cabled Jane; she'll understand. And I'll be back at the office on time, in a fortnight. I've booked as far as Port Said.' He took both her hands. 'When I was just eight years old, I kissed the Blarney Stone. With the help of that, and just a little Irish luck, we'll both fly back to London from Cairo.'

She had not expected to be invited to sit at the Captain's table; it was a custom of which she had been unaware. On her arrival in the dining saloon for dinner, with Lewis at her side, she was asked her name by the chief steward, who checked his list for her table. Lewis's presence caused the chief steward concern when she explained they were friends and travelling companions. He excused himself and consulted the Captain who was already at his table with the early dinner arrivals.

While the steward was away, Lewis explained the custom to her. 'Favoured guests ... titled gentry ... directors of the company. It's supposed to be an honour to share the Captain's table. I don't think you should refuse, even if they can't fit me in.'

'But what will he expect me to talk about?'

'Just talk about the things you would have talked about if I wasn't here.'

The chief steward arrived back smiling. Contented passengers assured better tipping, and the Captain had agreed to an adjustment to his table. He led them across the dining saloon.

She realised she was attracting the same kind of attention she had received years before when she had first accompanied Gerald into the dining rooms of the Calcutta hotels. Eyes followed her; some merely curious, others with envy. But she no longer felt the acute embarrassment that had so often ruined her evenings; now, she could understand the eyes, even enjoy them, be amused by them.

The men at the table stood as she reached it. The Captain who already knew her name introduced her and then Lewis. Her worry about conversation proved needless; a titled woman at the table would have been enough to draw the attention of the other guests, that Lady Petrie, of the well-known Petrie India Company, was Indian, and beautiful, guaranteed it.

The *Celicia* had already become an unreal world in which the discomfort and sickness of the early days of the voyage were being forgotten, and with them much of the sorrow and stress of the past months. For the first time, she felt herself relaxing, experiencing forgotten pleasures.

It was dark beyond the windows of the dining saloon and the promenade deck by the time dinner was over, but the dark was not the cold frightening darkness of foggy, ill-lit London streets, but comforting, the warm breeze created by the *Celicia* herself as she cut her way through the soft air, massaging away tensions.

Lewis seemed changed, no longer so ready with his wit, or his willingness to tease her. Now he was more serious, more careful in his conversation and courtesies. He linked her arm through his as they strolled the deck, loath to return to the stuffiness of the ship's bars and accommodation. He led her to the bow.

Distantly, lights twinkled like dying stars against the silhouette of the land. Below the curve of the bow, the white waves broke in roaring phosphorescent streamers, curling, foaming, tumbling away from *Celicia*'s black hull to fade into peaceful death in hidden darkness long after the ship had passed.

Here at the bow the breeze was strong, pulling at clothing, tugging and dishevelling hair, still warm, exciting; beneath their feet throbbed the engines, as steadily and comforting as a heartbeat. Above, in the black sky, the stars were once again a fascinating canopy, their light reflected on the rippling surface of a sea as yet unbroken. Mary became aware of her vulnerability in such surroundings but knew there could be no escape.

Lewis had slipped his arm around her waist, drawing her closer to him. The strength of his muscles and his body close against her own added to a strange but almost attractive sense of danger she was experiencing, the danger of being carried beyond the limits of the emotional frontiers she was attempting to maintain.

With the roar of the bow wave as the ship clove sea and air there was no conversation between them, only the transmission of thoughts through the contact of their bodies. She felt and understood his needs, his desires, through the strength of his arm around her, and he the reluctance which he could overcome only with patience and gentleness.

Soon he led her back to her suite. At the cabin door he held her, his hands cupping her shoulders so she faced him. The boyish grin had returned. 'They say there is no more romantic place than a good ship on a calm sea, on a warm star-lit evening. I'd say they were right.' He leant forward and kissed her on the forehead, his lips touching her skin for only a brief second. He let his broad hands slide down her arms, as though his hands were unwilling to leave her.

She said, 'Goodnight,' softly.

She showered, found herself a nighdress, and then discarded it with the realisation the cold nights were behind her. She lay on the bed with only its small lamp illuminating the cabin, the sounds of the living hull of the *Celicia* hypnotic, fading to unconscious acceptance with familiarity, soporific, the gentle movement adding cradle comfort.

For the first time since Gerald's death she felt able to question her own future, to explore its possibilities, its meanings. The desperate urge to fulfil all Gerald's wishes had eased as though his mind had withdrawn from her own. There was still sadness at his memory, but there was now acceptance. A future which had seemed, only weeks ago, to have been lost, dead, buried with the man she had so deeply loved, had emerged as might the sun from below a bank of deep cloud. There could be pleasure, perhaps even happiness.

With Lewis?

Her mind was still reluctant to accept him as more than the friend he had been in London. He had formed an image, unintentionally, which he must destroy and re-create. It might not be possible for either of them. Lewis was ... just Lewis; funny, reassuring, helpful, kind. When she had first seen Gerald, first thought of him that night in the plantation line-room, she had been able to imagine herself in his arms, dreamed of the passions they might experience together and had longed for realisation. There were no feelings of this kind with Lewis, no fantasies. And yet there was a fondness, a trust, a liking.

As with Alan!

Alan. Dear Alan. He had been a friend for so long and like Lewis an image of their relationship had been implanted in her mind. Could she accept Lewis and reject Alan?

This is stupid, she thought, angry with herself. Why should I accept either of them? Momentarily she was resentful of their proposals, blaming them for the confused emotions which now spun through her mind, attaching themselves to her thoughts so reasoning had become impossible.

I am a tool, she suddenly thought, a tool which everyone is using for their own purposes. I have been a wife to my late husband, and a mother to my son. It's true I enjoyed the situation, still enjoy the situation with James, but I am still being used. It has been James's future I have been shaping, not my own. Alan sees me as part of his future, as his wife, his hostess ... and Lewis pictures me in the same role. Simon Petrie sees me involved with the development of India Petrie. Why should I be involved with anything, with anyone, unless it is in my own interests? Unless it is particularly what I want? Perhaps I have been too unselfish for too long; perhaps I have given so much of myself that I have become a bearer again, everyone's bearer. Perhaps that is all I am capable of being ... despite everything, despite my marriage, my education, the British title which I have, the wealth, Kimberley; perhaps I am still no more than a house servant.

What then would I really want for my own future?

The gentle movement of the ship calmed her towards sleep, but planning, she found, was an impossibility. Whatever direction she attempted to lead her mind, the picture of her need remained unchanged. It was late afternoon, the ghat crowded, dusty, noisy. Lorries, soldiers, the thrashing of the great paddle-wheels in the muddy water of the river. And on the steamer's deck a tall, slender, young British officer, his hair bleached almost white by the sun, his eyes as blue as the sky ... so very, very blue.

Lewis was not so foolish as to attempt to force his company on her for every minute of the following days. There were meals when he did not appear, times when he left her to read in the afternoon sun of the deck, or in the solitude of her cabin after lunch. He was there only when he felt she might enjoy his company, or needed him. He had not again mentioned marriage. And sometimes, now, Mary found herself unconsciously searching for him, wondering what he might be doing, alone. More, she found herself using him to protect her from both the growing boredom of the voyage and the passengers who increased it for her. There were some for whom her title and connection with Petrie India was a magnet, who sought her out and unwittingly drove her away from them, a few who still resented her and attempted to use the ship-board situation to test or even embarrass her. One or two, with only wartime memories of India, still viewed any Indian girl as willing to share the bed of any Englishman, their normal sense of either decency or propriety removed by the duty-free liquor served at the *Celicia*'s bars.

Only in the evenings could she be certain of Lewis's presence; it had become almost ritual. They ate their dinners, then strolled the decks. The weather had become even warmer as the ship worked its way past Gozo and headed east-south-east towards the Suez Canal. After a while in the soothing air they would enter the quietest of the bars and drink together. Lewis his Irish whiskey, Mary wine.

With the weather settled and warm, a screen was erected on the foredeck and a film shown each night. Sometimes Mary and Lewis watched one; more often they avoided the crowded deck for the pleasure of each other's company.

He touched her now, often, and she had accepted the familiarity, even welcoming his hand in her own, or his arm around her.

Lewis told her again that he loved her.

This time she knew his statement was sincere, and enjoyed the balmy feeling of protection which his words seemed to cast around her. Once again she was sharing; her fears and misgivings halved by another, hope, optimism and pleasure doubled.

There were times now when she felt so light-hearted she suspected she might be intoxicated. The cares and worries which had stifled her for the past months were being swept away and replaced by near-euphoric sensations of happiness, even colours seemed brighter, the halcyon images clearer, more sharply defined as though everything in her life had been brought exquisitely into focus by some unexplainable and mystic lens. Her youth, which she had believed lost, had returned and with it its hedonistic delights. Once again she had become conscious of her body, its wants, hungers, so at times Lewis's proximity offered not only the promise of a welcome emotional haven but the satisfaction of a growing primitive need which had been forced into dormancy for so long.

The hot sun-filled days and soft, warm nights passed too quickly, spinning one into another. Each leading her towards the decision she knew Lewis expected of her, so desperately wanted her to make. As time shortened she became more aware that to reject him again might be to relinquish forever her rediscovered joys.

It was his last night on board the *Celicia*. It was already late. They had danced, holding each other close as the small orchestra had played their last waltz. During it the length of their bodies touched as they moved in the dimmed saloon lights. She had held his hand as he had said his farewells to ship-board acquaintances they had made, conscious even by his words to others that he was again reminding her how soon he would depart.

It had been an evening of champagne, at Lewis's insistence; an evening he wanted her to remember.

When they reached her cabin door, she was unable to leave him, unwilling to dismiss the arms which held her. The corridor was bleak, as impersonal as that of a hospital. She veiled her invitation, knowing he would understand. 'I'm afraid I've no coffee to offer, no night-cap.'

He nodded, followed her inside, but did not let go of her hand, bringing her close again as the door shut behind them. It was a cabin occupied by a woman, scented by her clothes, her body, her perfume; identifiable by a woman's possessions. It was lit by the bedside lamp, switched on by the attentive steward when he had pulled back the coverlet of the bed. Lewis held her head between his hands, raising it as he kissed her, softly, his lips finding hers. She needed to feel his body against her own, needed the touch of his flesh against her breasts. She slipped the fold of sari from her shoulder, unbuttoned her blouse, keeping her movements small so that they might be unnoticed. His tongue was tracing the outline of her lips, moving gently along her jawline to the hollows of her neck. He let her loosen his tie, open his shirt and press herself against him, her breasts soft against the muscles of his chest. She untied her waistband and the sari tumbled around her feet. His hands followed the lines of her shoulders, arms, hips, slipping around her to caress the hollow of her back, the fingers gently easing beneath the elastic waistband of her briefs to slide them from her. She felt a satisfaction in her nakedness before him, a growing rapture at his touch. She wanted him to take her quickly, almost violently. She wanted to feel the powerful thrust of his body as his penis was forced deep inside her, needed to experience an explosive union of orgasms that might somehow irreversibly bind them forever.

She felt his hands, strong, turning her away from him, resisted at first but then followed his movement. She saw herself in the long dressing mirror of the cabin wardrobe, saw Lewis holding her, his hands resting on her hips. He wanted to see her, examine her without a loss of contact. The broad hands found her breasts, nipples, his fingers sensed their hardening. She felt like a child as she watched, her body so small and slender against his, so naked, pale, against his clothing.

Her mind was unwillingly detaching itself from the reality so she was becoming a voyeur and not a participant. Suddenly distressed, she attempted to recapture the fading enchantment, facing him quickly, stripping away his clothing with distraught hands which fumbled buttons, then held him to her with possessive fierceness. He mistook her growing fear for passion, lifted her to the bed, carrying her easily, setting her down lightly, gently, while she clung to him.

Still in the mirror, she could see the reflection of the white mourning sari on the cabin floor, see the broad hirsute back of the man, his heavy masculine thighs above a delicate feminine body which was no longer her own.

She watched him kneel beside the woman, saw his lips and hands on her breasts; saw him press the slender thighs apart and prepare the woman's body with his touch. But was it a woman, or a doll? There was no response to the caressing hands, the persuasive movement of the male body.

The woman-like doll lay on the ruffled bedclothes, one leg resting over the side of the bed, the small foot on the patterned carpet, the other leg drawn up, bent at the knee, the thighs wide so that the deep red sexual lips, no longer concealed by protective hair, accepted the gently forced penis until the man's body seemed to mould into all the passive curves beneath with undulating rhythm. The doll's arms lay at her sides; the dark eyes staring back at Mary from the mirror were emotionless, dead.

She saw the movements swelling, the heavy muscles of the man's back and hips rippling, pumping. The man hesitated, straightened quickly, and she saw the penis, moist, alive itself as it was withdrawn from the doll's body, spurt droplets white on olive thighs.

The man's face followed the doll's eyes to the mirror, and understood.

Mary seemed to awaken from a dream. Lewis stood above her, his muscular body damp, glistening with perspiration, his eyes searching hers. He spoke sadly, wryly. 'It didn't work for us, did it?' There was no need for her to answer him. He turned away from her and began dressing, slowly. She lay unmoving, silent, but when he had dressed completely he returned to her and knelt beside the bed. 'It wasn't you ... wasn't us who spoilt it.' He kissed her cheek, gently. 'It was other things; too many other things.' She nodded. 'Perhaps, one day ... the next time you come to London ...' he began, then smiled, grimly. 'Perhaps.' He kissed her again. She could see hurt in his expression, the pain of masculine failure, but she was unable to force herself to act the lie he needed.

Lewis sighed, then straightened himself. She knew he would leave her now, and closed her eyes so she might not see him go. A moment later the cabin door clicked shut behind him.

She lay still for a long time, until the gentle movement of the ship brought normality and reason to her mind, then she sat upright and stared at herself in the mirror. Strangely, she thought, her body had retained no feeling of the contact, the penetration. But for the glistening semen pearls on her thighs it might never have happened.

She walked to the bathroom and stood under the warm shower for a long time, catching the needle-fine spray on her uplifted face, slowly turning the temperature control until the water became jets of ice, tightening the skin of her face and neck, dragging her breath from her lungs. Then she towelled herself until her skin glowed. Afterwards she oiled herself carefully, enjoying the touch of her own hands on her skin, the rich scent of the balm. She opened the cabin ports to catch the soft night air, straightened the bed and lay on the coverlet. Her mind seemed to have been cleansed of all thought; she slept deeply.

The shouts of the Port Said bum-boat tradesmen awakened her the following day as they hurled their weighted mooring lines over the ship's rails and brandished their wares at the curious and amused passengers. It was noon, the high sun reflecting the desert heat, shimmering the outlines of the warehouses, wharves, cranes on the shoreline and distant low horizon.

The passengers who were to disembark at Port Said had left the *Celicia* two hours previously, and with them Lewis.

Mary dressed unhurriedly, and joined a group of passengers standing near the bow watching children diving for pennies tossed from the deck into the sea below. They caught the illusive glistening copper effortlessly, their lithe bodies twisting, lunging in the yellow waters of the canal dock. On the promenade deck a few yards away, a gully-gully man produced live chicks from his mouth, from folds of his jellaba, the passengers' pockets and any unlikely place momentarily attracting him.

A woman with whom Mary had formed a small acquaintanceship informed her the ship would be moored in the canal dock until six o'clock that evening. A party of the passengers were going ashore for a small escorted tour of Port Said and a visit to Simon Artz, the famous store. Would she care to join them?

She did so willingly, finding pleasure in the excitement of discovery, in the familiar dust on firm warm ground beneath her sandalled feet, the scent of spices, incense. In the great central hall of Simon Artz, she bought a pendant of heavy gold inlaid with enamels, the winged god Horus. It was the first piece of expensive jewellery she had ever purchased for herself. It seemed to signify the beginning of a new period of her life, a period where her future and destiny lay within her own hands and not the hands of others, to be controlled and directed only by herself.

*

Once through the Suez Canal Mary enjoyed a sense of homecoming in even the name of the sea across which the *Celicia* now cruised. Flying fish skittered from her bow waves, the flukes of distant whales breaking the clear blue water of the Indian Ocean as she turned her bow north-east towards Bombay.

It was late Friday afternoon when the converted Dakota of Air India ended its descent and coasted from the runway of Dum-Dum airport into its parking bay.

Mary had known Alan would be waiting for her. She could see him amongst the spectators beside the small huddle of airport buildings, a dapper, anxious figure, the mechanism of his gloved hand concealed by the cuff of his white shirt. A garland of red flowers of greeting waved as he recognised her on the aircraft steps. Beside him, Rai and Sekander, their faces split by wide grins of pleasure at her return.

That night she dined with Alan at the Grand. He had not mentioned his proposal until then, and waited until they had finished the meal, and were enjoying coffee and liqueurs.

He smiled at her. 'I know the answer to my question,' he told her, his grey eyes holding hers, 'but I don't want to hear you give it. You're wearing it; your white sari. But there's nothing like a forlorn hope for an old fool, and I want to go on hoping.'

She smiled back, grateful for his understanding, and knowing that through it their friendship would remain as firm and needed as ever. 'Thank you, Alan.'

'I'm not taking the Singapore job. Turned it down. There's far too much of India in my blood, far too much I need here to leave. I've bought myself into a partnership ... a partnership with a small transport company; lorries, that kind of thing, carrying hard stores up into the hills, to the mining camps. Bahadur and Jameson Limited.' He raised his glass of Cointreau. 'Want to drink to its success?'

She knew there were moments, moments like this, when their friendship teetered on the very brink of love. She lifted her own glass towards him. 'To success ...'

PART III

CHAPTER FOURTEEN

CALCUTTA. AUGUST 1962

Her private office in the India Petrie building had become so familiar to her over the years that Mary had long forgotten the awe with which she had first entered it. Then, it had been Gerald's office, still, many months after his death, containing small memories and relics of his occupation – a desk set she and James had chosen for him as a birthday gift, a battered cigarette lighter in one of the drawers that she had remembered from the first days of their meeting, so many small things he would have touched and held. For months the office, and her work with the company, brought its painful memories; Gerald's signature on documents, scrawled notes in his handwriting in files, casual references by the clerks to decisions he had made, orders he had issued.

Each time she had entered the office it had been with a sense of guilt; the feeling that it was still his and that she was no more than an intruder. There had been a painful year during which she had felt herself an imposter maintaining her position only by some strange form of default; even mentally questioning the loyalty of those of her staff who had previously been Gerald's; conscious that it was they who were conducting the business of India Petrie and that she was little more than a figurehead. But slowly her confidence had matured.

Under her control the Company's profits grew, its position in the Indian sub-continent more secure under her directorship. Her instinctive bargaining capability and keen eye for good business brought her the respect and friendship of the British shareholders. Simon Petrie's personal attitude towards her had changed completely. His visits to Calcutta were quite different from those he had made formerly. He always stayed with her at Kimberley and although he still enjoyed his round of business contacts, his trips had assumed far more the proportions of vacations during which there was time for him to relax in the solitude and quiet of Kimberley's gardens. Mary had appreciated the compliment he paid her, knowing that it was only at Kimberley, and in her company, that he discarded the shield behind which he concealed himself in London.

His relationship with Mary had grown to the intimacy of father and daughter, as though he had been unable to resist qualities in her lacking in his own son William. It had been Simon Petrie's suggestion to her that the Calcutta offices should be modernised, and she had realised then his concern was not with the buildings themselves but with her own almost reverent attitude towards them.

'Do some spring cleaning. Rip the whole damned lot out,' he had told her. 'Disgraceful old mausoleum. Best thing that ever happened to the London office was the Blitz. Blitz this place yourself. Modernise it.' He had chuckled as though some secret joke amused him. 'Make Picey Petrie turn in his grave. Do an Anna Leipsiger to the place.'

She had taken his advice. Office by office she had gutted the building, impatient as labourers tore out the heavy Victorian woodwork, disturbing the aggravated clerks and typists with swirling dust that settled on their ledgers, racks of files and old machinery. Ancient cabinets, desks, clerical stools and typewriters were sold to Chowringhee traders, to be replaced by up-to-date office equipment imported from America. The last internal work was her own office. For a few minutes before the labourers moved in she stood there experiencing mingled feelings of remorse and unexpected sadness, realising that by her action she was destroying even more of the fading memories of a man she had loved so fiercely. Should she, she had wondered, stop the renovation at this point, leaving this one office untouched as some kind of a memorial to the past? To have done so, she knew, would have made the entire rebuilding pointless. The furniture had already been removed, the room seemed much larger and almost hostile towards her in its raw state, its faded walls still showing the positions once occupied by the mahogany bookcases, old brown photographs in teak frames. The foreman of the demolition labourers stood close behind her, a small man, his clothing grubby and ragged, his dark eyes greedy with anticipation like those of a hungry death-watch beetle.

She had turned her back on the room and with a chill sense of finality, as though ordering an execution, had said: 'You may begin now, babu.'

As Simon Petrie had believed, his advice removed the final constraints which Mary's working environment had been imposing upon her. The new offices of India Petrie became her own, no longer those of all the Petrie men who had preceded her and where a hundred eyes in old photographs and paintings had stared at her as though questioning her every judgement, and where even the furniture itself, age-scented, seemed to retain the personalities of former users. Although the façade of the building remained unchanged, beyond it all was new, all was the creation of Mary herself.

As the building itself had changed, so too had its occupants. Despite London directors' initial fears, there had been no mass resignations by the Calcutta British staff when Mary had first received her appointment as joint chairman of the company. To their surprise all of them had remained until, as they reached retirement age, they were replaced by Indian nationals. Now, the only Englishmen employed in Calcutta were those sent out from London to gain experience of the tea trade in India for brief spells of overseas training before returning to the UK offices. With roles completely reversed in less than a decade, young Britons learnt their trades from Indian departmental managers.

In 1958, long past the age when he should have accepted retirement, Simon Petrie died. He did so with a calm efficiency which surprised none of his business acquaintances. At eleven-twenty on a Tuesday morning he buzzed his secretary and quietly requested her to summon the company doctor; he did not suggest that it was urgent, and sounded quite normal. When the Harley Street doctor was shown into the chairman's office three-quarters of an hour later, Simon Petrie was sitting upright in his chair, his pipe in his hand, dead; in front of him, neatly stacked on his desk, were his will, car and house keys, wallet and a brief memo ordering his son William to a luncheon appointment his father would no longer be able to fulfil.

With the improved communications systems between England and India, Mary was able to attend the funeral. It was formal, drab and, she felt, emotionless. At the graveside she wept; no one else displayed grief. William and his wife, unaccompanied by their daughter, appeared bored by the entire proceedings. His fellow directors, most of them relatives, stood in a line, all dressed alike in City suits with navy blue overcoats as though they had all stepped from the window of the same Savile Row tailor, while the vicar of the Kingston church read a short service. Afterwards, they had lunched at a nearby hotel overlooking the river Thames and the following day attended an emergency board meeting at the Mincing Lane offices.

The meeting had been brief, stormy, and resulted in the resignation of William Petrie from his post of managing director and eventually the Company itself.

The board had seen no reason to automatically elevate William to the position held by his late father. Nor would they, they made it clear, even be prepared to support such a proposal at a shareholders' meeting. They were delighted with their present chairman, Lady Petrie, whose annual balance sheets showed continuously rising profits for them. There was no longer, they felt, any reason why a chairman should be based in London. In emergencies Lady Petrie could be in the London office, travelling from Calcutta by air, in less than twenty-four hours – and if faster decisions were required there was always the telephone or telex by which the offices were now adequately linked.

William, in a fit of pique, instantly resigned his position as managing director. He had stormed from the meeting, and was even more angry later when he discovered that Jane Petrie had been immediately voted to his former post. He had subsequently disposed of his shares. It was rumoured he was working as secretary of a Surrey golf club.

From a rather introverted and thin child, James grew into a handsome young man, as tall as his father had been. To Mary's disappointment, he had never accepted England as his home, and lived for the times when he could join her in India. He had made few close friends at his school, and spent those of his vacations which he was forced to spend in England either with Jane in London, if her annual holiday coincided with his own, or on rare occasions at Ash Park Manor. He had developed few hobbies, the only lasting one being trout fishing, to which he had been introduced by Lewis. His scholastic progress, however, filled Mary with pride. His reports were glowing. She had no doubts that once his education was completed he would be ready to join her in India Petrie and looked forward eagerly to the time when he would do so. For several years

Lewis had maintained a contact with James, despite the fact that Mary had never met him again since their parting on board the *Celicia* at Port Said. She knew that on her visits to London Lewis avoided her, although for a time he still visited Jane regularly. Jane had mentioned Lewis's trip with Mary only once, to comment: 'I'm sorry things didn't work out.' When Mary had appeared reluctant to discuss the matter Jane had never raised it again. Lewis married the daughter of one of his senior partners, unexpectedly, some six years after Mary's first return to India. Once his daughter had been born a year later, he was lost to all his former friends, including James.

With manhood, James had developed a persuasive charm, and an air of confidence Mary identified with her own memories of Gerald. She compared the two men, son and father, often seeking any small vestige of Gerald's behaviour in James, but the years of English schooling since Gerald's death had cast the young man in a different mould and erased childhood ways so that she found more of herself and others in him than his father. It was in his voice she sometimes heard distant echoes of Gerald. There was a rich, aristocratic Englishness about it with no trace of an Indian accent, and sometimes when he spoke she could close her eyes and allow herself to be transported back through the lonely years.

For the past two months James had been with her at Kimberley and soon he would begin his studies for a degree at Calcutta University. Now he was taking a vacation in the Naga Hills. She missed him, missed the sound of his voice, his laughter, his teasing conversations with Rai, who loved him like a son of his own; missed the chaos he left in his wake, discarded clothing, books, magazines, and all the paraphenalia of enthusiastic youth. And Kimberley, as always, felt empty without him. Just as she had done during the years of James's schooling in England, Mary counted the days until his return.

Aurobindo Das was an old man. The years had stolen his upright elegant stance, and with it his height. He walked slowly, aided by a rattan stick, his shoulders rounded. He disliked the sticky August weather in Calcutta when the air was so humid that cloth of a freshly pressed jacket felt damp after only a few minutes' wearing.

It had required great effort for him to walk the few yards from his chauffeur-driven car to the foyer of the India Petrie building, where he stood for a few moments enjoying the crisp chill of its air-conditioning. He could remember the heavy panelling which had once clad the walls; now pale marble reflected the sunlight and his own stooped figure like a smoke-dimmed mirror.

With the right of age, he ignored the reception desk but heard the sari-clad receptionist who had recognised him dial through to Mary's secretary. He knew it would be Mary herself who would meet him at the lift door on the fifth floor of the offices; it was a courtesy she never failed to observe. As the lift doors slid apart, she was waiting for him.

She smiled a welcome, then spoke a little crossly. 'Aurobindo, there is no need to tire yourself by coming here. If you had telephoned I would have come to your house.' She knew he had been unwell for several weeks. In fact, for the first time in all the years she had known him, he had been unable to attend the recent Congress Party's meetings. She linked her arm through his and steered him towards her suite. She had been signing the authorisations for the latest shipments when her secretary had informed her of his arrival and as she entered her office the shipping manager was collecting the documents from her desk. 'You can complete them,' she told the man as he bowed slightly towards Aurobindo. 'But please make sure the shipping company appreciates the urgency.'

'Certainly, madam.' The shipping manager left them.

Aurobindo said: 'I'm interfering with your business, as usual.'

'Of course not.' She led him to an armchair and watched anxiously as he lowered himself, awkwardly. His ageing caused her sadness. 'Let me order some tea.' She gave him no time to answer but flicked the intercom switch and spoke to her secretary in Hindi. 'There.' She brought a small chair to his side, rather than use her own which would place her desk between them. 'So why have you been so naughty, tiring yourself by coming here?' Now he was seated his ageing was not so obvious. His deep brown eyes were as quick as ever; without the strain movement imposed on him he was still handsome, she thought.

'My diaries ...' he smiled at her.

'Diaries?'

'And an anniversary,' he added, mysteriously. 'An excuse for a small celebration, perhaps.'

'Your birthday?'

Aurobindo shook his head, rocking it sideways. 'Oh, no. Something far more important. Something I only discovered last night. You see, I have been indulging myself. I have always kept diaries, all my life. A very British habit, I'm afraid. At first I kept them simply as reminders for myself, references. There is nothing more annoying than having someone correct you in public, so my diaries were my encyclopaedias. For instance, I know the exact minute the Congress Party agreed to Jinnah's insistence on Partition ... and I know who said what, exactly, at that time. Better than that, I also know what many people were thinking, but didn't speak. Everything I noted as a journalist, but was sometimes unable to publish in my newspaper, is in my diaries.' He shook his head again, this time a little sadly. 'So, I wondered what should be done with all the information I have collected during my lifetime. As a publisher, I have taken a natural step ... I am editing them for publication.' He laughed drily. 'To be truthful, in my lifetime I seem to have written a library rather than a single volume.' He paused, and then held her eyes with his own. 'However, the importance of my diaries today is only that they have reminded me of this special anniversary.' He reached out a thin hand and rested it on Mary's. 'It is eighteen years today since I first learnt of you.'

'Learnt of me?' Mary searched her memory. It was now August, the month when she and Gerald had first arrived in Calcutta from the military base at Dimapur. Surely she had first met Aurobindo at Kimberley ... and had they not purchased Kimberley until late September? Aurobindo had first interviewed Gerald alone following the death of his father. 'Of course, when you wrote the obituary for Gerald's father.' Was it already so long ago? Eighteen years!

Aurobindo surprised her. 'I learnt of you before that. There is a special mark in my diary of the date. Of course, I didn't meet you then, but later. But today is the anniversary of the day I learnt of you from my brother, Mahant Surendranath. A temple priest.'

Mary frowned, puzzled. 'I don't think I've ever ...' Aurobindo had never mentioned having a brother who was a priest. She suddenly remembered her visit to the temple at Alipore. It had been long forgotten and she felt herself blush deeply. She had thought it a secret known only to herself. And the priest had been Aurobindo's brother!

Aurobindo tightened his grip on her hand, reassuringly. 'Of course, I don't know why you visited him. You were such a young girl then ... only a child really. My brother was a very confidential man,' he assured her. 'I only know you visited him, and he told me you were the new Indian wife of the son of the British Petrie family. Later, the untimely death of your husband's father gave me an opportunity to meet you. But I would have met you anyway.'

'But why?' Mary felt her blush fading. Now she was curious.

Aurobindo laughed again. 'Because my brother informed me you were a most attractive young woman. And you still are. That is why I have used this excuse to see you today.'

They were momentarily interrupted by one of the company servants knocking at the office door, and entering with a tray of tea and biscuits. He poured their cups before leaving, which gave Mary time to absorb some of Aurobindo's words.

When they were alone again, she waved a finger at him in mock severity. 'I suspect you have been manipulating me, all this time. Now I am very angry. You are a very wicked man, Aurobindo Das.'

He chuckled. 'I have not been manipulating you.'

'You made me go to university. Made me do lots of things.'

'I suggested you made better use of your talents, Mary. Was that the wrong thing to do?'

'And look at the work you have given me. I seldom have one evening to call my own. And if I dream at night, it is of the workings of the Congress Party ... of all its committees. I am beginning to suspect that had it not been for you, I would be one of those genteel ladies who spend their time in leisure at the racecourse or their clubs ...'

He interrupted her. 'You would have preferred to be like a memsah'b?'

'Of course not. But you are a puppeteer, and I have been like one of your puppets.'

'Nonsense, you have been nothing but your own woman.'

'No, Aurobindo. I am everyone else's woman. I am India Petrie's woman, I am the Congress Party's woman, I am my household's woman. How can I be my own woman? Sometimes, I am completely exhausted by it all.' She remembered nights when she was so tired it took all her remaining strength to undress and shower before reaching her bed and then her sleep would be disturbed by thoughts of the work still ahead of her.

'Because you have not yet learnt one important thing,' said Aurobindo seriously. 'You have not yet learnt to share your complete life with another.'

Mary raised her eyebrows. 'Not learnt to share? My life is shared by the entire population of Calcutta, of India.'

'Only parts of it. Some parts you deny to others.'

'You are an impossible man.'

'How old are you,' he asked unexpectedly, his eyes quizzical and the fine lines on his forehead deepening.

She hesitated, realising there was no intended impertinence in his question. 'I am not absolutely certain. I have no true record of my birth date.' She mentally added up the years. 'Thirty-six ... thirty-seven.'

Aurobindo smiled. 'I should have asked how young you are. Thirty-six or thirty-seven is nothing. I am over seventy years old. I have great grandchildren. Most of your life is still ahead of you, mine is almost finished. You must share what is ahead of you with a man, with a lover, with a confidant, with someone who can really share everything.'

'I have James.'

'You have him for only a short while to come. Yes, he is in India now, but he will make his own life and you will be alone again. And, in any case, do you share everything with him? Of course not. The relationship which you need cannot be that between son and mother. You must have a husband ... perhaps even more children.' His eyes examined her sari. 'You have been wearing your widow's weeds for too long.'

'I am quite contented as I am, Aurobindo. Don't tell me you have come here as a marriage broker as well.'

'You have no need for one, my dear,' said Aurobindo, softly. 'There are a hundred men here in Calcutta who would lay themselves down at your feet. And the first would be a certain British captain ...'

Much later, when she had sent out for a lunch which they shared in the cool of her office, and Aurobindo had reminisced of the early days when they had first met, she accompanied him from the offices to the car which waited in the shade of the buildings. When his chauffeur had assisted him into the vehicle she returned Aurobindo's wave as he was driven away. Sadly, she was aware that it would not be long before she lost yet another of her closest and oldest friends.

MON, NAGALAND. AUGUST 1962

The rice fields on the slopes were already turning to gold as they ripened. As the sun dropped lower towards the hills, its rich rays brought a hint of metal to the landscape so that it seemed as if the terraces where the dense forest had been cleared and the crops sown had been plated with burnished bronze.

The stream, bright, gin-clear water tumbling from pool to pool over rocky ledges and narrow waterfalls from its hidden jungle source, lay a mile below the townships which had once been the capital of the powerful Ang of Mon, but were now the district headquarters of the Nagaland administration.

Jungle trees shaded the water, tall, majestic, vine-draped, their roots locked in fractured boulders. Above them, birds shrilled in the canopies, their bright plumage as garish as their cries.

A young man was fly-fishing a broad pool from the shallows of its neck. He was exceptionally tall for an Indian, slender-waisted and narrow-hipped, but with broad shoulders. His face was angular, his cheekbones pronounced, his jaw narrow but strong. He was wearing khaki shorts and a bush jacket, but his feet on the narrow platform of rock from which he was casting were bare. It was the stream and its surroundings that interested him more than the fish he knew he might catch; compared with the brown trout of Hampshire or Kashmir, they were small and poor fighters, but they provided him with the excuse to enjoy the solitude of the only British pastime he had learned to love ... taught to him by an Irishman during the long unpleasant years of his schooling in the distant, hated land where he had been made to feel he could never be more than a foreigner.

Calcutta was little better for him. Even there he was obviously not of local stock. His title, which he had come to dislike, gave him a position with its white population which they could not ignore, but openly resented; his height, build, features and family wealth prevented his acceptance by many of the Bengalis. He had few friends among them and knew they envied him his British education and his assured future with his family business.

He had begun to live only for the time he could spend in Assam during his vacations, the time alone in the forests with his gun, or by the banks of the rivers and streams with his rod. Here he could breathe the clean air and enjoy the hills and jungle. He knew it was here he belonged.

It was not his first visit to Nagaland. But it was his first without the company of his mother. Since the movement for separatism had begun a few years previously, tourists of any kind were discouraged, the territory virtually sealed. It had been only through the influence of his mother's political friends that his present trip was possible and he had been allowed a temporary permit by the Governor of Assam and Nagaland, in Shillong. A gun had been forbidden, his fishing rod was acceptable. He was staying in Mon as a guest of the Additional Deputy Commissioner. Here, in a land of rolling jungle-covered hills, he felt at home; he knew it was home.

He had been fishing the stream down for the past couple of hours, and the few fish he had caught were in a basketwork creel he carried over his shoulder. He was conscious of the girl who was watching him from the shade of the trees beyond the track which led alongside the stream. She was Naga, and, by the length of her black hair, drawn back and held in place by a narrow headband, unmarried. She wore traditional Naga dress and ornaments, several rows of beads around her neck, silver and beaded bracelets on her arms. Above her narrow skirt, which reached less than halfway down her thighs, incongruously she wore a cotton blouse, unbuttoned like a waistcoat, so that when she moved one or both of her small firm breasts were exposed. She had been watching him for the past half an hour.

He was now only some fifteen yards away from her.

He stepped from the rocks on to the shore and began changing his fly.

She called to him in Assamese. 'Why are you beating the water?'

He laughed. 'I am fishing.'

'It is not a very good way to try to catch fish. A net is better.' She stood and walked towards him. 'We fish this pool sometimes. The men hold a net at the bottom and we drive the fish down towards them.'

She was only a few feet from him, a slightly built, attractive girl, her figure supple, athletic. He opened the top of his creel and held it towards her. 'I've caught some.' There were five in the creel, none more than six inches in length.

She was not very impressed and pouted, prettily. 'They are all babies. There are much bigger fish. You are obviously catching the stupid ones.' She examined his clothing. Now she was closer to him she saw that his skin was unusually smooth and unblemished. He was taller than any of the young men of her village, and his eyes met her own with an intriguing lack of embarrassment. 'Are you a teacher?'

'No. A visitor.' His smile encouraged her.

'The man who is staying at the house of the ADC?' She already knew the answer. 'You have stayed there before. I can remember you. You have been often.'

He corrected her. 'A few times.'

'The people talk about you. They say you are a Naga whose family are famous in India.'

He rested the rod against an overhanging branch and sat on a small outcrop of rock. He wanted to prolong the conversation, encourage the girl to talk more to him. When he had first stayed in Nagaland, he had been only twelve years old and it had been easy to make friends with the other children, though this had been discouraged by his mother. As he had grown older, it had become more difficult. Now, considered an adult by his mother's friends, he was expected to spend most of his time in their company. 'My mother's father was Lushai, from Sachema, but her mother was a Zemi Naga from the North Cachar District.' He did not mention his British blood.

'Naga blood is stronger than Lushai blood,' observed the girl, positively. 'So you are Naga.'

It flattered him to have her think so, and seemed to confirm his love for the hills. 'What is your name?' he asked her, as gently as if he were questioning a small child.

'Lipung. I am a Wangsa. My father was a son of the last Ang.'

He knew the complicated social structure. There were three main classes. The Wangyem were sons and daughters of the offspring of the great Angs and had wives of equal status; beneath them were the Wangsa, the children of Wangyem men who had married wives of a lower status; beneath them were the Wangsu who were the lowest strata of Naga nobility, and then the peasants of the commonest clans. It seemed probable that this girl would have received some formal education. 'Can you speak English?'

'Of course. It is taught here. I am a pupil at the government school.'

'A Christian?' Most of the educated Nagas seemed to have accepted Christianity.

'Yes. And you?'

He shrugged. He had accepted the teachings of Christianity until he had been fifteen, and then questioned them. He had felt a greater affinity to the more philosophical religions of India but when he had delved more deeply into them had found no more satisfaction. He was now in a period of doubt when political solutions seemed to offer more than religion.

'Do you work for the administration?'

'No. I'm a student, too.'

The girl's face showed surprise. 'You are at school?' His manner, bearing and confidence made it impossible for her to relate him to the boys with whom she shared her own studies. They were immature, childish.

'I go to university soon.'

'Ah. My brother is at university. He has been there for a year; in Calcutta.' She spoke with obvious pride at her brother's achievement.

'I shall be going to Calcutta University.' He remembered the terrible argument there had been with his mother when he had announced his decision. She had intended him to study at an English university and as his final school examinations had been good, had expected him to apply for a place at either Oxford or Cambridge. He had refused to do so. He had decided he had spent far too much time already in England. If he was to take a degree, then it would only be at an Indian university. It was one of the few times he had ever experienced his mother's anger; it had been hard to resist, but he had succeeded.

'Then you must meet him. He is here now. And later when you are at the university he can be your friend. There are other Nagas there, too.'

'I'd like to meet him ... and them.'

'Tomorrow,' the girl promised. 'Do you smoke cigarettes?' she asked quickly.

Momentarily, he felt guilty. It was a habit he had begun only in the past few months, and which his mother discouraged. 'Yes, sometimes.'

The girl smiled at him. 'Then you will have matches. Give them to me and I'll make a fire and cook your fish for you.' It was a suggestion he understood was intended to imply that she wanted to develop their friendship.

'I'd like that.' He found the matches in his pocket, gave them to her, then emptied his creel on the rock between them.

The girl leant forward, her blouse opening as she moved so he could see the firm, youthful swell of her breasts. There had been no girls in his life in England, none yet in India; those he met at his mother's house parties, or those of her friends, were over-sophisticated, sometimes thrust at him by their mothers as obvious candidates for a marriage some time in his future. He resented the planning of his life; resented the Indian attitude that wealth should be combed with wealth regardless of the feelings of the individuals.

The girl examined the fish, weighing and turning them in her slender hands. She shook her head sadly. 'You are not a very good fisherman,' she told him. Silently her mind added, 'But you are going to be my man, one day.'

There were two towns of Mon. The old Naga town, built on the high ridge above a massive eight-hundred-foot precipice from which the adulterous had once been thrown, was shrouded with jungle, its houses still built in the traditional form, their eaves decorated with carved 'house horns'. Beside the chief's house were mounds of stones representing the ceremonies of the old head-hunting rites, a tally of the heads lost in a fire which had destroyed the clan's trophies some years before. A little below the village, on a track so steep and narrow it was impossible to reach the old town even in a jeep, was the cemetery with its pointed stakes for the male dead, the forked ones for females.

On more accessible lower ground was the new town of Mon, the administrative centre of the region. Founded since the war, it was a collection of white buildings with corrugated iron roofs, centred around the Additional Deputy Commissioner's bungalow on one of the hillocks. The new town had plumbing and electricity in its buildings, it even had street lighting at night, out of place in its setting against the jungle-clad hills. Nlamo Petrie hated it as much as he hated the British name with which he had been christened; James! It was as incongruous as this reminder of colonial development, this ugly jumble of harsh white buildings totally out of character with the countryside in which it had been built.

He could not remember exactly when he had begun hating his British Christian name, but he could remember why. There had been other boys called James at school and to identify them there had been appendaged nicknames; Jimmy the One had been the English house captain ... they had referred to James Petrie as Jimmy the Nig, a cruel parody of Jimmy the Kid of wild west history. There had been pupils at the school whose skin colouring was deeper than his own, but he had noticed that if they had been given a name in keeping with their national background, then the British pupils used it, perhaps because its strangeness amused them, or because by its use they were able to produce in their own minds the sense of racial superiority they seemed to need. In time his name had been shortened, by constant usage, first to Nig, and in his last two years, to Ni. Its origins had been forgotten by his fellows, but never by himself. If he had been asked to explain it, he said it was an abbreviation of the name he now used, Nlamo.

Nlamo Petrie did not hate everything British; he did not hate the memories of his father, although he had hidden that part of his blood from Lipung when he first met her. Over the years, reinforced by conversations with his mother, with Alan Jameson, even with his late grandmother, the picture of his father in his mind had become that of an almost mythical warrior, who had fought and given his life for the Naga hills. That a cobra had eventually killed him was irrelevant; had he not been wounded fighting for the hills, he would not have died. But things which the young James Petrie had never noticed or understood had become obvious to Nlamo Petrie. Many times he had stared at the photographs of his father and attempted to find any resemblance between them and himself; there was none. His mother and Alan had talked of similarities in height and build, but these were not obvious in photographs taken when his father had been forced to use a wheelchair. Only once, when examining those of his grandmother, had he thought perhaps they were right; the photograph had been taken when his father was first commissioned. But there had been other young officers with him, and most of them were of similar build.

It was as though his father had fertilised the ovum from which his son had developed, without the passing of a single gene, as though the act had been committed jealously, so that white should not be seen to mingle with brown, whereas his mother had given herself totally and generously. Sometimes he had resented this cruelty; but it had never led to hatred.

The final two weeks of his vacation at Mon were spent either in the surrounding hills, exploring in the company of Lipung and her brother Lupok, fishing the streams with them, or chatting with their friends in the huts of the old town of Mon. He was aware he was neglecting his duties as a guest of the ADC, but had sensed no criticism from either the man or his wife. He still ate most of his meals with them, played with their children, and occasionally accompanied the ADC to one of the outlying villages; but whenever it was possible, he spent his time with the Nagas.

The friendships had developed. Lipung's brother Lupok was eighteen months older than Nlamo. He was a wiry young man, several inches shorter than Nlamo, darker skinned, and with his coarse hair cut so short it seemed to sprout in every direction from his head, giving him a continuously dishevelled appearance. He wore European clothes during the day, but in the evening he would change into tribal dress. He was intelligent and well educated, his voice softer and less harsh than many of the other Nagas. He was reading Law at Calcutta and intensely nationalistic, often speaking of the time when he would be qualified and might put his studies to use for the benefit of the Naga territories. He saw Nagaland as an independent country, administered by a Naga council, elected by the free vote of its own people; a socialist state.

Lipung, though loyal to her brother's views, was less interested in politics. She was sixteen years old. A few years before, she would have been expected to be offered by her father for marriage to some suitable young man of similar family. Her father's own education and Christian upbringing and views had altered that. She would have a free choice of a husband when she chose to marry. She already knew that Nlamo was attracted to her, but he was very shy compared to the boys of the town. She intended to encourage him, and had already extracted a promise that he would return to Mon, with her brother, for the spring vacation.

Five months passed, and Nlamo returned to Mon. This time he was more self-assured, more confident. Lupok and him had become close friends in Calcutta, and he had begun to learn Naga, already speaking it well. Although at different colleges, for Nlamo was taking a degree in Business Studies, they spent most of their free time together and despite Nlamo having his family home in the city, were contemplating sharing an apartment near the university. They talked politics excitedly, discussing Marxism and the works of Engels with an enthusiasm which was almost fanatical. Lipung tolerated it because it was necessary to do so to be close to Nlamo, but she found it boring and sought every opportunity to draw him away from

Lupok's company. It became less difficult after the first few days of his visit; she had allowed him to discover her body. He had been so timid at first, his hands finding her breasts so gently in the privacy of the forest, that his fingers had felt like the gentle breath of a summer breeze. But it had awakened all the masculine feelings imprisoned for so long; as he held her, she had felt the stiffening of his penis between them and had known that at a special time she would choose, it would enter her body.

The special time did not arrive until the last few days of his vacation. She had led him far from the village, several miles up the rocky stream bed to where she had promised he would find fish so innocent, so undisturbed by men, even he would be able to catch the monsters hidden beneath the rock of the pools with the cane rod and tiny bunches of feathers he threw at them.

Even though they had left the village shortly after dawn it was almost noon by the time she found the pool. She had visited it as a child and it had been no more than a memory of the pleasure it had provided then. The pool was almost a hundred yards long, far wider than the stream which entered it by a fifty-foot waterfall which thundered on to the water-fashioned rocks below. For several thousand rainy seasons the waterfall had cut the pool deeper and deeper into a long ledge of grey rock, with overhanging shelves, moss-covered and draped by the vines of the jungle. Boulders had scoured and polished the bottom and walls, dug basins and underwater caverns. To one side of the pool, near the shallow run that drained it, was a fine pebble beach, open enough to the sky for its shingle to catch and hold the heat of the sun.

She sat and watched him set up his tackle, tie the miniscule fly to the gut leader, and begin to fish the shaded side of the pool where the eddies of the current produced small backwaters beneath the moss ledges. He had stripped off his shirt, damp after the long hike up the steadily rising ground beneath the jungle. He shouted exuberantly and she heard the brake of his reel scream. He waded backwards towards her as a dark shape beneath the surface of the pool ripped the line through the water. He was laughing, and the sound was boyish happiness, excitement. The fish broke the surface at the far end of the pool, a silver crescent, powerful, hurling itself up towards the jungle canopy as if escape lay only in the sky above it, then crashed its broad side into the pool to cascade water on to the dry rocks.

He fought the fish for twenty minutes, sometimes with the concentration of silence, at other moments with noisy exasperation at his own clumsiness, or joy at the cunning of his foe. At last, he drew the fish carefully on to the fine shingle, hooked his fingers into its gills and carried it to her. He examined it, the bright scales already dulling.

His voice was breathless. He squatted by her side. 'Look at it. It must weigh eleven or twelve pounds. Isn't it beautiful?'

She spoke quietly. 'Look at me, Nlamo. Am I not also just a little beautiful?'

The strangeness of the invitation in her voice drew his eyes. She sat on the shingle beach, naked, her clothes in a small pile beyond her. As he watched, she lay back and held her arms towards him.

CHAPTER FIFTEEN

CALCUTTA. 16 DECEMBER 1963

It seemed to Mary that over the years Kimberley had grown in size. It had always been a large and spacious villa, but now she had become conscious that it was far too big. It contained rooms she seldom entered or used, even when entertaining guests. There was a boxroom where James had once played; it still contained a railway layout and many of his childhood toys, but it had been silent, empty, and forgotten by him for the past three years. She had opened the door once, several months previously, and peered inside; it had been like searching for a ghost, and for a few moments she had seen one there, a child kneeling on the carpeted floor, engrossed in its play, ignoring the calls of its parents.

In a second boxroom, wedged between trunks and storage chests, was a dusty wheelchair, its once polished aluminium grey with verdigris, its rubber tyres cracked and perished by Calcutta humidity. She had been unable to touch it, was still unwilling to ask Rai to put it out amongst the rubbish. And Rai would have been unable to carry it himself, frail with age, his white hair thin, his shoulders rounded, and his legs even more bowed with the passing years; but he would have dutifully obeyed her instructions and would have ordered one of the younger housestaff to clear the room. Rai was an old friend now, company for her when she needed him, no longer considered a servant though he still controlled the staff and received a salary.

Soon, she had decided, she would sell Kimberley, unless James married and wanted it as his own, which seemed unlikely at the moment. She had not seen him for a week, although he had telephoned her two days ago to confirm that he would join Alan and herself to celebrate his birthday on 17 December. He was expressing his independence at the moment, she realised. The apartment sharing was simply youthful rebellion. In time it would change, and he would return to her. It was the way of his generation; a resentment of any form of establishment, of the old ways, even of money. To judge by the dress he wore, the furniture of his apartment and the old and rusted Austin which he drove, he might be almost penniless.

Often, she wondered how Gerald would judge James now, might judge her. Had she produced the man he would have wanted as a son? She thought so, hoped it was so. James had been given the education Gerald had wanted for him. It was a pity he had refused to complete it at an English university, but judging by his examination results and from conversations she held with his tutors, he was a fine student who promised to qualify at a high standard. He did not appear to object to the suggestions she had made for his future once he left university. In fact, it seemed to appeal to him to begin his work in India Petrie as a plantation under-manager; he spent so much of his time in the Assam hills that they were already familiar to him. It was hard now to persuade him to spend any of his vacations in Calcutta. It was all part of his growing up, she told herself. Like preferring to call himself Nlamo; he was seeking identification, seeking himself. There had been many young students like him when she had taken her own degree; she had been older than most of them even then, and had recognised that once they entered the real world they would conform, unwillingly perhaps at first, but eventually. Some of them had become friends whom she still met, and their wildness had left them as they had matured. It would be no different with James.

His absence did not make her lonely. His years at school in England had conditioned her and her time while he had been away had been filled by her absorbing work. She enjoyed James when he was with her, loved the sound of his voice in Kimberley, but accepted the partings. Kimberley might be large but it was seldom empty. She had a wide circle of friends in Calcutta, and her political committee work had increased rather than decreased following Aurobindo's death. Thoughts of that made her sad; it had been so long, so slow, so painful. She was glad that Gerald's death had been quick, painless. Poor Aurobindo's had dragged on for months until even his closest friends had prayed for his release to end his torment.

When he had died and she was returning from the ghat where his body had been burned, she realised that she had never really known his motives for the interest he had shown in her during all their years of friendship. Though she had questioned him, his replies had always been turned to jokes. It was far too simple to believe he had been captivated by the charm of a naive hill girl as he professed. Perhaps, she had thought, at first it had been done out of sympathy for Gerald, who had sufficient disabilities without those imposed upon him by an ignorant wife. Later, once Aurobindo had become a friend, it had been continued by a genuine liking for her.

His diary, *Notes on Freedom*, published only a month after his death, had startled and embarrassed her. In them, she found herself mentioned several times with glowing praise for the development of the committees under her control. He had even quoted from speeches she had made. She was, according to his notes even of the earliest days, 'a rising political star above the hills of Assam'. For weeks after the publication of his book she was uncomfortably self-conscious when she met her political friends and acquaintances, knowing that they too would have read the publication but uncertain as to their feelings towards her.

There had been countless invitations from Congress Party branches throughout the country for her to speak at their meetings, and pressure was growing for her to accept a nomination to stand as a representative. This and much more she sensed as Aurobindo's ambitions for her, the real motives; somehow she had become the arrow driven from his bow, and which he believed would find the mark at which he aimed. Circumstances, the years of delay before freedom from British rule was achieved, had prevented him from fulfilling ambitions which must have been his own in his youth.

The high-pitched klaxon of one of the steamers on the river brought her mind back to the present. She had rested after lunch, a habitual siesta in the quiet of her room, ended by Rai bringing her a tray of tea. Normally she would have worked in her office for the next couple of hours or in the party committee rooms. Her mornings were usually spent at the India Petrie offices, but she limited her company work to four hours a day, beginning with the other office workers at eight a.m. but ending at noon. Today and tomorrow she had taken as leave. She was waiting for Alan's arrival. He had always shared James's birthday and Christmas with them; James's nineteenth was no exception. Alan was due to arrive at Dum-Dum at four p.m. She checked her watch; it was four-thirty. Sekander would have already met him and they would be driving through the crowded streets of Calcutta at this very moment.

She closed the book on her lap and walked from the gardens into the house. The old punkahs had gone, replaced by modern air-conditioning, and the house felt cool. At times, though, the air was too dry and gave her headaches.

In her room, she checked her make-up and re-tied her white sari, knowing that at some time during the next few days Alan would be unable to resist making a comment; it had become a joke between them. Sometimes he would affectionately refer to her as his snowdrop, or his lily ... nothing more, but she understood it was intended to show that his feelings had never changed throughout all the years.

She studied herself and thought: 'I have changed. Every time Alan sees me there is another grey strand in my hair, another fine line on my face.' True, it was necessary to search for the grey hairs and fine lines, but they were there. In only two more years she would be forty. The thought depressed her. Where had her youth gone? It had slipped away unnoticed.

Broad tyres crunched the gravel on the drive outside the villa. She heard Rai's voice welcoming Alan, and experienced a glow of pleasure at the thought of his company.

Sitting across the table from him that evening, she thought the years had been kinder to him than herself. Although he was a little over fifty, he was still handsome, his face deeply tanned by the constant sun, his hair still thick and only slightly tinted with grey above his ears. He had retained his military bearing, and his step still had a spring to it. The years had brought him success too, after early misgivings about his trucking business. His enthusiasm and optimism had carried him through the difficult period of expansion and eventually he had been able to buy out his partner.

They seldom talked now about the war, about Gerald. They had their own memories if it was necessary to reminisce. They were comfortable in each other's company, relaxed, easy; there was no competition, no need for cleverness. His humour still amused her, and she found satisfaction in the knowledge that he still found her attractive, still enjoyed complimenting her.

In the ten years since his proposal, he had never asked her again and she knew he would not do so without a sign from her. There had been times when she had considered it deeply, attempted to prime herself to give one and always failed; something, and she did not know what it might be, prevented her.

She smiled, inwardly; he was what the British, and the Indians, liked to refer to as 'one of the old school'. A very English Englishman, with a true love of India; she remembered how rare they had always been. They were even rarer today.

He had been joking with her, during the meal, comforting her with tales of his own rebellion when he had first left school. James was no different, he told her. He had a spirit which would carry him far in his life. It had confirmed her own feelings and relaxed her.

She was finding the room now over-cool and suggested they should have their drinks on the verandah. She rang the bell for Rai, and Alan led her outside.

It was the time of the year she enjoyed in Calcutta. Although it was always humid, in December it was bearable, pleasant after the heavy monsoon months. The night was completely still, disturbed only by the sound of distant traffic and the croaking of the frogs in the reed beds beside the silent river. There was a full moon and its bright light illuminated the garden, adding mystery with its deep shadows, creating grottoes out of the flower beds and shrubberies.

Rai, slow, a little unsure in his movements, his face now as gnarled and furrowed as the bark of an ancient tree, brought the drinks and set them on a table. He poured them, knowing what they would want, knowing they would replenish them themselves, later. There had been no need for him to work tonight, but he had chosen to do so. He spoke to Alan. 'It was a good thing you came by air, captain sahib. There has been a big explosion at the railway station.'

Mary said, 'Not another!' There had been a series of bombings in Delhi in November, and two only the week previously in Calcutta. There had been several deaths.

'On the wireless, it is saying there are very many people killed. Perhaps one hundred.' Rai stood the bottle on the table and straightened himself painfully. 'Will you want more tonight, madam?'

'No thank you, Rai. We will look after ourselves now.' She knew it was only because of Alan's presence he had called her madam, just as it had been when Gerald was alive. Alone, Rai always addressed her as daughter; now the formal manner of address sounded unfamiliar, unfriendly, almost as though she had somehow offended him. 'Goodnight, Rai.'

'Goodnight, madam.' She was pleased to see an amused twinkle in his eyes, as though they were sharing a secret. She smiled back at him.

Alan tilted his glass, watching the moonlight reflecting silver from its deeply engraved surface. He sounded angry. 'Damned fools. As if we didn't have enough killing in the war ... after the war ... during Partition. It never ends; it achieves nothing.' He paused. 'I suppose our generation is to blame. We showed how easy it was to kill. We gave it glory. We justified it.'

She consoled him, quietened him. 'It was necessary then. You didn't want to kill.'

Alan grimaced. 'Oh yes, I wanted! Most of us wanted. The first Japanese I killed was scrambling up the hill towards me. I certainly wanted to kill him. I waited until I couldn't miss, and blew him right off the end of my bayonet. The only thing I didn't realise was that I would never forget. I never forgot any of the ones I saw; sometimes, if I shut my eyes I can see them with as much detail as if I was meeting them face to face again in Chowringhee market. I suppose, in some ways, I never killed them. Instead I gave them an obscene kind of immortality.'

The police Champ swung into Kimberley's drive past the startled chokidar at a quarter to six the following morning. Its ribbed tyres caught the pebbles, flinging them on to the lawn while cutting deep furrows through to the earth as its driver braked fiercely to a halt in front of the entrance steps.

A second vehicle, a camouflaged Bedford lorry, slowed outside the gates. Even before it stopped, a platoon of uniformed police carrying rifles leapt from beneath its tarpaulin-covered body, and were directed by a sergeant to positions twenty-five yards apart around the perimeter of Kimberley's gardens.

Outside the front of the house, the two passengers of the jeep, a chief superintendent and a deputy superintendent, stepped out of the vehicle, then knocked loudly at the door. Before the door was opened by Rai, another jeep entered the compound and the two officers were joined by a corporal and two constables carrying Sterling sub-machine-guns.

In the kitchen, Rai had been setting the trays for the morning's chota hazri; the water for the tea had not yet boiled. Normally he served it at six-thirty; but from old army habits he rose himself at five-thirty; he enjoyed the early hour of silence in the house before the other servants began their daily duties.

To his annoyance, the officers would not reveal the purpose of their visit, but the chief superintendent's manner was brusque: he wished to speak with Lady Petrie immediately. He did not wait to be asked to enter the house, but stepped past Rai, followed by his fellow officer and the armed policemen. Rai was quick to notice that the Sterlings they carried were cocked and ready for use. The thought that it might be some crude form of assassination attempt, or kidnapping, crossed his mind, though it seemed only a remote possibility. He wished he had kept his kukri in the house, but it was in his own quarters above the garages; there was a sporting rifle, in a case in the billiards room, but he could think of no excuse to go there and the chief superintendent was already becoming impatient. Rai wished he was younger, so that if necessary he could have fought them with his bare hands.

He awakened Mary, gently, knocking softly at her bedroom door until he heard her move in the bed, only then entering the room. 'Daughter, there are men at the door. Policemen. An officer wishes to speak with you.' She had not yet fully awakened and stared at him, puzzled. 'I don't know the reason for their visit, but it is very early. Not yet six.'

'Tell them I will come shortly.'

He left the room, but stopped outside her door. If there was to be trouble, then two men were better than one. He awakened Alan before returning to the police officers.

Alan did not dress. He pulled on his dressing-grown, strapped on his artificial hand and went immediately to the lounge. Rai had been unusually agitated and concerned. Alan could think of no reason for the police visit, especially in the numbers which Rai had described, and when he had looked from his window and seen the lorry and further guards outside the villa boundary his own disquiet deepened. The only reason he had been able to find was political; the possibility there had been some kind of coup which might lead to the arrest of the new government's opposition. It horrified him to think Mary might be one of them. But whatever the reason might be, it was serious enough for the police to deploy themselves as though they were expecting some kind of trouble.

He found the chief superintendent waiting impatiently, a

short and portly Bengali, dapper, his uniform immaculate. He had removed his hat which he was holding under one arm with his swagger cane. There was a polished leather revolver holster clipped to his Sam Browne, its flap unbuttoned and the black plastic butt of the weapon visible. A corporal was standing beside the lounge door, a sub-machine-gun held in both hands, ready for use.

Alan introduced himself. 'Captain Jameson.' Normally he never used his rank, but in these circumstances it might prove useful.

'Chief Superintendent Gopal Rupali, Twenty-three District.' The officer did not smile, but held out his hand. He had a black moustache, neatly curled, its ends waxed. His handshake was firm, brief; simply a courtesy.

'I wonder if I can help you ...' began Alan.

He was interrupted by Mary's voice. 'Chief Superintendent Rupali?' There was recognition in the way she spoke his name, and the police officer's face softened. He bowed formally.

'Lady Mary.' He smiled, slightly. 'Please forgive me calling at this ungodly hour. I would not have dreamed of doing so had it not been imperative. I hope you will understand.'

Mary explained to Alan. 'I know the chief superintendent very well. We are old friends of many years. Is that not so, Gopal?' There was concern in her eyes. 'How can I help you?'

Gopal Rupali looked uncomfortable. 'It is official business, Lady Mary. My duty, of course. I have first to request your permission to search your property.' He anticipated Alan's protest. 'Please, Captain Jameson, this is not of my own choosing. I would rather be anywhere else than here at this moment.'

Mary experienced a rising feeling of dread. 'What has happened.'

'First I must have the property searched,' insisted Rupali. He spoke quickly, apologetically. 'I give you my word my men will search with care; they are fully trained in this kind of thing. It is a regrettable necessity ...'

'You have my permission, Gopal.'

He looked relieved. 'Deputy Superintendent, you may begin now ...'

'Sir ...'

Rupali stopped the man as he turned away. 'However, I expect it to be done with consideration for Lady Mary's property.'

*

There had been twenty minutes of almost complete silence, Mary, Alan and the chief superintendent alone in the lounge. Rai had brought them tea, but Gopal Rupali had drunk his cup standing at the French windows, staring into the garden. When Mary had attempted to question the reason for his visit, he had politely refused her an answer; a quick flaring of Alan's temper had been no more rewarded.

The sergeant appeared at the lounge door. He spoke in Hindi. 'Sir. Something has been found.'

Rupali put his cup and saucer carefully on the tray. He spoke to Mary. 'I had hoped this might not happen ... that a search would be fruitless. It would have been better, easier. Perhaps we should go together, Lady Mary.' He caught Alan's eyes. 'You may accompany us, captain.'

The sergeant led them through the billiards room, and the narrow corridor beyond, to the boxrooms. Inside was the deputy superintendent and two more of the men. The deputy superintendent was kneeling beside a box which had held some of James's childhood railway equipment. Beside him, on the floor, were a pile of spare tracks, several carriages and a transformer.

He held a candle-sized cylinder encased in oiled brown paper towards Rupali, and said one word: 'Gelignite.'

Mary heard herself say: 'That's impossible.' Gelignite! It was an explosive! Why should there be explosive here? She refused to acknowledge the only answer that was attempting to force itself into her mind; it was not believable.

Alan stared down into the trunk. There were two thick cardboard boxes of gelignite at the bottom. He recognised them; commercial blasting charges. Beside them were two cylindrical tins of detonators, one tin for use with the coil of cordex fuse which lay on the explosives, the other electrical detonators. Twenty pounds of explosives; enough to demolish Kimberley! It was sweating nitroglycerine, dangerously old, and overheating in the unventilated room. He warned the deputy superintendent: 'Put it back carefully. Don't try to move it.'

'Alan?' Mary's voice was questioning, needing some form of reassurance he was unable to give her.

He put his arm around her shoulders. 'It is explosive. Perhaps there's an explanation. Perhaps it has been here for a very long time.'

He knew that was not so. The explosive had only recently been placed in the trunk; had it been there for more than a few days the wood of the trunk would have absorbed some of the glycerine the gelignite was exuding and which had already stained the cardboard boxes like spilt oil. He spoke to Rupali. 'I believe it would be sensible to evacuate your men from the building until you can get an expert in to remove this stuff.'

Rupali nodded. He could see the beads of glycerine on the explosive and feel the tickling irritation of nervous sweat on his own body. The worst, he knew, was yet to come.

The house was empty. Rupali had radioed police headquarters, and a military bomb disposal unit had already arrived at Kimberley. The servants were standing in a bewildered group beneath the neems near the river gate of the gardens. Alan and Mary waited for Gopal Rupali to join them as they sat waiting at one of the ornamental iron garden tables.

Mary's mind was full of questions she knew Alan was incapable of answering. She felt she had become involved in something beyond her understanding, something more terrible than anything that had happened to her before, and over which she had no control. Although she prayed it was, perhaps, one of the young servants who had been responsible for the explosives which had been discovered in her house, inside her she knew it could not be so. James was the only person who came and went as he pleased, who would never be questioned by Rai or even herself. But why should he want explosives? The reasons were too terrible to consider.

She watched Chief Superintendent Rupali walk towards them. He was alone, and there was a disconcerting way in which he held himself, moving stiffly, a wooden soldier on parade, not proud or arrogant, but steel tense with the knowledge of some unpleasant duty he must perform, every muscle of his body taut.

Mary looked away from him, trying to shut the moment from her mind. Rupali's eyes sought Alan's, begging help but knowing he could expect none. Alan had seen the look before, recognised it as one of a bearer of bad news, understood the emotions Rupali was experiencing; protectively, he took Mary's hand.

Rupali spoke nervously. 'Lady Mary, God knows, I wish I

was not the man to tell you. I also wish you to know that you have my deepest sympathies. It is in regard to your son, Sir James Petrie.' Alan saw the man was shaking with nervousness, and felt Mary's hand tense with anticipation in his own.

She turned her head slowly and faced Rupali. The firmness of her voice astonished him. 'You are about to tell me of the explosion, last night in the railway station.'

Rupali bit his lip. 'No, Lady Mary. Not that. At least, not directly. Sir James was not responsible, it was the work of religious extremists.' He took a deep breath. 'Unfortunately, without your knowledge, I am sure, your son was a member of a group of Naga separatists ...'

Was a member? The words were a warning which pierced her brain like the needle point of a stiletto.

Rupali continued. 'The group was known to our security department. It was not active but it was known, as were the names of its members. Last night, when the appalling explosion occurred with so many deaths, it was decided that all the cells of various insurgents should be brought to Police Headquarters for questioning. It was not our intention they should be imprisoned without trial; those not guilty of last night's terrorism will be released.'

Mary felt the physical weakness of relief. Rupali was telling her James had been arrested. Unfortunately, though, with the discovery of the explosives he would probably now be charged. It was bad enough that he might face a prison sentence but perhaps he had been forced to hide the explosives, was an unwilling dupe of the separatists? There would be ways she could help him. 'So you are holding him in custody?'

'No.' Rupali dropped his eyes and studied the polished toecaps of his brown shoes. 'Regrettably, one of the Naga separatists shot at the police. It became necessary for us to use our weapons to subdue them. The building caught fire, and only one, seriously wounded, was able to jump from a window. We interrogated him for a few minutes before he too died.'

Rupali was still avoiding telling Mary directly. Alan forced a direct answer. 'You are telling Lady Petrie her son has been killed?'

'I am afraid that all those within the building have perished.'

Mary was on her feet, quickly. Alan took her hand and felt her fingers tighten on his own. 'I must go to him.' She spoke as though James was alive, her child needing comfort.

Rupali shook his head. 'No, Lady Mary. I am sorry but it is not yet possible. The building was very combustible; the ruins are being searched now. There may be difficulties with identification.'

Alan asked the one remaining question knowing that the pain Mary was experiencing must be terminated. 'Are you absolutely sure that Sir James was in the building, superintendent?'

The superintendent shrugged hopelessly. 'There were witnesses, Captain Jameson.' Rupali was obviously relieved he had completed his unpleasant task. His respect and liking for Mary had made it almost impossible for him. He spoke more confidently to Alan. 'We were informed that explosives had been concealed in this house. I had hoped it would not be so; without them the role of Sir James within the group would have been questionable and the embarrassment which will add to the sadness would have been prevented.' He lowered the tone of his voice sympathetically. 'Lady Mary, there will be unavoidable formalities, identification, a statement ... eventually an inquest.' He glanced towards the house. A young engineers officer was carrying one of the boxes of explosives to a bomb disposal vehicle near the gate. 'The house should be cleared in a few minutes. There were also a few documents in Sir James's bedroom which I have also removed—separatist literature. But, I shall leave you now, and you will not be disturbed again today. Naturally, captain, if you wish to speak with me about this matter, I will always be available.' He saluted, and left them.

Alan turned Mary gently to him and held her tightly in his arms. He felt inadequate, helpless, knowing that the feelings of the woman he loved were beyond his reach—perhaps beyond his comprehension—during these terrible moments.

She did not cry, because tears were impossible. Instead, for a long time in the solitude of her room, she felt only a strange emptiness, her body a void which contained no emotion, neither sadness nor grief. She was thinking and yet not thinking, wondering if she was experiencing a form of insanity which she might end by screaming, to open the shock-induced flood gates surely restraining her true feelings. Like the tears, the scream did not yet exist.

'James would have been nineteen years old today.' She spoke the words aloud to herself, hoping they would bring her sorrow. They did not. 'Nineteen years ago, I lay in this room with my son in my arms, and loved him.' She loved him now; would always love him. Why was there no sorrow? Was it, she wondered, because she had already lost her son to his manhood, accepted her loss, known throughout all his childhood that one day it must happen? Conditioned herself? But that kind of loss was not death! Was death no longer important to her?

Gradually, she realised grief would come in its own time. That it should not be invited, yet. It would arrive like the first unnoticed falling leaf ending a summer, and might grow to overwhelm her.

Long empty days followed during which she remained in the solitude of her room despite Rai's anxious pleas. She was conscious that Alan was near her, knew that he was waiting for her while understanding her present need for seclusion. At times she heard his footsteps in the corridor, his voice in the gardens or house. She had heard his anger at the visit of reporters from the Calcutta press and his orders to the chokidar to bolt the gates once they had left. He was protecting her.

There was still only the frightening sense of bleakness in her mind as though the news of James's death, a lightning bolt searing the heart from a tree, had created a vacuum in her mind within which no emotion could exist. Perhaps, she thought, it would always be so, now.

She saw the anguish in Alan's eyes when he came to her, the official request to identify James's body in his hand. His demands that he, and not Mary, should be allowed to perform the task had been denied; the circumstances of the young man's death had made her attendance a necessity.

She did not experience the fear which Alan had anticipated, only the feeling that her body now was of lead, not living flesh, so that all her thoughts and movements seemed slow, heavy, while beyond her the activities of the normal world were quickened and unreal.

The mortuary was ice-cold, scented by disinfectant, echoing silence between harsh whitewashed walls. A deferential and apologetic clerk led them to the vaults and then hovered in the doorway, as though loath to go further into the depths of the building once he had introduced them to one of the attendants.

A steel door opened, frost crisping the air and turning their breath to pale mist. Beyond were a dozen mortuary slabs, some empty white marble reflecting the stark unshaded light bulbs above, others shroud-draped over stiffened corpses.

The attendant paused, checked numbers pinned to shrouds.

Alan's eyes caught Mary's questioningly. It seemed to him the cold air had frozen her mind and body beyond response.

The silence was so deep she heard the soft rustle of chilled linen as the attendant swept the covering from the nearest body.

It was not James who lay before her. Instantly her mind was carried back through the years to the countless bodies of the young who had died at Kohima; the scarred blackened flesh, the gaping wounds, torn limbs, seared and blistered skin. There was no likeness to the calm and gentle face of Gerald as he too had lain in death before her; here, coarse fire had stripped bones naked, scorched unfamiliar clothing into crisped charred skin. This was not James.

She heard the attendant's voice, distantly. 'Look, lady, here...' The man was pointing.

One unburnt limb, one smooth youthful thigh; a thin, old scar, barely visible against the pale olive skin.

She heard James's cry as he fell, a child, adventurous, daring, from the gnarled roots of the old tree on to the sharp rocks which lined the garden path; saw the deep red blood darken the sandy ground, remembered the warm sensuous feeling of his young body in her arms as she held him, as Rai had bound the wound.

This blackened corpse was flesh of her womb, conceived in her body, carried, nurtured, loved ... her son.

She screamed.

A solitary, long, high-pitched shriek of pain that wrenched itself from her lungs.

Her mind destroyed the truth, so that later, in memory, the body of her son had been perfect. But with the acceptance of his death and the grief which enveloped her came the knowledge that with him had died the last physical bond which had held her to Gerald.

Kimberley, hushed behind its shuttered windows, mourned with its inhabitants. Alan waited alone with the patience of tragedy, his sadness laced with a depressing sense of failure. Throughout the years of his love for Mary he had sought only to protect her, but when that protection had been most needed he had been unable to help. It was as though a heartless fate always placed him one step behind the events which threatened her, so that he was no more than a warrior arriving at battles already fought and lost.

In the mortuary he had felt her grief as keenly as if it had been his own. Her tears, as he had held her to him, had been so fierce on his chilled skin that they had seemed to burn themselves deep into his body.

What, he wondered sadly, would she feel was left for her now? How much of herself would she be forced to bury with James's tortured body? Her strength had often amazed him. He had witnessed it at Kohima, in the military hospital at Dimapur, in the early days of her marriage to Gerald ... and at his death. But there was a limit to such fortitude, and to the courage and determination which sustained it; he had seen it drained from the bravest of men. Did enough of Mary's strength remain for her to survive?

It was dusk. Shadows lengthened in Kimberley's gardens and faded with the coming twilight. The evening air was heavy with the rich perfume of flowers.

Recent memories of James, and the great waves of sorrow they carried with them, seemed also to have faded and for the past hours Mary's mind had been occupied by her thoughts of Alan. She had feared self-deceit; that the need she felt for him, the longing for his closeness, his touch, was no more than the child of her sorrow. Her grief had mellowed with Alan constantly at her side through the harsh days; now she realised it had always been so and that he was part of everything she had ever done. Alan had reunited her with her lover, stood beside her at her wedding, been close to her room when she had given birth to her son, grieved with her at the loss of her husband, and now comforted her in her present bereavement. He had shared life and death with her, from the savage battlefields of Kohima to the peaceful sadness of Kimberley.

Since James's death she had eaten dinner alone in her bedroom, but now with an inexplicable sense of calmness she undressed, freshened herself at the vanity unit, then cleansed her face and applied make-up. She searched the drawers of the tallboy; folded carefully between tissues were the saris she had not worn since Gerald's death. She found one of pale green silk embroidered with silver flowers, remembering it had once been a favourite. It was scented faintly of mothballs, but she shook it out and then sprayed it with perfume. She dressed slowly and carefully, adjusting the folds so they hung like multiple pleats from her waist. She sleeked back her hair and held it in place with a small diamond clip. She stared at herself in the mirror; the woman she saw seemed younger, prettier.

Alan sat at the dining-table. The cutlery had not been disturbed, but he was holding a cut-glass goblet of red wine. The dinner jacket, almost as military in its cut as a uniform, contrasted sharply with the grey hair of his temples but made him an elegant, masculine figure. He sipped the wine thoughtfully but looked up quickly as she entered the room, then stood, his eyes studying her.

She felt self-conscious and uncertainty showed in her voice: 'Good evening, Alan.'

He hurried to help her with her chair, moving it gently beneath her at the table. His eyes never left her. He filled her glass from the carafe, then returned to his own seat.

'Forgive me, I wasn't expecting you down this evening.'

She said to him: 'Alan, I can't exist alone.'

'I didn't intend you to.' His grey eyes were softer than they had ever appeared to her before. 'I'll stay as long as you need me.'

'No.' She experienced a sudden surge of panic. Her voice quickened. 'That isn't what I want. I want to go with you. Back to Assam. Back to the hills. Away from here.'

He calmed her. 'I'll make all the arrangements.'

She was silent for a few seconds, knowing he was watching her, waiting. 'Alan, once you judged my answer by the colour of my sari. Would you ask me again knowing the only thing I am sure about is that I love you today . . . at this moment.' The words seemed to echo from the forgotten past.

His voice was warm with emotion. 'There has never been a day when my heart has not asked you. Will you marry me, Mary?'

She felt like a girl as she answered. 'Yes, Alan.' She knew once his arms were around her that she would be protected by his love . . . by their love . . . always.